A PHONE CALL HOME

David dialed home with the excuse that he was in the mood for Chinese food that night. You didn't just call home and tell your wife that you wanted to hear her voice, not if you were the type of husband who got his romance outside the house.

"I cashed my paycheck yesterday, so I think I could swing dinner for you and Julie." He looked at the picture of his wife and child that stood in the oversized brass frame on his desk. The photograph was almost ten years old and David refused to replace it. He just couldn't advertise his daughter now.

"So, I'll see you later and I'll put the chicken back in the freezer," Marjorie said. Just the reminder that they shared a major appliance took them both out of the dating mood. By the time they both hung up, David was feeling better. It was a brief phone call but it grounded him. He had managed to replace Elizabeth and predictions of death with Marjorie and egg foo yong.

Pinnacle books by Gail Parent

Sheila Levine Is Dead and Living in New York

A Little Bit Married

A Little Bit Married

Gail Parent

PINNACLE BOOKS   NEW YORK

This novel is a work of fiction. Names, characters, places, and in-
cidents are either the product of the author's imagination or are
used fictitiously. Any resemblance to actual events or places or
persons, living or dead, is entirely coincidental.

A LITTLE BIT MARRIED

Copyright © 1984 by Gail Parent

Pinnacle Books edition, published by special arrangement with
G. P. Putnam's Sons.

Putnam's edition/April 1984
Pinnacle edition/March 1985

ISBN: 0-523-42448-5
Can. ISBN: 0-523-43428-6

Printed in the United States of America

PINNACLE BOOKS, INC.
1430 Broadway
New York, New York 10018

9 8 7 6 5 4 3 2 1

For my Parents

Acknowledgments

With total appreciation to Phyllis Grann, Owen Laster, Rhea Kohan, Peter Wylan, and Dr. Martin Grotjahn.

A
Little Bit
Married

One

Marjorie should have known that there were rough times ahead when her husband announced, over ordinary coffee, that he felt like God. He had, over the years, felt godlike, and like a God, but this was the closest he had ever come to being the ruler of the universe Himself. It should have alarmed Marjorie, because God had never taken a wife.

David had a right to his feelings. He was worshiped. People bowed their heads when they talked to him and they kissed both his hands. When a woman's husband lay ill in intensive care, David was the one she turned to. It wasn't the real God's shoulders she sobbed on when she wept, "Please, Doctor, save him. Our daughter is having a baby in April and he's looking forward to it," David saved them. Their families thought they would die, but Dr. David Weissman fixed them so they could see the children their children were giving birth to. He had touched men who were pronounced dead and they lived to play a little pinochle and eat a little Danish. Marjorie worshiped him, too. He had her heart to love, to be indifferent to, to pound on if anything went wrong.

"Did you save someone's life last night?" Marjorie asked, assuming he had. She refilled his cup, giving him as much coffee as the cup would hold. She was good at pouring and he held his cup well.

1

''No. Why?'' He put the cup down, knowing it was too hot to drink and too full to blow cool.

''I just figured since you're feeling like God, it must have been because you saved a mortal.'' He looked at her and past her, through the window and into the sun. He felt warmth from everything he saw.

''Nope.'' His hands surrounded the cup. They were definitely doctor's hands, strong, square, perfect tools of the trade. ''I saw Mike Rosen the other day.'' Marjorie brought her hand to her chest only because their family physician was named. The hand would stay there until she found out the results of the examination.

''Why didn't you tell me?'' Her concern was sincere and he would milk it. He swallowed before speaking, even though he hadn't tackled the coffee yet.

''It was just a check-up and everything is fine.'' Her hand left her heart. ''He said I had a prostate of a twenty-one-year-old black athlete.'' David grinned so broadly that Marjorie understood why he felt immortal. She couldn't help feeling jealous. Her gynecologist wasn't telling her that she had anything young or black.

''That's too bad,'' she said.

''Bad?''

''Well, not for you. It's good for you. I just feel sorry for the young black athlete who is missing a prostate.'' He laughed. It wasn't easy to get David to laugh, but Marjorie could do it.

''He's probably not missing one altogether. He probably got mine. He's playing pro basketball at a million and a half a year and is on the road so much he doesn't know he has the prostate of a forty-two-year-old Jewish doctor.'' She laughed. Marjorie was careful. She wasn't an easy laugh, but David could get her to.

''I think I've seen him,'' she said. ''He's always feeling around in his pants after a good shot.'' He laughed again and wound it down into a smile. They had always enjoyed quipping over coffee and since their marriage was not yet in trouble they were having a good time. He especially. Marjorie was willing to pull away, rinse a cup, water the ivy. David wanted the moment to last longer, but he couldn't stop it from passing. The coffee was cooling and so were they, not because they didn't care about each other, but because they did. They had the confidence that there would be hundreds of conversations like this in their lifetimes, so there was no need to extend this one.

She asked him what time he would get home and he told her not to wait for him for dinner. She had been the wife of a cardiologist for eighteen years and knew he would never know in the morning what time he would get home. She kept asking because it always comforted them both when she did. He kissed her at the sink, but she followed him to the door anyway. She told him that Julie needed Band-Aids and Tylenol for camp and to bring them home if he remembered. He took a pen from his jacket pocket and wrote a note to himself on his hand. "Julie-camp," the flesh of his palm said, as he waved good-bye. "See you later," she yelled from the doorway, assured that she would, even though he drove his Porsche too fast. (He laughed at people who cared too much about their cars and yet he loved his.)

Marjorie went back to her country kitchen. She hadn't meant to go country and yet she had, a full year before *The New York Times* design section even mentioned country was desirable. The house had originally been electric and then she had gotten attracted to quilts, some stretched on walls, some on the backs of couches, some that had doubled in price. Then she got fascinated by weathervanes and paintings of other people's ancestors. (Her own were from Russia and Austria and were too busy running from enemies to sit for portraits.) When the eagle came in, everything that wasn't American went out. An antique dealer told her that she had a good eye and she convinced David that the ox harness was charming over the fireplace. She even got him to sleep in the wrought-iron bed, which she bastardized by making it king-sized. (She laughed at people who knew too much about antiques and yet she knew too much about hers.)

She put David's cup into the dishwasher. There was a time in the seventies that she had demanded that they share in the straightening up, but all that demanding seemed unimportant now. Taking care of her husband's cup in the eighties seemed more like a sign of affection than a warning of subservience. Blanca would be there soon to take care of their floors and walls. Thank God for Blanca. (They laughed at people who depended on their maids, but called Blanca a jewel and gave her no-good son a Christmas present every year.)

Marjorie went to the den to phone Amanda. If she didn't let Amanda Fine in on all the details of her life, her day could not begin. Every morning she conformed to the curves of the love seat, placed the red phone on her stomach and punched out the numbers that would bring her friend.

Amanda Fine and Marjorie Weissman had shared it all. They had talked about their vaginas in the sixties, their cunts in the seventies and their pussies in the eighties. They told each other of itches and drips that even their gynecologists never found out about. They got their resale numbers and real estate licenses together. When Amanda had a breast removed, it was Marjorie who had to go to a psychiatrist. They loved each other more than friends were supposed to.

Instead of hello, Amanda said, "You wouldn't believe what's happening. Somebody turned the pool heater up so high if I threw in a couple of chickens, I could have soup for every Jew on the North Shore." Not for a minute did Amanda doubt that she was talking to Marjorie.

"Do you want me to call back?" She would be disappointed if Amanda couldn't talk. Everything was in place for a good conversation.

"Absolutely not. People are out there turning switches down and getting their sunglasses steamed up. I want nothing to do with them. Hold on while I get you on my other phone.'' Amanda liked lying on her bed, her head on three pillows while she talked.

Marjorie waited. She imagined her friend, still in her bathrobe, rushing through the many rooms of her large home. She would be holding her robe as she ran. Just as Marjorie pictured her landing on the bed, there she was saying hello and asking what was new.

"David told me he felt like God," said Marjorie, hoping for a big reaction.

"And you're not panicking?"

"Why should I panic?"

"Haven't you ever noticed that God never had a good relationship?"

"You're right. Maybe because He's always busy on holidays."

"And He's untrustworthy . . . He made what's-her-name pregnant."

"And never sent a support payment." They knew they were on a roll and neither one of them wanted to give it up.

"How is God in bed?"

"All right."

"Just all right?"

Marjorie thought before answering and since her mind always worked quickly when she was talking to Amanda (or David when they were hot), only a couple of seconds passed before she felt the joke coming on. She laughed even before she spoke.

"You've heard perhaps of the big bang theory?" By the time she finished her question, Marjorie's laughter was deep and full.

"Yes." Amanda laughed too just because Marjorie was.

"Well, you can't have both. Either you get God or the big bang." Amanda snorted and Marjorie's eyes teared. They yelled at each other to stop. Marjorie choked out more than once that it wasn't that funny.

Soon they were sighing and catching their breath and telling each other that it was good to laugh. This was something that Marjorie had always known. It was no accident that she had a funny husband and funny best friend.

"I hate to ruin your joy," Amanda said when they were sober enough to talk again, "but do you remember what we have to do today?"

"Of course I remember. Have I ever missed a clean-up session? I'll be there at ten."

"I'll be there at ten-thirty, after you do all the dirty work."

There were no stars in the North Shore Players. So even though Marjorie had played Rose in *Gypsy* the week before, she was still obligated to pitch in and help clean up. By ten o'clock she was walking down the rows of seats of the small basement theater with a paper cup in her hand. She picked up candy wrappers and cigarette butts and hoped that she wouldn't find gum, which she would have to free from the floor with newly manicured nails.

At the same time, Blanca was cleaning her house.

Two

Dr. David Weissman fled down the hall trying to escape from compliments. Still he was caught at the elevator by Evelyn Goldblat, a woman half his size and weight. She looked into his very blue eyes and told him he had worked miracles on her husband. "Myron is sitting up in bed and asking for Häagen Dazs. I tell you, Doctor, it's a pleasure. He even yelled at me today—that's how good he feels. I didn't bring him the right slippers, and you should have heard him screaming about how stupid I am. I tell you, it was just like before the operation. You're an angel from heaven." David had saved other men who lived to yell at their wives and the wives were always thankful. He had learned long ago to treat the heart and not worry about the man.

David held both of Evelyn Goldblat's hands. He wanted to tell her to yell back. If anything happened to Myron, he would paste him together again. "Mrs. Goldblat," he said, "when you came to my office and asked me to see your husband, I had every intention of telling you the truth, that I was too busy to take on any more patients. The minute, the second, I met you I knew that I'd have to see him. There was something about you that made me say yes. I hope your husband appreciates you."

He saw in her face that she was flattered. She straightened one still curl in front of her ear and became flirtatious. Before she had talked with her hands, but now it was with her

eyes. She had heard he was a charmer, but she hadn't expected to fall in love.

She took his face in her hands, using his ears as handles,
pulled him toward her and planted a big one on his cheek.
''So, go. I've kept you long enough. Go work your miracles
on someone else.''

David stopped an elevator from leaving without him with
his forearm. He was in a hurry to do something wrong. He
was after what he had not gotten in his exhausting sexual
youth, and that was romance. Not the kind of romance that
can falsely be put together on winter vacations in Bermuda
with a wife, but the first glimmer of romance, burgeoning
love, something that he could only get with someone new.
The two women he had tried it with before had enjoyed it at
first, and then when he refused to go to bed with them, had
gotten angry. If they were willing to give their bodies, then
he was wrong not to take them. David never understood
their anger. Why couldn't they fall in love, enjoy it and go
home without each other? Didn't they know that the fucking
wasn't the really good part? What had they said about him at
Columbia: he would fuck anything that moved and if it
didn't move he would just go for a dry hump. Those days
were too much alike, available bodies in his small, dark student's apartment. He hadn't known romance then. No one
got flowers or even had her hand held at breakfast. The wife
of the friend had felt betrayed and the nurse still hated him
for the attention he had given her. He really should leave
Elizabeth Pringle alone. But there she was, her hair brushed
and looking capable of taking long walks in the rain, even
though she was ordered to lie in her hospital bed. As David
got into his Porsche, he knew it was wrong to send roses to a
young heart patient whom he wanted to know, yet he needed
to feel the first shy minutes of being with a woman again.

He heard an annoying sound deep within the body of his
Porsche. It was not one of the usual ones that he could tinker
with, but one of those noises that would cost over two hun-

dred dollars and never be gone. When he fixed bodies, they never rattled again.

He pulled into the parking lot at Leo's florist shop and decided since he could see his car at all times from the shop that he would leave it unlocked. Before opening the door that let you know they would wire flowers anywhere, David checked to see if he had enough cash. If you were sending flowers to a woman with alabaster skin, you didn't want it showing up on your MasterCharge.

"Hiya, Doc," said Leo, who was poking wired carnations into a square of green foam. Leo was not artistic and his arrangements were common, but he was conveniently located, a block and a half from the hospital, and he was one of the people who owed David his life.

"Hello, Leo. You're looking good." David meant his words as a casual greeting, but Leo reacted as if he had just been examined.

"You really think so? I was feeling some muscle strain, but I'm sure it's just muscle strain. I've been down at Nautilus and it's in both arms." Leo moved both arms in a circular motion, proving nothing.

"We all get muscle strain." David looked into the glass case that caged the better flowers. He was attracted to some purplish-blue ones, iris, he thought, but he remembered that women had a thing for roses. He pointed out the ones that he wanted sent.

"That's good to know, Doc. I'm going to remember that and I'm going to be relaxed about it. I have a new lease on life now. I'm enjoying life more these days since I looked death in the face. Thursday afternoon I'm going to close the shop up and drive out to Jersey. Just for the pure pleasure of it." Leo grinned, revealing a history of poor dental care. "Did your wife like the flowers you sent for her opening night? I sent the freshest ones in the place and I threw in some baby's breath free of charge."

"She loved them," David said, not wanting to be reminded of a wife while sending roses to another woman.

He paid while Leo assured him that these would be just as fresh because the doc had saved his life. David left feeling like a good guy even though he was about to cloud up lives.

Damn it! The Porsche was making that fucking sound again. He didn't like noises, especially new ones. Why, then, the flowers to Elizabeth Pringle? Why had he spent hours in her room since she had been admitted to the hospital? Why did he want to buy her a tiny diamond on a chain, hoping it would be the first diamond she ever owned. (He laughed at middle-aged men who made fools of themselves with young women, but he was going to the jewelers anyway.)

Elizabeth was sleeping when he looked through the window of her room. Asleep, she looked to him like a child of the sixties, her hair not attended to by beauticians, allowed to wave exactly where it wanted to. He could imagine her in a long dress, walking barefoot in the street, wishing strangers peace and handing out his yellow roses. She was meant to sleep on a mattress on the floor rather than in a hospital bed. He and Majorie had been too adult, too busy getting degrees and too busy having Julie to have ever been flower children. Majorie had had a long white dress and he had enjoyed his grass, but mostly they were too responsible to feel it was the dawning of the Age of Aquarius. He hoped Elizabeth Pringle could get him back there.

David slipped from her room and once again headed to the elevator, this time to get to his office. Again he was stopped, a handful of bony fingers grabbed him from behind. He turned to find Mildred Shullman, an elderly woman, barely five feet tall, stretching to look directly into his eyes.

"Thank you, Doctor," she said, holding on to his arm. Her grasp was too light to keep him there, but he had no intention of leaving. "Thank you for saving my Saul."

"He's fine, Mrs. Shullman. You don't have to thank me, because we didn't have to do anything."

"It was gas, wasn't it? I said, 'Saul, don't worry, it's

gas,' but he kept insisting it was his heart. Thank you, thank you.''

David had trouble saying she was welcome, because he hadn't done anything for Saul. He thought of tactfully removing her hand from his arm and backing away, sort of nodding as he went. It was getting late and if he wanted to get back and see Elizabeth awake before he left the hospital, he would have to get away from all this appreciation. Before he could, Saul walked out of his room, his leather slippers shuffling along the hospital linoleum, his tailored robe exposing skinny white legs. He had meant to enter the hallway with a frown, but upon seeing David, he couldn't help smiling, throwing his arms open and shuffling forward as quickly as he could.

''Doctor David! The man who saved me! You wanna give me a hug or what, you Messiah, you. The Chinese think you save a man's life and you're responsible for him, you know.''

David had to get away from all this unwanted, unwarranted praise. It was fair when they adored him when he used his talent. He was used to those embraces, but he couldn't be a savior for someone he didn't save. He thought of explaining to them once again that all he did was run a few tests and keep Saul there for observation, but that would take more time than he had, so he convinced himself that the kinder thing to do was to let them believe he had healed. Once he had accepted their thank-yous, he decided he had to get the next elevator. He escaped from their petting and the Shullmans watched as he raced down the hall. With each outstretched step he got away not only from them, but also from any guilt he might have picked up. Saul Shullman would praise David to the skies until he got his bill and then his heart attack would become gas again. Mildred would always remember that Dr. David Weissman saved her husband's life and she was the one who knew it was gas from the beginning.

Maybe Elizabeth was awake by now.

Three

These were the lazy days of summer for Julie, the few days between the end of school and the beginning of camp where she lay around the house. Most of the day she had a Sony Walkman attached to her and never heard anyone ask her to pick her curled underwear up off the floor. Julie, weighing in at a hundred and seventy-three pounds, was being forced to go to a fat girls' camp where the owner swore that last year the hundred and fourteen girls who attended had lost over two thousand pounds. The statistics were good enough for David, who was so embarrassed over his offspring that he found an emergency at the hospital to attend to the morning of the father-daughter breakfast at school. Marjorie wanted to know from the camp director if the loss of the two thousand pounds was distributed fairly evenly among the campers or if some found ways of arriving home in the same condition they left.

"We can't guarantee. With some it's glandular," Mrs. Morrison, the director's wife, said.

"She's been checked out. It's just too much food," David said with medical authority.

"She'll lose. They all do, unless it's glandular," Mrs. Morrison guaranteed.

"It's not glandular."

"She has such a pretty face," Mrs. Morrison said, but the

Weissmans couldn't agree, because all they saw was a fat face that cried when it couldn't get enough Mexican food.

David wrote out a check to Camp Cottonwood as the Morrisons were packing up the movie equipment they had brought to show rows of girls, their bodies shaking as they jumped into the blue lake. When they left, Julie cried and said there was no way that she was going to a place where they starved you. She said Madeline Minsk was just as fat as she was and her parents were going to buy her a car if she lost weight. Marjorie and David didn't offer any bribes.

"I'd rather die than go to one of those places. You know what they give you for lunch?" Julie asked, throwing herself on the den couch, taking up too much of it and threatening the springs.

"Fish, vegetables . . ."

"Wrong. They make some cole slaw or something out of shredded cabbage and they say there's meat in it, but there isn't. They never give you protein and everyone is so hungry and malnutritioned that they faint all over the tennis courts. Really, everyone gets anemic and faints and they make you run around in the heat all day until you get dehydrated and then, when you lose all your body fluids, you weigh less."

Marjorie squeezed in next to her daughter. When they sat side by side the tragedy of the daughter was greater. "They have a doctor up there the whole time."

"They have to have doctors because of all those girls who lose all their body fluids and have to be fed intravenously. And they teach you how to vomit. They don't show you that in the movies, the part where the counselors teach the girls how to vomit. Is that how you want me to spend my summer, puking?"

"You're going to Cottonwood," David said, remotely turning on the television, ending the discussion.

"It's your fault I'm fat." And her stomach shook as she screeched.

* * *

Marjorie was cleaning the theater floor and David was examining a forty-five-year-old man who complained of pain in his left arm by the time their daughter awakened.

Julie was getting up feeling queasy and sluggish these days. She got out of bed and threw up before crawling back in. What a laugh that her parents were sending her to camp to lose weight when she was already two months pregnant, maybe three. She didn't know exactly when you started counting from. She didn't know anything about being pregnant except that she probably was. She couldn't call Dr. Rosen because he would bring her parents into it and there would be hell to pay. They had warned her about letting boys into her body. They had been up front and straight about it and let her know in no uncertain terms that she would get pregnant if she had intercourse. Well, they were right. She had had intercourse with Finkle eight times and here she had a baby growing inside her. Her parents had once told her not to open the door to strangers and that if she did she would be punished severely. Well, she had opened her door to Finkle and the punishment had to be much worse than anything she could imagine. Your parents didn't just stop your allowance, or send you to your room, or ground you for getting pregnant.

And it wasn't really the punishment she feared. It was the explosion. There was bound to be some major explosion when they found out. There would be yelling and choking voices and angry sounds bouncing off of walls. She would make her father disappointed and her happy mother sad. She couldn't stand bringing them pain. If she had been thin maybe the bulge of a baby would have given her away by now, but her fat kept her secret. How she was going to survive Cottonwood was another problem. Maybe as her stomach grew they would just consider her one of their failures. Maybe she could convince them it was glandular. Maybe the whole thing would go away. Finkle had.

Julie rolled herself out of bed. Her body didn't want to move, but she had promised Emily that she would come over. She had to do what Emily wanted because she was the only one who knew about Julie being pregnant and was trying to help her figure out what to do. Emily's continual suggestion was for Julie to tell her parents, but she knew them as Mr. and Mrs. Weissman, reasonable people who smiled and asked unimportant questions like "How's it going?" She didn't know the mother and father who looked toward heaven and asked "Why is this happening to me?"

Also, Emily felt Finkle had to be told, but neither girl really knew why they had to tell him, especially since Julie didn't even really like Michael Finkle. It was just that she needed someone besides her parents to love her and he had been willing to do it eight times. With difficulty, she reached down and picked up the jeans she had left on the floor the night before. Without leaving the bed, she lifted her body and pulled them on. She had trouble zipping them, but she always had trouble zipping them. She threw on a big gray polo shirt that advertised Harvard and made her feel small, since it was a man's extra-large. Her mother was always trying to get her to wear neat, feminine clothes but she liked big tops where people couldn't exactly tell where the clothes ended and she began. Maybe the best way of announcing the news to her family was to put on one of those maternity tops that said "Baby" and had an arrow pointing down.

On the top of the stairs was a note from her mother. Rather than bend down and pick it up, it seemed easier to sit beside it and read.

Dear Julie,
   I'm at the theater and will probably be here most of the day. Don't bother making your bed, since Blanca is changing the sheets today. (Not that you ever make your bed.) Please try on the shorts that are on top of the washing machine. You need eight pairs for camp and we better get started.

Love,
Mommy

Fuck the shorts. Nothing fits.

Julie slowly walked the three and a half blocks from her house to Emily's, pulling an occasional leaf off a tree and bending it. She didn't feel good, like she was going to get her period, but it was probably just another false alarm. When she was only a few days late she kept feeling like she was getting it and she ran to the bathroom between every class, and about every five minutes on weekends. The blood she was looking for never came and soon a whole month went by and then two months and she stopped looking. She had read this awful story once about a nun who had gone through nine months of pregnancy without anybody knowing and delivered the baby herself on her bare bed at the convent. Julie supposed that the young nun's habit concealed her pregnancy in the same way her fat was concealing hers.

There was a strange car in Emily's driveway. That meant Mrs. Griffing had a man over. Julie, who didn't know any other man in her mother's bed besides her father, found it exciting that Emily's mother had lovers.

"You can say that because you don't know what it's like. One of them used my toothbrush once. I swear," Emily had said, still annoyed by the act.

"You probably just thought he did."

"I know he did. I brushed my teeth in my mom's room because I was watching TV in there one night when she was out on a date. So I didn't want to miss something and I ran and got my toothbrush and brushed my teeth watching the show, you know? And I left the toothbrush in her bathroom and I swear this guy used it, because it was wet the next morning and there was a dark hair on it. I assume he had dark hair. I don't know because I didn't get to meet that one. Some of them sneak out early so they don't have to meet me and Marcie."

"Maybe they're embarrassed."

"My mom is the one who should be embarrassed. I'll bet she has more sex than the Plasmatics."

"She has to have sex."

"I know she has needs, but she's oversexed or something. There are guys here at least twice a month."

Emily answered the door in small, tight jeans and a white tank top that revealed she still had hopes of developing. She rolled her eyes toward her mother's room, letting Julie know that she was not happy with the situation. Julie looked down the long hallway toward Mrs. Griffing's doorway and saw it was closed. Emily shrugged more than her shoulders. Her whole body shrugged as she talked about her mother's latest escapade.

"This is the third time this schmuck has stayed over and I'm going to have to do something about it."

"How do you know he's a schmuck?"

"Do you see what he's driving? Does a nice guy sleep over some woman's house knowing her kids are right down the hall? It's after twelve o'clock for Chris'sake."

They turned into Emily's room. Emily landed on the pink shag rug, giving Julie, in consideration of her pregnancy, the bed. Julie, whose favorite thing in life besides eating was lying on beds, had argued that the floor had made her nauseated. Emily said she could always have the bed, but only for nine months.

"Would you rather your mother spend the night in a cheap hotel somewhere?"

"Why is that my choice always? I don't want some low-level creep here and I don't want her in a cheap hotel."

"What's she supposed to do? She needs sex."

"Where did you and Finkle do it?"

"All over. Seven times in his room and twice in his car."

"I thought you only did it eight times."

"Oh, yeah. I guess it was six times in his room. He has these pictures of dolphins hanging all over the walls because he says that dolphins will show us the way to the future and help us harvest the ocean. He once said that the best thing you could do was get friendly with a dolphin because it's only a matter of years before we run out of food and the ocean has to be harvested."

"Dumb."

"Yeah."

Emily pulled on her rug. Her room had been done for her when she was eleven years old and then it was just what she wanted. Lately she had been trying to convince her mother that she had to get rid of the pink and lavender and all that white wicker, which was coming apart anyway. In the meantime, she was doing a good job of balding her rug.

"Remember that guy in electronics? At least he had a good business going, and I said to my mother that she really should get serious about him."

"What'd she say?"

"She said something was holding her back. Christ, she's thirty-seven years old. She's lucky someone like that was really serious about her. I told her to stop waiting for Prince Charles, since he was taken."

"She'll find someone."

"That's what I'm afraid of. Most of the guys she hangs out with don't even have houses. They have apartments with all this stereo stuff. The one that's in there now doesn't own a house." Emily had been to his brown and black and chrome apartment and felt the bachelorhood there.

"But you do, and if they get married he could live here." Julie tapped on her stomach. It sounded hollow and she wished it were.

"You don't know about these things, because you've never been divorced. According to the agreement, we only own half of a house and my father owns the other half on account of community property. If some creep without a house married my mom he couldn't move in because my father wouldn't want this stranger to be living in his half or something like that and we'd have to move."

There was a long pause while the girls thought. The good friends were used to silences like these. Having been best friends since junior high, they had spent hours just being close, whether they talked or not. Emily rolled onto her back, and at practically the same time, Julie rolled onto her stomach. One of her arms dangled off the bed and she too began working on the rug that asked to be picked. "Whaddya thinking about?" asked Emily, knowing Julie's worry.

"What am I always thinking about?"

"You've got to tell your parents."

"Oh, yeah. Sure."

"What's the worst thing that could happen?"

"The worst thing that could happen. I dunno. The worst thing that could happen is that my parents hate me."

"They won't hate you. Parents don't do things like that."

"Yeah, but it can feel like they do."

Four

Marjorie and David had started out as equals, two glorious, strong young people who could love each other as much as they loved themselves.

He was the only child of two short parents from Great Neck. They expected their son to be a doctor. (Jack Weissman was a dentist who would have been a surgeon if his family had had the ten thousand dollars more it would have taken.) They were further rewarded when they saw him grow to be six feet tall. He was forty-two years old and they were still measuring him.

She was the younger daughter of Max and Esther Weinstein. They smiled behind her back from the moment she was born and asked her to sing for relatives. When she told them she was going to be an actress or die, Esther clutched her heart, knowing the theater could hurt her child. Marjorie not only insisted that she was going to make it, she made her whole family eat in the dining room even though it wasn't a holiday. (She was sure at thirteen that people who ate in the dining room for no reason were better than people who didn't.)

She was playing the lead in the NYU production of *Little Mary Sunshine* when David first saw her. Since he knew nothing of the theater, he didn't know that the glow she had came from carefully hung lights. Since she knew nothing of life and was determined to make it as an actress, she told him she wasn't interested in marriage. Since they both realized that they were the best of their generation and a perfectly matched pair, they were married a year after they met.

Through the eighteen years of their marriage, they had loved and tortured each other. He had come to the marriage with a history of fucking around and enjoyed the quiet, loving sex he had with his wife. She arrived in David's life after two mild affairs and a couple of months in high school with a great make-out man. He gave her a two-carat diamond and her first orgasm. She recognized the diamond, but not the orgasm.

During the sixties, they sometimes got stoned and made love with a tie-dyed scarf over the closest lamp. She learned to stiffen her body and squeeze and became responsible for her own orgasms.

During the seventies, she had the feeling that every woman in the world was having a better time in bed than she was.

During the eighties, which she already knew was a middle-aged decade, their lovemaking was more erratic than erotic and they had definitely settled into married sex. It wasn't the type of sex that sells novels or that Italian directors are interested in. It was a familiar love where she knew all of his moves. There were no new feels or smells. His body was almost as familiar to her as her own and he could shape his hand, knowing before she got there that she would fit the curve he created. Sometimes they went for a month without touching just because they knew that they were always there and tomorrow would be as good as today. For some reason they stopped kissing.

Marjorie and David had learned to tell each other when they wanted to have sex. She talked softer, brushed her hair in front of him, knowing it was seductive. He walked tall with whatever stomach he had accumulated over the years tucked in. Her nightgown went on in front of him, her arms outstretched as they found the sleeves. As they performed this pre-foreplay dance for each other, lights and covers were turned down. Never was their passion so strong that Marjorie forgot to take off the custom-made quilt. Once they were under the sheets they knew where to turn and how to touch. Unfortunately for Marjorie, her sexual appetite was not what it used to be. Less than fifty times a year used to be enough, but Marjorie at thirty-eight was—in Amanda's words—like a seventeen-year-old boy with a constant boner.

"You used to look in their eyes and now you look in their pants."

"I'll bet you know which side Warren wears his on," Amanda said over chicken salad.

She didn't want to be turned on all the time, but an innocent Twinkie on a grocery shelf was a phallic symbol to her. She could hardly deal with hot dogs.

Marjorie had arrived home late after a long day of cleaning the theater and getting the costumes and props back in place. She should have been tired. She was. She had skipped dinner, but she couldn't skip sex. Last year after dress rehearsals, she had needed a glass of warm milk to relax. This year only a man could wind her up and wind her down again.

He didn't want to. She knew he didn't want to because she had been reading his body language for years. (She now knew English, a little conversational French, and David's body language.) He was at the far side of the bed smelling beautiful and changing the channels. Funny, in their youth he wanted to fuck his brains out and she wanted romance and now she wanted to fuck her brains out and he was sending yellow roses.

She wanted him in her as quickly as possible. It was risky. Lately he had been stopping her advances, not aggressively, but removing her searching hand from his body, kissing it and returning it to her. They had discussed it as openly as married people could and decided that they should never have sex unless both of them wanted to. In principle the concept worked. In reality it left her in bed, hating David's peaceful rest and needing sex before she could hope to fall asleep. (I have sex, therefore I am alive, therefore I can surrender to sleep which is the closest thing to death.) "For Chris'sake, Marge, I'm not a machine, you know," he had said a couple of weeks ago after the fourth day in a row she had tried to get him as a love partner. She wished he was a machine, a man with a vibrator instead of a penis. It could be a pain in the ass replacing the batteries, but it was a hell of a lot easier than these organs that seemed to have a life of their own.

She, like every other woman who had tasted life in the fifties, could never get used to a man not wanting to do it. Back then they all wanted to do it all the time and you had better watch out or they would do it to you. Now, these same penises were content to rest, pointing towards their owners' thighs. Sometimes, they would stand up and be counted, but not necessarily often enough and definitely not often enough for Marjorie.

The scariest thing in bed was when she was needing to be plugged into and "it" selfishly would not respond. "Don't worry about it," David would say, rolling over, yawning, dragging more than his share of the covers with him. But she would worry about it. She'd worry about those limp inches for hours. What if it had resigned and left her service for life? What if it greeted other women, saying its own hello?

Should she risk it tonight? He could remove her hand. "It" could not respond. It could half-heartedly respond, not doing anyone any good. Better just leave it alone, let it rest so there would be more for everyone tomorrow. It looked right resting and wrong erect so what was the big deal in pushing it into service? Her own body couldn't pull any tricks. When you had an opening like all women did, you couldn't lock it up sometimes. You could feel like not doing it, but you always *could* do it, which seemed like an unfair disadvantage. "Vaginas should be more like mouths," Marjorie thought. Somehow they should be able to be sealed tight or at least shut down for the night. Not that she wanted to have the capability of non-functioning the way men did. It would just be nice to have a zipper in the vicinity. Tonight she would unzip herself and stuff him in.

It was eleven o'clock and David had settled in with the CBS news. Marjorie drew in close and threw her most available leg across his stomach. It was a good sign that he left it there. Sometimes he slowly squirmed away or complained that a leg was too much for his full stomach. David watched the news as Marjorie watched the room. She loved the blue bedroom that she had carefully put together during her decorating days. Opposite the white iron and brass bed was the pine chest that housed the television and several quilts, above the chest a carved horse that had possibly been part of a weathervane. At first Marjorie felt that the horse had nothing to do with them, since neither of them rode and the only horses the Weinsteins or Weissmans had ever come in contact with had Cossacks on them, but then she got used to the Americana in her life. There was a rocking chair with a quilt draped over the back between the windows and on the wall closest to the bathroom an old pine chest that looked great, but that David hated because the drawers didn't work well. Marjorie's things were in another pine chest with drawers that also didn't work well, but she wouldn't admit it. The furniture gave her splinters, but it also gave her a sense of owning a part of a country that none of her relatives had anything to do with in 1890.

David changed the channel to NBC and a story about a diner being robbed caught Marjorie's attention. This was no ordinary robbery, they were saying. Four masked armed robbers emptied the cash registers, took the wallets of the customers and then had everybody lie on the floor. At gunpoint, the victims were forced to have sexual activity with each other. There was a shot of the outside of the New Jersey diner and then the friendly news team moved on to the weather. Marjorie didn't move with them.

''Did you hear that?'' Marjorie asked, her leg still draped around her husband.

"What?" David was sleepy and gently pulled the hairs on his chest. He wore pajama tops but never buttoned them. He said he enjoyed the breeze. Marjorie always thought he enjoyed playing with the hairs.

"Did they say that the people on the diner floor were forced to have sex? How can they do that, force people to have sex?" Marjorie was outraged and curious and hoped that David had answers. It was at times too strange a world for her and, like a small child who expected her father to know everything, Marjorie expected David to make sense out of senseless situations. He usually didn't. Marjorie was the sense maker in the family.

"They obviously tied people up. No. You can't tie everyone up and then have them do anything, I don't know." She rolled over on her back and tried to figure it out. She pictured the robbers, the staff, the customers, but couldn't figure out what was demanded or what was done. They could have been forced to disrobe, but what about the erections? Erections couldn't be forced by gunpoint. It chilled her, repulsed her, and like all things repulsive, it wouldn't leave her head.

"It's so perverted." she said. "If they wanted money . . . they got the money. If they wanted to see live sex acts, they could have gone to one of those places on Forty-second Street." Marjorie sat against the brass of the bed, her knees under her chin, her arms wrapped around her knees. One hand reached to the lace at the bottom of her nightgown.

"They must get their kicks out of watching poor souls squirm." It wasn't like David to use an expression like "poor souls." Marjorie didn't know if he was trying to come up with an answer or tired of the whole subject. He flicked the television off and said something about packing it in. Marjorie couldn't let him do that.

"If they wanted to torture them, they didn't have to have them do anything sexual. I think the big questions are: one, what did they make them do, since you can't rape a man, and two, why would four robbers have the same sexual perversion and how did they meet?'' Marjorie tilted her head toward David, once again expecting him to have the answers.

''That's three,'' he said. He was going to turn off his lamp, a simple antique jug wired for light, but he decided not to for the moment. Marjorie was happy because a darkened light in the bedroom was like a curtain coming down in the theater.

''There were four robbers. That I remember.''

''But it was three questions. One, you can't force a man to have an erection. Maybe it was just the women who were molested.''

''They said they forced the victims to perform sexual acts. So that was the victims among themselves. That's what they said.'' Marjorie pointed toward the dead television for her proof.

''To answer your second question, in crimes where two or more criminals are involved, there is often a leader who influences the other into submission. That's the truth. I saw it on a *Hill Street Blues*. And three, I don't know how they met, but I'll take a wild guess and say in a laundromat where the dryers didn't work.''

''Nah. More likely at one of those phone centers with the Mickey Mouse phones that cost ridiculous amounts of money.'' Marjorie slid under the covers. She hoped she would be pursued.

''Goodnight.'' David had a thing about saying goodnight. It was a part of his schedule as was brushing his teeth. Marjorie saddened. Saying goodnight was final. After that there was sleep. In one gesture he turned away and turned out his lamp. He had shut his door.

Marjorie thought that she would let sex go for the night. Then she thought she wouldn't. Then she thought she would. Then she thought of the people on the diner floor and that turned her off.

Or on.

She turned her light off and found her favorite position for sleeping, facing away from David on her stomach. She tried to sleep—not for long, but she tried. There had been times when there was one piece of cheesecake in the refrigerator. She could pass up anything but cheesecake and when it was there, on a plate covered with aluminum foil, she'd hear it calling to her. If Julie hadn't devoured it, she would get it, and using her special cheesecake fork she would stand by the sink and eat it barefoot. There was no way she could ever sleep while that cake was in the refrigerator. Tonight her body was calling to her. The opening between her legs was screaming to be filled and it didn't matter how many positions she crawled into, the opening didn't forget that it was open.

She wanted to leave David alone. He was probably sleeping by now. He didn't want to. There was a risk of rejection. She could wait until he fell asleep and then take care of herself.

Then there she was reaching out for him, sneakily through the back, forcefully separating his thighs so that she could get to the part that had the power to satisfy. Surprisingly, he didn't stop her and her hand got more aggressive. It had just been there the night before, but once again it examined the merchandise. It was all there, the balls and the bat in the middle, all that was needed to play the game. The object, of course, was to get the bat hard enough, long enough so that it would fit inside home plate.

' You sure you want to tonight, Marge?'' David asked sleepily. He had remained very still during these first few moments.

"Yes. Positive." What more could she do to convince him not to take his balls and go home? She worked harder, pressed her breasts against his back. She moved her legs under his, conforming to his form, and sighed as if things were happening to her instead of just him.

"Don't you ever get tired?" he said, not unkindly, finally, turning toward his wife.

"I worry that I'm insatiable." Marjorie reached for David again. She had meant to be playful with her words and less than a year ago they would have been taken as light-hearted seduction, but David looked worried. "Don't worry, darling. It's just a phase. You know that thirty-eight-year-old women are like seventeen-year-old boys." She didn't want to have to explain her sexuality, especially while she was having sex. Discussion ended.

David gently, he was always gentle, that was the problem, lifted her nightgown. She wanted him to take it off, but he seemed content to open only that part of the present that he needed. He raised it to just above her breast. Instinctively, she raised her left shoulder thinking her breasts would look even. (For months she had been sure that her right breast was sagging faster than her left.) He touched her right nipple and then with one light finger circled it. The man of her fantasy, the one she had never had, grabbed a handful of breast, with dirty fingernails. When she first married David and was still scared of men, she was grateful for his light touch and the tickling. Now, even as she lay there being fondled, she wondered if she shouldn't have started anything tonight. She could have pulled the polish off her big toe. Sometimes that relaxed her.

They foreplayed nicely and when she felt he had been hard enough long enough, she eased him onto his side, facing her, and locked her left thigh over his right one. She forced them to fuck in this democratic position. She had learned that when they faced each other if she stiffened her body hard enough and moved to her own rhythm, she had a chance of coming while he was still inside her. A chance. On this night, although she tried and tried and tried again, her body hitting against his stomach, she felt that she was taking too long and probably not going to make it. She worked harder. Her face tightened. Sounds she didn't want to make escaped from her. Soon it was not ecstasy she was experiencing, but work. He climaxed in her and for the moment she was jealous. He had been writhing too, but his pleasure seemed more easily had, while hers took hard work. Never in a sex scene in a movie had she seen the heroine strain. She kept going, assuming it was all right with him. She held his back to let him know to stay in place, and pushed ahead knowing he was ready to call it a night. Finally, finally, it was there, not strong, weak, but relieving her from the tension that had been started minutes before. When her body relaxed, he knew that they had both been successful. Immediately she was happy she had gone for it, and glad that she hadn't been too lazy to have sex and glad that there was sex to have. She held him tightly and he held her and, even though she had done the work for both of them, she was grateful and in love. This was their sex. She wanted to tell him to work harder and someday she would. She would as soon as she got her mother's voice out of her head saying "He's a doctor. He works hard all day." Once, in an honest conversation in a Connecticut hotel, she had asked him to be more forceful. He promised he would, but never did.

He fell asleep and she was restless and jealous. He came easily. He peed easily. He slept easily while she stayed up and concentrated on her wanting vagina. It was ready to go again. It wanted to boogie and it had just been given a delicate waltz.

Marjorie got out of bed and in the dark found her way to the vibrator that Amanda had given her as a joke. Amanda didn't know it, but Marjorie had gotten a lot of use out of the joke, on mornings after baths, on nights when David wasn't home, on nights when David wasn't enough.

She took the vibrator out of the pale blue lingerie case and stole away to the guest bathroom down the hall. There she lay on the bathroom rug, a peach one that she had bought at B. Altman's for its softness. She raised her gown and pushed the button on the white plastic cone. Hell. The batteries were gone. Weren't they supposed to be ever ready for times like this? OK. Don't give up hope, faith or orgasms. There were batteries in the electric mixer, the flashlight. There were batteries in Simon, that game with the lights.

She was down in the den and back in the bathroom and on the peach rug in record time. She locked the door, but wished David could see her.

Julie didn't hear her mother's movement. She lay in her bed thinking of Streisand. She was thinking of how lucky Barbra was to be famous and rich and talented and not pregnant. Julie had a pretty good voice. Maybe if she became a singer, not as big as Barbra Streisand, because she was the biggest and the best, her parents wouldn't be so pissed off that she was pregnant. Not that they wouldn't notice, or wouldn't care or wouldn't scream and yell, but somehow singers got away with things that other people didn't. Grace Slick got away with murder. She could have ten kids without being married and no one would bat an eyelash. Even Streisand had lived with someone and not married him and her mother came to visit. It was in the magazines all the time.

Julie put her Sony Walkman on and sang with Deborah Harry. She thought they sounded pretty good together. Maybe she could be one of her back-up singers or a Harlette. If she could be a Harlette and have a baby, her parents would be confused, because singing was considered a good thing in her household, especially by her mother, who was always telling her to use her chest voice.

Rock singers get away with everything. Wasn't it Grace Slick who had a baby without being married? Yeah, it was Grace and the father was Paul something. Paul . . . Paul from Jefferson Starship. Paul Kantner and the baby was named God. Grace changed it later to China, but it was named God. Rock singers get away with everything.

Her mother laughed when Julie did an impression of Bette Midler and kept making her do it for Amanda and whoever else was around. Once she burst into her parents' room with this Bette Midler-type wig and a towel wrapped around her and sang "Swanee" and they applauded when she was finished. It was real applause and she could tell that they thought she had talent because they were both getting dressed for some big party or something, but they stopped buttoning and zipping to listen to her. And they didn't have to applaud. Maybe she could do a demo record and get it heard. Emily's uncle was actually in the music business. He knew Streisand when she was just starting out and he knew right from the beginning that she would go far.

Maybe the uncle would listen to the demo. They said "demo" in the music business, that much she knew. If you said demonstration record you were really from nowhere. It was possible that the uncle would recognize Julie's talent, everyone said she had perfect pitch, and help her to get an agent or a contact. It sure would help this pregnancy problem. Too bad she didn't know how to get a demo made or how to do anything about this baby.

Five

When Marjorie first moved to Syosset with a baby in her arms, and the feeling that her child would grow, but she would shrink, Amanda Fine saved her artistic life. They found each other in the supermarket about a month after Marjorie moved into the house that David had loved and she had thought she could do things to. (They laughed at people who had mortgages, but had one in their twenties.) She was passing through the cereals when a squat woman in too much purple deposited her two-year-old daughter in Marjorie's shopping cart and took off after her three-year-old son, who was happily walking through the electric doors. Marjorie expected her back immediately, but the lady retrieved her older child and casually worked her way back to cereals, shopping along the way.

"She likes you," Amanda said, making no effort to take her daughter back.

"Can I give her a cookie?" The child was trying to open a box of Oreos and eating the paper it was wrapped in. "Sure. You want her?" The question was asked seriously.

"Want her?" Marjorie was unsure of what this woman was asking.

"Yeah. If you want her, you can have her. Think about it." Amanda Fine and her other child moved down the aisle and Marjorie could do nothing but watch her. This purple woman chose food with no interest, her small arms emerg-

32

ing from the huge cape, grabbing cans as she made her quick decisions. It all seemed silly, since she was about the size of a small sixth-grader. She reminded Marjorie of the type of woman she had left behind in the city rather than the ones who usually guided their carts in the clean, suburban markets. Those women always wore versions of their college clothes and looked like they were on their way to a foursome.

Marjorie continued shopping with the unasked-for little girl in her basket and didn't run across Amanda until paper products. "I know you're supposed to match toilet papers to bathrooms, but when it really comes down to it, I don't think people care if they wipe their asses with flowers or not. Do you?" Once again the question was earnestly asked. The small woman waited for an answer.

"It just looks nicer."

"You're not one of those women who puts crocheted dolls over the extra roll of paper are you? You know, where the skirt covers the roll because no one wants to admit it's there."

"No."

"Good. I don't want my kid growing up in a home where they have to hide toilet paper. How's she doing?"

"Fine. That's her second cookie . . ."

"You've got to do me a favor. Please, *please* invite me to her sweet sixteen. I won't mind missing her sixth-grade graduation because I understand they only give two tickets and you and your husband will want to go, but what would it hurt you to have me there for her sixteenth birthday? That way I can see how she's blossomed into a young lady. I promise you, I'll put it in writing, I'll never tell her who her real mother is. . . . It would be odd if I just showed up as one of the guests. Maybe I could arrive with the caterers and wear a maid's uniform. I just want to see her almost all grown up. You wouldn't deny me that, would you?" Amanda kissed her baby on both cheeks, European style, and took off again. Marjorie followed her into fresh produce.

Marjorie Weinstein had learned how to shop for groceries at her mother's side at the local Gristedes on Columbus Avenue before she even attended kindergarten. Her mother often told her that it was better to pay a little more in order not to be subjected to bruised fruit. Mrs. Weinstein picked cautiously, handling each peach even though a hand-printed sign warned her not to. She carefully looked for the slightest blemish and totally trusted her own judgment. The Weinstein daughters shopped like their mother.

Amanda was filling a large brown bag with fruits and vegetables. Not only was she not inspecting anything, she wasn't even looking, and a handful of string beans, three tangerines, two potatoes and a banana went into one bag and another combined apples and brussels sprouts. Esther Weinstein would have whispered "That woman needs help," and she wouldn't have meant in bagging produce.

"What a lovely little girl. My husband and I can't have children," Amanda said sadly, looking into Marjorie's cart.

Marjorie looked toward Amanda's son who was by now under her arm and the image of her, including the sparse red hair. Noticing Marjorie's momentary stare Amanda quickly added, "Oh, him. He's just a friend," and she took a bite out of a cucumber before placing it in the bag along with the grapes.

This time Marjorie moved away. The game she was forced into playing with this smiley woman was fun and not that different from the improvisations she had had to do in acting class. It was certainly better than methodically filling her basket with the same foods that she would have to buy again next week. The little girl in her cart was leaving a trail of crumbs Hansel and Gretel style so there was no doubt that her mother would find her.

After finishing her shopping and doing a mediocre search for her new purple acquaintance, Marjorie headed for the cashier, sure that the woman in the cape was about to appear and reclaim her child, who was standing up and pulling packages of Juicy Fruit gum into the cart. The cashier, a teenager who was trying to hide her acne, ignored Marjorie, the child and the groceries, her fingers working quickly to add up the total.

"Is that it?" she asked.

"That's it for now," and she handed over three twenties, expecting change.

"There's a special on dented peas. I mean the cans are dented. The peas are fine." She indicated a shopping cart that had been filled with cans of peas with unattractive dents. A sign said they could be had for twenty-one cents apiece.

"No, thanks." Marjorie was sure there was botulism in every can. She wouldn't even buy one with a ripped label.

"It's real weird how we can't get rid of those and the peas are fine. People are scared of the dents or something."

"I don't need peas."

"You could stock up." She held the change in her hand as if she was going to convince her customer to buy the peas.

"Peas are just not my husband's favorite."

"Maybe for company or something. They wouldn't have to know you got them on special. You could throw the cans in the garbage before they come."

"Really, no. I don't need any," and Marjorie held her hand out.

"Too bad. It's a really good special and you can't tell a book by its cover . . . you want gum? 'Cause if you do I'm gonna have to ring it up separate." By now the child had over a dozen packs of gum in the cart.

"No, thanks. No gum either."

"You're going to have to take the one your kid opened. We don't take back opened gum. Store policy."

"Just take it out of my change." The cashier carefully gave Marjorie the money which was owed her, her receipt for the groceries and her receipt for the gum. Marjorie took the gum from the child fearing that she would swallow it.

Since Julie was only about eight months at the time she had no idea when gum and children got together. The child, who had been perfectly behaved up to then, howled, her heart breaking. Her world was that gum. "Have you seen a woman in a purple cape with a little boy?" The girl with the acne was on to her next customer and talked over her shoulder.

"Yeah. She checked out."

"She couldn't have."

"She did. She bought about six of those peas and had the exact change. Exactly. Hardly anyone has the exact change, but if they did the world would be much more efficient. You know what I mean? Because I could probably check through three more people an hour if I didn't have to give change."

"You sure she checked out?"

"I'm sure. She had the exact change."

Marjorie checked up and down the aisles for the woman she would learn to know as Amanda Fine. At first she figured they were just missing each other, but gradually she panicked when it was evident that she was no longer in the store and that she had no way of reaching her. As she walked the aisles, her mind was running down the dialogue she would have to tell the police. The hardest part would be why she had accepted the child in the first place. The authorities could rightfully doubt the true story and change her from recipient to suspect. And what if the mother reported her as a kidnaper? Mrs. Weinstein would have said that anyone who mixed fruits and vegetables in the same bag was capable of other craziness. Damn it, David would have a right to be mad. She was supposed to help him start a practice by meeting nice women whose husbands might have heart attacks. She wasn't supposed to be arrested for kidnapping. She wasn't even supposed to let a bag of Oreos be opened before they were paid for. The little girl was perfectly calm as Marjorie took her to the car. Not thinking clearly, her priorities were off. It seemed more important to get the ice cream she had just bought into the freezer than to get the child to the police and beat the kidnaping rap. It wasn't until she started loading the station wagon (they laughed at people who had station wagons, but bought a new one every other year) that she realized that the woman was sitting in the front seat, her son on her lap. They were both eating raw string beans, enjoying the crunch as much as the taste.

"Can you drop me off?" she asked harmlessly.

"You petrified me. Why didn't you tell me you were leaving the store?" Marjorie's anger showed.

"I don't know why. Who can know why, when it comes to these things. I spotted you in there and I had this compulsion to add some drama to your life."

"My life has enough drama in it."

"In Syosset? Are you kidding? People out here don't even fuck. My pussy has been asleep for a week."

"Do you do this often?"

"I come shopping often but I have never, *never* given away one of my kids before. Come to mama, Tallulah." She reached for her little girl and made room for her on her lap. "I wanted to meet you ever since I saw you in *The Glass Menagerie* at NYU, but I was too shy to come backstage. Today when I saw you I wanted to come over and introduce myself. The first thing I thought of doing was giving you Tallulah. I figured if you had my kid, I'd have to meet you sometime. I mean, if I gave you a lamb chop we might never have gotten to talk. I'm Amanda Fine and you're Marjorie Morningstar."

"Marjorie Weinstein, Weissman now."

"Everyone called you Marjorie Morningstar."

"That's because of Herman Wouk's book. There was this—"

"I read it fifteen times. If I had been tall enough I would have been Marjorie Morningstar."

"I guess we all would have been."

"So what happened to her?"

"What always happened to her? She had a destiny to fulfill. She married a doctor, had a baby. She shops in supermarkets and isn't even brave enough to buy dented cans of peas."

"You were good in that show. I cried and I'm not a crier."

Amanda managed to get her arms past her children and behind the wheel in order to embrace Marjorie, who got to taste Amanda's cape. It felt good for Marjorie to have a fan again. Her last performance, the birth of Julie, was big, but rapidly fading.

"Thank you. I can't believe you remember. Where can I drop you?"

"You're rejecting me," Amanda sulked.

"No. No, really. I just have to get home. I don't like to leave the baby too long with the housekeeper."

"If she speaks anything but English, you can leave it. The ones who speak English are the real killers."

"Really. I have to—"

"I didn't know you had a baby. If I knew I wouldn't have given you one of mine . . . You were supposed to laugh at that. You're rejecting my friendship. I understand because I was just a little nobody at NYU, majoring in elementary education with a lot of dull girls, and you were a big star in the drama department."

"That was years ago and totally unimportant."

"So, take me to your place. I'll get a ride from there." Marjorie drove Amanda Fine to her split-level house although she feared that once she let this woman into her home she would never leave. (She had already prematurely hugged her and had given signs of clinging.) However, she surprised Marjorie. She handled her two children well, complimented the matching gold carpet and drapes, loved the peacock-blue accent, marveled over the baby Julie, and telephoned for a ride within five minutes of entering the Weissman home. A short time later, after she had refused even a glass of water and praised Marjorie again on her performance in *The Glass Menagerie*, a chauffeur-driven Rolls-Royce pulled into the driveway to take her home. Marjorie tried not to be impressed and Amanda tried not to impress her.

"Nice meeting you, Amanda. I hope to see you again."

"I'll call you tomorrow. I got your number off the phone . . . and Marjorie, maybe I was only an elementary education major, but I can act circles around you. I'm brilliant. Brilliant. I would have been a huge star if I had been taller. Name one star as short as me and don't say Judy Garland, I'm shorter than she was at her shortest."

Eventually Marjorie Weissman would realize that Amanda hadn't lied. She was a brilliant actress. Brilliant. She was also one of the richest women in the world. Amanda, as promised, called the following day and her life and Marjorie's began to mingle.

It was because of Warren Fine's generosity, which David always thought was a bit too showy, that Amanda and Marjorie were able to start their community theater group. Warren donated a hefty sum to the Greater Syosset Sisterhood, earmarked for special events, and Amanda stepped right in and took over what was to become the North Shore Players. She made one thing clear from the start. She and her good friend Marjorie Weissman would be doing most of the female leads. Consequently the part of Lorelei Lee in *Gentlemen Prefer Blondes*, which calls for a young, beautiful blonde, was played by Amanda Fine while she was six months pregnant.

Six

Amanda started honking five houses away from Marjorie's. They were late for the North Shore Theater Board meeting and she was letting the neighborhood know. On the tenth honk, Marjorie opened the front door and gave Amanda the finger. Amanda yelled, "Fuck you, bitch!" and gestured in broad Italian, turning the lovely treelined Syosset street into the South Bronx. Marjorie had asked her to keep her trashy mouth shut on her block, but Amanda had insisted that you could say anything you wanted out the window of a really expensive car.

Marjorie emerged minutes later, smiling and looking great in the tailored linen pants and shirt that had always been her summer uniform. "You look good enough to eat," yelled Amanda, hoping at least Blanca, who fooling around with the garbage, heard her.

Marjorie swung into the car and Amanda took off before the door was closed. She looked like a child when she drove. Her short legs barely reached the pedal. Her eyes barely peeked over the steering wheel. She always drove too fast and considered her passengers victims, laughing as they clutched any of the handles that were available to them. As she screeched around corners, she actually enjoyed seeing Marjorie slam her foot on brakes that weren't there.

"Where were you last night? I called more than once," Marjorie asked on a calm stretch of road.

"My husband took me dancing."

"No."

"How come you know it's no? Just like that you know everything about my life?"

"Everything. I know when you're going to have to scratch your ass."

"That's an interesting talent."

"You weren't dancing last night. If you had been dancing, I would have felt the movement."

"So we weren't dancing, but we did go to see a movie with dancing in it so it's practically the same thing. I could have been a fabulous dancer if only I had been taller. Audiences don't like little dancers. It reminds them of all those Munchkins in the *The Wizard of Oz*. Maybe if I had found a little Fred Astaire we could have done movies with little scenery behind us." Amanda took another sharp turn and Marjorie refused to show her fear, knowing her friend was looking for it.

"I called to tell you that Eleanor doesn't think I need any more therapy. For some strange reason she thinks I'm fit enough to lead a normal life."

"She's getting senile."

"Anyway, since you weren't home I figured out how much it cost me to go to her. You owe me approximately thirty-six hundred dollars. I'll settle for four thousand."

"You never should have gone to that cockamamie philosopher in the first place. You don't go running off to a shrink every time a friend goes into the hospital for a trim."

"I only went because you were sitting there laughing your head off."

"Of course I was laughing. The Valium was flowing. The Demerol was there for the asking. Morphine was not out of the question. What I lost in flesh, I gained in drugs. I was too doped up to take anything seriously, especially the loss of part of a body I'm not too crazy about in the first place. I cried when I got home."

"You never told me."

Amanda got serious for the moment. They were forced to wait for a red light and Amanda did more than wait. She rested her head against the seat, her eyes closed. Marjorie figured she would have to watch for changing lights. "I liked you worried about me," Amanda said, her eyes still closed. "I've always looked so capable. My hands always looked like they could open jars and they can. Everyone else, including Warren, thought that I was joking around, that I was perfectly OK. And I was. Maybe not perfectly OK but I would really rather lose a tit than anything else. If you're not breast-feeding twins, you really don't need two. Anyway, everyone else in my life cried for me, but they continued their lives. You were the only one who fell apart enough to go to a shrink."

"I only went because you wouldn't."

"When you did, I didn't have to."

The light had already changed, but since there were no cars behind them, there was no reason to go. When Amanda felt rested and wordless, she shot forward, taking a long country road as if it were hers.

Marjorie never loved Amanda more. She would have reached out and put her arms around her if she hadn't been afraid of dying. They were going too fast to touch, so Marjorie had to do it with words. "You're the best," she screamed. "You can collapse on me any time. I swear I can take it. It was that fake strength that scared the shit out of me."

"Next time I feel like crying I'll come over so you can see me do it."

"You promise?"

"I promise, and if I ever have another tit removed, you'll see me fall apart."

"That's not going to happen."

"And if it does, it won't be the end of the world. Everyone in *Vogue* looks like they've had a double mastectomy. I'll be able to wear those size one T-shirts."

By now they were at the theater, which was housed in the

basement of Temple Emanu-El. Amanda raced into a parking spot that said "Reserved for Rabbi Fleischer" and braked just before hitting the wall. "OK, time to think clearly." Amanda turned to get a large leather briefcase with overflowing papers from the back of the car. The case had old scripts, swatches from their decorating days, contracts on houses from their real estate days. It held nothing that she would need for today's meeting, but she always carried it when she was in the official capacity of producer of the North Shore Players. "It's filled with crap," she said, "but the leather is so good it makes people shut up." Amanda couldn't reach it but Marjorie's longer arms dragged it into the front seat.

"We're going to be late," Marjorie said when she noticed that Amanda had her arms folded in front of her and was making no attempt to leave the car.

"Before we go in there, you and I have got to be in sync."

"I thought we were. Am I crazy or did we sit by your pool last week and figure out the four shows we wanted to do?"

"We start out with *Camelot* and you play Guinevere. Right?" Amanda turned the car back on so that they could have use of the air conditioner. Marjorie sensed that their mini-meeting was going to take longer than she hoped it would.

"Right, as long as you know that I'm only doing it because I think it will be a commercial success. I hate the idea of playing a virgin."

"That's only because you're oversexed right now. You'll calm down by September and we'll move the first four rows back. The second show should be *Irma La Douce*, starring *moi*." Amanda smiled broadly, enthusiastically looking forward.

"Thank God you don't mind playing a whore as much as I mind playing a virgin."

Amanda tried to strike a sexy pose behind the steering wheel. It worked and it didn't work. The pose was as sexy as she could make it but her elbow hit the horn. "OK, I'll be doing the whore around the beginning of November, which is great because I'm going to lose half my body fat by then. In March, you'll knock them dead with *A Little Night Music*. You can't complain about that part. Who can play an actress who gives up her personal life for the theater better than you?"

"I'm not complaining. I hope I can do it."

"You'll do it. You'll do it. What does Martha Rosenberg always say? That Marjorie Weissman is better than you get on Broadway for a million dollars a ticket."

"And we end the season with both of us in *Fiddler*," Marjorie said as she opened the car door. Amanda pulled her back.

"We've done *Fiddler on the Roof* three fucking times in the last seven years," Amanda said, ready for a fight. All her features narrowed and her hands automatically closed into fists.

Marjorie turned toward her, leaning on the car door, something her mother told her never to do. "We had this fight already. We settled it two days ago."

"I had a change of heart," said Amanda, trying for sympathy.

"We looked at the box office receipts. Nothing does better than *Fiddler*." Marjorie was exasperated. On Saturday they had gotten together to put together the fall schedule. They had agreed on the first three shows and spent an hour arguing about the fourth. Amanda wanted them to expand, she said. They had to take risks. Marjorie reminded her that every time they tried something different, nobody came. Neither one of them had the stomach to play to empty seats. *Chorus Line* came up more than once with Amanda pushing for it and Marjorie shooting it down. "Amanda, the youngest member of our company is thirty-six and I think she's lying. We're going to look like assholes singing about getting a chance in show business." Amanda's solution to the "too old" problem was to turn down the lighting. "We'll use pink gels and stand toward the back of the stage.'' Marjorie won, only because it was going to be an expensive season and they already had the sets and costumes for *Fiddler on the Roof*. She thought the season was settled and now there was Amanda pushing again.

"The great thing about having a community theater is that we don't have to look at the receipts. We can experiment.''

"If you're talking about *Chorus Line* it's not exactly experimental. It opened on Broadway years ago. We're too old. We could call it *Chorus Lines*.'' Marjorie was happy with her argument and considered herself the winner. "I wanted to do *Evita*, but the rights cost too much so I'm giving it up. I wanted to do *Agnes of God* but I know a play about a nun having a baby wouldn't go over in a temple.'' Marjorie knew she had painted herself as a saint, but she didn't feel like taking any of it back.

"Where's your courage?'' asked Amanda.

"I thought we were going to do a commercially successful year so that we could help build a gym for the temple.''

"I decided we should fuck the gym. When I was a kid in the Bronx, my temple didn't have a gym. Where is it written that a temple has to provide basketball?''

"Most of our company will look like jerks in leotards.''

"You're going to have to give in,'' Amanda said, showing she had aces up her sleeve.

"Why?'' said Marjorie, vowing to herself she wouldn't. The result was becoming much less important than the fight.

"Because I'm sick.'' Amanda pointed to her missing breast. She had replaced the breast with a form so the outsider couldn't tell, but Marjorie squirmed at the reminder of what was missing.

"You told me the doctor told you you were disease-free.'' Marjorie was scared. She had been comfortable minutes before but now shivered, having to rub her arms to keep warm. Amanda saw Marjorie suffering and rushed to relieve her. "I am disease-free. Those were his exact words, only with cancer they never think of you as cured and they only stop worrying if it doesn't show up anywhere else after seven years." She saw Marjorie relax, close her eyes and get angry.

"So for the next seven years you're going to point to your missing boob and blackmail me?"

"I guess so. It's one of the few weapons I have and it makes me puke to think of doing *Fiddler on the Roof* again."

Marjorie gave in. She opened the car door and headed for the temple entrance. Amanda was always faster, but Marjorie's long legs took her farther and she won the race to the door.

"It's settled then?" Amanda screamed after her down the temple hall. "The last show is *Chorus Line* and I get to do the number 'Tits and Ass.' I swear to God it'll be great and a very interesting comment on society."

The meeting lasted no longer than forty minutes. The board met in a religious school classroom and sat on chairs that made their knees reach their chests. Herm, the director, was anxious to get back to his restaurant. Rose Lehman made a motion that they try to sell season tickets and Amanda Fine pushed her season through. There was some question about whether *Chorus Line* would work, but Amanda reminded everyone who owned the lights and two hundred of the four hundred chairs.

When they got into the car, Amanda sang "There's No Business Like Show Business" exactly the way Ethel Merman would. Most of the time, in order to really sell the song, both her hands were off the wheel waving and punching out the tune. Marjorie tried to think of herself hours ahead at dinner with Julie, just to prove she would survive the trip.

"Did you ever think this wasn't supposed to be your life?" Marjorie asked when she started taking the song seriously. There had always been times in her life when she realized there was no business like show business.

"This wasn't supposed to be my life. I was supposed to

meet someone on the stoop in front of my house and be aggravated by him. Warren gave me no aggravation and a pool. I'm one of your overachievers.''

"I was supposed to be an actress. I was determined. I don't know where my determination went.''

"You're an actress. You act all winter. Those real actresses in New York don't get to work.''

"I meant professional." Marjorie put the car visor down, and seeing herself in direct sunlight, she wanted to put it right back up. She left it down to see if she had the face of a professional.

"You know you do this to me every year. We set the schedule and you go soppy on me. We are professional. Jack Pomerance was with the Met and you've played opposite him. How much more professional can you get?''

"He owns a chain of hardware stores.''

"Only because it's more profitable than singing with a spear. And Thelma Meyerson was under contract to David Merrick.''

"That's what she says.''

"The show closed in Boston. Are you going to blame Thelma for that? All I'm saying is we have a semiprofessional group and we do good work.''

"We do great work," Marjorie said, throwing the visor up.

"And we sell out.''

"Yep, we sell out.''

Seven

Julie tried on three pairs of shorts, but none of them would close. They lay in a pile on the floor that she knew she would be yelled at for, but yelling was easier to take than putting them away. She didn't have the energy for anything these days; even flopping on her bed took all she had. What was she going to do at that goddamn fat camp when they made her do things like play basketball? "Exercise is a big part of our program," the camp brochure warned. Damn it. How was she going to play basketball when she felt like she had swallowed one?

She heard her mother singing in her bedroom and thought she was wasting a great voice. She could have been a rock singer if she wanted to. Barbra Streisand was almost exactly her mother's age. It would be great to be Barbra's kid. She would probably be thin for one thing. She would send her to one of those places in Switzerland that Emily told her about once where they put you to sleep for about a month and a half and you wake up skinny. Barbra Streisand would also probably get her a recording contract or she would at least have some of her important record people over and maybe she would ask her to sing and eventually someone would recognize her talent. Her mother had her sing for friends, and especially her grandmother, but what was her grandmother going to do about it? All her grandmother did was kiss her too close to her lips and smell old. Sometimes

Grandma tried to get her to sing, as she put it, "more cultural music," but she could listen for hours, she said. Who knows, maybe Barbra Streisand's mother could listen for hours too. If she was Streisand's daughter she wouldn't have known Finkle.

Thinking of Finkle made her go to her desk, open the drawer, get out her stationery box and take out the postcard that she had received from the Fink that morning.

"Dear Julie, just got here this afternoon. Camp is great. The lake is great. The kids are great. Write if you get a chance. Mike."

What a dope thinking everything was so great after being there less than twenty-four hours. Finkle was like that. He took in the whole picture at once and made an instant opinion. When they went to see *Superman II* he decided that it wasn't as good as the first one in about three minutes. They had a fight because he wanted to leave even though they had paid five bucks apiece to get in. That was before they had sex and she couldn't get him to pay for the movies just by saying she would never do it again.

Everyone had said they better be careful and they were pretty careful. He always wore rubbers, although they both knew from sex education that it was not the safest contraception. He wanted her to get something better, but she didn't want to go to a gynecologist and those rubbers looked safe. When he took them off, they were full of sperm so she was sure that they had captured all the possible babymakers. She had a feeling that sex was better without rubbers, like holding hands was better without gloves, but she never once suggested that they do it without protection because she didn't want to get in trouble. Hah. She was in trouble anyway and her mother, who was singing sweetly in the next room, was going to shatter like glass and all the broken pieces were going to rain on her, a continuous rainfall of sharp, jagged edges that were going to hurt. Her father's wrath was easier to take because he said what he had to and left you alone. Her mother didn't stop. When she wanted Julie to go to this crummy weight camp she talked about it until you had to find some drawer to hide in or you had to wear a Walkman twenty-four hours a day. Jesus, she wished she could forget about this baby business but she couldn't get it or Finkle out of her head. She should have stopped him. All she had to do was be there and he took off all her clothes and everything. He took her hands and put them where he wanted them, which was always the same place. She held his penis as if it were a microphone and Finkle put his hands on hers and guided them up and down. (She wished it was a microphone. It would be more fun singing into it than moving it.)

In the meantime, before intercourse began, he kissed her breasts and moved his finger inside her, doing more for her than the Ivory Soap she had let float up between her legs when she was in the bathtub ever did. If it had been up to her, they would never had had intercourse because that was her least favorite part of the whole thing. She liked the feelings and she liked the really good part at the end, but she always felt guilty when he was in her. It wasn't up to her. Finkle always got on top and pushed himself into her body. The eight times they did it, she had tried to get him not to do it, but he always got his way, not only because he was stronger than she was. He was smarter, able to come up with more reasons why he should than she could why he shouldn't.

"Don't," she said.

"I have to."

"You don't have to."

"Do you know what'll happen if I stop now?"

"Nothing."

"Nothing physically maybe, but cutting off at this point can be very castrating."

She didn't want to be a castrating woman. Emily's mother had been castrating, yelling at her father all the time and she was suffering the consequences, having no husband and having to sleep with a lot of different men. Julie's mother cheered up her father and he was still with her. The only way of cheering up Finkle when he wanted to fuck was to fuck.

Marjorie knocked on and opened her daughter's door at the same time, which drove Julie crazy. Why bother to knock if you're going to open the door and come in without being asked to anyway? She hid Finkle's postcard behind her back, as if hiding her pregnancy. There was no reason to be secret. The card said nothing and, not knowing the dirty things he did with her daughter, her mother liked Mike Finkle. Through an adult's eyes he was a nice boy. Adults didn't think of teenagers as failures if they were just failures with each other.

Marjorie knew her daughter was hiding something and assumed it was food. Julie had been sneak-eating since she was six. "You'll be sorry if you eat that," she said, and Julie thought for once that her mother was right.

"It's not food. It's personal."

"If you lose twenty pounds this summer I'll get you a completely new wardrobe." Julie thought they would have to be maternity clothes and wondered why her mother was talking about pounds constantly. She didn't realize that her body was a constant reminder to her parents that something was wrong.

"I have to meet Emily. We're going to a movie. Daddy said he would drive us there since Emily can't get the car tonight."

"How come you're not driving?" Julie hated the question. She had stopped driving at night because she was just too tired. She wanted the conversation ended and the postcard back in the drawer.

"I have a headache," said Julie as an excuse for not taking the car. Immediately Marjorie looked worried. Mountains of snow meant broken legs and headaches could lead to tumors if you didn't lie down. (She laughed at Jewish mothers, but she tore her hair out.)

"Maybe you shouldn't go to a movie with a headache." Marjorie was already heading for the Tylenol.

"No, the unusual thing about me is that movies actually cure me. That's why I'm going and Mom, you sounded great just now. Your voice I mean."

Marjorie almost cried because of the compliment and because they lived in a house where they hardly ever complimented one another.

"Thanks, baby. You know, sometimes I hear you, I can't help it, you have those headphones on and . . . you're loud. And I'm impressed. Really. You've got a good, strong voice."

Julie beamed. Marjorie beamed. It felt soothing to both of them to be good to each other.

"When I listen to you sometimes I think it's the radio. You could have made money with your voice."

"No." Sometimes Marjorie thought she could have but she always said "no" when somebody suggested she could have been a professional.

"Yeah. You sound just like those real singers. Sometimes you sound like a white Diana Ross."

"Thanks, baby." She kissed Julie's cheek and liked that her hair smelled from the same baby shampoo that it always had.

"Maybe I'll go into show business." Marjorie was surprised that Julie had an ambition. Whenever they asked her what she wanted to be or do they got a shoulder shrug.

"It's a lot of hard work," Marjorie said, as if she'd been there.

"That's OK," said Julie, who felt it was too hard to empty the dishwasher.

"You'll have to lose weight . . ."

"Why don't you stop! Why don't you and Daddy just shut up? It's your fault I'm fat. You always bring home cupcakes on holidays. Remember? Green ones for St. Patrick's Day and everything. How was I supposed to grow up right with all those cupcakes around?" Julie caught her breath and began again. "You're driving me crazy. We can be talking about . . . I don't know . . . Egypt and somehow you relate it to me being fat. Shut up! Just shut up. Being fat isn't the worst thing you can be. What if . . . what if I were pregnant or something?''

''Don't be silly.''

''I'm not being silly.'' The tears came. She was big and puffy from pregnancy and her mother thought it was silly.

Maybe she had told her.

Eight

The roses had all opened and stood erect in the typical green lumpy vase that florists always provide. It was nice of him. More than nice. It was like he wanted something. So far he just wanted to look at her, but how much looking could one man do? He kept coming to her room and looking down at her and asking how she was, as if she knew. He talked to her like they had met before, but she didn't remember him and most of the time she was too tired to find out. Maybe he had been there when she was brought into emergency. Funny how he sat there on the edge of her bed, maybe closer, for what seemed like hours. Maybe not hours. She was losing track of time in this hospital. It was so peculiar how he was there so much of the time when she opened her eyes. He must watch her sleep. What kind of kicks could a man get out of watching someone just lie there? And he sent her roses. This guy was acting more like a lover than anything else.

Elizabeth was sitting up in bed. Her eyes left the roses and went to a large red book that rested on her legs. She didn't see David, which gave him the chance to study her studying. David appreciated what he saw, Elizabeth Pringle was a beautiful woman, but he wasn't going to have an affair with her. He had come here for love, and sex had nothing to do with it. He had had his share of sex with assorted women.

From the time he lost his virginity to the camp nurse at fifteen, which may or may not have spurred his interest in medicine, to the time he promised to forsake all others for his blushing bride, who had no reason to blush, he had had sex with enough women to last a lifetime. He had shiksas and more than one black woman at a time when most Jewish med students didn't know black was beautiful. He had smoked dope in the early sixties and made love to a number of arms and legs in a last-minute orgy. He had spent weekends in bed, two days of nakedness with tireless girls who sulked on Sunday nights when Ed Sullivan came on and he had to crawl back to his books. He had sex with every waitress at Al's coffee shop around the corner from his Riverside Drive apartment. He had sex under the influence of coke, acid and by mistake, angel dust. He had gotten girls pregnant and had to pay for abortions in Puerto Rico. He had everything that moved and a few that didn't, including his cousin Beth. He had older women who were extremely hot and older women who were extremely grateful. He had a virgin who lied. He had paid for sex with five other ZBT's. From the time he met Marjorie every woman who came into view and wasn't a blood relative was a possibility and now and then even a blood relative was not out of the question. He had sex with his cousin Beth on her parents' bed under the family coats. The whole experience smelled of wool. From Elizabeth he wanted shy smiles. Most of all he wanted them to hold hands with their clothes on.

"You sneak," Elizabeth said when she saw she was being watched.

"What's the book?"

"Astrology. I do charts, not professionally or anything like that, but you can find out incredible things about people, and sometimes they pay me. Although that's not how I make a living. I work for an insurance company, which is good because they gave me tons and tons of medical insurance so I can pay for you guys."

"Whose chart are you doing?" David leaned against the wall, his arms crossed, looking very safe.

"Winston Churchill's. It's really incredible. It shows right from the beginning that he was going to be an important world leader. I mean he had to do what he did. When you have your planets lined up like that you can't get away from being great. After his I'm going to do Gypsy Rose Lee's. Of course neither one of them is going to pay."

"You think it'll show right from the start that she was going to run around naked?"

"It's never that specific, but I'll bet you anything that there's a strong Leo influence somewhere on her chart. Did you know most strippers are Leos?"

"I didn't."

"Oh yeah. It's incredible how it turns up every time. We've also had more Leo presidents than anything else, of course." David didn't follow her logic, but it wasn't worth questioning. She could say anything she wanted to as long as she let him watch her say it.

"I didn't know that."

"Yeah, well, there are a lot of things you can learn from astrology, like what's going to happen to you and all. I knew I wasn't going to die from this heart business because I already know when I'm going to die. June sixth, 2041. It freaked me out at first to know the exact date and everything, but once I got used to it, it took away a lot of the scary things in life. Like once I was coming back to my apartment and this guy was standing there with a knife and it was great because I knew the worst thing that could happen was that he would rob me and cut me up."

"What happened?"

"He took my whole purse. I tried to talk him into just taking the money because I knew once my license was gone I would never get another one. I'm really bad at keeping my personal business in order. But he insisted on the whole purse and when he brought the knife up to my neck I gave him the whole thing."

"But you knew you weren't going to die."

"Yeah, but I didn't want the whole hassle of a bloody throat. When's your birthday?"

"April seventh."

"God, I knew you had Aries in there. Maybe I'll do your chart before I do Gypsy Rose Lee's."

"If you do all that work for me, I'll have to find you a nice souvenir to go home with." He thought of the tiny diamond that he wanted to buy.

"Nah. I'm doing it for the fun of it. I don't want to get paid or anything. You've already given me too many presents." She looked from David to the flowers. "What year?"

"Nineteen forty," he said, thinking she would think he was old.

"Gosh," she said. She reached for a pencil and wrote his birth date down on the inside of the book.

"Get some rest and I'll see you tomorrow," he said with a smile and a salute.

"You work on Sunday?"

"No, but I'll be here. You need anything?"

"Could you tell me the truth about something?"

"If I can." David instinctively knew that Elizabeth's next question was going to be medical.

"Is this PAT thing that I have very serious? I know I'm not going to die from it, but I really don't want to be a vegetable on account of it, although I really shouldn't put vegetables down. I'm crazy about banana squash."

"My heart should be as good as yours." David had said this to many of his patients and it always seemed to relax them. He never knew how grandfatherly he sounded.

"You wouldn't want it as good as mine. As good as mine means you have to be hooked up."

"They're just monitoring you. I'm telling you everything is going to be fine. You're going to get out of this hospital before I am." When he thought of her leaving, he missed her. This was love as he knew it.

She smiled and relaxed hard into her pillow.

He felt well enough to leave.

Nine

"Dear Finkle, thanks for the postcard. Nothing new on the home front. Have to go, my father's honking. Julie."

It wasn't much of a letter, but she hadn't intended to write Finkle at all. And it was true. Her father was honking. She looked out her bedroom window to see him sitting there in the Porsche, tapping the steering wheel in rhythm to something he was listening to on the radio. Probably some country and western junk. She didn't mind real country like they had a few years ago, but now everyone was cashing in on it and there was this commercial trash all over the airwaves.

Under ordinary circumstances Julie was not the type of teenager who would run down to the car, but for her father she moved quickly. She wanted to be a perky daughter for him, the kind who wore pony tails and skirts with poodles on them in all those fifties movies. Those kind of teenaged daughters were always overindulged by their fathers. There was one movie, maybe it had Sandra Dee or Hayley Mills in it, where the mother was really furious because the father and daughter went shopping and the father was so dumb he bought everything in the store for his kid. They arrived home with dresses and hats and the mother was furious because the kid had her old man wrapped around her finger. Julie thought it was great how the father and daughter snuck around behind the mother's back. Her father would never do that. He would never ever take her shopping. The only times they ever went into a store together was to get a Mother's Day present when she was too young to shop alone. They never went anywhere alone together except once he took her to a baseball game, which she hated but pretended to love. They also went to the temple together on nights that her mom was in a play. Even though it was real ugly that Emily's parents were divorced and everything, at least Emily got to spend whole weekends with her father. According to Emily, her father wanted her to feel at home at his place, so he bought her a second stereo and all the same albums she had at her mother's. That way she didn't have to carry anything back and forth. That, to Julie, was just as good as shopping with your father.

Julie slid into the car next to her father and strapped herself in. Her mother was right. He drove the Porsche like a madman.

"You got here early. I didn't get a chance to have dinner," she said, just to start the conversation.

"It's not bad to go without a meal sometimes." Jesus, every time she even got near to mentioning food they turned it into an object lesson.

"What if I don't lose weight at this camp?"

"You will. Everyone does."

"Well, what if for some reason I don't? What if for some reason my glands go out of whack?"

"You don't have a glandular problem."

"I don't know, but I read somewhere that it can develop overnight." That wasn't true. She had never read anything about glands.

"Don't worry about it, Princess. They know what they're doing. I'll bet you lose more than anybody there." She knew a lot of fathers called their daughters "princess," but it made her feel great. It made her feel like he really loved her when he called her things like that.

"I guess so." They drove for a while not talking, listening to the radio. She was right. It was that country and western crap. Her dad must have listened to it a lot because he was singing along, using this phony cowboy voice. She hated to hear him twang like that, but she didn't know how to stop it without making him feel lousy.

David turned the radio off when Emily slid into the car and Julie realized that the music had protected them from each other. They drove to Great Neck, the three of them in the two-seater. Julie's one wish was that she wouldn't break her father's car.

David was always very nice to Emily, saying things like "Hi ya, kiddo. Is the world treating you OK?" Julie knew it was trite, but she still liked the warmth her father gave her friend. Tonight when he asked her what was new, Emily had plenty to say. She held on to her pocketbook tightly, the way church ladies do, and in a very straight voice that Julie had never heard before, she began her strange story. "Well, to tell you the truth, Dr. Weissman," she said, her eyes on the road as if she was driving, "I had this problem that I was scared to tell my parents about. I arranged to buy this puppy, which cost me over a hundred dollars. I get paid for baby-sitting my sister, which isn't exactly fair because I would be home anyway and I had some money from my birthday. Anyway here I was bringing this living thing into my house and my dad's house on weekends, and I was real scared that they would be upset by it. I didn't tell them for months." Emily knew she could get caught by her last statement and quickly rearranged her thoughts. "I knew about the puppy long before it was born so I was worrying all those months. Anyway, I didn't have to go through that aggravation. I spoke to my mom and I called my dad and I found out they were pretty decent people. When they understood that in my heart I couldn't get rid of the puppy, they were happy for me. I should have told them a long time ago. Don't you think, Dr. Weissman?"

"Sure," said David. Emily was disappointed. She had expected a speech on the virtues of children being honest with their parents, which she hoped would open the way for Julie to talk about her pregnancy. "Sure" wasn't going to do it.

Julie, of course, knew exactly what Emily was doing and enjoyed seeing her fail. She had told her her father was impossible to talk to. "What are you going to call it?" Julie asked, as if there was a puppy to be named.

"Arthur," said Emily quietly.

"Arthur, like in *Arthur* the movie we're going to?"

"You're seeing it again? How many times is that now?" David reached for the radio dial and then, realizing he had asked a question, withdrew his hand.

"We've only seen it twice, but it's one of Emily's favorite movies so I guess that's why she's naming her dog that. I'm glad she wasn't that crazy about *Harold and Maude* or she would have had to get two dogs."

Emily tried to shoot Julie a dirty look but since they were crammed in so tightly, the luxury of looks was gone. David dropped them off in front of the theater and asked Julie if she needed money. She did. There were big boxes of M&M's to buy.

"That was some shaggy dog story," said Julie as they waited to buy tickets.

"I thought he was going to say something about how great it was that I could be truthful and honest and then you could have snuck the pregnancy in, maybe not on the spot, but soon."

"Parents only talk about truth and honesty when they bring it up *and* my father's going to think that you're a very dishonest person when he learns you don't even have a puppy."

"He's going to think you're a lot more than dishonest when this baby comes out."

"Right. I know. Why don't we both get popcorns and then you get peanut butter cups and I'll get M&M's?"

"You've got to tell them sooner or later."

"Later," said Julie.

David had meant to go home. He was a third of the way there when he pulled over to a telephone booth and called Marjorie. He had to go back to the hospital, he said. That was true. What Marjorie didn't know was that he had to go back for love, not medicine.

Ten

Elizabeth Pringle had been told four times to turn her light off and go to bed. Each time the nurses left she sat up in bed, turned the light back on and went back to the red book. God, this was too exciting to stop. If only these goddamn nurses knew what she was doing. Even Ashley would be excited about this, and the whole time they had lived together, he had never gotten excited about her astrology, arguing that it was an inexact science when that wasn't true at all. It had to be exact. That was the whole point. God, she had even taken a course in it. You can't teach interpretation, she would scream, and he would scream back that she wasn't doing chemistry and she shouldn't think she was. When she had been with Ashley for about . . . God, it must have been about a year, during one slow week she did Jesus' chart. She told her grandmother about it, but Gran thought it was sacrilegious to do the son of God's chart, so she didn't talk to her about it a lot. She knew she would never forget Jesus' chart, because it was all there, everything she had heard about since she first went to Sunday school. It showed the Pisces and Aquarian influences. It showed the missing years and his early death.

Tonight, when she began Dr. Weissman's chart, she saw immediately that he was an extraordinary man, but it wasn't until she was . . . God, about half an hour into it that she realized that she had done this chart before and about ten minutes later she knew that Dr. Weissman had almost the same chart as Jesus! Not exactly the same, of course. Dr. Weissman was almost ten years older now than Jesus had been when he was crucified, but except for some of the time differences, it was all there, the devotion, the followers, the early death. She wondered how the doctor was going to react to her information and she thought about what it would be like to fuck the closest thing to Christ.

David stood watching Elizabeth through the window of her room the whole time that Julie was in the movie. He didn't know that she was doing his chart and thinking of fucking. He didn't even know that the hospital staff in cardiology thought he was strange.

Eleven

Marjorie sank into the bathtub. It was white and square and not as comfortable as she thought it would be when she ordered it. (They laughed at people who decorated bathrooms, but when the bedroom was finished, they went on to theirs.)

Amanda was right. Marjorie did go soppy every year when they went over the following year's schedule. She had completely given up thoughts of becoming a professional actress except on days like this, behind closed doors and underwater. She reminded herself that Walter Matthau made it late in life and tried to convince herself that if she really tried, gave herself a year of trying to get an agent, of going to every audition, of hanging out in all the right Manhattan drugstores that maybe she could get her late start. At first, she wouldn't ask for much, just a small commercial where she swore some peanut butter was more peanutty tasting than her ordinary brand. She saw women like her on television every day and figured that if she showed up at one of their auditions at the right time she could be chosen. Doing commercials would just be the beginning. This was, after all, a bathtub fantasy, so there was no need to have herself pushing dandruff shampoo for the rest of her life. Martin Scorsese would spot her while he was lying in bed watching television one night. He would bring her in to audition with De Niro. Even is she was nominated for best supporting actress she wouldn't go to the awards. She would buy a fabulous dress, make David wear a tuxedo, get a new, thin Julie some princess outfit and the three of them would watch on television, sipping champagne out of fluted glasses. (They laughed at people who made a big deal out of only drinking good champagne, but David swore cheap wine gave him a headache.) Just when the film industry was willing to support her, she would return to her first love, the theater.

As she raised her arm to shave under it, Marjorie planned her next few career moves. When Julie was in camp she would take the train into New York every morning. She saw herself boarding, riding, arriving. OK, then what? She'd get the trades, check out the open auditions like she used to, go to everything whether she was right for it or not. Let them see her.

She stretched one leg out for washing and it was as if she had taken a step forward. She would do more than audition. She'd join one of those little theater groups that were always having showcases. If necessary she'd run the candy concession at first, just until the members of the company trusted her enough to be part of them. Most of them would be very young, not much older than Julie, all with a passion for show business.

Maybe the best thing for her to do was to take a serious acting course. Not one of those Mickey Mouse ones for housewives, something serious. One where professional actors go to continue improving their craft.

She slipped the bar of Ivory soap between her thighs and let it float up. She had discovered this means of masturbation in pre-puberty. Ivory was the only soap she knew of that had a life of its own and was therefore able to make her happy. She never knew that Julie had found the same secret.

Marjorie had always linked what she considered her struggle to have orgasms with her struggle to act. She was sure that the same demon that had deprived her of her career deprived her of the sexual explosions that some women were treated to. Maybe if she had found the right coach or director, somehow he would have had the key to open up her sexuality and make her able to do those Clorox commercials. David never tried pushing open the door she so heavily leaned on.

She would find a good acting teacher in New York, she thought, as she placed the wash cloth over the tub, signaling the end of her bath. As she stepped out of the tub and wrapped herself with monogrammed towels (she and David laughed at people with monogrammed towels, but were never without them), Marjorie figured there were two ways to go: she could get an acting coach to help her with her loving or get a lover to help her with her acting.

She stretched out on her side of the bed and propped *Rabbit Is Rich* on her stomach. Her mother would be concerned that she had gone from *Rabbit Run* to the third in the trilogy, skipping *Redux*, and Marjorie would probably end up promising that she would go back and read the middle volume. Esther would shake her head, trying to figure out what she could possibly do with a daughter who read a trilogy out of order. Updike never failed to capture Marjorie and the heavy hard volume felt good. She read close to fifty pages before she thought of calling David. She wanted him to sneak some Häagen Dazs chocolate chocolate-chip into their bedroom. She stopped after dialing the first five numbers. This was the year she had promised to learn how to do the plumbing and make her own ice cream runs. In one continuous motion she put the phone back and pulled on terry cloth jogging pants and was halfway down the stairs before she got her top on.

On the way to Häagen Dazs, she passed Summit's Diner and remembered the diner robbery she heard about on television. Her fantasy was she was lying there on the floor in that diner, the linoleum cold against her face, the dirt of thousands of shoes soiling her clothes. She was lying next to David and whispered in his ear, "Please, don't fight them." One of her worst fears was that she would be witness to her husband's impotence against a weapon. She pictured ketchup bottles, napkin holders, the stiff yellow uniforms of the waitresses, the runs in their stockings, sugar spilled from the counter that she could reach with her tongue, the truck driver next to her, whose wool jacket smelled of the hot summer rain, hurt and crying from humiliation, the gun at her head that wouldn't feel real, the stained apron of the Puerto Rican short order cook, the women sobbing and praying, the smell of the diner coffee.

Her scenario had four different endings. One had David not being able to have sex with her, explaining to three masked maniacs that he had decided of his own free will to be celibate. In that version, David was smashed in the face and Marjorie was also beaten. Then there was a scene where she and David were both forced to strip from the waist down and he climbed on top of her. She worried about sticking to the dirty floor and there was her husband pumping on top of her and not able to get hard enough to insert himself. She screamed for mercy but the robbers insisted they continue the fruitless, painful pumping. Marjorie pleaded for David to stop but David continued, bruising her from both sides.

The third fantasy was the most satisfying. He was hard and the sex was incredible. She had an orgasm during intercourse that was so powerful she couldn't keep it a secret. Her head was pushed against a booth and the violence of their love caused a plate with a half-eaten grilled cheese sandwich to fall to the floor. The plate was too heavy to break, but until it settled, the sound was loud and helped muffle Marjorie's cry of pleasure. It took three guys with a gun and stockings over their heads, but it worked.

Version number four had Marjorie with the gun, no diner, no other villain, just a frustrated wife at the foot of her king-size bed forcing her husband to have sex with her. She would never pull the trigger, but neither would he.

Twelve

"You're spilling it. That's disgusting."

"I am not. Not one drop."

"It's disgusting even if you don't spill it," said Emily, opening up the refrigerator door. Julie, one step at a time, moved slowly across Emily's kitchen floor holding a vial of urine that she was planning to put in the refrigerator. It took her forever, for the fear of spilling even one drop made her crazy. Even if she got to wash it off right away she didn't want anything spilled because she would get sick and Emily would make a big deal out of it, saying she was ruining her mother's kitchen or something.

They had chosen to do the EPT test on a Thursday morning because Emily's mom had a standing hair appointment at the beauty parlor and she got a manicure too and the whole thing took her till at least one-thirty. If you put the urine in the refrigerator, you could get the results in a couple of hours, so they knew they had plenty of time to find out whether Julie was pregnant.

"Done," said Emily, closing the refrigerator door.

"What if it doesn't work?"

"It always works, but you gotta remember it isn't always a hundred percent accurate."

"So why did I spend almost fourteen bucks on it?" Julie pouted. She had tried to convince Emily to chip in, but Emily flatly refused, saying she would have chipped in for a diaphragm.

"Do you want to find out if you're pregnant or not?"

"I know I'm pregnant. I know from health class and that was free."

"I mean you have to know scientifically. You may know it in your head, but you've got to know scientifically too."

"How scientific can it be if it isn't a hundred percent accurate?"

Julie opened the refrigerator door and looked at the vial. In case things spilled by themselves, they had taken the precaution of putting a newspaper down on the shelf they were using.

"A watched pot never boils," said Emily, causing Julie to slam the door.

"You wanna go back to my house?"

"You think we should leave it alone?"

"It's not gonna walk out of here."

"What if my mother comes back, which she won't, just what if?"

"Let's hope she doesn't think it's apple juice."

Ordinarily they would have had a good laugh over Emily's mother drinking urine, but today they were forced to be in a somber mood. They sat down at the kitchen table and Emily poured them each a cup of coffee. Julie always felt like part of the world when the two of them sat down to drink the instant Yuban together. She didn't like the taste as much as the adult camaraderie it brought. It had been over cups of coffee that they decided their futures. Emily was going to be a writer who used men when she needed them sexually and Julie was going to have it all, home, husband, children, and stardom. Emily told her she couldn't have it all, but it was the one thing Julie wouldn't back down on. Emily always won their arguments, except the ones that had to do with Julie's having it all.

Today they were less talkative than usual because any conversation seemed too light compared to what was going on in the refrigerator. They took seriously what was brewing inside.

"You want to have some coffee cake or something?" Julie suggested.

"I don't think we have any."

"Yes you do. Behind the Jell-O, on the bottom shelf. I saw it."

"You really look into a refrigerator good," said Emily, standing to retrieve the cake.

"Sometimes I think I know where every cake in the world is."

Emily got the cinnamon cake, a knife, one plate, and sat down again. It amazed Julie that anyone could pass up coffee cake, especially when she was having coffee.

"Maybe all this junk isn't good for you, in your condition," Emily said as she watched Julie cut too big a slice.

"We don't know what condition I'm in yet."

"Well, just in case, I don't know if you're supposed to eat things like heavy cake."

"I never heard that." Julie was eating by now.

"We never heard a lot of things about pregnancy. I'm sure there's a lot you have to do that we don't even know about."

"Like what?"

"Like eat right and get plenty of rest."

"I know about that. Even if you just have a bad cold you're supposed to eat right and get plenty of rest." Emily had to agree and, in doing so, agreed that being pregnant was in the same league as being sick.

When Julie finished and Emily had put their things in the dishwasher the girls headed back to Emily's room. On the way Julie got a wave of nausea and headed for the hall bathroom, almost throwing up before she got to the toilet. Emily posted herself outside the bathroom door, not wanting to get too close, but being responsible enough to be in the vicinity in case she was needed. Julie emerged from the bathroom triumphant. She had had the pleasure of eating, but had gotten rid of the calories.

"You OK?"

"Yeah. Isn't it great that all that cake didn't count?"

"What if you have to throw up at camp?"

"I don't know. I don't want to think about camp."

"You have to. What if you do what your parents want and go and you have to vomit?"

"They have toilets."

"Suppose you're playing baseball or something? What if you're in the lake?"

"I can't go to that place."

"You've got to tell your parents you're pregnant."

"We don't know that for sure yet."

"People just don't throw up for no reason," said Emily wisely as she headed for her room.

"Maybe it's just the heat," said Julie, following.

"Did the heat take your period away too?" Julie flopped down on the bed, landing hard on her stomach, hoping to flatten it out.

They wasted time talking about Finkle, Emily's mother, and how Emily's room could be fixed. They listened to Janis Ian. Julie rolled on the bed and Emily continued to pull strands of her rug out. Finally, after two hours, Emily made the trip to the kitchen and when she returned Julie looked at her face for results.

"It'll be OK," Emily said, the vial in one hand, the rest of the coffee cake in the other.

"It'll be OK because I'm not pregnant?" Julie hoped.

"You are, but it'll be OK," Emily pushed the coffee cake forward, hoping the sweet would soften the blow.

"You're sure?" Julie said, shaky.

"There's a brown ring." Emily couldn't help crying, not the scared tears of a child, but the concerned ones of an adult.

"I can't go to that camp," said Julie, terrified of it all. Emily tried to control her own tears and brought Julie's head to her underdeveloped chest.

"You have to tell your parents, Julie. You *have* to."

"I'll go away some place."

"Where? You don't have money."

"I'll go on welfare."

"You couldn't live on welfare. They live in slums with black and white TV's. They don't even have stuff like end tables."

"Maybe I better get married. They wouldn't hate me so much if I was married or something." Emily rocked Julie as her tears came faster. Her T-shirt felt as if she had put it on wet.

"Who are you going to marry?"

"I don't know . . . Finkle."

"You want to marry Finkle? You'd have to live with him and have more of his kids. You'll have to have sex with him every night. Every single morning when you wake up for the rest of your life the first thing you'll see is Mike Finkle."

"I could marry him now so they won't yell so much and then later we could get a divorce." Emily pulled herself away. The thought of divorce made her stiffen.

"What about having an abortion?"

"I told you no. I have some morals, you know." Emily understood. At sixteen they were both anti-abortion and scared not to believe in God. They had discussed abortion even before they were old enough to understand what it was and had never wavered from their original decision that it was murder. Julie imagined it as a knife entering the mother and stabbing the baby in the heart.

"You have to tell your mother."

"I'm going to tell her. I'll tell her before camp. I can't go to that rotten place. Cindy Pinkus went to one like it last year and she said they give you this punch all day long that dyes your teeth red."

"Cindy Pinkus exaggerates everything."

"I saw her teeth two weeks after she got home and they were still pink."

"So, look at the good side. Now that you're pregnant you won't have to go."

Julie sank deeply into the bed and hugged a pillow on top of her. There was a good side. She hated going to a camp where they applauded you when your shorts fell off. When they heard she was pregnant, they would let her stay home and lie around.

For the next few moments, Emily watched Julie sadden and Julie saw Emily become a middle-aged woman. She stood up and bent over Julie. Looking straight into her eyes, she began her lecture.

"We're going to take you to a doctor," Emily said with authority. Julie said nothing, but Emily, assuming she was going to argue, quickly went on. "I mean it, Julie. I've got it all arranged and everything. I knew in my heart what that test was going to tell us today. Pregnant women have to do those things. Remember when I had the flu in February and I was out of school and the only thing I could do was watch TV all day? One day I was watching *Donahue* and everyone was talking about how important prenatal care is for the mother and the child and those people were doctors."

"Some care I'm giving this kid. I'm taking it to a fat girls' camp."

"You can't go. I mean they're going to make you play basketball and everything."

"Exercise isn't bad."

"Exercise yes . . . but stuff like basketball? You can't do anything where a ball could actually hit your stomach."

"It'll look like I'm hiding the ball under my shirt."

"Anyway, we'll go to this doctor in New York and then you can ask him questions like whether you can go to camp or not. He's very reputable. I got his name from my aunt Shirl. You know my aunt Shirl, she's the only hip relative I have. When I told her I had a friend who *might* be pregnant she thought it *might* be me and she didn't even yell or anything. She said she would take me to this guy and everything would be fine. So, then I had to swear it wasn't me and she believed me and everything and she made me an appointment on Friday." Emily made it definite by lying on the rug again.

"He'll tell my parents."

"He won't tell your parents. We'll use a fake name and make you look married. We'll do some makeup and get your hair up or something."

"Not everybody who is married wears their hair up. Both Pat Benatar and Kim Carnes are married and they wear their hair down."

"I meant that we could get a more mature look and I'm gonna lend you my mother's old wedding band."

"We couldn't take that. She'll miss it." Julie usually trusted Emily's sensibility, but this time had the feeling she was going too far.

"She's divorced. Divorced women don't go running around looking for their old wedding bands. She probably doesn't even know where it is. It's just lying there on the bottom of her jewelry box. Come on, I'll show you." Emily headed for her mother's room and although Julie didn't feel like moving, she felt that she had to follow.

Emily fished around the tangled chains and bracelets that her mother no longer had interest in, occasionally throwing a necklace over her head or slipping a bracelet on. Julie, not that far away from being a child, got interested in the adventure and slipped on several heavy chains. It wasn't until they were loaded down and feeling rich that Emily found the small gold band that she was looking for. She delicately lifted it and sadly examined it as if it were her own. For the first time, she noticed that there was an inscription inside. "From D.G. to L.G. forever."

"What a lie," said Emily.

"What?"

"This D.G. to L.G. forever." She showed Julie the ring. "Can you believe that lie?"

"Maybe he wasn't lying. Maybe when he gave it to her he really believed it was true."

"Maybe." And in order to hide the inscription and protect herself from any further pain she shoved the ring onto Julie's left hand. Julie lifted her hand and admired the ring as if she were a new bride.

"So, now we're married, you and me," said Julie, liking the look of the ring on her finger and trying to get some significance out of the occasion.

"Yeah, forever."

Julie looked at her hand again and then, having enough of married life, tried to pull the ring from her finger. It hardly moved. She tried again and then panicked. "I can't get it off. Your mother is going to kill me."

"Don't get crazy. My mother doesn't even know it's around. You can have it for good."

"What if she and your dad decide to get back together and they go looking for the ring?"

"You're as bad as Marcie. She thinks my parents are going to get back together too, but that's just not going to happen."

"I can't just steal your mother's ring."

"You can for now."

Julie raced for the bathroom, moving more quickly than she was accustomed to. She was encumbered by the jewelry around her neck and had to hold it down so that it wouldn't beat against her chest. Since everything about her tended to get fatter, she had gotten rings stuck on her round fingers before and knew that the only hope she had of rescuing her own finger from its imprisonment was soapy water. If that didn't work it would have to be cut off by a jeweler who would ask questions.

"I don't know what all the panic is about," said Emily, watching Julie struggle. "You can keep the ring forever."

"It's real gold probably."

"So what. My mom doesn't care."

"She could probably sell it and get money for it," said Julie, trying to get the ring past her first knuckle.

"We don't need the money. I swear we don't. We want the doctor to think you're married so you'd just better leave it on."

"I can't go to the doctor."

"Why not? I made all the arrangements. I promised we'd be there on time, because he wants to get out of the city before all the traffic."

"I don't know why not. I don't want some crazy doctor putting his hands all over me." Julie gave up on the ring and turned off the water.

"You have to go. It's very dangerous not to. Being pregnant is like being sick so you have to go and you really don't have to worry about anything because my aunt Shirl wouldn't go to a crazy doctor. He might not even have to touch you or anything. Maybe the first time he's just going to ask a lot of questions." Neither girl had ever had an internal examination and although it had been covered in health class, with no practical application, it was not information that they had retained.

"You think it's going to cost a lot of money to see him? I mean if he's on Park Avenue it might cost a small fortune."

"How much do you have?"

"Less than eighty dollars. My grandpa usually gives me ten when he sees me, but he's not coming up this year because he doesn't like New York anymore so I don't know whether I'm going to get the ten from my grandmother who's coming tomorrow or not."

"So, I'll call my aunt and find out how much she thinks it's going to cost. She should have some idea." Emily led Julie back to the bedroom, once again giving her the bed. They had been happy together and now they worried together.

"I don't want to give all the money I have in the world to some doctor to tell me something I already know."

"Yeah, but when a doctor says it, then you really know."

"It's not fair that I have to pay for the whole thing myself. I didn't do the whole thing myself."

"So, what are you going to do, get Finkle to chip in or something? Maybe you could write to him and tell him how much it cost and he could send you some cash. Counselors make about five hundred dollars without tips so he could really afford it."

"Yeah. Maybe." She wondered if Finkle had another girlfriend and didn't seem to care if he did. When her parents found out she was pregnant they would ask her who the father was. If she told them, they would have a big meeting with the

Finkles, probably at her house and her mother would serve cake. She hoped her mother got enough. Sometimes she only got one cake for everyone and that was never enough. That would mean there would be none left and no sweetness to come down to the kitchen for in the middle of the night.

The Finkles would face the Weissmans, her mother would be the only one standing, as if on the middle of the stage. Julie would like to be sitting on the top of the stairs overhearing only what she wanted to, but they would probably make her be in the room. Finkle, luckily, would be at Camp Pontiac.

The Finkles wouldn't want to believe that their kid would trick anybody into getting pregnant, but Julie's father would convince them it was true. Since he was an important doctor he never lost an argument. Her father would force Finkle to admit it, but he was too nice a man to force him to marry her.

"I wish I was the type of kid who could make it on her own." Julie looked at the ring on her finger as she spoke. "I just don't see myself in a small midwestern town, living in a rented room with a cot and a stained mattress, working in a luncheonette and pretending that my husband is dead."

"You can't run away."

"Right. I can't run away. It takes too much energy and too much money. Do you know how much cash it takes?" She didn't. Julie didn't either. "I probably have enough money to get someplace, but then I wouldn't have anything left when I got there." She had already thought about a bank account that was for her college education. She was sure that she needed her mother's signature to get any money out and she wasn't about to try anything at the bank for fear that they would handcuff her to a pole and call her family in to pick her up.

"Tell your parents," Emily said louder than the last time.

"Wouldn't it be great if I could get a job as a backup singer in a group and travel around the country in one of those buses with the toilets in them? Maybe I could find a friend, not as good a friend as you, but be friendly in the way that poor Patsy Cline and Loretta Lynn were. I would eventually tell the group I was pregnant, but it would be no big deal because they had kids all the time for no reason at all. When I have the baby, they could announce it from the stage and that's how my parents could find out.''

''You sure know how to dream.''

''You have any better ideas?''

''No, but you're not getting a job as a backup singer so you don't have any great ideas either.'' Emily got up to look at the washing machine working. She wanted to relax, but she always had to check everything twice before she could. While she was gone Julie didn't move. She had always been able to rest. Since the pregnancy she was capable of being motionless. She started speaking when she heard her friend's Nikes in the hall.

''I wish I could hide. You know I never even had a secret hiding place as a kid. I went to my room but that doesn't really count.''

Emily looked at Julie and thought she would be hard to conceal. ''What's the real reason you won't tell your mom? She always wants to talk about your problems.''

''That's the problem. They talk. They both talk until you can't take it anymore. They both think they're real psychological and they don't leave you alone.''

''Your mom is great. She smiles more than anyone I know.''

''Yeah.'' Julie almost cried. ''I absolutely don't want to be the one to get that smile off her face.''

''She'll have to know eventually. She'll have to.''

''She loves the summer. At least I can let her have a nice summer.'' Julie yawned and stretched as if she didn't have problems.

''So you'll go to camp?''

''I can't go to camp. I'm too tired to go to camp.'' She closed her eyes.

''We should leave early tomorrow to make sure we get to the doctor in time.'' Emily moved two stuffed animals from her recent youth around and then placed them carefully back where they had been.

"I think we should go in real early and see *E.T.* If we get there early enough we shouldn't have any problem getting in."

"We could see it after the doctor."

"It'll be crowded after. We have a good chance of getting in before."

Emily thought through what she was going to say before she spoke. She picked up Snoopy, who looked sadder than usual, and hoped she wasn't going to have another argument on her hands. It was hard being Julie's advisor these days.

"I don't think we should see *E.T.* until we see the doctor and ask him if it's OK. It's a really weird movie and I don't know if it would be good for your system. I read an article once that said the emotional state of the mother can have an effect on the unborn child and it was in one of those good magazines that my mother spends a fortune on."

"I'm not going to get into any emotional state. I'm just going to see a movie."

"Not just any movie. *E.T.* is supposedly a total experience and I don't know whether your kid is ready for it."

"What do you think, that the kid is going to look at the movie through my bellybutton?"

"All I'm saying is you don't have to believe me. Just ask the doctor if you can go."

"This doctor is going to think we are really weird. What am I going to say? Doctor, I have two questions. One . . . am I pregnant? And two . . . can I see a movie about an extraterrestrial? What would you think if you were a doctor if some teenager waddled in and asked you that?"

Emily had to smile and the second she did, Julie did, too.

Thirteen

David hardly ever spoke to Solomon, so young Dr. Burke was flattered when Dr. Weissman asked him to come to his office for a cup of coffee. He figured that David had noticed his work and was going to ask him if he could refer his overload. This was just the break he needed. He was a hell of a cardiologist, but he hadn't been able to pull it together in the bedside manner area. He didn't have the personality to deal with hysterical relatives and he hadn't the ability to kiss the asses of the administration, which wanted you to be an excellent surgeon and tell great jokes in elevators. He didn't dress right or look right. No matter how many showers he took, he always looked dirty—short, dark and dirty. His classmates all seemed to be ahead of him with thriving practices, even those who barely got through while he was getting A's. One of his teachers had told him he wasn't going to make it if he didn't keep his nails clean. He had looked down at his short, fat fingers to see his surgeon's hands topped with nails that were bitten. He had always hated doctors like David Weissman, who had huge private practices, plenty of money and plenty of love while he had a short, dark, pregnant wife and a kid in an apartment in Queens and all the emergency patients he could handle. It embarrassed him to be on salary while all the other doctors spent half their time looking for tax shelters. He knew some day someone would see the brilliance under his dry, flaky hair. He was surprised that it was Weissman because he thought Weissman didn't notice anything besides potential patients and women.

The coffee was Scotch and the reason for getting together had nothing to do with medicine or money. Solomon found himself sitting opposite David in the wood-paneled office he wanted, talking about Elizabeth Pringle, not as a patient, but as a woman. David was confiding that he was attracted to her. He talked about her lips, breasts, eyes, but never once brought up her heart, even though he knew Solomon was her primary physician. David, who should have been embarrassed, spoke as if he had nothing to hide, and Solomon correctly supposed that being successful did that to a man.

"No one says you don't have great taste in women. Your wife is good looking too," said Solomon tactlessly.

"Are you bringing up my wife to remind me I have one?" said David, draining Scotch, making ice cubes bang against each other.

"Why not?" said Solomon with the same air that lost him patients.

"I would never cheat on my wife," David said indignantly, and Solomon couldn't figure out when he got to be the bad guy. Having never been taken into David's confidence before, he had yet to learn that David was never impure or wrong.

"You're a saint." Now that he knew David Weissman wasn't going to improve the quality of his life, he felt he could call it like it was, or at least be very sarcastic.

"Why so much anger?"

"I don't know. Maybe it's because I don't know why I'm here and you do."

"You're a good doctor, Sol." Solomon tensed. Maybe he had been called in for business reasons and he had fucked it up again. He had this bad habit of reading people wrong.

"Thanks." He tried to look clean. He moved his nails out of sight.

"I just wanted you to know that I'm visiting Miss Pringle

now and then and that I'm not in there to try and win her over as a patient.''

Solomon nodded, disappointed that the afternoon drink led to nothing more than his giving his colleague visitation rights. He had learned, in situations like this, to leave quickly before his disappointment turned to anger. He was known as a good staff doctor with the ability to tell anyone to fuck off.

"See you around," Solomon said on his exit.

"How long are you going to keep her here?" David's words stopped Solomon in the doorway. He wondered if David was asking him to keep the girl in the hospital longer than she had to be there.

"Just long enough to rule out myocardial infarction. If she doesn't have another run of PAT she'll be out day after tomorrow." Solomon tried to see disappointment on David's face, but he wasn't showing any.

"Well, thanks a lot for stopping by." Solomon hated that he was being dismissed rather than getting out when he wanted to.

"Yeah, sure."

"Anything I can do for you, pal?"

"Referrals," said Solomon, blunt as usual.

"I didn't know you wanted a private practice."

"Yeah? Well now you know." Solomon didn't mean to sneer all the time, but he had long ago lost control of his facial expressions.

"I hope I can help you out real soon."

"Good," said Solomon Burke, closing the door behind him.

David left his office minutes after Solomon did. He just took the time to get out of his jacket and into his white coat. There was no need for him to be in his whites, but he had learned that people loved him even more when he was dressed as a doctor, and he was on his way to Elizabeth Pringle's room.

Elizabeth was in bed as usual and looking much healthier

than any hospital patient should. It was a good time of the day for her. It was early afternoon and the sun streamed in and let you know that her hair had strands of red in it. This against a blue blanket was enough to make even a less romantic man than David think of light kisses, stolen from young girls who would still blush even though they long ago gave away their virginity. Elizabeth was with her big red book again, but snapped it closed as soon as she saw David.

"You're looking beautiful," David said from across the room.

"Does that mean I get to go home?"

"That wasn't a medical opinion."

"I'm not sick and we know I'm not going to die so you might as well let me out of here. I know I'm going to be fine on account of I've done my chart about a million times. When I'm thirty-six I'm going to write a hit song and I can't even read music yet. They might as well let me out of here because I really know astrology and there's no way that I'm going to die in this century."

"They'll let you out. And then I won't be able to come visit." David leaned against the far wall of the room, far enough away to be polite, close enough for them to seduce each other.

Elizabeth smiled at the knowledge she was about to reveal. She sat up straight in bed and became a child about to pop a secret. "You've been married for somewhere around twenty years. Maybe a little less." She looked toward David for amazement, but he gave none.

"I guess so." The number twenty was a strong one. It almost covered Elizabeth's whole life.

"Don't you want to know how I know?"

"You asked someone."

"No. I did your chart. I know everything about you."

"Does my chart show when you come into my life?"

"Sure, look, there are women popping up all over the place." She handed him a piece of paper with symbols that meant nothing to him. He handed it back to her. She studied it for a few moments and the studying sobered her. "Dr. Weissman, do you know how much like Christ you are?" He sat in the visitor's chair before answering.

"How do you know Christ was Jewish?" David asked, remembering a joke.

"How?" Marjorie would have known the joke was coming. Elizabeth didn't.

"He was thirty-three, single and his mother thought he was God." Elizabeth nodded, taking the joke as information. Marjorie had laughed.

"Anyway, there are so many similarities between you and Christ our Lord." David was not comfortable. The people he knew didn't talk about Christ as their Lord.

"Surely there were no women popping up all over the place in Christ's life."

"Yes there were. He was close to a lot of women. He didn't sleep with them like you do."

"Is that in my chart? Sleeping around?"

"No. It was more of my interpretation. I saw the women and I just guessed about the rest." David took Elizabeth's hand and traced her fingers against the blanket before he spoke.

"You know I'm married and I don't cheat on my wife," he said seductively. She did not believe him. She felt his touch not only on her hand, but deep inside.

"Good," she said, and couldn't help feeling rejected.

"You don't mind, do you?"

"That you're faithful to your wife?"

"Yes." He still had her hand, which made it harder to answer. In her twenty-four years she had so many men touching her, it seemed impossible that Dr. Weissman's hand was doing so much.

"How could I mind that? Do you love her?"

"Sure I do." She tried to read his face because she didn't like the words she was hearing. The face was calm, which she resented, since she was starting to feel nervous.

"That's nice," Elizabeth said, trying to look like she

meant it. She ached a little and didn't want David to see it. "You can show her your chart."

"She wouldn't understand it," David said, and Elizabeth swore he winked. She didn't actually see it because it happened so quickly, but the twinkle lingered and was still there. And he still had her hand.

"I'll write it all out. That way you'll know about all the important things that are going to happen." She picked up the chart with her free hand, hoping that David wouldn't release the hand he had. She studied her chart heavily, concentrating on the symbols. "It's all here. You were born . . ."

"I know when I was born. As a matter of fact, I know everything that has happened up to the time we met. Why don't you go on from there?" David, like any conceited man, enjoyed the attention that he was getting. He had the girl's hand and her mind. Her heart, although slightly malfunctioning, was probably also his.

"Somewhere in the next eighteen months to two years, I can be exact, but not exactly exact, you are going to receive great honors." David was pleased. He didn't believe in this horoscope junk, but he did believe in honors and couldn't see any reason why, as long as they were being constantly given anyway, they shouldn't be bestowed on him. "Around that time or maybe even before that there will be some stormy times at home." What Elizabeth actually saw in her scratches was that there would be marital disharmony, but that David would have only one wife. She chose not to deliver this information. "Don't worry about it, though. It's nothing important. Really minor stuff." As Elizabeth tried to minimize what was going on in his household, David squeezed her hand, which brought delight and pleasant aching.

"Want to know when you're going to die?" Elizabeth asked cheerfully, and David nodded as if he had been asked if he wanted ice cream. As a child he had felt immortal, as all children do, and as a doctor he felt immortal, as all doctors do. "OK, let's see. You know a lot of people believe you can't show death in a chart, but it's always real obvious to me. Hang on. Oh yeah. Here you go, when you're forty-three. Crist died when he was thirty-three, but maybe they counted years differently then." David's expression didn't change. No part of him moved, including the part that held on to Elizabeth Pringle. He didn't believe. He saw no reason why a crazy girl with a problem heart should know when he would expire. Still he felt uneasy, not panicked or overly concerned, because this was silly, but uneasy because no man wants to hear of his untimely death. David bent over and kissed Elizabeth on the forehead. He straightened the blanket out even though it had hardly moved at all. As he started to go, saying goodbye on his way, Elizabeth decided to keep him awhile. "You're not upset are you, finding out when you're going to die and all?"

"I don't take it very seriously."

"The important thing is not to worry about it. You can ruin your whole life worrying about when you're going to die." She was sorry she had told him. He looked worried and her job was to delight him. His wife probably worried him and even though he loved her, it had to be that worry that drove him into Elizabeth's room every day. "Anyhow, what's the difference when you die anyway? I mean life is just a transition, it's not as if death is permanent or anything." David didn't look consoled. He threw a kiss and moved through the door. "I mean there really is no such thing as death," Elizabeth shouted and never knew if he heard her. He did. He heard it all, but the only thing he kept hearing was that somewhere it was written that he had less than a year of life left.

David went back to his office, moving slower than he usually did. By the time he sat in the leather chair, that still smelled like leather, he had decided there was to be no more Elizabeth Pringle. He liked her hair catching the sun, but that was no reason to be running around her listening to her predictions of death. Christian girls did that to you. You would invite them into your life for a little fun and before you knew it they were spooking you with astrology or prayers or you would find out that they really believed in the little baby Jesus and that half their head was filled with thoughts of salvation. David was a scientist. The Elizabeths of the world were beautiful to watch, but if you let them get close they could make you worry about your own mortality. What if he had been crazy enough to marry a girl like that? He would be going to the hospital to try to save a life and she would be telling him it wouldn't matter if the patient died because death was not permanent. Crazy kid. He should have told her that he had just had his physical and that everything was better than OK. She should know about his prostate. He didn't like hearing that his time was up. He especially didn't like that she didn't cry about it. Marjorie cried. In her softest moods she would look toward heaven or into his eyes and wish that she would die first. He would cite the statistics about women living longer than men, but she wasn't interested in statistics. Marjorie wanted him alive. Elizabeth didn't care if he was crucified.

David dialed home with the excuse that he was in the mood for Chinese food that night. He knew it was wrong that a man needed an excuse to call his wife, but he felt he always had to have one. You didn't just call home and tell your wife that you wanted to hear her voice, not if you were the type of husband who got his romance outside of the house.

Marjorie answered on the third ring. She sounded as if she was in the middle of something, which surprised David. He knew she had a life, but most days, he found her where he left her, so he had every reason to believe that her time stood still while he was gone. "David?" she said, as if she was guessing the caller's name.

"Yes, David. Your husband for life."

"Oh, that one," Marjorie sat on the bed and stretched out her legs the way a teenager would while talking to a boyfriend. In person they refused to flirt with each other, but the phone gave them the protection they needed.

"I'm asking you out for Chinese food tonight."

"I've got to warn you, I come with a child. I told you I have a child, didn't I?" Julie flashed before him. She was enjoying an extra large egg roll, which annoyed David even though he had conjured it up.

"I remember you saying something about . . . let me think . . . a daughter. Am I right?"

"Right. A little girl." He saw Julie again and wondered how Marjorie could refer to her as little.

"She could come too. I cashed my paycheck yesterday, so I think I could swing dinner for the two of you." He looked at the picture of his wife and child that stood in the oversized brass frame on his desk. It had been taken the only time they had been sailing. Marjorie was tan and shiny; the small white shorts and bathing suit top helped show off her perfect body. She was hugging Julie, who at seven years old was her mother's miniature down to the small white shorts. The photograph was almost ten years old and David refused to replace it. Marjorie was still in her prime, but Julie had lost it. He just couldn't advertise his daughter now.

"So, I'll see you later and I'll put the chicken back in the freezer." Just the reminder that they shared a major appliance took them both out of the dating mood. By the time they both hung up, David was feeling better. It was a brief phone call but it grounded him. He had managed to replace Elizabeth and predictions of death with Marjorie and egg foo yong.

Fourteen

Julie had planned to tell her mother about her pregnancy on the way into town. She was going to state it clearly so that her mother got what she was saying the first time. It would be horrible to have to repeat that she was pregnant with Finkle's child over and over again. She imagined her mother would pull the BMW off to the side of the road and the crying would begin. She expected, because of the eight times she had allowed herself to be taken by Mike Finkle, that the rest of her life would be tears, wet and salty. As she got in the car Julie found herself wishing that she was old enough to leave home. She knew she couldn't leave because she didn't know how. She didn't even know how to find a place to sleep. She had been to hotels with her parents, but checking in was a mystery of credit cards that belonged to her father and the rest of the adult world. When you left home, you needed credit or money and she didn't have either of those things.

The first thing Marjorie did after starting the car and insisting that Julie belt herself in was to turn on the radio. She had only to push one button and Barbara Mandrell was telling them she was Country before Country was cool. Marjorie couldn't help singing along and Julie couldn't talk about Finkle. She wished she was Barbara Mandrell or even one of the silly sisters. She was willing to bet that Mom Mandrell smiled at everything her children did.

The songs kept coming and Marjorie sang or hummed. The commercials and station breaks were too short for Julie to tell her sad story. Unlike her father, her mother didn't use the radio for protection. She would have gladly turned it off to listen. Julie didn't want to ruin her mother's good time. Then they were in town.

"Do we really have to do this today?" Julie knew the answer, since they were already parking.

Marjorie turned off the ignition before answering. "We're here. How can you ask a question like that when we're already here?" Marjorie stressed her exasperation by brushing her hair hard. "You need clothes for camp." She got out of the car and expected Julie to do the same. Julie knew she needed clothes, but she didn't want to get them because it was going to hurt. Salesgirls' hands were going to be determined to zip up shorts with hard waists that would cut into her excess flesh. It would hurt in other ways too. The first sizes wouldn't fit and boxes would have to be brought down and drawers would have to be opened to find the extra-larges.

It all happened the way Julie imagined it would, except with the extra added horror of having a salesgirl named Karen, who was not much older than she was, but who had the decency to stay thin and unpregnant. The girl had a natural sweetness, which also didn't help. To Julie the purchasing of clothes was always a bitter experience and a cheerful salesperson only pointed out her own sullenness.

Julie gathered clothes with the same enthusiasm with which a prisoner would pick up the uniform he would have to wear for the next fifty years. Marjorie and Karen pointed out things they thought were great and Julie knew would hurt. "Can I, please, at least pick what I like?" she asked strongly enough so that Karen retreated and Marjorie sat down. She walked through the tables and racks of Sport Togs, Great Neck's best and biggest sports boutique, for those who knew looking good was more important than winning. People forgot scores faster than they forgot outfits.

When her arms were filled with the best money could buy, she headed for the dressing room. Karen, who could never be insulted, followed her. Marjorie remained seated, waiting for the fashion show that she really didn't want to see. Shopping with Julie was hard on her too. She had thought of a girl with long hair down a slender back in pink overalls. The child she had raised had store owners hoping they could fit her and cruelly suggesting she lose weight.

As Julie tried on shorts and shirts with difficulty, Karen smiled and talked too much. She seemed to be excited about the haul. "You're going to love all the Polo stuff," Karen bubbled. "Ralph's colors are really great this year. I have the pink and the purple and I'm going to get the light blue with the pink and white stripe this week." Julie could probably buy the pink and the light blue in one shot. She hoped she could make Karen jealous.

"My husband hates purple," said Julie and, when she saw Karen register shock, she added, "don't tell me I look too young to be married. I am so tired of hearing that." Julie looked at herself in a pink shirt and thought that she looked like three people stuffed into one. Karen's slim body with the no tits was really beginning to annoy her.

"Don't you go to Syosset High?" Karen asked, taking pins out of shirts.

"Yeah. There's no rule there that says you can't be married."

"Wow. That must be great. What does he do? I mean doing the daytime?"

"He's a senior," said Julie, slipping into a large football shirt that she had picked. It was big enough to feel good. It bore the number eighty-four on it and Julie wondered why.

"So do you and your husband do your homework together or what?"

"We both cook, and then we both do homework, but not exactly together since he's a senior, who just graduated and is going to college so we can have a better life. Then we sort of sit around singing and then we have sex and go to bed."

"So do you want it or what?" At first Julie thought Karen was talking about whether she wanted sex. Then she realized that she was referring to the shirt.

"Yeah. I'll take it. It'll be great for when we're watching football on Sundays." She removed the shirt and slipped into a green Polo exactly like the one Karen was wearing. She had wanted to like the shirt but the comparison made her sad and she ripped it off her body as quickly as she could. "He wouldn't like it," she said.

"Oh yeah, then you shouldn't take it for sure. Your mom said you were going to camp. How come if you're married you're going to camp?"

"We decided before that we were going to always have separate vacations to help keep the marriage exciting and he's maybe going to be counselor at the place and they've made provisions for us to have sex and everything."

Julie chose a pile of shirts mainly based on how comfortable they were. She felt some power over Karen in being able to acquire so many new things at once, but knew that being rich and fat was not better at sixteen than being poor and thin. She enjoyed being married and easily answered all of this young salesgirl's questions, including the one that asked where her wedding band was. "The jeweler is putting more stones into it." Karen accepted this explanation as she had accepted the whole marriage. She stayed envious and Julie realized for the first time in her brief life that some females are jealous of another woman just because she's married. Marjorie had always taught her daughter that she had more options in life than just being a wife, but by the time Julie emerged from the dressing room in a pair of men's size thirty-four tennis shorts she thought being married had it over everything.

"How're you doing?" Marjorie asked hopefully.

"She got all these shirts," said Karen, who was expecting the mother to veto the sale. In the few months since Karen had gotten the job, she had seen many fights between mother and daughter over tops and bottoms. The teenagers hated their mothers for depriving them of what they thought everyone else had and they often left the store angry and crying. Karen had no way of knowing that in the Weissman household Julie never begged for clothes and her mother was happy to buy anything that fit her daughter's body.

Marjorie said that the shirt purchase was fine without even checking it out. Her eyes were fixed on the men's shorts her daughter was wearing. She circled Julie, one hand on her chin, her head tilted. One would have thought she was involved with at least the splitting of the atom. When she finished her three hundred and sixty degrees, she called for the tailor. Julie protested since tailors were never her friends. They shook their heads in desperation and came close with their fingers, making her feel like a mound of wet mud that would never be firmed. Marjorie always got what she insisted on, and waists were let out and lifted, shoulders were brought in and hips were released beyond the better judgment of the doubting tailors. "You'll see, there'll be a mark," they warned, but Marjorie Weissman insisted and they always gave in. Julie didn't mind the results. When she put on the new altered clothes she actually felt pretty for the moment and mother and tailor agreed that it was worth the struggle.

Karen went for Mr. Rubin and Julie positioned herself in front of the mirror. The shorts fit her swollen waist but hung almost to her knees and left room for her backside to grow. She knew the tailor would say he couldn't make them fit and her mother would get him to take them apart and put them back together.

Mr. Rubin was older than she had expected. Instead of looking overwhelmed by her, as did all the other tailors in the world, Ben Rubin smiled and elegantly offered his arm to Julie, escorting her the one step up to the platform where she would be fitted. She liked this brief man with his faded blue eyes and coffee-stained moustache and was sure that he would cause her no trouble.

"So, we want it shorter, right?" said Rubin, already into pinning up the hem. As he folded the material back, the alligator on the bottom of the shorts disappeared. "So you need the animal or not? It's important to you?" Julie turned and looked at Marjorie for an answer. "You need your mama to tell you whether you need the alligator? Come on, you tell me if you love him."

"It doesn't matter to me," said Julie softly.

"Good. I like a woman who doesn't want to go around being a walking advertisement. We'll get rid of him. Send him back to Miami. The alligators love it there. Is that short enough or you want shorter?" Again Julie looked toward her mother, but this time she turned back before there was time for an answer.

"A little shorter," said Julie with confidence.

"Good, because shorts should be short. You didn't come here to buy a pair of longs." Julie, Marjorie and Karen were polite enough to laugh. Ben laughed too. Julie worried about him because he laughed freely with pins in his mouth. He continued to pin and tuck, turning men's shorts into ones that would fit a pregnant girl. No matter how many adjustments Marjorie asked for, Ben made them with good tailoring and bad jokes. She put on five pairs in different colors and he performed his magic with all of them. He never once mentioned Julie's weight or made her feel that he regretted taking on the job. Julie liked him and appreciated his kindness. When he was finished pulling and pinning, she didn't want to let him go. She surmised that he could help with more than a pair of La Coste pants.

"Sorry I'm fat," Julie said to Mr. Rubin. The grief and confession surprised Marjorie. Her daughter had never admitted to being fat or to being sorry about it. Marjorie reached out and hugged her.

"So, so what's the problem?" Ben Rubin asked. "Today you're fat, next month you may not be."

"I'll be even bigger next month." She hadn't meant to be so revealing. This man was accepting her as is and it felt right to talk.

"So, it's baby fat. So what?"

"It's sort of baby fat . . . I'm pregnant." Julie expected a stillness. She anticipated shock, including dropped jaws and tiny intakes of breath. What she got was laughter from Mr. Rubin, a sigh from her mother, who thought she was being silly. The only one who believed her was Karen, who mouthed a "wow." Julie got down off her mini-pedestal and walked to the dressing room.

Fifteen

David got home early for the first time in his life. He was not a man with hobbies and only knew how to do two things, work and go home. He had expected Marjorie to be there and was disappointed that she wasn't. On the way to the refrigerator he felt lonely. He opened it and closed it quickly, a little hungry, but impatient with the food. He sat on two different kitchen chairs before he decided to yawn. He caused it, as if he had nothing else to do but expel air. He sat knocking his knuckles against the kitchen table and enjoying it. David knew he had earned the right to have moments like this. He had proven his intelligence and his ability to earn a living. He had at least earned the right to do nothing.

His eyes left the table where they were watching his hands. Everything was familiar and yet he rarely saw it in the afternoon light. It was unlike David to get sentimental, especially about something as ordinary as a kitchen, but he was loving the kitchen and wanted nothing in it to change. Taking his thoughts further, he realized that he wanted nothing in his life to change. He wanted the same house with the same feelings forever. It would disturb him to have one flowered cup gone from the cupboard. He didn't want any of them to get any older, not even Julie. He wanted her always sixteen and always living with them. He wouldn't ask to be younger or richer. His one prayer was for more of the same. ''Just give me more of the same, God,'' he prayed to the rhythm of his knuckles, knowing it was the one thing he couldn't have. Part of more of the same would mean that he would stay attracted to Elizabeth Pringle even though she was the one who had put him in this mood with her charts and troubling predictions. The flowerpot that stood on the window ledge appeared too close to the edge and in danger of falling into the sink. David saved the pot and the consistency of his life.

He stretched and forced another yawn and decided on two things that were not in his daily routine. He drank coffee and showered every day. In an attempt to prove to himself not only that variety was the spice of life, but that it didn't kill, he decided to have a glass of milk and take a bath.

It wasn't until he got up the stairs and ran the water that he realized why his bath was drawn. David was agitated. Elizabeth had thrown him the ball and he had dropped it. He had started the game by sending the flowers, paying attention, doing all the nonphysical foreplay that any lover would. Because of his two previous experiences in the world of love since his marriage he thought he had learned to pull out in time. It was the look of love that he was looking for and when he found it, he had to retreat. With the nurse he had waited too long. She had confronted him with her feelings. It had taken her three cups of coffee in a hushed corner of the hospital cafeteria. She repeated herself over and over, looking for the key that would make David respond, not knowing that all he had come to her for he already had. She offered herself, which he refused, saying he was faithful to his wife. She cried. He apologized. He had offered to be her friend, he said, and she mistook it for passion. She wanted to know why the flowers, why the gold chain that he had placed around her neck. He said he wanted to give them to her and nothing more. She accused him of flirting and he said that he couldn't believe that there was no such thing as being a nice guy anymore and that he would be glad to take back the chain if that would help. She reached for the gold around her neck and begged him to sleep with her. He had to remove her hand from his arm and explain that he found her very attractive, but that he could never jeopardize his relationship with his wife. If he were free, she would be the type of woman he could really go for. Angry tears sprang forth. "You came on to me," she wept. He said he hadn't meant to. She bit her lip to hold back tears, but they refused to stop. He offered his handkerchief, but she threw it back at him, preferring the napkins that were readily available from the chrome dispenser on the table. She was making her nose redder than it had to be by wiping too hard. He wanted to offer his handkerchief again, but he was afraid she would mistake his concern for more love.

"Why did you say I looked compelling last Thursday?" she sobbed and blew.

"I don't remember the exact circumstance, but I'm sure if I said you looked compelling, I meant exactly that." His hands were folded on the table like the perfect gentleman's.

"Men don't say things like that if they don't mean to follow up."

"I'm not allowed to say you're compelling without having to go to bed with you?"

"You know what you are . . . you're a cock tease."

"That's impossible. You don't have one to tease."

"You know what I mean. The opposite of a cock tease. You go around turning women on and not following through. I have feelings too and I have a throbbing between my legs every time I see you." David knew he was in trouble, but he felt equal parts of guilt and pride.

"What about Dr. Peters? He's a good-looking guy." He actually felt he was doing a friend a favor.

"I don't want Dr. Peters. I want you." David could understand why he and another doctor were not interchangeable in bed, but he had to get back to work. They both knew by now that there was no relationship to talk about, but it took three more tear-soaked sessions before she stopped drinking her coffee and dumped it into David's lap.

The wife of the friend had been kinder when they broke

up. There was no hot coffee in his lap. She just left her husband and moved out to California to be near her sister.

David soaped his arms and promised himself that from now on Marjorie would be his hobby. He was lucky to have her. They made each other laugh. The sex was good. They could do more together, go on a great vacation this summer. Where? They could climb some mountain. Marjorie had accused him of being a "White-Water Man." She had suggested going rafting and he had said he would do it if it was all white water. "Why does it always have to be white water and dangerous mountains? Remember when you wanted to invest in silver, but you only wanted to buy a hundred thousand dollars' worth? The reason we never do anything is because you're a White-Water Man."

He would change. They could go on mild walks. He would be romantic with her and they could climb small hills rather than dream of mountains that they never got to. He would show her he loved her, maybe do something dumb like get an "I Love Marjorie" bumper sticker for his car. One thing was sure, he was through with the girl in the hospital. Infatuations weren't worth anything.

The phone rang and David had to decide whether to interrupt his bath. His body wanted desperately to stay in the tub, but he was a heart specialist with a heart and he felt compelled to ease himself out of the water, throw on a towel and head for the phone. By the time he got there, Marjorie had already picked it up and he thought, as she stood there outlined by the window, that she was beautiful.

"It's an Elizabeth Pringle?" she said as a question, the receiver limp in her hand.

"She's a patient." Marjorie handed over the phone and David wondered how he was going to keep his end of the conversation neutral both for Elizabeth and his wife.

"Hello, how can I help you?" he asked in his best doctor's voice.

"I'd really like to see you because I feel funny about how you left here today and everything."

"I'll be making rounds tonight. I'll drop in then."

"You mean just drop in and drop out quickly or drop in and hang out?" Before answering, David looked toward Marjorie, who was slipping out of her yellow sundress. If he hadn't known every inch of her he would have been incredibly turned on by her stripping. Before either of them could react to her bareness she was in a robe that covered much more of her body than the spare yellow dress had.

"I'll be there later. We can discuss it then." David hung up before Elizabeth had time to answer.

"How come you're going back to the hospital tonight and how come you're home early?" The answer to both questions was Elizabeth Pringle, but men don't give their wives such answers.

"I needed to relax a bit," he said, answering only half the inquisition. David lay down on the bed to prove his point.

"I thought we were going out to dinner." Marjorie sat on the bed and bent over to brush her hair. David enjoyed the show.

"We are. We'll go early and I'll get over to the hospital about nine." The thought of the hospital and "hanging out" with Elizabeth depressed him.

"I have the chicken defrosted if it's going to be a problem." Marjorie threw her hair back into place and David was ready to applaud. It almost fell in slow motion on her shoulders. She had been talking about cutting it and he had pretended to be supportive. Secretly, he wanted her to have the same hair he had known for the last eighteen years.

"If we leave by six-thirty, it won't be a problem. We could take two cars." Marjorie was tired of taking two cars. She had once described being a doctor's wife as having to take separate cars. "Why don't I just throw on the chicken. It would be better for Julie anyway." Marjorie joined David on the bed. It was unusual for them to be lying down together in the middle of the day and they both felt mildly excited by it. If they hadn't been talking about Julie and chicken, they might have made love.

"One meal in a Chinese restaurant isn't going to make a difference."

Marjorie saw Julie standing in front of the mirror in the men's shorts and felt she had to protect her. "The problem is it's a hundred nights at Chinese restaurants. You keep telling her not to eat and keep driving her to egg rolls."

"It's my fault she's fat?" David couldn't believe he was being accused. He wasn't home enough to ruin anyone's life.

"It's both our faults. We both feed her." Marjorie was very interested in a peaceful night. She smiled to show she wasn't interested in fighting and propped herself up on one elbow so David could see her friendly face.

David stayed accused. What Marjorie would never know was that it was Elizabeth Pringle and not her who caused the fight they were about to have. David had just realized that Elizabeth had his home phone number, which couldn't be good for any of them. "Julie could live on her own body fat for months," he said, being crueler than he planned to be. David's voice was loud and strong and Julie heard him.

"She's still a child," said Marjorie. Always she would try to save her.

"She's fat," he cried, with the pain of a father who wants to be in love with his daughter, but can't be.

"David, please, she'll hear you," Marjorie said. She got up and went to the door, standing between David's voice and her daughter.

"Maybe it's good that she hears me. Somebody has got to get through to her." Julie sat down on her bed to listen to the rest of the argument. She was hurting and glad that her parents were fighting. At least she wouldn't be the only sad one in the house.

"I tell her to go on a diet every day. I'm trying to help her. I'm sending her to that camp, aren't I?"

"The big mistake is you turned everything into food. Remember a couple of years ago when my aunt Rose couldn't come to her birthday until the following week and you had two cakes?'' David pointed a finger right at Marjorie's heart.

''You're the one who took her to baseball games and gave her hot dogs and peanuts and everything else you could get into her.''

''That was on special occasions.'' David by now had taken back his finger, but it still felt to Marjorie like he was pointing.

''Her birthday was a special occasion and I think it's insane that we're blaming each other for Julie's condition.''

''Maybe you're jealous.''

''Of what?''

''Of her youth. You know she looks like you. Maybe you have to be the star of the family and if Julie was thin she would be.''

''That's amateur psychiatry and totally untrue.''

''She looks just like you, Marjorie. If she was thin, she'd be you twenty-two years ago. That would be very hard for you to live with.'' David sat up in bed now and Marjorie paced back and forth in front of him.

''She's my daughter.''

''And who says a mother can't be jealous of her own daughter?''

''Are you suggesting I sabotage her?''

''Yes. You tell her to go on a diet and you bring home brownies. You say you'll help and you have junk down there. Helping is having celery and carrots in the refrigerator.''

''There is celery and carrots in the refrigerator,'' she said triumphantly.

''Yeah, but it's next to the apple butter.''

David's accusations became strangely comforting to Julie, who had to strain less to listen as the voices got louder. Up to now she had thought she was fat by her own hand, but if what her father was saying was true, then it wasn't her fault. There *was* apple butter in the refrigerator and she had a weakness for apple butter, and everything else. Daddy was right. Mommy was making her fat.

"It's just pureed fruit," she heard her mother scream. "Have you ever checked the calories in that stuff? It's like eating whipped cream."

"I get it at the health food store," Marjorie defended herself. "And how come you've kept this clever little theory to yourself?"

"I just thought of it. You really couldn't take not being the most beautiful woman in this house."

"You are so wrong," she snarled, and pulling her robe closed she went running down the stairs into the kitchen, yanked out a Glad bag and started throwing everything that was even suspected of being fattening into it. David followed, amused by the theatrics that he had caused, and Julie listened, trying to hear what was being thrown out of her life.

When the storm was over, they all got dressed and went to Su Ling's. Julie was confused. How could both of her parents, the same people who had been calling her fat an hour before, let her eat the moo shu pork and egg rolls? Did they have a pact that this was to be her last good meal ever? Maybe she should tell them about the baby. She knew from health class that babies had to be taken care of even before they were born. Surely her parents wouldn't dream of starving their unborn grandchild. As she looked into their faces for disapproval over her shoveling pork fried rice into her mouth, she wondered if she should just come out and tell them. They couldn't scream in a Chinese restaurant. They couldn't throw things and the most they could drop would be chopsticks. It would be good to get it off her chest and maybe they would let her eat in peace. Maybe, just maybe, if they knew she was going to have a baby, they would stop calculating her calories in their heads. However, after each mouthful, there was another mouthful to enjoy and by the time dinner was over her courage had faded. By the time the Chinese waiter came to clean the table, her mind was more on whether her parents would let her have dessert than on whether she would reveal the baby. Vanilla ice cream and almond cookies were calling to her from the kitchen and she couldn't quite understand why her father was asking for the check.

"Don't you want dessert?" Julie asked, feeling safe because the decision would be theirs.

"Do you?" asked her father, and immediately Julie felt that it was a trick question. Perhaps behind closed bedroom doors they had decided to change their psychology. They had asked her to diet, helped her to diet, bribed her to diet (there was a promise of a whole new wardrobe), punished her to diet (there were threats of not allowing her to use the car, once they found out she was driving to supermarkets, buying quarts of ice cream and eating them in the parking lot), but there was never, since the time she had grown fat, the theory that if she were left alone, she would get her fat under control herself.

"Of course I want dessert. Who in their right mind doesn't want dessert?" They had wanted her smart and, now that she was, they didn't have the energy for it. "Can't we have one goddamn meal without talking about how much food I'm eating?"

"No one's talking about how much anybody ate. We're asking you if you want dessert," David said coolly.

"Why? How come all of a sudden? For years you've been slapping things out of my mouth. For years you've made me feel like scum just because I ate. Now you want me to have dessert? I'm scared to have dessert in front of you. You'll hate me."

Julie pounded the table with a fat fist. They were all in pain, mother, father and child. The handfuls of baby thighs they once loved to pinch were now too big for them to appreciate. Tears rolled down the cheeks that they once thought were adorable.

David reached out and grabbed one of Julie's hands and Marjorie held the other. Julie let them. It had been a long time since she had been stroked and even longer since she felt loved merely for existing. All of their arms stuck to the bare table but nobody minded. It was important that they hold on to their daughter before she learned to hate them.

"I'm sorry," said Marjorie when she could speak.

"It's not your fault. I'm the one who does all the eating. Every night I promise myself I won't and every morning I do." Julie was so sad about the failure that David felt compelled to squeeze her hand when her pediatrician gave her a shot. She used to squeeze back hard because if she held on tightly, and hurt her father a little, the pain wasn't so great. Tonight she squeezed back, too.

"I should have helped more. I should have gone on a diet with you." Marjorie looked into Julie's eyes and saw her own eyes look back. Same color. Same pain.

"No. You're perfect," said Julie.

"Oh, Julie, I'm not." Marjorie clasped her daughter's head in her hands and kissed her forehead. David watched the connection between mother and daughter and felt happy they were attached to him.

"You're pretty," Julie sighed.

"You're pretty," her father told her and Julie wanted to believe him. If she didn't avoid mirrors, she might have even seen it herself.

"I'm not. I'm a blimp."

"No," they both said.

"Yes," she insisted. "You know those blue pants that you just got me? I put them on the other day. I had to lie down on the bed to zip them up and afterwards I was brushing my teeth, just brushing my teeth, and they split. They were really made well 'cause we paid a lot of money for them, so the only reason they split is on account of me. I hid them under the mattress. So, I guess that proves I'm a blimp."

They were all bleeding. Both parents shook their heads "no" to let their daughter know that they disagreed with her. They were on the verge of letting her know that they would accept her the way she was, and she was on the verge of telling them she was pregnant. Nothing was said because the waiter shuffled over with the check, which was nestled among four fortune cookies.

Julie couldn't help focusing on the cookies. She wasn't interested in the fortunes, they never had anything to do with her life. She didn't even like the taste of the cookies, but she wanted them. They would be at least as soothing as her parents' words or gestures. They could shake their heads, insisting that she wasn't a blimp, but she knew she was, and a blimp needed fuel.

"How can we help?" David wanted to know and Julie tried looking at him when he talked. Unfortunately, the cookies were still there.

"I think that camp is really going to work. I know I've been bitching about going, but this one kid I know said she had a cousin who went and lost tons of weight. So, I'm going to come back really thin." Julie felt her parents' smiles even before they appeared on their faces. It was so easy to make them happy with promises she knew she couldn't keep. Pregnant people, she knew, didn't lose tons of weight.

"You'll be happier," David said, reaching for his MasterCard.

"Maybe you'll take some pictures of me and put them on your desk." David realized, with shame, that Julie, who hadn't been to his office in almost a year, remembered the picture of her taken on the sailboat. Julie looked like an all-American child on board and, as the son of immigrant parents, that was something he was comfortable with. Her heaviness reminded him of the Old World and the dangers his parents told him were there.

"We'll take pictures tomorrow if you want. I've wanted to get new ones for a long time."

"You don't want a blimp on your desk, Daddy." She was right. He would much rather have a sailboat.

Julie was pushing all the right buttons. Everything she

said made her parents feel bad, which only served to soothe her. The more she put herself down, the more they insisted that she was just a few pounds from perfect. Soon they were seeming to accept her at the size she was. It was at that moment that Julie ate all four fortune cookies without even consulting the fortunes. Marjorie and David tried to smile through it, but seeing the crumbs on Julie's large chest made them want to warn her about the evils of food all over again.

By the time David was on his way back to the hospital he was no longer rattled by Elizabeth Pringle's astrological predictions. The few hours he had been away from her allowed his sense of logic to take over. WNEW was telling him that it was a beautiful balmy summer night. It was Sandra Dee weather, the kind of night when boys and girls get together to torture each other sexually.

He went to his office before going to Elizabeth. Sitting in his large desk chair, he took Julie's picture in both of his hands. He loved the little girl in that picture. He hoped he loved the girl he had taken to dinner. He opened his top drawer and took out the class picture that Julie had taken the previous fall. He counted three chins before he tucked the more recent picture into the corner of the frame and put both pictures on display. He studied the face of the girl and couldn't find the younger one in the older.

David entered Elizabeth's room without knocking, knowing she would not question the intrusion. He found her sitting up in bed, a pencil in her disarranged hair, a pencil in her perfectly arranged mouth and horoscope source books and papers resting on her legs on the bed. Seeing the books attached to Elizabeth again gave him the strange feeling that she knew what she was doing.

"How did you get my number?" he demanded, trying to break any spells.

"I called your office and they gave it to me. How come you're not dressed like a doctor?" David realized that he was in his civilian clothes. It embarrassed him to have come like that because it broadcast to everyone who saw him that his immediate business was personal rather than professional.

"You can't call me at home whenever you want."

"Why not, it's a free country."

"I . . . I have responsibilities at home, a wife." Elizabeth giggled. She liked the complication of his life.

"I know you have a wife. I did your chart, remember. I know all about you." He sat on the chair next to her bed and took her hand, knowing that even if someone were to see them, he would only think of him as an outstanding physician who gave all the comfort he could to his patients.

"You can't call me at home because that violates the patient-doctor relationship," he said, hanging on gently.

"You're not my own private doctor."

"But I am one of the physicians at this hospital."

"Do doctors usually send their patients flowers?"

"They can." He wasn't about to get caught.

"I know they can. I was asking about usually."

"Not usually. Sometimes."

"But not usually."

"No." Caught.

"Did you ever send anybody flowers before, one of your patients, I mean?"

"I don't remember."

"If you don't remember it means you don't do it a lot." She was so pleased with her interrogation that David enjoyed her triumph also.

"I don't do it a lot," he admitted. Since Elizabeth Pringle led the totally selfish life of the very young, this was the most scared he had ever gotten. Calling him at home was only the first indication that she didn't think of wives.

"Then you can't say that we have a typical patient-doctor relationship, so I can call you at home." She was clearly flirting with him and with trouble. He let go of her hand, but she didn't take it as a rejection.

"Do you want to hurt your wife?"

"No. Of course not."

"So, how come you sent me flowers?"

David started with a lie, but continued with the truth. He said that he probably wanted her to like him, but now that she did it petrified him. He chose the wrong woman to be honest with. Elizabeth was armed with what she believed to be the facts.

"It really doesn't matter what you think or what I think about anything," she explained. "I've been working on my chart in relationship to your chart." She displayed a few of the scattered pieces of paper. With their symbols of suns and moons it reminded David of illustrations he had seen in mythology books. "Look, it's right here, clear as day. We're going to fuck."

"You know we can't," he said, hoping that that would end things, knowing that it wouldn't.

"Dr. Burke said we could." For a moment David thought she had asked Solomon's permission to sleep with him, but she went on. "He said it was absolutely, perfectly all right to have sex. He said it was actually good for my heart."

"He's right and I'm sure there are a lot of young men who would care to join you." David was retreating to the farthest corner of the room. He had no desire to be trapped by Solomon's instructions.

"I can't go running around with a lot of young men. Look." She held up a single piece of paper, but from where David stood he couldn't see it. "Check out where my house of Venus crosses yours. I mean I'm not so hot to chase after a guy who doesn't want to lay me, but it's not something we're going to be able to help." David stayed close to the door. Elizabeth was getting too hard to handle, probably because she was so uncomplicated.

"You could find one or two," suggested David, knowing she would not take his advice.

"No, I can't. Jesus had the same color eyes as you, you know."

"No one knows the color of his eyes. The Italians make him look Italian. The Scandinavians gave him blue eyes."

"Sort of like how people created God in their own image?"

"Exactly. Some people believe that Jesus was the son of God and others don't, but that's a long discussion, and one we really shouldn't get into now." David thought of throwing a kiss and exiting. He moved toward the door but never expected to get out.

"So are you going to fuck me or what?" She was no longer playing around with her questions.

"Jesus was celibate." David felt he had at least won a major round.

"How do you know for sure he was? I mean, come on, you don't even know what color his eyes were, but you know all about his sex life? Just suppose, I'm not saying it's true, but just suppose once or twice in his life he got so hot he couldn't stand it anymore and he got it on with a couple of women. So what? Why would that be so terrible? I mean he is still our Savior, so what he chose to do in his private life is really none of our business. There are even some people who say he was homosexual, maybe because he wore those long dresses and everything, but it really doesn't matter to me because he still died for our sins."

"You are a very beautiful woman and I would love to make love to you—"

"You would be making love with me. It's really chauvinistic to say 'to you' because I'm going to be there and doing half the work."

David wondered what type of "work" she would do. Still he wanted out more than he wanted in. "I can't. I don't cheat on my wife."

"Your chart is so close to Christ's," Elizabeth argued, pleading strongly.

"Maybe it's not me you want. Maybe it's your fantasy to sleep with the son of God."

"Maybe, and that would be really great because then I

could have God's grandchild.'' This panicked David. She was obviously insane enough to steal his sperm.

"It's not going to happen! I have a wife!'' With these words he expected to end the discussion, but Elizabeth got on her knees to fight.

"According to a lot of people we might as well have fucked already.'' She expected him to follow a logic that wasn't there.

"I don't understand.''

"I mean since you've been coming to my room, with me in a nightgown and the bed here and everything, we've been in an occasion of sin.''

"So I am already guilty?'' He saw she wasn't buying it, but at least he was staying in the room.

"Yeah. Like if two kids are in the back seat of a car, even if they don't do anything, they *could* do something so it's still wrong. If you really want to stay pure, you don't put yourself in an occasion that could lead to something.''

"This is a hospital,'' he said, trying to absolve himself.

"But you've had adultery in your heart.'' She had tried to scare him but saw he was just exasperated. His hand landed on the door behind him, ready to push.

"Goodnight, Elizabeth.''

"If we're going to burn in hell for it anyway, we might as well fuck.'' When she spoke of hell, there was mischief in her voice.

"I have to get home.'' And this time he made his escape.

Had David not been conscientious enough to stop at the nurses' station to ask about one of his patients, he would not have known about Elizabeth's attack until the next day. His eyes were on the telemetry unit that monitored her heart. There he saw a run of PAT at two hundred and forty. Elizabeth Pringle's heart was racing. Very quickly, before any help could find her, the problem aborted itself. David was guilty and thankful. He raced back to her room and gently made her lie down. Since she was in no pain, it might have seemed that he was about to make love to her.

"You've having a minor attack. Lie still. You're going to be OK."

"Who says you're not going to die for our sins?" said Elizabeth Pringle softly.

David was very scared. He tried to get her to believe that she was going to be fine, but his voice revealed his nervousness. She hardly believed him.

"What about tonight?" she asked. He had dealt with patients all his life, but he didn't understand her question.

"Tonight you'll be fine, too. It was very minor. You're OK." She started to sit up, but he gently pushed her back down and reached for her pulse.

"I mean, could you stay here tonight?" Assured that the attack had passed, he gave her back her hand and ignored her question.

"You'll be fine."

"I was fine until you left before." Clearly this was blackmail.

"I have to get home."

"Just tonight." This time she reached for him. She got two of his fingers.

"You'll be taken care of. There are very good doctors on duty." He moved like an animal that knew it was going to be caged, two steps in each direction. She held on.

"But how do I know how my heart is going to react when you leave again?"

"Just tonight." Once he gave in, he didn't mind as much as he thought he would.

"What if you're not here when I open my eyes?"

"I'll be here."

"Promise?"

She made him promise. He sat down and she closed her eyes, opening them again seconds later to see if she really had her catch.

Sixteen

It wasn't the first call from the hospital that upset Marjorie. The first call was from David, who explained he doubted he could make it home. Marjorie had gotten dozens of calls just like this one during her marriage and had learned to understand. She said goodnight to Julie and got into bed with *Rabbit*. With the book resting on her breast, her finger holding her place, she thought once again of the bizarre robbery in the diner. Her mind made up more details. By now she imagined what the robbers were wearing, cheap plaid shirts and ski masks, and what some of the diners were eating, according to Marjorie at least two were having hot turkey sandwiches. There had been a few hot turkey sandwiches in her life and always under pleasant circumstances. Therefore, she couldn't figure out why more than one person in the robbed diner of her imagination was having this meal. She didn't tamper with it, however, and let them eat in peace before they were pushed to the floor.

She had just made up a woman in the bathroom who was washing her hands when the phone rang again. She expected it to be Amanda and was surprised when she didn't recognize the woman's voice. After Marjorie's friendly ''hello'' the voice hesitantly began its story.

''We've never met,'' the voice said, ''but I'd like to tell you something about your husband.'' The staff at North Shore Hospital would have recognized her voice as that of

Marsha Hines, the young nurse who had been seen following Dr. David Weissman around a year and a half ago. Her
friends knew he had given her a gold chain and never come
through.

"What about my husband?" Marjorie was scared by the
voice. It sounded friendly, almost sweet, but the circumstances were too unusual to make her feel comfortable.

"He's trying to make a patient fall in love with him. I
know what he's doing because he did the exact same thing to
me."

"Are you a patient of his?" Marjorie was not yet concerned. All of David's patients were in love with him. She
had the needlepoint pillows and the banana breads to prove
it.

Marsha Hines got flustered. She had meant to deliver her
two-sentence message, make her impact and hang up. Now
that she heard the wife's voice, she couldn't put the phone
back on to the receiver.

"I work here at the hospital and . . . and I just wanted to
tell you that almost a couple of years ago he made me fall in
love with him, although I swear on a pack of bibles that we
never did anything. Now he's making a patient in cardiology fall for him and I think you should know." Marsha had
counted on feeling better after talking to Mrs. Weissman.
She felt guilty and pulled off a nail.

Marjorie wanted to put this in the category of a crank call,
but there were too many facts to deal with. In the same conversation, her husband and love were mentioned, compelling her to stay on the phone and defend David. "My
husband is a good doctor, the best."

"You don't understand, Mrs. Weissman. I'm not talking
about him as a doctor. He's a great doctor. Who doesn't
know that? I'm talking about him as a man. To put it
bluntly, your husband is falling all over a patient named
Elizabeth Pringle. He bought her flowers. He spends all his
free time in her room looking at her like he used to look at
me. She's not even in critical condition and he's not even

her actual doctor. If you don't believe me, why don't you drive down to the hospital tonight and check for yourself. He's spending the night in her room. You could walk right in since there are no locks on the patients' doors.''

"He's a cardiologist. He spends time with patients." Marjorie was blaming the caller far more than she was blaming her husband.

"The patient is fine. He's just a big flirt. He gave me a gold chain. I don't wear it anymore because it's too painful.'' Marsha wanted the conversation to end, but she didn't want to get off the phone until she was believed.

"Who is this?" Marjorie asked

"I'm a friend," Marsha said, and added quickly, "I'm your friend, not his. I think he is a total rat.''

Marjorie heard the sorrow in the young woman's voice. She had witnessed phone calls like this in movies and on television. The other woman called to tell the trusting wife that her husband was having an affair. This call was different because the crime was not infidelity, but flirtation. "My husband makes women fall in love with him. Is that what you're telling me?" It had always been a compulsion of Marjorie's to clarify things.

"Yes. He did it to me and now he's doing it to her and I feel bad for all of us because it's crazy, but there's never enough love to go around. I have to go now." Marsha Hines hung up the phone. She didn't have to go. Her dinner break wasn't over for another twenty minutes. She opened the door of the phone booth and tried to breathe fresh air. Maybe she had done it. Maybe she had gotten the great Dr. Weissman with his dangerous blue eyes in trouble.

While Marjorie was deciding whether to believe what she had just heard, she kept holding the receiver. It was hard to understand why this stranger was trying to interrupt her life. Once when she and David were first married, the phone rang in the middle of the night and Marjorie answered it, saying a very sleepy hello.

"I know you're sleeping with my husband," the voice said.

"You must have the wrong number," Marjorie answered in her private girls' school voice, trying to sound innocent.

"I have the right number, sister, put him on."

"Really, he isn't here. Really." Marjorie felt sorry for this woman who was making painful phone calls in the middle of the night.

"I know he's there and let me tell you something, sister, if you ever come near Roy again I'm going to whip your white ass," and the phone was slammed again. Marjorie was sorry that the woman hung up. She wanted to assure her that she would never sleep with someone else's husband. She didn't fall back to sleep for hours because although she knew the woman had a wrong number, she still didn't like her white ass to be in question.

Tonight it was David's ass that was on the line. Five years ago when Marjorie felt secure she had told David that she would understand if he went out and had an insignificant affair. "I can understand you wanting to have a young, firm blonde," she said while cradled in his arms. David said he wasn't going to and Marjorie said he should and he said she should and they fell asleep together with the assurance that they weren't going to. This was different. The voice on the phone talked about David and love, not sex. The young woman had left her with a very clear thought; there wasn't enough love. If David was sprinkling his around, she would leave him, kill him, and get Marvin Mitchelson to represent her.

Marjorie called Amanda and told her what had just happened and Amanda explained it as "Some frustrated nurse with a moustache and space shoes who thought love was a ride in an elevator where nobody farted."

"He gave her a gold chain."

"You can get one of those little, light ones at Fortunoff's for about twenty bucks, so you're still not talking love."

"What if I go down to the hospital and check it out?" Although she was asking Amanda if she should go, she was already planning what to wear. As she talked, she took the telephone into the bathroom with her and carefully started putting on makeup.

"What the fuck are you going to check out? You expect him to be fucking a patient in a hospital room?"

"He's not fucking. He's just down there spending time with her. My time."

"Great, you're going over there to catch him looking at someone. That's some great jealous wife scene."

"So, it's not the greatest, but how many chances do I get to bring a little drama into my life." Marjorie checked her eyeliner and was happy with the simple black line that she had drawn on her lid.

"What if you get there and he's working or in surgery?"

"Then I'm the supportive wife who showed up because she desperately misses her husband." Marjorie decided to wear a black cotton dress just because the nurses wore white.

"I don't get it. Do you believe this woman who called?"

"I believe her."

"Then how come you're not crying? This is inappropriate behavior, Marjorie. Your husband is stealing your time. Shouldn't you be crying?"

Marjorie carefully brushed Clinique's Pink Blush onto her cheeks and was satisfied with the vulnerability it gave her. "Maybe."

"What do you mean maybe? Your husband is drooling over a stranger when he should be home so you could drape your thighs over him."

"I don't feel like crying. I feel like going down to the hospital and slugging it out."

"You're in big trouble. You've been to hospitals. They have pictures all over the walls with nurses who look like they matured in 1920 telling us to be quiet. Those nurses have their fingers on their lips and are saying 'Shhhh!' You think you're going down there to scream and yell?"

"I don't have to scream and yell. Just going down there will be my statement."

"You don't believe that woman who called."

"How do you know?"

"I know you. I've been your best friend since from before I had to use a really good moisturizer, so don't tell me about you. I'm an expert on you. If you really thought your husband was thinking of sticking his thing into some other woman or even cared about another woman, you would be crying your eyes out."

"You're right."

"Of course I'm right. I was born right and, Marjorie, I was put here on earth to guide you. I know I have other functions, but you are my main one. Stay home."

"That's so boring. Here I have a chance to catch my husband doing something wrong and you're suggesting I stay home and watch reruns."

"What if he is cheating on you in his own prepubescent way? What if they're holding hands and thinking of fucking?" Marjorie flashed on the night, this same week, when she had gone to the hospital and found David nurturing a patient. She had been there long enough to see the woman in the bed was young and beautiful. Then there was nothing to worry about. Now there had been a phone call.

"I'm going to get hurt." Marjorie was resigned to this and for the first time since the phone call she was taking the warning seriously.

"I'll lick your wounds and then you'll forgive him."

"Why?"

"Because if you don't forgive him you'll leave him and if you leave him, you'll have to leave me and nobody leaves anybody for mind fucking."

"I'd never leave you."

"If you don't forgive him you'll run and you'll be running away from me too. Do you expect me to survive without you? I won't. Warren and the kids are part of my life, but you're my girlfriend. Do you know how hard it is to find

a really good girlfriend?'' Marjorie, recognizing the serious-
ness in Amanda's voice, got serious too. She took the phone
back into the bedroom and sat down on the bed.

"Of course I know. I know."

"Forgive him."

"Do you think David is with another woman?"

"Yes."

"How do you know?"

"Nurses don't make crank phone calls."

"I'm going over to the hospital. I'll call you the minute I
get back."

"Don't leave me."

"I'll forgive him, Amanda. I will."

Since Marjorie knew her way to the cardiology floor she
didn't stop at reception. Visiting hours were over and the
hospital was cool, quiet and empty. A small staff was working quietly, cleaning and healing. Mops were being moved
across long, narrow already sparkling hallways. Marjorie
never walked across wet floors, in respect for the people
who were cleaning them, but tonight she did, leaving her
high-heeled footprints behind.

At the desk in Cardiac Care, four nurses were doing their
job. Two were doing paperwork, one was checking medication, and one, a young Oriental girl with a look too serious
for her years, was checking the monitors. Marjorie ordinarily would have felt guilty disrupting anyone, but tonight she
spoke right up, asking for Elizabeth Pringle's room. The
nurse checking medication—short, gray hair, just the type
you'd expect to be available for the night shift—informed
her that visiting hours were over. Marjorie told the woman
that she was Dr. Weissman's wife and that her husband had
asked her to pick him up in a Miss Elizabeth Pringle's room.
The nurse became charming. She not only told Marjorie the
room was 1508, she stepped out from behind the desk to
point her in the right direction. Marjorie didn't get away
without hearing what a wonderful man Dr. Weissman was.
"Such a good doctor and such a nice person," the nurse said

before Marjorie headed down the hall to catch this nice person betraying her.

Bravely she looked into 1508 and immediately knew that this was the same room she had looked into before. This time the patient was sleeping, her long hair reaching to the far corners of the pillow. David too was asleep, too peacefully she thought. In an uncomfortable chair, Marjorie had caught her husband sleeping with another woman.

She had to wake him up because she needed the confrontation she came for. She quickly entered the room, bent over and shook his nearest shoulder. Unlike other men, he didn't need time to adjust to his wakefulness. Instead of being disoriented, David went from deep sleep to complete alertness in seconds. "Marjorie, what the hell are you doing here?" he asked softly. Marjorie motioned him out of the room and walked out in front of him. Once in the hall, she realized that Amanda was right. Hospitals are no place for confrontations. She wanted to use the full range of her emotions, but everything had to be reduced to whispers.

David, with one hand scratching the back of his neck, spoke with enthusiasm. "I was having this incredible dream," he said. "I was in a car dealership, only it wasn't one specific one. I was being given the chance to put together the absolutely perfect car. You wouldn't believe it, Marge, I could have anything I wanted. Money didn't come into it at all. So I chose the interior of a Maserati. It had Italian tan glove leather with a walnut veneer. I could smell it. I don't remember ever smelling in a dream before. I thought about it and then I chose the body of the Ferrari. You remember that Ferrari I pointed out to you a couple of weeks ago, well that's the one, the Ferrari Dino, but I wasn't going to have them do the paint job. Italians don't know how to paint so I was going for a Porsche paint job and without hesitation I knew I wanted that iridescent lavender. It was going to have the engine of the Porsche 928 and the suspension of the Citroën. It's air suspension. I kept asking for all these preposterous things and the salesman kept saying I could have them, so I kept asking for more.''

''Was your girlfriend in the dream?'' Marjorie asked, forcing David to focus on her pain.

''What girlfriend?''

''The girlfriend you were spending the night with.''

''We weren't doing anything,'' David said, the boy again, the fire blazing behind him and still denying that he enjoyed the matches.

''I saw you in there with her.''

''You didn't see anything.''

''What I saw was enough.'' And then she found what she said so significant she repeated it. ''It was enough.'' It was then that David realized the importance of the confrontation. He had been caught with a woman, but he had been dressed and somehow he felt that would be enough to protect him. He saw now it wasn't. Marjorie was angry and they both knew if they weren't in a hospital her voice would be heard.

David led Marjorie to the lounge and she agreed to be led because there were things to sort out between them. She remembered that Amanda had said to forgive, but she was so angry that forgiveness was not going to be something that she was going to offer easily, if at all. She wasn't going to walk out before David had a chance to bleed and explain, but she might walk after the explanation, leaving the hospital staff to deal with him and the mess he created.

Amidst the black plastic couches, David began his plea. Marjorie sat as far away as possible and gave him no assurances that she would soften and laugh with him again. ''This is crazy,'' he began. ''How could you be accusing me of having an affair in the hospital where I work?'' David tried to look innocent as he cleverly placed the ball in Marjorie's court.

''It doesn't matter if you were actually doing anything. The intent was there.'' Since David stood accused, he took some time to build his case. He faced away from Marjorie and knew that if he didn't think quickly he could lose this round.

"You wouldn't believe what I've been through these past days. That woman in there, that girl, is blackmailing me. Look, Margie, I made the mistake of sending her flowers, of giving her some extra time, she's a kid, nobody was coming to visit . . ."

"So you slept with her."

"I didn't sleep with her. I slept by her."

"When were you going to sleep with her?"

"I'm not. I told her I can't because I'm married." David expected praise, but when he looked at Marjorie and saw her hand was a fist, he knew he wasn't going to get it.

"I don't think that's how it works. I think they have discovered a new thing in fucking. You can be married *and* do it with someone else."

"I can't, and you would be doing me a big favor if you told her that. Look, I was wrong to do anything extra for her. I'll admit that. If you have to blame me for anything, it's for being too nice."

"I didn't know nice people lied to their wives. You did at least indicate that you were staying to work tonight. I pictured you pumping someone's heart." They shifted positions slightly. Marjorie got up and stared out into the parking lot. She noticed that her and David's cars were closer than their owners were. David retreated to a corner of the lounge that had a coffee machine and a dull painting of mountains.

"For some reason she fell for me," David said, shrugging.

"And the flowers and the extra time had nothing to do with it?" By now Marjorie felt she had won, but the fight was still in her. It would be hard to forgive someone who considered himself guilt-free. She looked at him standing there, pretending that he didn't want to start something with that girl, and didn't want him. He looked at her and thought she was beautiful and that he was safe.

"She's blackmailing me, Margie. If anything, you should feel sorry for me. I was nice to her, maybe a little flirtatious, but mainly nice, and she got it in her head that she wanted to sleep with me. She's a little crazy, you know. She does these cockamamie astrology charts all day and she sees in the charts that the two of us are supposed to have an affair. So I said no. You think I'm crazy? You think I want to fuck a heart patient? The second I said no, she had a mild attack right then and there. I'm caught." David was working hard for Marjorie's sympathy. He wanted her to take him in her arms, bury his head between her breasts and tell him that they would conquer Elizabeth Pringle together. She was almost ready to give him the benefit of all her doubts when he added, "You can't be mad at me. I'm just trying to do the best job I can." Telling Marjorie that she couldn't be mad made her angrier. She wanted to slap him, but she was afraid she couldn't hurt him enough.

"I can be mad at you! I caught you!"

"All right. All right. Be mad. Maybe it's good you get it all out." He tried to touch her, but she preferred to hug the wall. "I'm sorry, Margie. I'm sorry you had to come and see me like this. How come you came, anyway?"

"Someone called me and said you were getting that woman . . . girl to fall in love with you." David didn't ask further questions, because he knew exactly who the caller was. Fucking unions wouldn't let him get her fired.

"I'm sorry," David yelled. They had had many fights during their marriage, but David always found a way never to be wrong. When they were too tired or didn't care enough to continue the argument he always came to the conclusion that it was nobody's fault, everybody's fault or Marjorie's fault. He rarely said he was sorry. Marjorie was so relieved to hear him admit fault that she was willing to open her mind. He seemed weaker and less muscular than she had known him, standing there, hoping to be forgiven. She didn't particularly like him tonight, but there was enough love left to take him home.

"You're really sorry?"

"I'm sorry I hurt you. I'm sorry Elizabeth had a heart attack. I'm sorry I was ever infatuated with her. I'm sorry I'm failing you as a husband." David didn't look sorry anymore, he looked annoyed, but Marjorie found her way to his arms. They hugged each other as proof that nothing had changed when it had.

"I'm getting makeup all over your jacket."

"It's OK. It's all OK."

"I wish I didn't have my car here. All of a sudden I'm too tired to drive home. Maybe I should just go with you and pick my car up in the morning," she said, still leaning against him.

"Leave it here. I don't want you driving when you're tired. I'll drop you off."

"Drop me off? What do you mean drop me off? Aren't you coming home?" Marjorie untangled herself from David so she could see his expression while she heard his words.

"I thought you understood what the problem was." He reached for her hand, but she wouldn't let him have it.

"The problem is you were spending time with another woman."

"I had to promise her I'd be here when she wakes up. I swear I don't want to stay, but I gave her my word. Believe me, the second she's well I'm going to make her cut the crap and let me go. I'm never and I mean never going to fall in love with anyone again." He had through the years forgotten how powerful the word "love" was. When he saw how shocked Marjorie was, he raced on. "I don't mean real love like you and I have. This is nothing." It didn't feel like nothing to Marjorie. It felt like she had been mugged, her security stolen.

"You're never going to fall in love with anyone again?" she spat.

"I shouldn't have said love."

"You shouldn't have been here tonight."

"I couldn't help it. I told you she was practically black-mailing me."

"You were here with her on my time. My time. You don't get to love someone else and have me waiting at home or taking the skin off your chicken before I cook it." She looked sadder than he had ever seen her. The corners of her mouth were down.

"I shouldn't have said 'love.' It's not love. It's a stupid infatuation."

"Guess what, David. You don't even get to be infatuated with someone else. All I have is your love and infatuation. I don't share those things. I don't let my husband spend the love he owes me on someone else." She stood firm, directly in front of him, face-to-face, ready to punch.

"I didn't even sleep with her," he said, getting back to an old argument.

"If you had had an affair, it might have been easier to take. At least that's just two bodies touching. You led with your heart." Her anger turned to sadness, which he moved away from.

"Are you saying you would rather I had slept with her?"

"Is that my choice . . . either you fuck her or you love her? I choose none of the above. No. Wait. I choose fucking. Fucking is better than flowers every time. You fuck a piece of fluff, but you love or get stupidly infatuated with something that lives."

Marjorie retreated, not physically, but in such a way that she could no longer be reached. David talked on about how he had made a terrible mistake, but as a physician he didn't see any way out, short of returning to his patient. He was sure Marjorie would understand and they would pull through this nightmare together. Marjorie didn't under-stand. She hurt. She saw David standing there talking to her, but he had nothing to do with her life. It all had to do with Elizabeth Pringle's life and how important it was that she survive. Marjorie, who was fighting for her own survival and was losing the other body in her bed, didn't want to hear another word. "Do what you have to," she said, angrier than she had ever been. David heard her words as permission to stay. He started to follow her to the elevator but she waved him away and he didn't try again. When she got home to her blue bedroom that had always been more hers than theirs, she spent the whole night being angry.

How dare he not love only her?

How dare he publicize his infatuation throughout the hospital?

How dare he make her his mother by asking her help?

All she had was his love. How dare he make her share it?

She had married for love. She had stayed with him for love. She had given up her ambition for love. She had counted on his loving her back. Always. She was the one he had to be infatuated with.

At five A.M. she threw away the Aramis soap that she had bought him.

By the time it was really morning, she had remembered for the first time in eighteen years that she never wanted to get married.

Seventeen

Emily and Julie could not have chosen a worse day to confirm the pregnancy. They took a nine-thirty train into the city and went directly to the Times Square theater where *E.T.* was playing. They almost didn't get to see the eleven o'clock show because they were toward the back of the line and by the time they got into the theater the only seats left were in the first five rows. Emily thought they would ruin their eyes. Julie refused to leave and Emily, knowing there was no way to get her friend out of the theater, gave in. They loved the movie as much as the rest of the world. They came out of the theater saying "E.T. phone home" in their best alien voices.

They went to lunch at Howard Johnson's at Forty-sixth and Broadway and were seated near the window. Every time Julie looked out she saw brides and grooms in the street. First there were four, then two, then maybe twenty. She hadn't heard that this was the day that the Reverend Moon was marrying over four thousand people and each bride, in her long white gown, reminded her that she was a single mother.

They walked to Dr. Birnbaum's office because there was time and cabs were expensive. Again there were brides and grooms to taunt Julie. They all seemed to be hurrying somewhere, the women lifting the hems of their white skirts, as they crossed the street. Julie was jealous of all of them. She had no information on the circumstances of their marriages, but it seemed like they were headed toward a better life than she was.

"What's going on?" Julie asked, as if Emily had an answer.

"I don't know. It's June so maybe a lot of people are getting married."

"What do you mean, maybe? The place is crawling with brides and grooms. It's like they're multiplying."

"It's that time of year."

"It's more than the time of year. How many people have you ever seen walking around in veils in your whole life?"

"I don't know. I feel sorry for them. They'll be all tied down with each other and snot-nosed kids. Sorry."

"What are you sorry about?"

"I'm sorry I said that about being tied down with snot-nosed kids, since you might be in that situation soon."

"My kid will never have snot."

"All kids have snot," a practical Emily said.

There was nothing Julie liked about the visit to Dr. Birnbaum's office. Emily's aunt Shirl showed up, despite Emily's promise that she wouldn't. She put her arm around Julie and said that she was there if she needed her. Julie dodged her affection and the Tea Rose perfume that was making her nauseated. Once inside the examining room, the nurse looked over the form she had filled out and raised one eyebrow at a time, letting Julie know that she knew the information was lies. And then she weighed her. Julie closed her eyes so she wouldn't see the numbers, but she heard the weights being moved around, easily finding their slots.

Julie felt getting weighed was the most humiliation she would have to suffer, but then she was asked to get undressed and put on a frail paper robe with the opening in the front. She sat at the edge of the examining table, waiting, she thought, for the doctor to come and feel her stomach. Dr. Birnbaum was not what she expected. (He was both older and whiter than she thought he would be.) And the examination was not what she expected. The doctor and nurse kindly helped her into the stirrups, but she didn't want to be positioned like that and her legs fought them.

"Have you ever had an internal examination before?" Dr. Birnbaum asked sweetly, holding her hand.

"No. I never had to," Julie said, her eyes filling with tears.

"It won't hurt," Dr. Birnbaum reassured her.

"What're you going to do?" Julie asked, wishing she could run out and join the brides in the street.

"I'm going to put a rubber glove on and I'll feel your uterus to see if it's enlarged and firm and I'm going to check your cervical coloration."

Julie still didn't know what he was going to do but she asked, "Do you have to?"

"We'd like to find out if you're pregnant. That's the only way we can help you. It won't hurt. I promise."

"My father is a doctor," Julie said as she gave in. She hoped there was some code of ethics that kept physicians from hurting one another's children.

"What kind of a doctor is he?" Dr. Birnbaum felt that if he kept up the flow of conversation it would make the examination easier on this young patient. When he touched her, he felt her body stiffen.

"A cardiologist," said Julie. "He's a great heart specialist." During the rest of the examination, she cried softly and tried very hard not to reveal her emotion. Actually, she thought the doctor was doing something terribly wrong. She was sure that he could tell whether she was pregnant by feeling the outside of her stomach and she felt violated by the intrusion. Finally, finally Dr. Birnbaum relinquished the stool he was sitting on.

"And when was the last time you menstruated?" he asked kindly. Julie was angry at him for what he had just put her through, but she managed to politely tell him that the last time she got her period was around Easter vacation and that was around the beginning of April.

"Why don't you get dressed and meet me in my office? Mrs. Rothstein will show you where."

"Am I pregnant?"

"We'll talk about it in my office." Dr. Birnbaum left, but not before patting her on the shoulder. He knew she didn't like what he had had to do and was trying to make it up to her with sincere pats. Julie pulled back. If she was pregnant, it was Dr. Birnbaum who was going to be blamed for it.

When Julie entered the office she was relieved to see Emily already there. She wanted to let Emily know she had been through a horrible ordeal, but instead she just sat down. Aunt Shirl was seated on the worn leather couch and Julie didn't question her being there. Dr. Birnbaum sat behind a large, old desk that had dozens of crystal paperweights on it. He was holding one with a blue flower in it, but he put it down as soon as Julie was seated. Julie looked at Emily and realized that she was too young to protect her.

"I estimate that our young lady here is about eleven weeks pregnant," Dr. Birnbaum began. Julie cried and the doctor came around his desk to give her a Kleenex even though the box stood on the edge of the desk and could be easily reached. She felt sad and scared and caught by all the adults in the room.

"Are you sure? I mean absolutely sure," Emily demanded. She was watching Julie crumble and couldn't help crying herself. Dr. Birnbaum offered Emily a Kleenex, but she refused, preferring to use one of her own that she got from a little package in her pocketbook. Julie had once described Emily as the only kid she knew who carried her own Kleenex around even when she didn't have a cold.

"I'm sure," said Birnbaum, retreating behind his desk.

"I thought a rabbit had to die, not that we would want to hurt any living thing." Emily was clearly challenging his diagnosis.

"I can tell," he said kindly.

"Is it too late for an abortion?" Aunt Shirl asked.

"She's not going to have an abortion," Emily said. "We talked about it a lot of times, even before Julie was pregnant, and we decided that we would never have an abortion. So, don't even bother to bring it up because the answer is—never." Emily was satisfied that she had made herself clear. Julie nodded to show her total agreement with her friend's stand and being encouraged, Emily went on. "Not that we think everyone should think our way. We really believe that every woman has the right to decide what to do because it's her own body and everything, but we're deciding not to get rid of anything," Dr. Birnbaum started to speak, but Aunt Shirl got there first. Speaking directly to Julie she said something about in cases where there is no husband . . . Emily stopped her. "There is a husband. He's a great husband and he and Julie are crazy about each other. That's why they wanted to have a kid, to even strengthen the great marriage they have and they're hoping it's a boy. They want a boy first and then a girl because they figure he'll protect her and get her dates and the only reason Julie's husband isn't here today is because he's out of town on business."

"That's right. He's at camp," Julie said.

Emily, in an attempt to salvage the plausibility of the husband, quickly added, "He's head counselor so he's making quite a lot of money for the baby and everything."

Dr. Birnbaum did some thinking before he spoke. "Julie," he said very carefully. "You are pregnant. Do you understand that?"

"Don't worry. She does," said Emily, but Birnbaum looked toward Julie for confirmation of her understanding. Julie shook her head yes and wiped her nose into the Kleenex, which was falling apart.

"What I want you to do, Julie, is to come back here on Monday with your parents. If both of them can't come, then one of them. We'll talk about the options you have and we'll go through this as a team. Will you promise me you'll do that?"

"She promises," said Emily, relieved that someone with authority was demanding that Julie's parents be told. She also liked the idea that there was going to be a team. It sounded almost playful, like their team could beat another pregnant team in baseball.

"You'll be here on Monday with your parents, honey?" Aunt Shirl leaned forward to ask.

"They don't even know I came here today. They don't know anything. They think I'm good. Mainly they think I'm fat, but also they think I'm good."

"I'll help you tell them," said Dr. Birnbaum. "Just bring them here and we'll tell them together. I've been through this before, Julie, so I've gotten very good at it. It'll be all right."

"Dr. Birnbaum can charm the pants off anybody," said Aunt Shirl, using such a bad metaphor that even kind Doctor Birnbaum looked sour.

"What do I tell them to get them to come? I mean what do I say without telling them what's going on?"

"Do you want me to call them?" Birnbaum asked.

"No. I'll lie or something."

"Tell them that I want to see them about you. That's all you have to say. If they want to call I'll be available over the weekend. Just call my office and my service will put them through."

"Didn't I tell you he was a doll?" said Aunt Shirl. "Do you girls know how hard it is to find a doll like this in the medical profession?" Neither girl answered and the question, which was embarrassing the hell out of Birnbaum, was dropped.

"Is there anything else you want to know, Julie?"

"Is it unwise for her to do anything strange? Like do you think it's wrong for her, considering she's really pregnant and everything, to do something like see *E.T.*?"

Birnbaum smiled. "I think it would be perfectly fine for her to see *E.T.* I think she should have a terrific weekend and not worry about anything."

Julie was about to tell Dr. Birnbaum that she was supposed to go to camp on Sunday, but he stood up and said he had to leave for the Hamptons before he was in big trouble. Julie wished her troubles had only to do with traffic conditions. Birnbaum kissed Aunt Shirl on the cheek and Emily and Julie on the tops of their heads before he left. As Aunt Shirl gathered up her pocketbook and an overflowing shopping bag from Bendel's she smiled and said, "Such a terrific man. It's a crying shame he's gay." Emily refused to believe her and Julie got sick to her stomach at the thought that somebody who touched men had been inside her.

"Maybe he was wrong. Doctors are sometimes wrong, you know," Julie said on the train on the way home.

"He's not wrong. There's too much evidence. I mean you took that EPT test *and* you went to the doctor *and* you had sex with Finkle. What did he do to you anyway?"

"Who, the doctor or Finkle?"

"The doctor. I know what Finkle did to you. I'm not that stupid."

"You know, he just felt around down there and stuff. You know, with his finger. I didn't know he was gay then."

"Did he give you an internal?"

"What's an internal?"

"For someone who has had sex and everything you really don't know anything about your body. An internal is when they put their fingers in. They went over that in health. You probably were absent or something. So, did he do that or what?"

"Yeah. He did that."

"Oh, God, how could you stand it? Didn't you want to die? Were you naked or what? Did he just feel or did he look too?"

"He looked too. The whole thing was disgusting. I don't want to talk about it."

"Oh, God. I can't believe he looked. I wasn't planning on having children, but now I'm really not going to have any. Did you at least get to keep your underwear on?"

"They cover you with a sheet."

"I think I would have run out of the room."

"Oh, yeah, sure. You would have gone running around without any underwear."

"Maybe that's why they make you take your pants off in the first place."

Emily made Julie promise to tell her parents but there was no way she could. When she got home, her mother was packing her trunk and Daddy had been spending a lot of time at the hospital these days.

Eighteen

What Marjorie thought was most unfair was that David had
never given her the chance to walk out on him. She was, after all, the injured party. She was the one who had the right
to rant and rave and leave. David continued to spend extra
time at the hospital, giving himself the advantage of being
the adulterer and the deserter both. He had called home at
least six times during the next few days to tell Marjorie he
loved her and that the only reason he continued to check in
on Elizabeth was her faulty heart. When he was sure the patient was strong enough, he would never see her again.
Maybe they could go away for the weekend, maybe to Cape
Cod. (The location he picked was the only clue that he
would be totally Marjorie's before the snow fell.)

The first few calls took at least half an hour, but as all husbands and wives do, David and Marjorie soon developed a
shorthand. The fifth call, in which they repeated the essentials, he loved her, she was having trouble forgiving him,
took no more than ten minutes. Elizabeth was a crazy
woman whom he couldn't desert because of her heart condition. Marjorie felt deserted. Eventually, David would call
just to see if she would pick up the phone.

Marjorie knew she had to stay at home and pretend everything was fine until Julie left for camp. She was sure that
nothing seemed strange to her daughter since this wasn't the
first time that David had spent a lot of time away from the

house. (One of the reasons his patients loved him was that he did a lot of hand-holding.) Julie knew when Daddy wasn't at home he was at the hospital making people well. In fact, Julie was so consumed by her own problem that she didn't notice that her mother was really suffering.

Once Julie was sent away, the situation would change and Marjorie felt she could take control of her own life. Maybe she would leave Syosset for a while and spend a few days with her mother in Manhattan. She wanted to leave David's bed as empty as he had made hers. The problem was that when Marjorie had been sure she was safely trapped at home, she could easily fantasize about her escape to the big city. Now that Julie was going off to camp and David was betraying her, leaving seemed too difficult. Every time she pictured herself in the streets of Manhattan, she worried about who would be at home to let the men from Pest Control in.

"I can't believe this is happening to me," Amanda said after hearing the full story of what had gone on at the hospital.

"I thought it was happening to me. This is my desertion, not yours."

"So, if it's happening to you how come I feel like shit?"

"You're a good friend. You know when to hit the gutter."

"So what are you going to do? It better not be anything."

"What can I do? He's a good doctor. The girl is a heart patient. He's done this before, you know . . . fallen for someone . . . the nurse on the phone said so."

"He's a flirt, your husband."

"He's supposed to flirt with me."

"Husbands don't flirt with their wives." They were both sad at this thought, which they knew to be true.

"I don't know, maybe I'll spend some time at my mother's. I don't like her being all alone in the city anyway, and I feel like a schmuck sitting here while that young thing is taking my time."

"You can't go to New York. That's much too far. It's what . . . forty minutes, but it's a whole different world. They don't walk around in sweatsuits. They have shoes to match everything, high heels that they can walk in. They don't know their butchers. They think they're better than us. They think we don't cover our sofas with the same expensive crap they do. They think they got to live in Manhattan because they have stronger wills than we do."

"They do. I was supposed to live there. I'm leading the wrong life."

"You can't walk in high heels."

"I should have stayed. I could have learned. I should have made David take a job in a New York hospital."

"You wouldn't have met me."

"We would have met in the ladies' room at Bloomingdale's. You would have been nice enough to tell me that I was dragging toilet paper with my shoe."

"That's why you can't leave me."

"What am I going to do . . . sit here and wait around for David? He'll hate me if I wait. Only mothers wait. And men don't sleep with their mothers."

"David is a middle-aged man with a hard-on for youth. What he did wasn't so terrible. The man kept it in his pants. Are you sure this isn't your excuse to escape?"

Marjorie didn't answer. When Amanda was perceptive enough to be exactly right they both knew her questions were answers themselves.

As she packed Julie's trunk, Marjorie wasn't thinking about whether she would stay or go once Julie was on the train. Her mind was back in the diner. This time a small, blonde waitress came to life. She was unlike anybody Marjorie knew and the only thing she had in common with her was that her boyfriend was battering her and she wasn't leaving him. The waitress had put Max Factor over the scar on her eye so no one would know she had been hit.

Julie interrupted her mother's imagination. She said

"Hi" as she dragged herself to the bed. Marjorie smiled and said "Hi" back. She looked so beautiful to Julie, kneeling there beside her trunk, that Julie couldn't bear to hurt her by telling her about the pregnancy. There were four polo players lined up ready for battle waiting to be packed.

"You really don't want to go to camp, do you? Because if you really don't want to go, you don't have to." If Julie stayed home, Marjorie wouldn't be able to leave, but she wasn't offering her daughter refuge for selfish reasons. Julie wasn't surprised by her mother's sudden compassion. She had always known that Marjorie would never hurt her and that Julie felt love had always been part of the package.

"I really don't want to go, but I really should, you know to get thin and everything. Maybe it won't be so bad. Maybe." Julie wanted her mother to have the daughter that she needed. She wanted fat camp to work so that they could steal each other's clothes the way Emily and her mother did. If even her hands were thinner, she could feel, when the two of them walked down the street hand in hand, that they were truly extensions of each other.

Marjorie stopped packing, pulled the rubber band out of her hair and sat on the bed. "If it's terrible, you call me and I'll come get you. I promise. I'll be there as soon as I can."

"What do you mean by terrible? Terrible, like my counselor is a rotten person who makes us give her money to be nice to us or terrible because I'm starving to death? OK, maybe not starving to death, but very, very hungry and my stomach is making so much noise it keeps everyone in my bunk up?" They smiled at each other and intertwined their fingers as they had done since Julie's hands were large enough. Marjorie lost her hand inside her daughter's. Fortunately, it was the one without the wedding band.

"Even if you are just hungry. For any reason. I mean it, Julie. Call and I'll be there."

"Will you bring brownies, the ones with macadamia nuts that you get in Great Neck?"

"Only if you're dying and five doctors confirm that's the only thing that will cure you."

"They won't let me call you. You know those camps. They think telephones and poison ivy are equally harmful to the welfare of children. And besides Daddy would never let you bring me home early." Marjorie tried not to show any pain at the intrusion of David's name. It was important that Julie go off to camp with no worry of the separation that her parents had already begun.

"Don't worry. I'll get you. I'm your mother. I'll know if you need me." Marjorie went back to packing. The position she was in made Julie remember a painting she once saw of an early American woman placing sheets in a basket of laundry. If that were her mother and they were living in the 1800's, she wouldn't be going to a fat girls' camp. There was a chance, however, that she would be stoned in the streets for having slept with Finkle.

Nineteen

Elizabeth Pringle had once wished for a man who was interested in more than fucking. Ever since she was old enough to notice, she realized that people, especially men, talked about her as if she wasn't there. Because of the perfect face they saw, they didn't think she was hearing them. Out of all the people in her life, only Gran was honest enough to point out her beauty as the curse it was. "Men will want you," Gran said, her hands busy slicing strawberries in half. "I believe in having sexual relations. I think it's a very healthy thing to do and I tell you, Elizabeth, I even think it can be done for pure pleasure. I believe in God, but, unlike some members of our church, I believe in the pleasures of the flesh. There are few things on this earth as wonderful as lying stomach to stomach with a respectable build. This of course should never be done outside of marriage, but who here on earth is capable of defining what a marriage is in the eyes of the Lord? I say, and I'm only taking an educated guess, that a marriage takes place when a man and a woman lie down next to each other and make love for more than two weeks."

Gran stopped to rinse the red of the strawberries from her stained hands and Elizabeth hoped she would go on. Gran's advice was always precise, but rarely was it so grown up. Elizabeth, feeling the joy of her new bra and hearing her grandmother talk about men's bodies, wanted the conversation to continue forever. She saw that the container that Gran was drawing strawberries from was still half full and the chore and the philosophy seemed to go hand in hand. She felt there was more and she was right. After drying her hands, Gran continued. "I pick two weeks because that is the customary and usual time for a honeymoon. You must promise me two things, child. You must not bed down with any man until your formal education is over. The laziness of sex and the quest for knowledge always cancel each other out. And secondly, you must give me your solemn word that you will never be with any man for less than half a month. You will think twice before getting into bed with a man you have to spend two weeks with. If he is devoted enough to be around for fourteen days and you want him longer, with your good looks you could have him for a lifetime."

Elizabeth never did swear to follow Gran's wishes but she obeyed them almost exactly. She slept with one man she disliked so much that she couldn't bear to be with him for two weeks, but other than that, she lived by Gran's words.

Elizabeth had slept in the same room with David and he was confusing her. She knew they weren't going to have sex in the hospital (although she thought they should, since it was a real turn-on), and every time she talked about fucking he brought up this wife. She knew she should be flattered by a man who wanted more than a physical relationship and even remembered wishing for one. The problem was it was getting boring, all this being adored from afar. It was sad that it hadn't worked out because Gran's only other request was as interesting as the first. "Marry a Jewish man if you can, Elizabeth. You keep going to your own church, but marry a Jew because they make the best husbands. Jewish men don't have jobs, they have businesses and one of the best things about them is they do all their thinking out of bed." Elizabeth didn't have to ask Gran to explain because she went on. This time the setting was her own bedroom, where she was making her bed. Elizabeth didn't realize it at the time but Gran made a bed with art and grace. Sheets and blankets danced over the mattress until they were secured by strong arms. The pillows were forced into submission by quick punches. All this was done with a combination of co-ordination and muscle, and since Gran never taught Elizabeth the skills, it was to become a lost art. "Thinking should never be done in bed. Jewish men think all day long and then when they get into bed they just do what they have to. I think the reason is that in their church they don't teach them to be guilty about making love when they're little boys. That's why I want you to go to that junior college that the city has to offer. Seems you could meet a Jewish boy there." Gran was wise, but she didn't know that Jewish boys didn't go to junior college.

If Elizabeth had been lectured to on many subjects, she probably wouldn't have listened. Since the only two things Gran ever told her were to spend at least two weeks with a man and to marry a Jew, Elizabeth took her grandmother's advice very seriously, and it was evident that David was not going to bed her or husband her.

"Good morning," David said when he realized she was awake.

"The same to you. Would you do me a favor? Would you look outside and see if the parking lot is full?" David shrugged, asking why, and Elizabeth said she just wanted to know. David walked over to the window and took more time looking out than Elizabeth thought he needed.

"It's not," David said, turning back to her. "You look beautiful." He couldn't help saying it. He thought Marjorie was beautiful too, only the words didn't slip out to her anymore.

"Are you going now?" He was standing in her space and she needed him out. Maybe the question would drive him away.

"I should." He apologized, not knowing that he didn't have to. "I have to take my daughter to camp today. Maybe I'll be back later." The thought of its taking awhile was fine with Elizabeth. She needed some hours with no one else's breathing but her own.

"OK, well you know where I'll be until the day after tomorrow when they finally let me out."

When David left, she wondered if her chart hadn't meant her to be with a different Jewish Christ.

For the second time that morning David stood near a bed with a woman. This was a marital bed and the woman was his wife. Julie was off, they thought, saying goodbye to Emily. She was at Emily's but she wasn't saying goodbye. She was telling Emily that she had told her parents about the pregnancy and that fat girl camp was canceled.

It should have been a good time for a husband-wife talk but Marjorie felt too forsaken for conversation. She had a suitcase on the bed, which she was packing to take to her mother's. That's where she would be until she could figure out how to really hurt David.

"You're leaving me?" David asked, lost in his own home.

"Let's not be that dramatic," said Marjorie, punching socks into the sides of the case. "You're not home a lot these days so I figured I'd spend some time in the city."

"Why does it feel like you're leaving me?"

"I'm not leaving you. You're not around enough to leave."

"You're being very punishing." David sat on the edge of the bed and hung his head.

"You're spending time with another woman and I'm being punishing?"

"We're not doing anything."

Marjorie stopped packing. She looked at her husband's back and spoke directly to it. "Oh, yes you are. You're doing everything. You're talking to each other. Don't tell me you're not doing anything. The two of you are sitting there and dating each other."

"We're not dating."

"Sure you are, with flowers and everything. And you've done it before with the nurse and God knows who else."

David hung his head lower, asking for pity. "I know I'm behaving like an asshole. I just don't know how to stop. She'll be out of the hospital in a few days. I'm telling you I'm doing what every good doctor would do under the circumstances. Did you ever read Dr. Lynch's book, *The Broken Heart*?" He didn't wait for Marjorie's answer. "You should read it. He points out some absolutely frightening things, I'm telling you, Marjorie. There is a connection between the lack of love and heart attacks. I've got to take that seriously."

"I take it seriously, too. You think I want to harm her? I just don't want to sit around here while you're dating."

"I just feel like you're deserting me."

"I'll be at my mother's. You know the number. Call me, David. Maybe we can date too."

"You are punishing me."

"Did it ever occur to you that while you're with that girl, I'm lacking love? I have a heart too, you know." Marjorie slammed the suitcase shut.

"I know you do." He drew her to him. Since she was still standing, his head rested on her heart. Marjorie didn't know whether he was making peace with her or listening for flaws. Before she could ask, the phone rang and she reached over and got it. After the hellos, Elizabeth asked to speak to David. Marjorie handed the phone over and snidely remarked that she thought it was his girlfriend. While David spoke, she removed the suitcase and hid it under the bed. It was heavy for her to handle, but she wasn't going to ask for help.

Elizabeth made no apology for calling him at home. She just wanted to tell him that she had called her friend Carol, who was absolutely accurate on past lives, and that Carol had traced David back to Christ. Elizabeth sounded breathy and too excited for a heart patient. Instinctively he knew that the only thing that would calm her down sufficiently would be for him to share her enthusiasm. If he indicated that he thought it was nonsense, she would be hurt or argumentative. Therefore he said, "Yes, Elizabeth. Yes. There are times when I feel I will be crucified all over again." He snuck a look at Marjorie, who almost smiled. He could hear a calmness in Elizabeth's voice by the time she said goodbye and David felt that he had done a good job, considering the text of the conversation. His only problem was that as Elizabeth calmed down, Marjorie flared. He thought how unlucky he was to be caught between the emotions of these two women, not realizing that he was the one who caused the pleasure and the anguish.

"She's totally crazy. She's convinced that I'm Christ reincarnated. I'm telling you, Margie, she's crazed."

"She is nuts. If she knew you at all, she would realize that being the son is not lofty enough for you. You aspire to be God and have the prostate to prove you are."

"Who's talking about aspirations? All I'm saying is she thinks I'm Christ reborn."

"And all I'm saying is that you think you're God."

"That's ridiculous."

"I know it's ridiculous. I used to live with it." David sank both emotionally and physically. He still lived with Marjorie. He didn't want to change. Why did she insist on using the phrase "used to" when describing their lives? Why couldn't she understand what was happening wasn't his fault anymore?

Before either of them could say any more, they heard Julie. She had just started her ascent of the stairs, but her heaviness projected her approach long before she got there. In this case, it was a blessing, since it gave Marjorie and David the opportunity to stop fighting and focus on the daughter they were sending away. Without speaking, they told each other to become Julie's parents rather than husband and wife. When she reached the bedroom they both welcomed her. She, of course, first hugged the father who had abandoned her. Marjorie watched as David put his arms around his daughter. At that moment she wouldn't have minded being the sixteen-year-old girl in his arms. She wouldn't have even minded being the twenty-four-year-old he spent his time with. The only position Marjorie didn't want to settle for, at this time, was the one of wife. She slid her foot under the bed to reassure herself that her suitcase was still there.

They remained a family all the way to Grand Central Station. David drove. Marjorie and Julie sang. They were all scared for different reasons and they felt safe together in the car. Julie could reveal her pregnancy and stay home. David could give up the ego gratification he found in Elizabeth's room and Marjorie could unpack. Instead they headed toward Manhattan, enjoying the time they were having together and appearing, to anyone who could see into their car, as happy. That was no illusion. They were happy together. They just didn't know how to stay that way.

Platform sixteen at Grand Central was strong. It had to be for the weight it was carrying. About a hundred teenaged girls ranging from chubby to obese were being organized into groups of eight. The head counselor, a thin athletic type named Helen, pointed Julie toward bunk twelve. David and Marjorie followed, helping with their daughter's extra luggage. Julie spotted the sign for her bunk first and seeing three of her extra-large bunkmates already standing there she turned and said to her parents, "It looks like bunk twelve could use its own zip code." She got the laugh she needed from them.

Myrna, a large but firm counselor, welcomed Julie warmly to the group and introduced her around to a Susan, a Beth, and a Caroline. Julie's arrival was quickly followed by the arrival of Kim and Heather, identical twins, dressed alike and both carrying about a hundred extra pounds. Julie whispered to her parents, "It could have been worse. You could have had four of me." The twins were friendly and

Julie was happy to share her arrival with them. She got away from the center of the group just as Susan was asking Kim, "So, what's it like knowing there's someone exactly like you walking around?"

"They seem nice," Julie said, trying to make her parents feel they were doing the right thing.

"I thought so too, but you can still change your mind. Julie, really, nowhere is it written that you have to go," said Marjorie, holding on tight.

"Come on, you two. She wants to go." It was at that moment that Julie realized that her mother was more in sync with her feelings than her father would ever be. They were women together in a world where half the population would never understand their fears.

"It'll be fun," said Julie, still fooling her father.

Two more girls, not much different from the ones that had already gathered, arrived just as Helen made an announcement with the help of a bullhorn, telling everyone to start saying goodbye. The girls of bunk twelve regrouped to say hello to the newcomers, a very big Beth and a slightly overweight Karen, and then retreated to their parents.

Julie, Marjorie and David had no more real conversation for one another, but were happy to form their triangle again. Julie was proud of her parents. Almost all of the other girls had parents who were also heavyweights. The fathers had large, round stomachs straining under pants that were too high, with belts that were pulled too tight. The mothers had breasts with which they could smother their young.

"Do you need money?" David asked.

"I have some. Not that I'm going to need it. I'm sure they watch you like crazy. I mean they're not going to let you wander off and buy candy, not that I would since now that I'm actually going, I'm really committed to it."

"Don't keep your money where anyone can take it," David warned.

"I won't." She looked toward her bunkmates and had the

feeling that the only thing any of them would steal would be something to chew.

Helen was urging everyone to say brief goodbyes. "We want to have fun with your children now," she announced, as if the parents didn't want to let their daughters go.

Helen's request caused hugs, some crying, a little bit of advice like, "Don't forget to breathe in all that good air," and reminders to write. Some parents, including Marjorie and David, walked their children as far as they could before they filed through a gate that led to the train. Children and parents waved as they lost sight of each other and Helen told everyone not to worry, their kids were going to be fine. "You'll be proud of what they accomplish," she said, making hundreds of parents believe that this camp was going to work for their daughters.

"Why did we let her go?" Marjorie asked as they walked back to the car. "Shouldn't we be thinking she's a wonderful person and that's enough? Why did I spend the last ten years of my life teaching myself that men and women were equal and that makeup stinks? I won't go out of the house without mascara and I send my daughter to a fat girls' camp."

"We did the right thing. She'll feel better about herself. Without the weight maybe she'll start dating."

"Is that what this is all about? Are we just getting her ready for men? I can't believe that we sent our little girl to a place where they're going to get her ready for men."

"You're pissed at me."

"Of course I'm pissed. You let Julie go. You see other women in their beds."

"You're not going to understand, are you?"

"Nope. You pulled that girl's heart strings and her heart followed. I'm running home to Mama's." They weren't fighting. They both had their windows down and were letting the outside world be louder than they were.

"You're not doing this just to prove your independence, are you?"

"No, I made seventy thousand dollars in real estate to prove my independence."

"How long will you be gone?" David checked the rear view mirror, his side mirror and the traffic ahead of him.

"A few days," said Marjorie, remembering how heavy her suitcase was.

"How long exactly?"

"I'll be back as soon as I make it in show business or I'm sure you'll die without me, whichever comes first."

"I'll die without you."

"Maybe. I'll be back for your final words and they better be 'I've left everything to you.' "

"I feel deserted," he said.

"Me too." They took a chance and looked at each other. When they were close to home, David asked if she wanted to grab a bite at the diner. She didn't. There were too few fantasies in the world. Why give up one?

Twenty

There were no assigned seats on the train to Camp Cotton-wood, but the girls of bunk twelve sat near one another. Julie slipped in next to Caroline and they faced the twins. Since the seats had no handrest between them Caroline's thighs slipped over toward Julie's and it seemed like a friendly gesture.

"I swear I sat in the exact same seat last year. I remember because I got lunch last," Caroline said as she removed the paper from the back of her name tag so it would stick to her shirt.

"You went last year?" Julie asked.

"Yeah, and I lost twenty-seven pounds, but then I gained about thirty-three this winter on account of they put these junk food machines in the basement of my building. My mom was starving me out, but right next to the laundry room are Lorna Doones and HoHos. She never knew why I did so many washes." Caroline laughed at the memory.

"Any Oreos?" asked Heather.

"Yeah. Sometimes."

"Double-filled?" Julie wanted to know.

"No, no double-filled. I don't think they can fit those into machines. All the cookies have to be regulation size."

"I like double-filled," said Julie

"Who doesn't?" said Heather. Kim stayed quiet.

"It's great taking the tops off and then scraping the filling with your teeth," said Caroline, not having to demonstrate because the group knew what she was talking about. They nodded their heads to the rhythm of the train.

"We do that with mud pies," said Heather, speaking for herself and her sister.

"Do they starve you up there or what?" Julie asked her seatmate.

"Everything is mock something, if you know what I mean. Like they serve these little mock pizzas out of half an English muffin, hoping you're going to think it's great to eat pizza, but all it really does is remind you of the real thing." They all thought about pizza for a moment.

"My sister and I both eat everything off the top first and we don't like anchovies. If it has even been near an anchovy, we won't eat it." Heather again.

"You could pick the anchovies off," suggested Julie.

"We can always tell they've been there and it turns us off."

"Remind me not to order a pizza with everything on it," said Caroline.

"They let you order pizza?" were Kim's first words.

"I was only kidding. They'd rather you screw around with the Japanese chef than eat anything fattening. Their big thing every morning is announcing the total weight loss of everybody in the camp. It's all economics. They get a lot of money from our parents to get us to lose weight, so you can be sure as hell they're not going to let you eat anything but their little mock food."

"What do they do if they catch you eating something you're not supposed to, like candy or something?" Julie asked.

"Where are you going to get candy?" Caroline wanted to know.

"You're very naive if you think there's any way you are going to sneak food in there. Last year this girl, Francie Blumberg, had a friend of hers mail her some Sara Lee . . ."

"Banana or what?" asked Julie, focusing in on Sara Lee.

"What's the difference what kind? Did you ever eat one you didn't like?" Caroline said.

"No, but some I like better than others."

"I'm really not sure, but let's say it's banana for argument's sake." Caroline could tell she hit on the right one. She had everyone's attention and Julie even leaned forward. "Anyway, her friend sends her this cake disguised as a blouse or something. Don't ask me how she did it, but it got past the office and it wasn't confiscated because they thought it was clothes." Julie was already planning to write to Emily begging for cake in a blouse. "So, Francie brings the package back to her bunk, talking loudly all over the place about how happy she was to get some clothes to fit her because hers were falling off of her. They should have known right then and there that she was bullshitting because she had only lost about ten and a half and the camp average was past sixteen. I had lost exactly sixteen by then so I was right on schedule. Francie lugged the cake back to her bunk and started eating it when she thought no one was looking and her counselor, Miriam Levy, a dyke if I ever saw one, she had a dildo, came in and catches her. Believe me, Francie was very careful. She just took tiny, little pinches at a time. She left the cake completely hidden." Caroline didn't have to explain the process of sneak eating any further. They had all done it and they all knew the rules. You never took the chance of getting caught with the whole thing in your hands. "The problem was," Caroline continued, "these counselors are trained to find sneak eaters. True. It's all a matter of economics. If everybody loses weight, they get this fabulous reputation and raise their rates."

"What happened to Francie?" Julie had to know.

"Helen gave her one of her lectures."

"No yelling or anything?" from Heather.

"A lecture from Helen is worse than yelling. It's worse than any punishment you can imagine. For starters, she has the worst breath of any human being on this planet and she makes you feel like the worst shit who ever lived. She goes on and on about what your parents are trying to do for you and what she's trying to do for you, with her old dog's breath, and her armpits don't smell so great either.'' None of this frightened Julie to the point that she wasn't going to try and get Emily to send something up. Maybe she could disguise M&M's as buttons or something. Julie was committed to losing weight, but she was just as committed to not being hungry.

Julie decided to go to the bathroom, crawling over Caroline to get there. She hated going to bathrooms on trains, fearing that they would be dirty, but she had to go too badly to wait. Halfway down the aisle she saw Helen pushing a wagon, just a little smaller than the ones stewardesses used on airplanes. With the help of another counselor she was handing out box lunches. Julie rushed back to her seat. She didn't want to miss the food. ''Lunch is coming,'' she said as she crawled over fat thighs back to her seat.

''Wait until you get a load of this, that pressed turkey on two of the thinnest pieces of bread you've ever seen. You could type on that bread. In the meantime they send this disgustingly cheerful letter home to your parents saying, 'The girls enjoyed a healthy low-calorie turkey lunch on the way to camp.' You want to play chicken?''

''Chicken what?'' Heather wanted to know.

''I'm not talking chicken salad.'' Jennifer looked down the aisle before she continued. ''We take a bag of potato chips and pass it around, you know, like when you were a kid and played hot potato, and then the one who has it when Helen gets here loses or wins, depending on how you look at it.''

Julie was not at all interested in playing. She didn't like games. She hated losing. She didn't particularly like winning and she certainly didn't want to get caught by Helen and her dragon breath. Julie said she'd rather not but the twins were all for it so a small bag of Wise potato chips was slipped out of Caroline's pocket and the three girls started passing them around. Julie looked out the window at what started to look like real country. One of her sweetest child-hood memories was sitting on her mother's lap and looking out the window at what both her mother and father referred to as the country. When the scenery became farmland, Marjorie never once neglected to point out the cows. "Cows, Julie," she said endlessly and it became a family joke. Even when Julie was twelve, thirteen, fourteen and capable of sighting her own cows, Marjorie continued to point them out.

Julie was watching cows when Helen arrived to distribute lunch. As Julie got hers, Helen said she wanted to speak to her. She motioned for Julie to follow her immediately and asked Myrna to take over with the lunches. Julie was totally confused about why she was being summoned until she stood up and the bag of chips slipped to the floor. Julie looked at Caroline and the twins, but their faces were neutral, the way guilty faces can be.

As Julie followed Helen down the aisle to the back of the train she tried not to cry. She didn't want to be spoken to by Helen, but sadder was the knowledge that one of her three seatmates had betrayed her and the other two let her take the rap for the uncommitted crime. As she walked, carefully keeping her balance despite the rock of the train, she could hear the campers from previous years explaining to the new girls what probably happened. Helen slapped the bag of chips from one hand to the other, broadcasting what the violation was.

Helen sat opposite Julie and leaned in too far. First she said that Julie was only hurting herself. "Don't you want to have a successful summer?" she asked, and Julie was too humiliated to speak. She could only nod her head yes. Helen said everything five times, emphasizing that Julie's parents had sacrificed and worked hard to send her to such a wonderful place, where they could give her help. The worst part, besides the whole camp knowing she was a cheater, was that Helen hugged her before letting her go and Julie, not knowing what to do with her arms, hugged her back. On the way back to her seat, Julie got scattered applause and took a couple of bows as phony as the turkey in the sandwiches. It helped a little, but she still felt pained. She looked around for an empty seat near the bunk twelve group but there was none available so she was forced to climb in over Caroline again.

"I suppose you hate me," Caroline said. Julie didn't answer. At least she knew who had betrayed her. When they got to Cottonwood and settled into the bunks, Julie chose a bed as far away from Caroline as possible. Since Caroline was the only one of the eight girls who had been there before, she continued to hold the center of attention. They were all afraid of being hungry and Caroline was the only one who could give them exact information on the food situation.

Once they were unpacked, Myrna walked them up to the Social Hall, where Helen was scheduled to talk to the entire camp. The girls of bunk twelve were already forming friendships and some linked arms as they walked. Julie followed alone, still angry at having been set up.

They sat on well-supported wooden benches as Helen introduced herself and her excellent staff: Flo Browning, a black nurse, and Doctor Ino, a small man who looked about twelve and a half and who definitely came from a Third World country. Caroline leaned over and told her bunkmates that they were now in for Helen's "We're fortunate to be here" speech, and moments later it came.

"We are very fortunate to be here," she began and Julie realized she was about to hear a version of what she had already heard that day. "Our parents love and care for us and that's why they sent us to Cottonwood Camp for Overweight Girls. If they didn't love us they would just let us get heavier and heavier and I'm sure no one here wants to do that." A few girls laughed for no reason other than that was what they had been doing their whole lives. "I don't think that's very funny, do you?" All one hundred girls assumed Helen asked a rhetorical question until she asked again,

"Do you?" and practically everyone yelled back "No."
"We're lucky to be here because being here is going to give
us a chance at being our personal best. Do you want to lose
weight?" By this time, the group had learned that Helen
wanted her questions answered and a loud yes was heard
"Good, let's begin. Let's remember that food is fuel and
that if we exercise and participate fully in all sports we'll use
the fuel up faster, and let's have a good time doing it!"
Helen screamed this, hoping to excite the crowd, and there
was some applause, but it wasn't enough to satisfy her.
"Let's make this the biggest losing season that Cottonwood
has ever had!" The girls could get behind that and there was
more applause and some stomping of feet. It was still not
enough to satisfy Helen. "Let's forget everything I said,
never talk about food again, have a great time and go home
looking great!" This was a crowd pleaser and everyone, including Julie, who especially like forgetting everything
Helen said, cheered. Helen, who had worked them up, now
pretended that she wanted them to quiet down, which they
finally did. She paced across the stage, letting them know
what she was about to say was serious.

"There is only one word I must say to you before I let you
go for your first weigh-in, and that word is 'vomit.' If you
are really sick, that's one thing and that kind of vomit I understand, but last year one or two of our girls, a very small
number, three at the most, wanted to lose weight faster than
the good Lord intended them to, were putting their fingers
down their throats and causing themselves to vomit. Yes, I
can tell by your hushed silence that you are as shocked as I
was to hear about this. We had to send them home and they
missed the camp Carnival and the Olympics and all the other
wonderful things that Cottonwood has to offer. They disappointed their parents, who had sacrificed and worked very
hard to send them here and I hear that all of them were sent
to psychiatrists, which is where they belong. If we catch
anyone putting her finger down her throat that girl will be
sent home immediately."

"That's a bunch of bullshit," whispered Caroline. "Kids were vomiting all over the place last year, but on account of they would have to refund your money, no one was sent home. It's all economics."

"Enough from me. I'm sure you all want to begin your summer of fun so I'm going to send you back to your bunks so you can finish unpacking and then your counselors will bring you to the infirmary for your first weigh-in. Don't wear heavy clothes today and light ones tomorrow. You can't fool us."

Julie thought she could fool them. She doubted that this doctor-and-nurse team, who looked very small standing there next to Helen, was going to give her the same type of examination that Dr. Birnbaum had given her, and without all that probing she felt her secret was safe.

Julie weighed in at one seventy-three. The doctor, who said nothing and probably didn't speak English, took her blood pressure and her pulse while the nurse did some quick calculations. Julie didn't say anything to them and they didn't talk to her until the nurse handed her a small orange notebook.

"You've got to write down everything you eat and everything you do physically, every time you're hungry and what your inner feelings are in a psychological kind of way. Then we're going to look at it so we can tell what's going on inside your head."

"OK."

"So honey, according to your height and build, your goal is one hundred and thirty-six pounds." That was pure science fiction to Julie. She was about to say that she was born at a hundred thirty-six, but it had been a long day that included a betrayal and Julie didn't have the energy to joke. She nodded as the nurse told her that she wanted her to lose four pounds a week and gave her Diet Plan B. (What she didn't know yet was that everyone in the camp was advised to lose four pounds a week and Plan B was almost identical to A. And C.)

The after-dinner volleyball game tired everyone out, but none more than Julie. She was the first one ready for bed, and while Caroline was in the shower, with the full approval of everyone else in the bunk, Julie wrote in Caroline K's little orange diary. "I can't help eating Reese's Peanut Butter Cups, which I hide in my underwear." Julie almost got applause from the other girls, as she planted an empty candy wrapper she had found behind the dining room in Caroline's thirty-six double D bra. "It's all economics," Julie told her bunkmates as she drifted off to sleep.

Twenty-one

Amanda drove Marjorie to the Long Island Railroad, but when they got there she locked her in the car. "You're not going."

"I didn't say that when you went to Bermuda." Marjorie faked a smile, trying to get Amanda to do the same. She didn't succeed.

"There's no comparison. You knew I was coming back from Bermuda. You knew I couldn't stay in a place where men wear lime-green pants." Marjorie checked her watch and, seeing that her train was almost there, tried to get out of the car. She couldn't. Amanda had the controls.

"I'm coming back from New York."

"Then why are you going? If you're coming back, definitely coming back, there's no reason to go. This whole thing is totally unfair. Nobody ever feels sorry for the friend."

The train was due and there was no time for philosophy, but Marjorie asked, "Did you ever think that this wasn't the life you were supposed to lead?"

"I was supposed to stay in the Bronx and marry someone else."

"I was supposed to . . . I was supposed to do what I'm doing so why do I think this isn't my life? Out of all the hundreds of Jewish girls who get the lead in the school play, how many of them make it in show business?"

"Six," said Amanda. "Not counting Elizabeth Taylor who converted after she made it."

"I'll be back."

Amanda believed her and released her door.

Emily started worrying about nine o'clock. That morning Julie had said she was going to visit her grandmother in the city for the day. God Almighty, the day was over and where the hell was she? She tried the Weissmans again and still no answer. Emily hung up and lit a cigarette. She hardly ever smoked, maybe two cigarettes a month, but this was one of those times that she needed it. She put it out immediately because it was stale. That was the trouble with smoking two cigarettes a month, only the first one was good.

She sat down in the den, turned on the television and carefully took her knitting out. Maybe after this vest she would make a sweater for the baby. She only got through one row before trying Julie again. No answer again. Maybe there was traffic. Impossible. The traffic went from the Island into the city on Sunday nights. Maybe when they got into the city, her mother and father had told her grandmother about the pregnancy and she had made a scene. Maybe they were all on Valium. Emily went to her mother's medicine cabinet and had her choice of blue or yellow. She took Valium about as much as she smoked and promised herself that if she ever thought that she was getting hooked on it she would check herself into an institution. She chose yellow because blue put her to sleep and went back down into the den.

Maybe Julie's mother and father had decided to take her to a home for unwed mothers. Not a prison-type thing, just a place where Julie wuld be taken care of until she had the baby and it would be put up for adoption. Emily had seen a home like that in a movie. There were a lot of teenaged girls, including what's-her-name, Sissy Spacek, and they had all gotten into trouble and were in this place waiting to have their kids. Julie's mother would probably think one of those places was a good idea.

Maybe, goddamnit, they had talked her into an abortion and Julie was in some hospital being cleaned out of the baby. Marjorie and David might have decided that abortion was the best thing so that Julie could have a normal adolescence. That was crazy. It was abnormal already because Finkle couldn't control himself. They better not have talked her into having an abortion. The baby would be fine. Emily would make sure of that. If Julie had her baby and she made Emily the godmother or something, she definitely would give up smoking entirely.

The yellow Valium was working. The knitting was slow. Maybe they went out to dinner in Manhattan and Manhattan was a very chic town and you ate very late so they were probably just getting started. One good thing, her parents would let her eat now that they knew she was pregnant. Emily worried that they might not have milk in chic Manhattan restaurants.

Twenty-two

David refused to sit on the couch, not exactly refused, but he pointed to the chair and Dr. Sherman Bernstein, sitting behind his desk, nodded approval.

"The psychiatry couch is a bit too much for me," David said, pulling a chair away from the wall.

"You don't have to lie down."

"I'm not going into therapy." David sat and pointed a finger, lecturing the man he had come to see. "I don't have time to sit around and talk about all that childhood crap. My old man was a dentist, my mother was a mother, and they fucked me up in all the normal ways. My wife left me five days ago and the only thing I can do with her gone is take care of my patients, and I'm not sure I'm doing a great job at that. I think, and I'm not saying this to be funny, I think I have been wearing the same socks for three days."

"Why did she leave?" Bernstein asked.

"Haven't you heard? I was spending all my free time with a beautiful young coronary case that didn't need all that attention."

Neither man spoke for almost a full minute, Sherman Bernstein because he was taught not to, David because he was there for answers. He had chosen Sherman because he heard that he believed in crisis therapy. He had helped another doctor at North Shore when his kid was on drugs and he had helped him fast. Since David had always thought of

162

psychiatry as a soft science, he didn't want to end up with some guy who didn't talk for five years and then told you you were ready for group. David broke the silence.

"Look, if I tell you what's wrong, and I'm not guessing, I know what's wrong, will you take a stab at telling me what to do? I'm hurting."

"What if I don't know what you should do?"

"I'm just asking you to take a stab at it. I need her back. A patient, a good man, a very good man, he should be president, came to see me yesterday with a funny feeling in his left arm and the whole time I was examining him, I was holding back tears. Maybe I didn't hold them back. Maybe I just thought I did. I've been crying lately and don't give me that crap about being sensitive enough to cry. You don't cry in front of patients and you remember to brush your teeth before you go to work."

"What can stop the tears?"

"Having things the way they were. How do I do it?"

"I'll try, but first you have to tell me why she's left." Sherman folded his hands on the desk. It seemed to David that he was in too calm a mood, considering David's life had changed.

"She didn't exactly leave. She says she'll be back. The problem is I need her home before she needs to be there. I don't know why she's out there. I don't know. I don't know if it's her age, the articles she reads, being a doctor's wife, all of the above. It's crazy. We love each other. Most of the time we even like each other. We laugh in the kitchen. You've got to say something about married people who make each other laugh."

"How's the sex?" Sherman's voice was as neutral as he was taught to be.

"What the fuck is that supposed to mean?" David was out of his chair and then back into it.

"It seemed like the right question to ask."

"The sex is fine. The sex is good. I want to fuck her and she wants to be fucked. She used to say we didn't do it enough, but I haven't heard that in a while. It's good, nice and warm. I have some patients whose wives want them to do it hanging from a chandelier. No wonder they end up with massive coronaries. Your turn."

"I'm supposed to tell you how to get her back right away?"

"That was the deal." Sherman thought and as he did he removed a hanging cuticle from his left pinky with his teeth. David lost respect for him.

"Beg," Sherman said and David liked him again.

"OK."

"Just like that, OK?"

"I haven't tried begging. Maybe it'll work. If it does I'll pay you for three sessions a week for the next five years. I won't be able to show up, but it'll be worth it."

"You're too smart for this."

"I love her. Love makes you stupid."

"You have another forty minutes . . ."

"I don't see how it'll help. I'll let you know if the begging works."

Twenty-three

Esther knocked loudly on Marjorie's bedroom door, insisting that if she didn't get up immediately she was going to be late for class. While Marjorie was growing up, Esther had knocked on her door hundreds of times with the same plea, but neither one of them would have predicted that Esther would be giving Marjorie late-for-class warnings when she was thirty-eight. Marjorie had signed up for acting classes at the Berghof Studio and came home proud that she had done something professional. "More school?" said Esther when she heard, not exactly showing pleasure.

"This is where the professionals go. If you're really serious about your work, it's really important to continue taking classes." Marjorie followed her mother through the rooms of the apartment.

"What work?"

"Acting."

"I didn't think that was work," Esther said, as opposed to her daughter's career now as she had been when Marjorie was eighteen and in the drama department at NYU.

"Of course it's work. You don't think getting out on that stage eight times a week isn't work for Geraldine Page."

"For her, yes."

"But for me, no. Why doesn't anyone take my career seriously? That's why I haven't made it yet. My own family never considered me an actress." Marjorie threw herself onto the same couch that had received her eighteen-year-old behind.

"So, it's my fault you're not a star," Esther said, drying hands that weren't wet on her apron.

"Partially. None of you thought I could make it and I probably got it into my head that I couldn't make it either. You all thought that it was the greatest thing in the world to marry a doctor and that was the beginning of the end of my career."

"Without David there would be no Julie," Esther said sadly.

"Julie is the best thing that ever happened to me, but how did this get around to Julie? Julie is my life, you know that, but we were talking about me getting into the Berghof Studio. I think you should be proud of me."

"It's hard to get into this place? They don't take everyone?"

"Well, the program I'm in they do, but that's beside the point. You should be proud that I'm doing something. I know it's just classes, but maybe that will get my confidence up. At least I'll know if I'm any good. If I don't try now, it'll be too late."

"And David understands that you'll be away for weeks?"

"No. And I don't understand about the flowers he sends to other women."

"You don't leave your husband because of a few flowers and acting lessons." Esther started straightening pillows, something she often did in the middle of arguments.

"You left yours." Esther stopped straightening, got disgusted with her daughter and went back to a cushion.

"I didn't leave mine. Mine is in Miami Beach waiting for me."

"You left him there for the whole summer." Marjorie smiled and bent down so that her mother could see her face.

"I left him because Miami Beach is a cultural wasteland. Your father was happy to sit on our terrace until I get back."

"We don't have a terrace."

"Don't be fresh." It was a sincere warning and Marjorie was warned.

"Mom, maybe I'm here because Syosset is a cultural wasteland. David will be there when the course is over."

"You're very cocky." Marjorie turned Esther around and kissed her on the forehead.

"You're very cocky, too, Mom. There are a lot of widows in Florida." Esther pushed the thought of other women away.

Marjorie opened her eyes and was surprised to be in the room of her adolescence. The colors had faded, but they were all there. The purple roses still climbed the walls in structured rows. The pale green chair that was supposed to be the color of the leaves stood in the corner and the drapes, whose vibrance had long ago been stolen by the sun, showed off more purple in generous folds. It was through these curtains that Marjorie had taken her first bows. She had had to fight her mother for the room of her childhood dreams. Esther felt the wallpaper was too expensive, the chair too light and the drapes too dramatic. She pushed for everything in pink, but Marjorie knew pink was for girls and purple for royalty. The adult Marjorie smiled thinking of the battle she had won.

It was in this room that she had painted her future, the men she wouldn't marry, the real bows she would take, the purple apartment she would have. She remembered that she had kept none of her promises to herself, including the one that had her always wearing a black cape. On Esther's second series of knocks, Marjorie forgot the past and threw herself into the present.

She turned and looked at her alarm clock. Seven-twenty. Class didn't begin until nine and she didn't plan to get up until seven-thirty, grab a bite, and be out of the house by ten after eight, leaving her plenty of time to take a subway to the Village. The knocking was, therefore, an unnecessary and annoying intrusion, but Marjorie decided to be pleasant and thanked Esther for waking her. "You want eggs?" Esther asked before Marjorie had any idea whether she had an appetite. She yelled back that her only interest was coffee. Esther, who was sure that Marjorie was going to die from malnutrition, shuffled toward the kitchen mumbling about girls who didn't eat correctly.

Marjorie lifted one of her graceful arms and studied the lace on the sleeve of the gown. When she was sleepy, she enjoyed tracing the intricacies of the pattern. She stopped the alarm from screeching and got out of bed. She opened the closet door and stood looking at herself in the long folds of flowing beige silk. She decided she looked fuckable. "Looking fuckable" was Amanda's expression. They would be in Loehmann's and Marjorie would pick out some good-girl blouse. Amanda would take it out of her hands, put it back on the wrong rack, warning Marjorie that the blouse was for frigid women. "Marjorie, above all you want to look fuckable." Today Amanda would be proud of her.

Marjorie got dressed with the great anticipation of the first day of school. She used only blush and a little mascara and dressed in the youngest-looking clothes she had, flat shoes, jeans, a white T-shirt, a big canvas bag over her shoulder. When she was in acting classes as a young girl, every so often a middle-aged woman would enroll. Usually they were overly friendly and overly dressed, wearing cashmeres and lizards that the other students couldn't afford and didn't want. Marjorie and her friends treated these women as outsiders looking for a hobby while they were preparing for their futures. Nobody took them seriously and when it was time for lunch the women came only occasionally and usually picked up the bill. Marjorie was determined not to be those women. Her jeans were not designer and her T-shirt was Fruit of the Loom. She knew the way she was dressed was absolutely right when Esther said, "You're not going like that, are you?" Marjorie, who was drinking coffee over the sink, nodded as she drank.

"Without a bra?"

"Mother, please, it's the eighties."

"You're going to sag. I'm warning you, Marjorie, one of these days you'll sag and be sorry."

"I'm already sagging and the left one is going faster than the right."

"You don't look like a mother."

"Good," Marjorie said, running out the door exactly on schedule. "I'll call you if I'm not back by six."

She was all the way to the elevator before Esther asked, somewhere between a whisper and a yell, "What if I'm not here when you call?" It wasn't meant to be a serious question and it didn't get an answer. Marjorie, who looked no more than seventeen according to her mother's eyes, shrugged and slipped into the elevator.

It had been her intention to take the subway to class. Those older women, whom she and her fellow students once excluded, often arrived in cabs. They were always entering class with crushed dollar bills in their hands. Sometimes Marjorie and her group would be given a lift uptown and there would be no doubt that the older women would pay.

She stopped at the top of the stairs of the subway to check the time. It had been so long since she had taken the train that she had forgotten the importance of moving with the flow. At least six people bumped into her. She moved aside to get her balance and there, stopped at the light, was the cleanest, newest, most inviting cab she had ever seen. She never even had to flag it down. She just slipped into the back seat and told the driver she was going to Hudson Street and West Eleventh. She wouldn't be like those other older women, because even though she was taking the cab, she would be getting out a few blocks from the school and no one would see her arrival.

"What's going on?" Marjorie asked the driver at about Forty-fifth Street when they had been immobile for almost five minutes.

"Whaddya mean?" said José Martinez. "This is what you call traffic. You from out of town or something?"

"No," said Marjorie emphatically, "I just don't usually take cabs."

"Yeah, well the subway is faster this time of day. Walking is faster. You gonna be late for work or what?"

"I'm going to be late for acting class."

José, since he wasn't going anywhere, turned around and took a good look at Marjorie. She had no idea what he thought, because he was silent afterward and soon traffic started inching forward. She checked her watch again and found that there was still a chance she was going to make it.

They arrived at Hudson and Eleventh six minutes before she was due in class. Marjorie paid in crumpled bills and overtipped as usual. José didn't say anything. He was off before she got her bearings.

She walked the few blocks to the Berghof Studio and was only a minute late. She was up the stairs and at the door of room 302 before it was two minutes after nine. Through a window in the door, she saw that the eight chairs arranged in a semicircle were all taken by students. They faced one singular chair, obviously saved for an instructor. Seeing that the teacher was not there yet gave Marjorie the courage to enter.

As she approached her classmates, one of the seated men, a true Marlboro man in a work shirt and beautifully faded Levi's, stood and in a gesture from another century offered Marjorie his seat.

"That's OK," said Marjorie softly, dragging over a chair from the edge of the room. The Marlboro man stopped her by putting his muscular arm on hers.

"You're not taking my seat, I was taking yours." He went and turned around the one lone chair facing the eight, straddled it and faced his disciples. Marjorie slid past four pairs of legs and sat facing her teacher. She knew his name was Lucas Morgan and that his credits included one Broadway Show that closed in Philadelphia, three Off-Broadway shows that had fairly decent runs, three summers with Joseph Papp's Shakespeare in the Park and several semesters teaching at Carnegie Tech. What she hadn't known was that he looked like he belonged on a horse.

"Class will start promptly at nine." Lucas looked directly at Marjorie. "Acting is a discipline." Since he hadn't asked a question, Marjorie didn't think he wanted an answer. However, he paused and continued to look at her. When the silence lengthened, she felt she had to offer some explanation.

"Sorry. I got stuck in traffic," said Marjorie, giving away that she had gotten there by cab.

"Nine o'clock," said Lucas and Marjorie nodded, curling her legs under her seat.

"As you all know, this is an acting workshop." Lucas' voice was strong and too loud for the room. "What I want you to remember is that the emphasis is on the work. For every hour you spend here, I'll expect you to put in four on the outside." Marjorie looked away from Lucas long enough to notice the very large girl directly to her right was taking notes. She had written down "four for one" in very large letters. Marjorie wondered if she should take the notebook she had brought out of her bag, but she decided not to. "You'll be living and breathing this course, with no time to devote to anything else. Your boyfriends and girlfriends will hate you for it because just when they need your attention, you will be off memorizing lines or rehearsing scenes with other class members." Marjorie thought it was great that Mr. Morgan didn't mention husbands or wives. She liked that he assumed that none of them were married. The girl next to her wrote "BOYFRIEND-HATE." "Anybody who thinks that they don't have the time to devote to this class should drop out now before I kick them out. By the way, call me Lucas. Any questions?"

The girl who was taking notes continued to write, but raised her hand. Lucas acknowledged her by making his hand into a gun and shooting in her direction. Marjorie had always disliked that gesture, but on a cowboy it seemed perfect. "I have a part-time job of more or less twelve hours a week. Will that interfere because if it does I'll give it up . . . somehow?"

"My dear, we all have part-time jobs." The class laughed and Marjorie, carried along with the mood, laughed too. She realized that there would be more than age to differentiate her from her fellow students. She would have liked to have thought of herself as someone who could work as a waitress, but couldn't come up with a good enough reason to do it. "I realize you have to eat . . . just so you have the energy to act, mind you." On the "mind you," Lucas Morgan, who was born in Cleveland, sounded a bit English. Everyone in the class forgave him. "So if you are all willing to live with me for the next eight weeks, let's begin." Lucas stopped and looked around before continuing. It was if he was counting them, making sure everybody was there for the speech. "First of all, I'm going to warn you that I'm not going to teach this class. Together we are going to learn how to act. We are going to be learning by doing, in this workshop. We are purposely a small group, which will enable each one of you to perform in front of us at least twice a week. We will spend the whole four weeks working on a play. I will choose it and you will do it under my brutal supervision." The note-taker took a whole page to write "Brutal Supervision." "You will be surprised to see the parts you are given. I do that for one reason only, so that we can all stretch. Any questions?" There were none. One fragile-looking boy started to raise his hand but decided not to. "Good. By the way, no one has ever dropped out of my classes, but my ego won't let me take credit for it. My best friend is one of the biggest agents at William Morris. I force him down here the last week of class. Last year he signed two out of the eight class members. That I will take credit for." There were murmurs from the class, excitement over the chance they'd be getting. "OK," Lucas said, getting out of his chair as if it were a saddle. "Since we're going to be on top of each other for the next couple of months, let's introduce ourselves. I don't care if you use your real name or a stage name. Just let us know what you want to be called. And I want to hear something about you, not your credits. It's bad enough out there to have to announce all that crap. In here let's assume we're all stars." Marjorie, who had been uncertain at first, decided she liked this Lucas Morgan. She was feeling good enough to smile and she was sure he had caught it. He bent down and scratched his ankle way inside his sock and seemed to smile back. "Let's hear something personal, something you ordinarily wouldn't tell your best friend for five years. Let's throw up on each other so we get close fast. Since we all have to be on Broadway by January, let's not waste any time baring our souls. OK, me first."

Lucas leaped up onto the platform that was meant to be a stage, paced for a second and then with arms outstretched said, "My name is Lucas Morgan. I am one of six children and am in bad need of attention. I have never loved anyone in the way that they deserved to be loved because I am selfish. I think I'm beautiful and I am constantly constipated." Finishing his performance, Lucas took a step forward, bowed and drew applause from the group. He jumped from the platform, inviting the next "star" to follow. No one wanted to be second, but after a few quiet minutes the heavy note-taking girl and another girl who looked like a young Jane Fonda both got up at the same time. The note-taker deferred and the young Jane walked to the front of the room, but didn't feel secure enough to get up on stage.

"My name is Saucy Lange. I'm from Florida, but I live here now. I model and do TV commercials, but I really want to act. Last year I did two Off-Off Broadway things . . . oh, gosh, I'm sorry, we're not supposed to give credits. Let's see, what else?" Saucy shrugged her shoulders and her green eyes looked toward the ceiling for advice. She got none. "I guess that's it." She didn't bow and the class gave her the lightest applause possible.

The note-taker, Millie Klein, was next and she talked about how she always wanted to perform, but, even though acting was absolutely, positively her first love she wanted to be a producer and a director as well. She begged the class on bended knee, metaphorically, not physically, to help her improve her posture.

Millie was followed by a fragile man who said he was a homosexual before he said his name and he was followed by a tall, Bohemian type of woman who said she was a homosexual, which had helped her acting.

There was an exceptionally good-looking Mike who felt he had acting in his blood, a young woman, at least as beautiful as Saucy, but with no makeup and a noticeable limp. She had started acting in therapy and hoped one day to play Laura in *The Glass Menagerie*. Then came Jake, big and basic, trying to be Marlon Brando at his best. (Lucas had to ask him to speak up twice.) Right before Marjorie was Alec Glenhouser, a singer-dancer who wanted out of the chorus.

Marjorie had decided right from the beginning that since she couldn't be first, she was going to be last. Any fool knew that the star had the final bow. She waited until Alec sat down and then, in a very queenly fashion, rose. She was the first one in the class, with of course the exception of Mr. Morgan, to use the stage. She nodded to the class, giving them permission to listen. "My name is Marjorie Weissman and I am an actress. What I do every day has nothing to do with that. I am a totally sane person who daydreams about being in a diner during a robbery. The patrons are forced to lie down next to one another and have sex. In my latest fantasy I have locked myself in the bathroom while all this is happening. I am here in Mr. Morgan's class in order that I may leave the restroom and get on with my acting." Marjorie's bow was not nearly as flamboyant as Lucas' but her applause was just as loud. As she strode back to her seat she felt he had recognized his match. "That was really good," said Millie and Marjorie thought she was wiping away a tear. She, however, had learned a long time ago not to trust emotions in acting class.

"All right, stars. The one thing I noticed is that none of you, and I mean none of you, know how to bow. You may think it's strange to start your first class with a lesson in bowing, but I can't let you go out into the professional world without knowing how to collect your appreciation from the audience." Millie Klein wrote down "bowing—important." "So come on, everyone, up on your feet. We have just finished opening night of, let's say, *Mame*. All right, you're the cast; Jake, you're Angela Lansbury so you'll be the last. When I point to each one of you, you come out and bow, with happiness, relief, appreciation. You have sweated upon that stage for the last three hours. Now it's time for the audience to thank you."

Lucas, who was a great cheerleader, had them all excited. He pushed them into two separate groups, except for Jake, whose hair he fluffed up a bit. As an orchestra of one, he hummed his heart out and at the same time walked through their bows with them. He strutted with total self-assurance and the students strutted behind him with the shakiness that students have on the first day of class. When it was Marjorie's turn she had grace, even style, and it would have been perfection if her new sneakers hadn't insisted on squeaking. Jake turned out to be exquisite. Under Lucas' direction he threw one arm out, put the other under his chin and took a long deep bow to the floor.

He brought them back to reality by saying, "Now all we have to do is figure out what to do before the final curtain comes down." There was not a member of the class who wasn't ready to work. If Lucas' intention was to loosen them up and get their devotion, he had succeeded. He gave them a five-minute break. "To use the john or have the john use you." For the most part that's what everyone did and while they were standing by the sink, Saucy asked Marjorie if she had a Tampax on her. She didn't but Marjorie took it as a good sign. Once she didn't ask an older woman in her class for a Kotex because she was sure she had already gone through menopause.

By the time they got back to class, Lucas was stretched out on the stage asleep. On each of their chairs was a copy of *The Fifth of July* with the character's name on it. Marjorie's had Evie on hers and all of Evie's lines were underlined. She had seen the play and knew that Evie was a thirteen-year-old girl, a love child left over from the sixties. She thought there was some mistake until she saw her name was written on the inside of the cover. Millie Klein was totally surprised to be playing the Swoozie Kurtz role. Obviously Lucas, as promised, had mixed them up and given them the challenge of being cast against type.

Lucas Morgan lifted his head from the stage to see that everyone was in place and content that they were, he straddled his chair again. Still a bit sleepy, he scratched his head before speaking. "Many of my fellow teachers feel that I go about things incorrectly. They are wrong. They prepare their students for the theater by preparing them for auditions, callbacks and readings. I prefer to pretend that the minute you walk into my classroom you have already gotten the part. Congratulations to all of you, you are in a Broadway hit."

A few smiled and Lucas was not happy with the response. "You've got the parts! Come on, let's see a little joy here! Isn't this what we have worked toward all these years? Congratulations, my friends." There was movement from the group and only Marjorie saw that Lucas was not getting what he wanted.

"Thank you," said Marjorie, acting. "I really didn't expect . . . I mean I'm . . . you know, really honored to be working with you." Marjorie giggled the way a teenaged actress, who would have actually gotten the part, would have, and the others caught on. The class, doing spontaneous improvisation, became the actors on the first day of rehearsal. Lucas said he felt he had a hell of a cast and they told him what a great honor it was that they were getting to

work with him. Marjorie added that she thought it was really
dumb that they were making her have a tutor and kissed him
on the cheek and then sat back down with one foot up on her
chair the way a thirteen-year-old would.

"You already know that we open at the Brooks Atkinson
six weeks from today." Lucas was the director, pacing before his cast. "If I didn't think you could do it, I wouldn't
have asked you to. All right. First I want to read it straight
through. Then lunch, then we'll block Act One."

Everyone turned to the beginning of the play. Marjorie
couldn't understand why, since she knew it was a game, she
was getting such a rush. Marjorie Weinstein Weissman had
not been so nourished since NYU.

The eight classmates went to lunch together and there was
never any doubt that Marjorie would join them. They went
to the Silver Cup, the cheapest luncheonette in the neighborhood, and pushed two tables together. There among the
BLT's, tuna's on toast, and cheeseburgers, they talked
about nothing but Lucas. Saucy thought he was magnificent. Millie thought he really knew his stuff. The fragile boy
thought Lucas Morgan was the most wonderful thing that
had ever happened to him. Marjorie thought all of the
above. She said "He seems to be a terrific teacher" and
hoped the schoolgirl crush she already had wasn't noticeable. They divided the check evenly, even though, as Millie
pointed out, she had fries, and were back in class ten minutes early. Lucas was already there laying out the set with
tape on the floor. He had been working throughout the lunch
break and had dimensions laid down, clearly showing where
the entrances and exits were and where the doors would be.
The chairs that had been on the outskirts of the room had
been recruited for couches, tables, and other pieces of furniture. To do this job, he had taken his shirt off.

"What did you bring me?" Lucas asked the whole group,
since they had arrived together. They looked at each other,
embarrassed not to be bearing gifts. At least half of them,
including Marjorie, offered to go back and get him anything

he wanted. The fragile boy won by getting closest to the door first. Lucas asked for a bagel and cream cheese, hold the lox, coffee. Don't let the coffee drip on the bagel. The boy left hoping that he would get things right.

"All right. Let's get it up on its feet. Jake, you sit there on the edge of the porch. There's a pair of crutches there in the corner. I want you to get used to them. Use them twenty-four hours a day. Keep them beside your bed. Don't let your girlfriend talk you out of it."

"I don't have a girlfriend."

"Good. She'd probably complain about all the time you're spending preparing for class. If any of you are living with someone don't expect them to be around a month from now. Mike, stage left, get ready for your entrance, the rest of you down front and watching. Watching is part of it. I think actors who aren't totally familiar with the whole production are assholes." Marjorie and the others sat in front of the stage, some on chairs, some on the floor. Marjorie chose the floor and was sorry she did.

It was four o'clock by the time the first act was blocked, but no one minded that they had run an hour over. They were tired and happy and left in twos and threes, not yet willing to let one another go. Just as Marjorie was out the door, Lucas called to her and asked her to stay. Her first thought was that he was going to compliment her. She knew she had been extraordinary in her introduction and very good in the reading. She stood before him waiting for her praise. He was getting into his shirt and buttoning it wrong. Marjorie didn't feel she could reach out and correct the mistake, so she let it go. Lucas realized the mistake, but tucked his misbuttoned shirt into his pants.

"Don't fall in love with me," he said directly into Marjorie's eyes.

"What?"

"Didn't you hear me or didn't you understand what I said?" Lucas said sweetly. He sat down to fix his shoe and Marjorie sat opposite him.

"I heard you. I guess I didn't understand. I have no intention of falling in love with you."

"That's what Pamela Cohen said and Cindy, what the fuck was her last name, said, but they both fell."

"For you?"

"You find that hard to believe?"

"No, I find that easy."

"I don't know anything about you. I didn't read your application because I don't believe in paperwork. They put up with me here because I'm good. So, without knowing anything about you, let me guess. You're either separated or divorced."

"Neither."

"Married?"

"Yes, married. I just left for the summer."

"I'd call that separated."

"Nothing official . . . and I still love him."

"Where do you sleep? With him or without him?"

"At my mother's apartment. Without him and no wonder that Cindy and Pamela fell for you. You're a big flirt. You're flirting with me now."

Lucas smiled, letting Marjorie think she had discovered a truth.

"If I were flirting we'd be in the same chair. I gotta pee. Wait here. I'll be right back." Lucas wore the type of Levi's with a button fly. He started unbuttoning them as he headed toward the door. By the time he left the room, Marjorie had no idea whether he was coming on to her or she was coming on to him. He was back before she could do much thinking, this time entering buttoning and talking.

"Pamela was in my summer session two years ago. She was blonde, not natural, had a beautiful ass considering she was the mother of three, and had just left her husband. She had spent her youth on Broadway. Did you see *A Room Full of Roses*?" Marjorie shook her head no. "Not important. She was in it. Good little actress. She left the business, got married and when all three kids were teenagers she left her

husband and tried to go back to the one thing she knew . . .
acting. That's how she ended up in my pro workshop." Lucas paused, perhaps expecting Marjorie to say something.
She nodded to show she was listening, encouraging him to
go on. "Of course she fell for me. I know that sounds conceited, but it's not. I work very hard to get people to love
me. I put all my energy into it. I touch. You're right—I flirt.
I'm supportive. I tell people they're stars. If you're good-
looking and you do all these things, people fall." Lucas got
up and moved slowly toward the window. Marjorie couldn't
help noticing that he had neglected to button one of the buttons on his fly. "I loved Pamela back and she went back to
her husband," he said, putting both his hands in the back
pockets of his jeans. "Cindy was a different story. She was
a good actress, beautiful in a fragile way. If she hadn't disappeared into Connecticut with a successful businessman
husband she would have probably made it, not on stage, but
on film. Even at thirty-five she had that kind of movie-star
skin. She fell in love with me before I knew it. I thought we
were having a sensible affair. She left her husband before I
knew she had to. There were tears, hers, mine, ours." Lucas turned around and looked at Marjorie from across the
room. The distance was wise.

"I'm not here to fall in love. I'm here to learn. For the
last . . . well, over fifteen years I've wanted to get back to
acting professionally. I'm good. Really. I'm . . . over
thirty-five. At this point in my life learning is more important than loving, so you have nothing to be afraid of."

Lucas came close. His whisper was very seductive.
"What do you mean by getting back to acting professionally?"

Marjorie bit her lip before speaking. "You caught me.
I'm like Cindy except without the great skin. I disappeared
into the suburbs with a doctor. I don't mean getting back to
acting professionally. I mean getting there in the first
place."

"We're not going to make it."

"We're not?"

"You're over thirty-five. I'm over forty-six. I don't think either one of us should still be dreaming about stardom."

"I don't want stardom. My dream is to be a working actress."

"There is no such thing."

"There goes my dream." Marjorie wasn't giving it up, but it seemed safe to say she was.

"I realized I wasn't going to make a living at it years ago. It's a good thing I have a good trust fund and you have a good husband."

"My husband doesn't support me anymore. I'm . . ."

He couldn't wait to interrupt. ". . . in real estate."

"Am I that trite?"

"No. You're unique. I just like finishing your sentences."

"What we really need is a good agent," said Marjorie, surprised that she had made Lucas and herself a team.

"I have a good agent. He's a great agent. He only takes two weeks' vacation. If I go out to dinner with him, he pays. If I get drunk, I can sleep on his couch. He looks out for my career and the most he can get me is a job a year. My income from acting is a cool thousand every twelve months."

Marjorie started to tell him the money didn't count, but he spoke too soon. "And don't tell me the money doesn't count. The money doesn't count with me either. I'd pay them to be on Broadway."

"But you're good."

"Haven't you heard that doesn't necessarily lead to work?"

"What does?"

"Being twenty-four and good. Of course I didn't know that when I was twenty-four and good and decided to write poetry on Cape Cod."

"Lucille Ball was forty before *I Love Lucy* went on the air." Marjorie was trying to cheer them both up. She didn't have to. Lucas was totally content with the life he had found.

"Lucy was at it at twenty-four."

"So, you're just going to give up, just like that?"

"No. I'm the one with the reputation and the agent. You're the one who should run. It's too dangerous for you. I'm going to make you better than you are now and it's going to be very hard to retreat back to the house with the country kitchen."

"How do you know I have a country kitchen?"

"Pamela and Cindy had country kitchens. I'll bet you have pot holders with cows on them."

Marjorie stood. It was her turn to pace. "It's horrible to find out at this point in life that I'm a stereotype."

Lucas stopped her by standing in her path. "You are. You are the beautiful, talented Jewess who doesn't realize she's in her prime. She can do anything, be anything but a brain surgeon or an actress. Probably they wouldn't let you into medical school because you would be taking the place of someone younger, who could serve society longer." Seeing Marjorie darken, he quickly added, "You could still train as an archer for the Olympics if your eyes and biceps are in good shape."

Marjorie returned to her chair and pulled one leg up so that her chin could rest on a knee. She sulked in the same way she had sulked as a teenager when Esther told her she was too young to audition. "You'll finish your education," Esther ordered, and Marjorie said then what she was saying to Lucas now. "It's not fair." She spoke louder than she had meant to.

"It is fair." Lucas straddled his chair again. They sat facing each other. Marjorie still clung to her leg. "It's very fair when you think what we're selling is over thirty-five years old."

"Do you think I should drop out and let someone with more years to give to the theater have my place in your class?'' There was no way that Lucas could miss her sarcasm.

"I just wanted to warn you about falling for me. You can proceed with your career plans at your own risk.''

"I won't fall.''

"I don't quite believe you and I'm scared.'' Lucas knocked over the chair that was closest to him. Marjorie waited until he righted it before she spoke again.

"Why aren't you paying attention to what I'm saying? I want to be a better actress. I'm not going to fall in love and I better get home.'' She made no move to leave.

"I'll walk you.''

"I live a hundred blocks from here.''

"So what're we worried about? If you lived in the neighborhood maybe we would have had a miserable affair, but I never go above Fourteenth Street.'' Lucas punched Marjorie in the arm as if she were a football buddy. "See you tomorrow in class.''

"Will I really be a better actress in six weeks?'' Marjorie asked as they left the building together.

"Absolutely. Whether you take this course or not.''

Marjorie said goodbye and pretended to head toward the subway. In less than five minutes she was in a cab daydreaming about the man whom she couldn't let enter her life. Unfortunately, like all women, always, she forgot his warning and remembered the color of his eyes. She knew their color exactly because they were exactly like hers. He certainly was something to think about.

Twenty-four

July 6, 1982

Dear Emily,

First of all let me apologize for disappearing on you. I really couldn't help it. I've done a lot of thinking about what I've done and now I realize why I did it. My parents are really OK and I guess I could have told them about you know what without them killing me. (I don't want to say what you know what is, in case they read my mail here.) The truth is they would probably help. The real reason I couldn't tell them is that they were so happy that I was going off to be a thin, beautiful person that I didn't want to disappoint them. Look, I know they love me fat, but they want me thin both for their sakes (who doesn't want a daughter they can show off?) and mine (who doesn't want a daughter who is healthy and dates?). You should have seen my parents' faces when I was leaving. They were really hopeful, like I was on my way to having a much better life. They've been so good to me, buying me that KLH stereo with the great speakers and everything, that I couldn't hurt them. I'll tell you one thing, if this kid is a girl, I'm not going to let her get fat in the first place. The kid won't know what a cookie is until she's fifteen years old. Are you surprised that I'm talking about the baby? Remember I never used to? What if it has Finkle's chin? He doesn't have a chin, you know. I have to go now because rest period is over, but I'll continue this later, OK?

LATER

It's about four o'clock and everyone else in the bunk is at free swim. It's the only thing around here that they don't make you do so I am lying on my bed and writing to you.

I have great news! I've lost four pounds!! Can you believe it? I was so surprised when I got on the scale I thought I was going to die. The very first weigh-in I lost two pounds, which could have been the "Camp Loser For The Day" except that one of the kids in the next bunk lost three and a half. (A lot of people said she took a diuretic, but I don't think so, she seems like a nice kid.) The next day and the next day I lost a pound each so I was pretty happy about that. The weigh-in every morning is hysterical. We get weighed before we eat breakfast because that's supposed to be your true weight so everybody wears the lightest clothes they have even though it's freezing. One girl even wore a short-sleeved polo shirt (Ralph, white and pink stripes with a green pony) instead of a long-sleeved one because she said, "Sleeves have to weigh something." Someone else from a younger group took a Band-Aid off her arm because she thought it would make a difference. We stand on line to get weighed and one girl goes in at a time and it's a riot. Girls scream real loud when they've lost and some of them come out crying because they stayed the same. Helen keeps telling everyone not to expect to lose every day and doesn't stop talking about how you can get on a plateau and not lose for days, but the ones who don't lose are depressed. Also,

I think the self-inflicted vomiting has already begun.
(Thank God I haven't had any morning sickness up
here.) A couple of times I've come into the bunk thinking that it was empty and I heard the water running in
the bathroom and when I went to see who was here, I
heard the toilet flush and then heard someone leave
through the back door. I swear, Emily, the place
smelled like vomit. Of course I would never report the
person or anything, but I would like to know who it is
because I think she's really harming her body. Look
who's talking. I really made a mess of mine. Between
my rotten eating habits and what Finkle did I'm really
not a prize specimen. That's what my parents want me
to be—a prize specimen—and I used to be very mad at
them for that, but now I don't blame them anymore because, to tell you the truth, Emily, I want my child to
be a prize specimen too. Maybe it won't look like me
or Finkle. With any luck it'll look like my mother.

The food is strange. It's very nourishing and everything—I've got to go. Everyone is back and we have to
go up to dinner. More later.

LATER

I've made some really good friends here. All the girls,
except for this one bitch who was here last year, are
really nice. Don't get jealous. I'll never be as close to
them as I am with you. For example, I would never tell
them about you know what. What do you think of the
name Eloise? Remember Eloise at the Plaza?

So as you can tell by this long letter, this place isn't
as bad as I thought it would be. The lake is really beautiful. We haven't had rowing as an activity yet and I'm
sort of dreading it. (To tell you the truth, I'm kind of
scared of getting in a boat with some of those girls.)
The bunks are nice. The only problem I have is I'm

tired sometimes. So, don't worry about me. It's not as bad as I thought it would be AND DON'T FORGET, I'M LOSING WEIGHT.

Love,
Julie

Emily read the letter twice before putting it down. She didn't want to but she was going to have to tell Mrs. Weissman her daughter's secret. This camp with all its activities was no place for someone pregnant. She picked up the phone, dialed the Weissmans' and found nobody home. Damn it. Why didn't Julie tell her that her parents were going on vacation?

Emily rummaged through a kitchen drawer for the note paper that she knew was there and fished a pen out of a cup near the phone.

July 11, 1982

Dear Julie,

I received your letter and was very happy to hear from you. I'm also glad that you're having a good time, but I urge you to come home. You need the proper medical care and *you must not lose any more weight*. I mean it, Julie. Didn't you ever see a pregnant woman? They get fatter, not thinner.

Things are fine here. My mother is dating a really terrific guy. He got her flowers and me flowers and my sister a coloring book that was really too young for her, but the thought was nice. I think these were the first flowers that I have gotten from a man.

Yes, I like the name Eloise but whàt about Hillary? Come home. Your parents won't kill you.

Love,
Emily

Julie put Emily's letter in the bottom of her stationery box and turned her light out. Since hers was the last light out, the bunk was now dark. They were supposed to be sleeping but they were teenagers with things on their mind and they needed to talk.

"The real reason and only reason I want to lose weight is so that I can lose my virginity," said Shana, in a whisper that was louder than her regular voice. "I'll never get sex if I don't lose about fifty more."

"I don't think men care how much you weigh, if they really want to do it," said Kim.

"They care. Practically every cheerleader in our whole school has lost it already, but this one girl who's even bigger than I am tried to get this guy to fool around with her and he said he would if she lost weight and you know what she said? She said, 'I'm going on a diet tomorrow and I'm going to get beautiful but if you don't fuck me fat, you're not going to get me thin.' "

"I hear it's not so great. This girl I know went to bed with this guy and she said it hurt like hell. They did it three times in the same night and it didn't get any better."

"So why did she do it three times?" Julie asked.

"How am I supposed to know? Maybe he forced her to."

"That's rape," said three of the girls, shouting into the night.

"It wasn't exactly rape, because she liked everything but the actual fucking, but she was a nice person so she didn't want to deprive him of his ecstasy."

"So it was partial rape," said Julie, who felt for the first time that Finkle had partially raped her. She had gone willingly to his car, his home, his room, but in his bed she had said no a thousand times. She had on all occasions tried to squirm out from under him, but he had always managed to pin her down. The first time she had held both her hands firmly in front of her vagina but Finkle had moved them away because he was stronger than she was. Funny, she had always thought rapists were in dark alleys and held knives at your throat.

"You sound like a bunch of jealous virgins," said Caroline.

"We are," said Kim.

"So why don't you go out and do something about it?"

"First I have to get a date," someone said, as others were falling asleep.

Twenty-five

Esther, in an effort to get her two daughters to be close to each other despite their eleven years' difference in age, invited Nancy for pot roast and to spend the night. Since her apartment wasn't air conditioned, Nancy accepted. Esther slept well knowing her girls were safe. Nancy slept well and enjoyed not suffering from the heat and Marjorie purposely kept herself awake.

She didn't want to sleep. She wanted to sort out Lucas. He had asked her to stay and talk after class for the last three days. He continued to warn her not to fall for him, but it didn't feel like a warning. When he said it was a shame that they had known each other for three days and had never seen each other naked, she said she would describe herself in detail if he really wanted to know.

She took her mind back to the moment when Lucas had said, "See you tomorrow, stars, and I want Scene One memorized. Marjorie, you'll wait." Just like that, not a request, but a demand. She thought of disobeying, but didn't want to. She waved her classmates goodbye and returned to her seat. He drew a chair up and sat opposite her. It was the first time she had seen him sit in a chair the way it was designed to be sat in. "You've got a problem," he said.

"Not that I know of," said Marjorie, already enjoying the scene.

"Yes you do. You're hot."

"It's a hot day."

"I'm talking sexually. You're hot."

"So what's the problem?"

"You don't know what to do with your heat. You probably take long baths or something. You probably don't even know that your juices are flowing."

"You're right. I'm a married woman from the suburbs. We don't deal in flowing juices. We deal in orange juice."

"You're too hot for me, kid. I like my women cold."

"Then you would have liked me last week."

"Yeah. I want you to know something, so you don't go home and have me dancing in your head at night."

"What's that?" She leaned forward, interested.

"I'm not good in bed." He leaned forward, too. They were extremely close and she hoped he didn't study the gray in her hair.

"Thanks for the warning."

"You think I'm kidding."

"I don't think you're kidding," Marjorie said, being just as big a flirt as he was.

"You don't?" Lucas, who was six-two, was as disappointed as a very short boy somewhere at the beginning of puberty.

"Why would you kid about something as important about being lousy in bed?"

"I didn't say lousy. I said 'no good.' "

"Do you have any witnesses who would testify to that?"

"A couple of thousand."

"Well, if we were going to have an affair, I suppose I would have to interview, let's say about five hundred of them, but since we're not, I'll just take your word for it."

"I knew I was right about you. I knew you'd fall for me . . ."

"Which I haven't."

"You're falling. And I knew you didn't know the difference between love and sex."

Marjorie saddened. She remembered that her husband

had fallen in love with a young woman with wavy hair. She, more than anyone, knew the difference between love and making love. If David had just made love instead of fallen, she would still be in his bed. To her, the greater crime was not adultery, but what led up to it. She shook herself, not wanting to share her thoughts with Lucas. "I know the difference between love and sex," she said. "You don't tell your mother about sex and they don't teach love in the schools."

Lucas took one of her hands in two of his. He played with her fingers, moving them together and apart according to his own rhythm.

"Well, beautiful, when it comes to me, I'm no good at sex and I really stink at love. You want to get a cup of coffee?"

In the afternoon, Marjorie had felt he was becoming wonderfully honest, but there in her single bed at night, she was convinced that all these warnings were Valentines. Each time he told her to stay away, it felt like he was sending roses. She would never be unfaithful in the way David was. She would not sit by Lucas' bedside. But she might fuck and forget him.

Marjorie yawned and turned on her side and got tired. She fell asleep running the lines from *The Fifth of July* into her pillow. Her sleep was deep, but not long. She was awakened by the loud ringing of the doorbell and banging on the door. She got out of bed and followed the noise, walking cautiously as if there was danger already inside the apartment. Seeing that Marjorie was about to ask who it was, and afraid that her sister was going to use a voice not suitable for these types of New York occasions, Nancy pushed her out of the way, deepened her voice to male proportions and said "Yeah?"

"It's David," a voice screamed.

"It's David," Esther told Marjorie, as if she hadn't heard.

"Do you want him in or what?" Nancy asked Marjorie.

"Sure," said Marjorie, as she moved behind a large wing chair, protecting herself.

Nancy opened the three locks and Esther, holding her robe together, muttered something about waking all the neighbors. By the time the door was opened David was leaning against the wall opposite the apartment.

"I miss you," he said.

"You hardly know me," said Nancy and only she laughed. Esther and Marjorie knew that estranged husbands were serious business.

"You'd better come in. You'll get a cold out there," said Esther. Hallways always meant drafts to Esther, just as strange toilet seats always meant urinary-tract infections.

David came in and all three women stepped back as if they had committed a crime and he had flashed a badge. In reality he flashed an uncertain smile and Marjorie returned it. It had been a long time since she had seen David display any amount of uncertainty and she liked it. It was nice to see God falter.

"You want some tea?" asked Esther. She always asked if someone wanted tea during difficult times.

"No, thanks, Mom." Marjorie stiffened. She didn't want the man who had taken care of another woman's needs greeting her mother as "Mom."

"So, maybe we should go to sleep and let them talk," Esther said to Nancy.

"You better be good to her or your block isn't the only thing I'm going to knock off," Nancy said to David, doing what she could to protect her younger sister. She headed toward her room, the bedspread that protected her nakedness dragging behind. "Let's go, Ma," she said over her shoulder.

"It's good to see you," said David, talking to everyone's backs.

"Cut the crap, David," Nancy said as she disappeared into her childhood bedroom.

"You sure you don't want tea?" Esther asked again. She didn't wait for an answer before closing her bedroom door.

There was no light in the living room so Marjorie reached under the closest lamp and turned it on. She was not embarrassed to be in a nightgown while he was fully dressed. The years of their marriage had allowed them this freedom. David, taking the light as his invitation, moved onto the couch. Marjorie took the wing chair, feeling that its high curves would protect her. She looked directly at him, while he looked at his hands.

"You want a cup of tea?" she said, just to make him smile. The corners of his mouth almost turned up.

"Are you coming home?"

"No . . . not yet. The course is keeping me too busy to commute."

"It's driving me crazy. I can't sleep. I cry. I cried twice today."

"I cry too."

"Yeah but . . ."

"Yeah but what? Yeah, but you're a woman so you're supposed to cry?" said Marjorie, one eyebrow up.

"Don't give me that liberation shit."

"Why is it when I cry it's not as important as when you cry?"

"So we both cry. So we're both miserable. This isn't a contest. If you come home we'll both have drier eyes."

"I can't. I have class, rehearsals," said Marjorie. David threw his arms in the air, frustrated, confused. He sat for a moment searching for the words that would bring his wife home.

"Am I so terrible? Do you hate me so much? Do you want this marriage to go in the toilet?"

"No, to everything."

"Come on, I'll take you home. Please. I'm asking you please."

"I can't." Marjorie's voice was getting shaky.

"Why the fuck not?" David said, pounding his fist into his knee.

"I have class tomorrow."

"I'm talking about our lives here."

"I have a commitment."

"Oh, you have a commitment to it. What about your commitment to me? Have you looked at your left hand lately? There's a ring on it." Marjorie twisted her ring.

"I'm responsible to a lot of people in class. I like it . . . it's good for me."

"Please don't tell me you're one of those women who is finding herself. I like you now."

"I'm not finding myself. I know who I am. A wife, a mother . . . an actress."

"So, come home and be those things. You'll come in every day. Sometimes I'll drive you."

"I can't . . . look at it this way, I'm taking a vacation from you. We're taking a vacation from each other. I need to do a couple of things like earn some money as an actress. I don't care if it's one dollar. I need to know that somebody will pay me."

"You're thirty-eight years old."

"I know how old I am. You think nobody thirty-eight ever got paid for acting?"

"They have experience."

"I have experience. Lucille Ball was forty before *I Love Lucy* went on the air."

"I'm scared."

"Of what? That I'll work?"

"You'll work. You'll be successful. You'll get used to life without me." And then he spoke very slowly. "Remember I used to come over here and we'd wait for your parents to conk out, only your mother never did until four in the morning, and we'd sneak into your room and fuck like maniacs on that little bed?" Marjorie remembered having sex, but she didn't remember fucking like a maniac.

"How could they not know? We'd know if Julie was doing it in the next room."

"Maybe they didn't know. We were quiet." That Marjorie remembered, the quiet sex.

"You want to be quiet tonight?"

David and Marjorie ended up in the single bed. She imagined her sounds were known to her mother.

"How late did David stay last night?" Esther wanted to know at breakfast.

"Late," said Marjorie.

"I think you have him petrified," said Nancy. "It's always the men who fall apart when the marriage is over." She was already smoking and had the cigarette too close to her permanented hair.

"Who says it's over?" said Esther, and they both looked to Marjorie for confirmation.

"It's not over. It's on hold."

"I've never heard of such a thing. Who puts a marriage on hold? You make it sound like some telephone call or something."

"Your marriage is on hold, Ma," said Marjorie, buttering a small corner of her toast.

"It is no such thing. I think the real reason your father didn't come north this summer is because he gets a rash up here. He just didn't want to scratch this year." Nancy and Marjorie looked at each other, amazed that their mother could take their father's temporary desertion and turn it into an itch. Esther, knowing that she was making the rash up, turned away to get more coffee. She brought the pot back to the table and filled everyone's cups, hoping to close the subject of her own separation. Nancy didn't let her.

"You know, Ma, Daddy couldn't stand all the ballet and concerts you dragged him to every summer. He looked very unhappy in all those ties you made him wear." She bent down to strap her unmanicured feet into sturdy sandals.

"You want I should stay in Miami where they think culture is doing *Fiddler on the Roof* twelve times a year?" Esther was fighting for her cultural rights. Her love of ballet, concerts and theater and her knowledge of books was genuine. Marjorie and Nancy had been proud for years that their mother liked Eudora Welty.

"Nobody says you didn't do the right thing. You're both where you want to be for a couple of months." Marjorie took Esther's hand. When she first heard her mother would be coming north alone, she was upset. She wasn't old enough to have her parents separated.

"I think I was right." Esther got less shaky as she spoke. Her posture was rigid and her words were precise. "I know it helped my marriage. The night before I left your father was affectionate with me all night." Esther was proud. Her daughters were surprised that their parents were still doing it. "You think I shouldn't stay away till Labor Day?" This was asked of Nancy, who although she had never married, seemed to have all the answers about men.

"Stay in New York, Ma. Marjorie, you should go home. I'm the first one to say women shouldn't rely on men. But in your case, Marge, I say go home. You don't hate David. Anyone could have seen that last night and don't think I didn't hear you thumping away." Both Esther and Marjorie blushed. "You don't want New York. There are four women to every man and that's on a good day. The few men there are, are too scared to have a relationship and they have hair on their bodies in places you've never heard of." Esther choked. Marjorie listened hard. "You might never get to see the hair because they're all looking for twenty-two-year-olds who don't wear underwear."

"I'm not going home and I'm not looking for another man."

"With your luck, you'll probably get one. It's the ones that don't look that get them all." Nancy had a bit of sibling rivalry in her voice. "I used to wonder why you got them all, but now, a year away from fifty, I know. You're built like the Weinsteins and I'm built like the Fishmans. It's the curse of the Fishmans to walk around big and bulky with overgrown tits."

"Nancy, such talk."

"Not talk, Mom. Reality. They say if you can put a pencil underneath and it stays there you're big. I can put a whole pencil case under there." Nancy was clearly unhappy with her breasts. From the day she grew them, she hadn't stood up straight.

"Pencils are for writing." Esther was trying to end the conversation.

"Being busty was in until Marilyn Monroe killed herself and then it was as if cleavage and suicide went hand-in-hand." Nancy sat back in the kitchen chair and looked down.

Marjorie didn't like the mention of suicide and rushed for a solution. "They have those new bras that minimize you."

"Every bra I've ever liked has been discontinued." Marjorie and Esther nodded. Every bra that they had ever liked had been discontinued, too.

"Who started this crazy bust talk anyway?" Esther wanted to know.

"I was explaining why, when the women in this city are starving for men, why Marjorie might get one. Be careful if you do, Marge, they all have herpes."

"Mrs. Hammerstein has something strange on her lip," Esther said with fear.

"Ignore it, Mom." Esther couldn't seem to ignore it. She sank into a chair and worried.

"I kissed her," said Esther.

"You kissed Mrs. Hammerstein? You hardly know her."

"She told me her daughter was getting married. Ordinarily I wouldn't kiss, but we've lived on the same floor, for how many years? Twenty-three. So you think I have something?"

"No, Mom, and I don't think Mrs. Hammerstein has anything either," answered Nancy.

"She has a daughter getting married." As if choreographed, the three women lifted their cups and drank. Only Esther felt it necessary to wipe her mouth once her cup was back in place.

"Why'd you run home to Mother?" It was a direct question, said in Nancy's usual direct manner.

"Sometimes I think it's because I caught him giving love to another woman." Marjorie had trouble looking at anything but her coffee cup.

"She saw him in a patient's room. She doesn't know anything for sure." Esther pointed a finger as she spoke and Marjorie was the accused.

"And sometimes I think I ran because he thought he was God."

"He's a doctor," Esther explained. "The man does go around saving lives. I hear a lot of doctors can get a little crazy in the head."

"It was just hard living with someone that . . . heavenly."

"Look what she complains about." Esther spoke this toward the sky. Marjorie got up and put half an English muffin in the toaster. "Did you ever have really exciting sex?" she asked her sister. "I mean really exciting. The kind that you think other people have behind their closed doors."

"What kind of thing is that to ask at breakfast?" Esther wanted to know, ready to wash cups.

"Yes," said Nancy proudly. "You're talking about the kind where you're so involved you forget the rent is due. Right?"

"Like in the beginning of *The White Hotel*," offered Esther, talking into the sink.

Nancy smiled, remembering. "I was in Cape Cod, about ten summers ago, and I didn't even have to try for an orgasm. It came as sort of a hot wave that rolled over me. We did it again in the morning. He was one frisky guy."

Esther was trying to pretend that she really hadn't heard any of it. She had long ago realized that this was a new world and that her single daughter was having sex. Now she was finding out that Nancy was doing things that brought hot waves and that was a new worry. Esther was tired of worrying about Nancy in her no-doorman building and hoped she could forget the moaning and find a nice man who would maybe be calm in bed, but would bring her midtown.

"The sex in my life has always been . . . I don't know . . . sweet," said Marjorie, sliding crumbs into the garbage.

"That's too bad," said Nancy.

"That's bad?" said Esther. "That's not bad. With all the starving people around the world, you think that's bad?"

"A person should be excited in bed," said Nancy, who always enjoyed getting Esther crazy.

"Let me tell you something, excitement you can get on a ferris wheel. And you want moaning? Moaning you can get in a really good restaurant. Watch when they bring out the rack of lamb. The whole place moans. You get into bed with your husband, I'm not saying you shouldn't have a good time, but don't expect him to love you and earn a living and love your kids and take you to cloud nine. What's so terrible that the sex is just nice? Nice is nice or am I crazy?"

"I guess it all depends if you're orgasmic or not," said Nancy, kissing them both. She was out the door with promises to be back for dinner very soon. By the time Esther returned from locking the door, Marjorie was stacking the old dishwasher.

"You go. I'll take care of that."

"I'm almost done."

"So, almost doesn't count. Leave it. Leave it." Marjorie stopped loading the dishes and wiped her hands on the dish towel. "You had a good time with David last night?"

"It was . . . nice."

"He didn't have to sneak out like a bandit at five A.M." Marjorie looked to Esther for an explanation. "I was up reading. That Sedgwick family is really something. Such craziness going on there up in Santa Barbara. So, I heard him leaving and I couldn't imagine what was going on at that hour and I peeked through the crack in the door. You're going home soon?"

"I've got to get to class." Marjorie smiled and checked the time. She was happy it was early enough to take a cab to school.

Twenty-six

Lucas Morgan made great exits. He had gone to the john, walking backward, unbuttoning as he went. He had, without looking, missed bumping into the scattered pieces of furniture in his living room.

Marjorie was not the first student of Lucas' to go to his apartment to rehearse. They each had a turn, so she was not considering the visit a seduction. While he was gone, she studied the pieces of his life. The couch and two chairs were worn, but couldn't hide that they were once good and not meant for a small, dark room on West Thirteenth Street. There were huge posters in a pile from Lucas' modeling days, not on display, most were turned toward the wall. There were hundreds of books and no bookcases, just piles of them in every corner of the room. Against the only window was a beautiful antique desk, piled high with papers. The desk chair held a new, red IBM Selectric typewriter. On the walls were black-and-white photographs of Lucas and his college fraternity, smiling for their yearly pictures. If Marjorie had had to figure out the man from his surroundings, she would have guessed that he had come from a family with money, that he had gone to good schools and had inherited furniture and a substantial mind. She would have been right.

Lucas Morgan also made great entrances. In his own words, he had gone to take a shit, but he came back bleeding. He had a half a roll of toilet paper wrapped around his finger and was ready to cry like a four-year-old who needed a mother's lap.

"I was trying to straighten up the john in case you had to pee and I stepped on a razor blade." He screamed in pain, the kind of scream that adults usually stifle.

"If you stepped on it, how come your finger is bleeding?"

"Because I picked it up." He went over to the desk, opened a bottom drawer, took out a bottle of Chivas Regal and, after taking the top off, stuck his finger, including the toilet paper, into the Scotch. "Grandma always said that if you don't have iodine, use booze. If you don't have booze, use piss. It's a good thing I had this bottle because I'm fresh out of piss."

"Your grandma was a very smart woman."

"Is. She is a very smart woman. She lives in Vermont, alone. The cold has preserved her." He screamed again and lay down on the floor as if it were a hospital bed.

"Uh . . . listen . . . if you want to nurse that, we could go over the scene tomorrow." Marjorie made a move to gather her things, but Lucas stretched out an arm to stop her, grabbing her ankle.

"No, stay. Blood has always been good for me. It reminds me I'm alive. It makes me feel that I have survived disaster and that survival gives me energy. I like bleeding." He unwrapped the toilet paper and found that he had almost been cured. When a tiny trickle of red presented itself from the cut, he smiled, exhibited it to Marjorie and wiped it clean. "Do you mind if I lie here for just a few minutes?"

"No, of course not. Are you dizzy? Do you want me to get you something?"

"Nothing, thanks. You're a good Mommy. Don't worry, I'm going to throw out the Scotch."

"What's your mother like?" Marjorie was sitting very still on the couch while Lucas lay on the floor.

"Crazy. She's a total schizophrenic who stayed in bed

with the flu my entire childhood. When I was twelve, my father realized I was going to be taller than him and got pissed. That was when he stopped walking around nude. I can see up your skirt.'' Marjorie, who was sitting on the well-worn couch, quickly moved out of Lucas' sight lines.

''You're a goddamn virgin. A real woman would enjoy being looked at.''

''What about real men? How would you like it if I looked up your pants legs?''

''I'd like it. I like to be looked at more than I like doing anything.''

''Are you seducing me?''

''Yes, but I'm counting on you to be rejecting. Let's begin at your entrance on page three. Just the lines, don't bother moving.''

''You mean just start.''

''Just start.''

''All right . . . well, OK . . . all right, give me a minute to get into it.''

Lucas gave her the minute and then read her entrance cue. She came back with her first line and within twenty minutes they had run through the first act. Marjorie was elated by the time they were finished. Lucas was a good actor and he brought her up, so that she was doing her best work. She could feel the difference between what was going on now and her performance in class. She also knew, for the first time, that what she had been doing in Syosset all these years was not acting.

''You're good, Marjorie Weissman. You're good and comedy is hard.''

Marjorie received the compliments shyly. Instead of saying ''Thank you'' she could only nod her head and, like the schoolgirl she was, pick the threads from the inexpensive gauze skirt she had bought to go to class in. By the time she looked up, Lucas was standing directly over her.

''Don't you want to tell me I'm good?'' he said.

''You know you are.''

''Oh yeah, sure. You're the only one who needs applause.''

''I'm sorry. I thought you knew. You're wonderful. Really wonderful.'' He bowed and went into his tiny kitchen and made them each a cup of herbal tea. Marjorie felt comfortable enough by now to lie down on the couch, making sure the soles of her shoes didn't touch the faded green brocade. It was four-thirty and she figured her work was over for the day, but she wasn't ready to pull away from the glory that had just happened. A wave of sadness engulfed her when she thought once again of what an impossible talent she had. Even after good training all she would be able to do was perform in people's living rooms. She could act with Lucas Morgan or sing for Aunt Fanny, but she would always be incomplete without strangers in the audience. (Even the North Shore Players had a theater that was a living room extension. She always knew everyone who came to the shows.) If her talent had been writing, she could write her stories and poems at home. If they were any good, no one would care how old she was. They might even say she improved with age. If her talent had been painting, she could have emerged from the suburbs at thirty-eight years old behind canvases. She could have taken her work to galleries and if they were brilliant enough, they might have been taken, with nobody caring how old the artist was. At worst she could display what she had on Sundays on the streets in the Village, sitting beside the other artists, some of whom even took MasterCard. An actress needed so much more to sell her talent, a whole theater, and an audience of people all willing to sit down at the same time. Lucas placed the cup in her hands and even on this hot day, the tea failed to warm her. Lucas had been right. Now that she knew she was good, the pain would be worse.

''What's the matter?'' he asked.

''It makes me sad to know I'm never going to get to do what I do best.''

"Only the stars get to do that. Everybody else does what they're told."

"At least they're paid for it."

"At least you're eating."

That night Marjorie told Amanda about a sadness she never expected to have. She sat at the table in her mother's kitchen, softly speaking into the same phone that she had spoken to girlfriends on all during her childhood. "It's worse now that I know I'm good," she said. "If I knew I had nothing, I think I could come home."

"I told you you were great. Fuck you, Marjorie, for not believing me," said her best friend.

Twenty-seven

Ida Pinsky said that her husband was prepared to go. "He told me that he had all his papers in order and when I asked, 'Why, Ezra?' he said it was all right, that he was ready to die and of course I said he was talking nonsense. He just looked up with that sweet face of his and told me that it wasn't so bad. Can you imagine, Doctor, someone saying death isn't so bad? I guess we all get a little crazy at the end." Ida took time out to cry. Her tears were huge and instantly wet her face. David wanted to offer his shoulder and he stretched out his arms, inviting her in. She didn't come because she was more comfortable crying into the Kleenex she had brought for her tears. David was very still and very quiet. He used all of his energy to keep from crying. Through all the sadnesses of his life, he had never felt sadder. He felt Ezra's death was everyone's tragedy and his failure. When Ida's tears stopped coming and she had dried her face, she continued. "He wanted you to know that it wasn't your fault. You're going to think that I'm making this up, but you can ask that pretty black nurse, you know the one who wears her hair straight back . . . Smith, Connie Smith. You can ask her if you don't believe me. She was standing right there when Ezra said to tell Doctor Weissman that it was bershert. That's Yiddish for *que será*. That was his faith. I'm telling you the truth when I tell you he was never afraid. He said, and I'm quoting him as close as I can, 'This was my time. I got the best medical care in the world, but it was meant to be.' Ask Connie Smith. He was concerned that you would feel badly. Can you believe that? He made me promise to tell you thanks.''

David felt all his emotion in his stomach. He was used to thanks, but only from the living. He had lost patients before, but their bodies disappeared and so did the relatives. They never directly blamed him, even those in deep mourning felt that he did what he could. Ezra and Ida were different. They were thanking him even though he had lost.

David made his way to Elizabeth's room. His pain was so visible that Elizabeth got scared. She drew her large red book with all the astrological symbols to her chest as a protection for her small, malfunctioning heart.

"How am I?" Elizabeth asked and David realized for the first time that, in the world, people asked, "How are you?" but within the walls of a hospital, they asked about themselves.

"You're doing fine. Aren't you going home in the morning?"

"Something's wrong, isn't it? It's Virgo. It's fucking everything up."

"I just wanted you to know that I'm taking a leave of absence for a while. I know you'll be coming back for checkups and I . . . I might not be around."

"I'll probably go home with this guy Ashley," she said, partly to hurt him, breaking up a romance that never happened. "He was this guy I lived with before I worked in insurance. Our chemistry is good, only he sleeps during the day and I sleep at night."

"Is that what you want?"

"I hope so," said Elizabeth Pringle, looking for the hurt in David that she couldn't find. "Did you ever love me? I thought you did and now it looks iike you don't."

"Is it important that you know?" Elizabeth shook her head yes, forcing David to find the words to answer. "When I was sending you flowers and pursuing you, I guess I didn't, but I think I do now." She smiled, hearing what she wanted to.

"I have to go home with Ashley. He knows my moods and understands my work. You're nice, but Ashley is more spiritual and I need that now. Does it bother you that we never made it?"

"No. That part of life isn't very important to me."

"Yeah. I knew that. It's in your chart."

"Dr. Burke will take good care of you," David said to neutralize the situation.

"Yeah. You Jews make good healers." Elizabeth's words made her so unattractive that it was easy for him to leave her behind.

David visited all of his patients, telling them all that Dr. Burke would be taking over, but he would be right there, supervising. He told them all the same lie. He had been asked by the commissioner of Health, Education, and Welfare to prepare a special report on heart disease so that the heart association could get special funding. David would have never taken on the assignment, he said, if he didn't feel his patients were doing well, and he would be right there in the hospital if they needed him. They all had similar reactions, pride that their doctor was chosen to work for the president, yet fear of being left in strange hands.

Solomon Burke sat across the desk from David, not believing his good fortune. His Mustang was leaking and he and his wife had just gotten the estimate that morning. Eight hundred, the guy with the bad teeth had said, just to patch it. Their three-year-old was starting nursery school and that was going to be over two thousand for the year. They knew they had to take care of both the car and the child, but they had spent breakfast deciding which was more important in the long run. Now, here was David Weissman throwing ten, eleven patients his way. They could do the car and the kid. Since Burke was a man who didn't know how to be charming he asked, "What about the fees?"

"They're all yours, pal," David said since this was not the time for caring about money.

"And you're going on a long vacation or what?" Now that Solomon had dealt with the money, he figured he could afford to be polite.

"I'll be here. I promised my patients I'd stick around. You have a right to know why I'm doing this so why don't you ask me."

"OK . . . Why?"

"I lost an important patient this morning."

"We've all lost important patients and this isn't your first so that's not it." Seeing that David had stopped the conversation, Solomon repeated, "That's not it."

"How close are you to your wife?" David asked.

"Close. We have a kid and another one is coming. She doesn't give me problems. I thought we were talking about you."

"I'm so close to my wife that she's inside of me. She's part of my medicine. You know what I mean?"

"She's on your team."

"Exactly. Right there inside of me, giving me the peace I need to work. Only now she's living at her mother's and . . . I'm just not right. If I were in any other business I guess I would keep on going, but I look at those patients and I think they deserve the whole team. Am I making sense?"

"Yeah." Solomon figured he was supposed to assure David that he could go on without his wife, give some speech about how they would probably get back together again, but he was not the type to make speeches or give pep talks. He was the type to smile at someone's troubles if they in any way benefited him. He didn't like those heart-to-heart talks where somebody told him embarrassing things that he didn't want to know. What he hated most was a man on the verge of tears. He sensed that David was trying not to weep and purposely looked at his watch, to let him know that his time was limited.

"You have to go?" David had noticed Solomon's concern for time.

"I have to pick my kid up at school." Solomon had learned to use that excuse over a year ago. Nobody had ever tried to detain him, and risk leaving a child in the street. It worked this time, too. David got out patients' files and promised that by the morning he would have Xerox copies of everything and that they would go on rounds together.

"So, are you going to go fishing?" Solomon asked, just as he was leaving.

"I thought you understood." David looked directly at Solomon to make sure that he got his message this time. "I'm going to hang around the hospital. I have no intention of abandoning my patients. I just don't want them to be subjected to a doctor who isn't a whole man." Solomon nodded and left, hoping that David would remain unwhole long enough for the Burkes to pay for the essentials of their life.

Twenty-eight

The girls from bunk twelve were ready for visitors. They had weighed in, had their breakfasts, shined their bunks, only because they were forced to, and were lined up as close to the parking lot as the counselors would let them get. The parents weren't due until ten-thirty, but practically everyone was waiting by ten.

They looked good. Every girl in the whole camp had lost weight and most were already a whole size smaller. Some pulled in their pants with a belt, some with a safety pin. Some borrowed clothes for the day from friends who had come to camp smaller than they were. Caroline was in a pair of white shorts that belonged to Vanessa Weintraub, a girl in bunk nine. She had paid her two dollars just for the use of them for the day. "Vanessa says these are a size thirteen, but I'm sure they were mismarked because I'm smaller than that," she said, annoying everyone in her vicinity.

With the imminent arrival of the parents, Helen found herself a small hill in order to make her annual Parents Day speech. "Where are my girls?" Helen began as if she didn't see campers in front of her. Since none of them had heard her use this particular question before, a few of the younger ones answered "here," but generally no one knew what to say. "Oh, there you are," Helen yelled. "You're all so small I could hardly see you." There was some laughter, but not the amount that Helen had hoped for. "I know you're all

211

pretty excited about seeing your parents and you've done such a great job I know you can't wait for your parents to see you. It's almost time to open the gates, but first I want to tell you what happened on visiting day last year. One of our campers had lost nine pounds and she was very happy and we were all very proud of her, but she was a fool because she wrote home and asked her parents to bring up cookies. Well, the whole family must have been fools because her mother and father brought the cookies up.''

''What kind?'' one of the younger girls asked.

''It doesn't matter what kind. What matters is that her counselor found out and her counselor told me and we had no choice but to send the girl home with her parents. I just hope and pray that nothing like that happens this year. Have a good time and let's hear it for Cottonwood.'' That was the clue for the girls to jump in the air and yelp, which they all did.

Julie had missed the speech. She was lacking energy these days and had found a rock to sit on until her parents came through the gate.

Marjorie and David were near the front of the long line of expensive cars. They were determined to put on a united front for Julie and, in reality, had no trouble being with each other. The ride up to Connecticut had been pleasant. She didn't tell him that her teacher thought she was good and he didn't confess that without her he was mortal.

Bored and impatient, David kept rolling down the window to see what was happening. ''When they say ten-thirty, I guess they mean it,'' he said. Marjorie was quiet. Getting no satisfaction, he rolled the window up and leaned back and tried to relax. He hummed ''Enjoy Yourself, It's Later Than You Think,'' which was an unlikely choice for David. He began punching the steering wheel in time to the music. His fist slipped and hit the horn by mistake. The sound triggered the impatience of all the other waiting cars and at least ten fathers starting honking. David felt helpless to stop the noise.

"You see the third car up? That's a Mercedes 600. They only made about twenty-seven hundred of them. They are magnificent machines, like fine-tuned tanks, only they're a pain in the ass. They spend all the time in the shop."

"That car reminds me of you."

"I'm a pain in the ass."

"A magnificent machine who spends all his time in the shop."

"So are you going to trade me in?" David was almost scared.

"No. Don't be ridiculous. There are only twenty-seven hundred of you." The cars started moving and David put both his hands on the wheel as if he was ready for a race. As they inched ahead, he snuck quick looks at his wife and decided that he really liked her.

The campers had been warned not to go into the parking lot, but once the cars started coming in they couldn't be contained. A bouncy ten-year-old, recognizing her parents' car, broke loose from the crowd and the rest followed. When Marjorie and David drove through the gates, Julie was right there jumping up and down and throwing kisses. Marjorie rolled her window down and reached out for her daughter. "You look great. How're you doing?" Julie walked along the side of the car as David guided it into a parking spot.

"I'm doing great. I lost eleven pounds, but I'm on this plateau now. It's nothing to worry about."

"Who's worried? You're looking good, kid," said David, pulling up the emergency brake.

"We brought you the stationery and the sweater. They're in the trunk." Marjorie got out of the car and she and Julie hugged. "You sure you're OK? I still feel rotten for forcing you to come."

"Well, you don't have to. I mean it isn't Paris, not that I've been to Paris, but at least I'm losing weight."

"Do they give you enough to eat?" asked Marjorie while David opened up the trunk.

"I swear I'm not starving. Sometimes everything tastes

like cardboard, but there's plenty of cardboard to go around."

Julie took her parents to her bunk, walking between them and hugging them both. It was the warmest place she could find on earth. Just as they were about to approach the steps to bunk twelve, Julie felt a butterfly move inside her stomach and got scared that her secret would pop out and reveal itself. She tried to hide her fear, but the worry showed and Marjorie noticed. "What's wrong?" she asked instinctively.

"Nothing. I'm just excited you're here. Let me check to see if everyone is dressed." Julie thought she ran up the steps, but it was a slow run. As soon as the screen door closed, Marjorie turned to David. "There's something wrong."

"She's fine," said David and because he was a doctor Marjorie was used to believing him.

Once inside the bunk Julie went into the bathroom and lifted her shirt. She still hadn't gotten used to the baby's movement and checked each time to see if what was going on inside of her showed on the outside. When she saw the same stomach that she always had, she replaced her T-shirt, walked to the front of the bunk and invited her parents in. She thought her mother looked worried but she had learned, as all children do, not to investigate a mother's worries.

After looking at the bunk, the Weissmans went from activity to activity together, walking arm in arm, linked in a strong family chain. They walked with the same foot at the same time, a small marching band with secrets. Marjorie and David watched Julie play volleyball, bunk twelve against bunk eleven, and then watched while she swam in the lake.

"She just doesn't look right," said Marjorie while Julie was drying off.

"She looks thinner. She's starting to look good."

"She looks tired. You can see a strain. I don't know . . . you're the doctor."

"And she looks perfectly all right to me."

"I don't know. Look around her eyes."

"What for?"

"For the strain. She may be pushing too hard."

"Didn't she tell you she's having a good time?"

"You can't always believe that. Remember when she said she wasn't having any problems at school and the school psychologist called us in because she felt Julie's shyness was costing her friends."

"That woman was full of crap."

"Maybe, but I'm telling you she looks weak to me."

"She doesn't look weak. She looks smaller. Isn't that why we sent her here? I swear she's lost a whole chin."

Marjorie dropped her argument when she saw Julie approach. She seemed happy, her terry cloth robe wrapped tightly around her body, her wet bathing suit in her hand. Marjorie almost decided she was wrong.

The camp provided lunch, a luau on the lawn in front of the dining room. They insisted that this was a typical lunch, nothing special for the parents. "We never, ever had pineapple before," Julie said as she filled her plate with fruit, chicken salad and a dietetic Jell-O mold, which was threatening to collapse.

The Weissmans ate on Julie's blanket and David and Marjorie were impressed with the food and with Helen, who went from group to group thanking the parents for entrusting their daughters to her care. "She's the worst," Julie said when Helen was too far away to hear. "She gives us these big, long lectures about not vomiting that make you so sick, you want to throw up."

"You don't want to become anorexic," said Marjorie.

"Don't worry about it, Mom. I have wet dreams about Häagen Dazs." Julie collected empty paper plates, and with her own, walked to the nearest garbage can.

"Did you see that?" Marjorie said, as soon as she was gone.

"What?"

"She threw away half her food."

"Her stomach is shrinking."

"Something's wrong," said Marjorie.

The rest of the afternoon waa taken up with a show put on by the campers called *Summer Fantasy 1982*. Bunk twelve did the orphan number from *Annie* and it was hard for anybody in the audience to believe that these rather large girls were underfed orphans. When they stopped singing, and began to dance, one of the mothers started laughing so loudly that half the audience turned around. She tried everything to stop herself, covering her mouth, biting her lip, but nothing worked. Unfortunately, her laughter infected a couple of fathers around her. Soon most of the audience was chuckling. The woman who started it all managed to crawl out of her row and out of the Social Hall by the time the number was over, but the girls took half-hearted bows and got off the stage as quickly as possible, knowing that they had caused hysteria. Marjorie was worried that Julie was going to feel humiliated, but she came bouncing over the second the show was over thinking the whole thing was as funny as the audience.

At about four-thirty, Julie walked her parents back to the car, the daughter in the middle holding both their hands. "Oh, God, it went so fast. I mean I've been thinking about today for so long and now it's over. Wasn't it hysterical when we were bumping into each other all over the stage? The only big problem up here is that everyone has lost weight and they think they're ready to model bikinis. Since everyone is fat, they've forgotten what the rest of the world looks like."

"You're sure you're fine? You're absolutely welcome to come home with us." Marjorie hugged Julie tightly with no intention of ever letting her go.

"She's fine. She's fine. Aren't you, kid?"

"I want to hear it from her. Julie, do you want to come home?"

"She doesn't."

"I don't. I think that if I don't eat a lot at dinner today will be a losing day for me."

"You're sure, baby? You're sure?"

"I'm so sure, Mom. We're having a campfire tonight and they let us have two marshmallows apiece."

Marjorie had no more pleading left in her so she gracefully slipped into the Porsche. She wanted to grab Julie and stuff her into the small space behind the seats, but she knew that David wouldn't let her.

"I want chopped liver the first night I'm home," Julie screamed to the back of the car as it headed down the dirt road.

Since all the parents left Cottonwood at the same time, cars once again clogged the single-lane road. Marjorie and David, tired from the sun and the day, chose not to speak. They were a couple of miles down the Connecticut Turnpike before Marjorie asked David to pull over.

"Here?"

"Yes, here. There, right past the trees. I have a deal for you." David, intrigued, pulled over and turned off the ignition.

"I like deals."

"This is a relatively simple one. You want me back?"

"I want you back. You know I want you back. I ask you to come home every day. Are you coming?"

"I'll come home . . . if . . . if we go back and get Julie. I know you think I'm crazy, but I'm sure, David, that something didn't look right. No. It wasn't even how she looked. I just have this instinct."

"You know what the problem is? You want to know what the real true problem is? Julie is looking good and if she stays at camp, she's going to look better and better and you can't take it."

"That's not true."

"Yes it is." David leaned his head back and closed his eyes. That he was so sure of his analysis of the situation infuriated Marjorie.

"You're wrong and I'm not real crazy about your amateur psychiatric theories."

"So why do you want to bring her home, just when she's pulling herself together?"

"I don't know. I do know I don't need an overweight child around to make me feel attractive. How badly do you want me back?"

"A hundred percent badly, but I'm not going for her."

"Then you better take me home."

"Home?"

"To Seventy-sixth Street."

"Are you calling that home now?"

"I guess so," said Marjorie, so softly that only she could hear it.

Twenty-nine

Dear Julie,

First of all, I'm sending my tape of the Runaways. I know you wanted me to buy a new one, but I figured we could save eight dollars because I could part with it for a month. *Please,* please take good care of it. I beg you not to leave it in the sun because if you mess mine up, we'll both have to buy a new one and that'll cost us just a little less than sixteen dollars. I wrote my initials on the label so you know it's mine in case you get one. Don't you wish you were Melissa Manchester and could buy all the tapes you want?

I really wish you would tell your parents about your pregnancy when they come to visit you. (I'm writing about it because I figured you have the prerogative of whether to tear it up or throw it into the campfire or not.) At least you'll be home in less than a month and we can deal with it then. Can you believe that the summer is almost over? It's amazing that the baby is doing all that kicking. Is that normal or is it possible that the baby is upset or something? Maybe you can ask the camp doctor. Can you confide in him?

You know I was thinking, having a baby won't be so bad. I mean your mother could take care of it while we're in school and if we do most of our homework in study hall we'll have time to bathe it and stuff when we get home. The big problem will be going away to college like you always wanted to. Anyway, I can't wait to see you. Also, you really should write to Finkle and tell him where you are. Wouldn't it be crazy if you and Finkle didn't see each other for years and then long after he's grown up and married he finds out he has a kid? It sounds like something that could happen on *The Guiding Light,* and by the way, speaking of *The Guiding Light,* Alan and Hope are having marital problems.

I have to go now because Marcie is getting home from camp and my mother is having her hair done or her nails done or something done and I have to go meet her at the bus. I'm really into Melissa Manchester and hope you like her as much as I do.

Love,
Emily

Julie drew the letter nearer to her, partly to conceal the words about her pregnancy, partly to be closer to Emily. She thought maybe her friend was right that she should write to Finkle. Sometimes just before she fell asleep she missed him. (Not him exactly, but his masculinity.) When he first moved to Syosset he was more of a runt, but recently he had been working out with an elaborate set of weights that he had gotten for his sixteenth birthday and he had muscles. He flexed them all the time for Julie and sometimes she caught him admiring himself in the mirror, with everything sucked in and sticking out just the way he liked it. Often he asked her to feel his arm muscles and then he made her tell him how big they had gotten since the last time he had felt them. Maybe he used his muscles to make her do things she didn't want to do. Maybe the muscles acted like weights keeping her there under him and frightened. "Social rape," she thought. "Just plain old social rape." If he did all those terrible things to her why was she missing his muscles and thinking of writing? Did other girls miss their social rapists?

She got off her bed and pulled her stationery box from a high shelf in her cubby. It wouldn't be terrible to send him a nice letter, something with a few jokes in it, just to keep in touch. Maybe he would have stopped those nights they were together if she had really begged him to or if she had bit him or something. Maybe she wanted him to go on because it felt so good at the end. Someday she would have to figure out if he had raped her. Until then, it would be nice to keep in touch.

Thirty

"Line please," Marjorie yelled.

The class had just begun the run-through of *The Fifth of July* for the first time without scripts. Esther had cued Marjorie for three hours the night before and she knew her lines well. Now, in class and using a real couch for the first time, Marjorie was suffering from memory loss. She had been the first one to call for a line and before they were ten minutes into the first act, she asked for her line three more times. Each time had given her less confidence to remember the next.

Millie Klein was on script and feeding lines to anyone who was lost. She screamed Marjorie's line to her so that the rehearsal could continue. Since this was the first time without scripts, they were concentrating and the pacing of the play was off. As the students worried and tried to act, Lucas groaned in the corner. He knew that this always happened on the first day without pages, but it upset his insides anyway. He dropped his head into his arms, blocking his vision, but heard Marjorie request another line.

"You say, 'I have said repeatedly that I will stay here,' " said Millie Klein with a little too much impatience.

"Cut," Lucas screamed. "Take five. Take the rest of your life. Marjorie, I want to see you." The students walked away whispering and confused as Marjorie, scared of the principal, left the platform, and with her eyes down, approached her teacher. He motioned her out into the hall and once they got there, he spent the first thirty seconds too angry to speak. He paced, he groaned, and finally he lashed out. "Do you think that's fair?" he screamed.

"What?" Marjorie asked, studying his and her feet and knowing the answer to her question.

"Screwing everyone up."

"I forgot a few lines. I'm sorry."

"Those people in there are working their asses off. We're on a schedule here and you're ruining their whole day."

"I said I'm sorry."

"Not good enough. What the fuck did you think I meant when I said commit your lines to memory?"

"I did."

"You didn't. You're lost up there."

"I knew them last night."

"So, what's the problem, Mrs. Weissman? You got your period or something?"

"I resent that. I really resent that. Why do men always think when something is wrong that a woman is menstruating?"

"Men don't. I sure as hell don't. This is the first time I've ever thought of that. Am I right?"

"No. Not even close."

"You want to tell me what's wrong or do you want to flunk?"

"I didn't know you gave grades."

"I don't, but you'll always know that in my heart I would have flunked you."

Lucas leaned against the opposite wall and moaned too loudly. A student from another class walked between them not knowing what was going on, and took a second and third look at the odd little scene.

"It's Julie," said Marjorie, still faced away. "I have this feeling that something is wrong and it's throwing me." Having said what she had to, Marjorie turned around and found a softening Lucas.

"You've got to think of this as Broadway and the show must go on and all that shit."

"I'll try."

"No. You'll do it or you'll be fired."

"Can you do that?"

"Ask Lydia Lindstrom, I threw her out on her ass for not taking me seriously."

Marjorie nodded, and feeling sufficiently reprimanded, returned to the stage. She went right to the spot where she had dropped her last line and sat down. Although she had been beaten in the hall, she wasn't about to let the class know it.

"We're late, but let's take it from the top," Lucas said, causing Marjorie to leave the platform and wait in the wings at stage left, ready for her entrance. "Listen, stars, I know the first day without scripts is rough and I know I scared the shit out of you by stopping, but we're in Boston. This is Tuesday morning and previews are Thursday night. That audience has paid up to twenty-two fifty to see this and they deserve to be entertained. If we work our asses off, we'll be ready to give them a show. OK, curtain going up, house lights down, stage lights up and go."

Lucas sat in a chair in the middle of the room, expecting the best and getting it. Occasionally someone had to call for a line, but not Marjorie, and they were all acting again. When they finished Act One, he applauded loud and long and for the first time went to lunch with them.

They placed him at the head of the table where they felt he belonged and took up the position of king naturally. He started the meal with quaint backstage stories, such as the time Anna Marie Alberghetti forgot to turn off her mike when she went to the bathroom and the whole audience at *Carnival* heard the toilet flush. The students ate up these stories more greedily than they ate their lunches. By the end of the meal, when he had all their appreciation, he had gotten more serious and, knowing he had listeners, launched into his favorite philosophy. "I wish I wasn't so fucking lazy,'' he said, putting a coffee cup back into the saucer that was waiting for it. ''If I wasn't so lazy, I would get a Nobel Prize.'' Nobody at the table doubted him and, when he leaned in to tell them why, they all leaned in with him.

''I got this idea about a year ago and I've got to tell you I was thrilled to get an idea that didn't have to do with show business. At first I couldn't believe that I had stumbled upon something so valid and important. I mean, it's the type of theory you would expect an anthropologist to come up with. It still blows my mind when I think it came out of my show-business brain.'' Lucas stopped long enough to take a cigarette out of his shirt pocket and light it. Since this wasn't a conversation, but rather a one-man show, no one spoke while he was quiet. Marjorie was worried that the match he had struck was still lit and about to burn his fingers. Just before that could happen he put the match in a glass of water and continued. ''Darwin only figured out half of it,'' he said, believing it. ''He got into the physical evolution of animals and man, but the emotional evolution was completely ignored. I realized this when I was up at my sister's in Vermont and looking at my nephew's drawings. I looked at those pictures and saw that a five-year-old today produces art very similar to that of Neanderthal man. Those Neanderthals drew things they wished for, things they feared. Are you with me so far?'' There was a unanimous nodding of heads. Knowing that he had them, he took time out to take a long drink of coffee and a long drag of his cigarette. A waitress came over to the table with a fresh pot of coffee, but Lucas motioned her away. It was clear that the only interruptions were going to come from him. ''It took me a long time from the time I made the drawing connection to develop the theory further, then one morning when I shouldn't have had a coherent thought, considering what I had done the night before, my brain was flooded. Right there in my crummy kitchen I realized that during Neanderthal times the whole world was emotionally five years old. From there, the whole history of the world unfolded before my eyes, not the history we learned about in those boring classroom years, but an emotional history.'' Knowing that he had his audience, Lucas winked the waitress over and held out his cup. After getting refilled, he motioned that the rest of them should get refilled too. He dumped too much sugar into his cup and seeing the coffee was too hot, he went on with his lecture. ''Human beings have had an emotional as well as physical evolution. It was a five-year-old world that did those drawings and hit each other on the head just the way five-year-olds do today. It was a ten-year-old world that accepted the Virgin Mary and Christ. Think about it. At ten we all want to think of our mothers as virgins. You can parallel history and emotion all the way down the line. When we launched out way into space that was the ultimate adolescent ejaculation.'' Lucas punctuated his last remark with an excited fist. ''A great, big ejaculation went into space because everyone in the whole world was an adolescent. We had just come out of the fifties, which was an era of innocent puberty, and we couldn't hold back. The present is the most interesting. Everyone in the world today is around eighteen years old. I'm just using eighteen as a number so that we can understand one another. Don't you see? We're only eighteen and that's why we feel sad when we have to leave our eighteen-year-old bodies behind. When the world is emotionally forty, we'll be happy about flab.'' Lucas smiled, knowing he had impressed his group.

''Wow,'' said Saucy, speaking for all of them. There was not one of them who wasn't totally impressed.

''Hey, don't take me too seriously,'' said Lucas. ''I'm just a starving actor who is full of crap like the rest of the world. I was kidding about the Nobel Prize.''

''No, you should get it,'' said Marjorie, feeling that she was in the company of greatness.

''Enough already,'' said Esther.

''Enough what?''

''Enough talking about this Lucas Morgan character. You

have a husband who loves you, you know." Marjorie knew that Esther was serious because she had turned her back on her cooking. In the frying pan behind her was an omelette that she had talked Marjorie into and it needed attention. "I hear something in your voice that I don't like, something that tells me that this Morgan is getting under your skin." Esther turned and rescued the omelette.

"He's my teacher. That's all."

"I hope so. I really hope so. I sure don't like that you talk about him twenty-four hours a day and what I don't like even more is all that rehearsing you do up at his place. To me rehearsing is done in a theater with a stage and seats, a lot of seats. It seems to me that a teacher who takes students to his apartment should be arrested." With this, Esther put Marjorie's eggs in front of her, letting the plate hit the table a little too hard. She never could hide her anger. "Eat. It'll get cold."

Marjorie ate and when the time was right she looked up at her mother, who felt she had to stand over her daughter or there would be food left. "You're being very silly, Mom. He rehearses people in his apartment because the school is closed at night. In a couple of years, I'll be forty years old. Do you think a man in his forties should be jailed for allowing me to come to his apartment?"

"Age doesn't matter. You have a husband. You know in *Fear of Flying*, when she runs off with that crazy man who gives her all those lies about being an existentialist and living for the moment?"

"I remember."

"Well, she practically ruins her marriage and let that be a lesson to you."

Marjorie stood up, rinsed her plate off and carefully placed it in the dishwasher. "You're right, Mom. I will never run all over Europe with a no-good lying existentialist. Lucas Morgan, who I am not at all interested in, is not like that. He's honest and . . . I don't know . . . terrific. The other day, after we did a complete run-through and he gave us notes, he had trays of delicatessen brought in because that's what they would do on the road. And—''

"And that's why you go to his apartment, because he gives you delicatessen? You want delicatessen? I'll give you platters. I'll give you whole deli trays . . . You have a husband who loves you."

"I just go to Lucas' to rehearse."

"You talk about him all the time, Marjorie. Do you realize that you smile when you tell me about what he does in class? You keep telling me he's going to win the Nobel Prize. When you came back from his apartment last week you were like a girl coming home from a dance that she was too young to go to. I'm no fortune teller, but I can see disaster if you continue to be mesmerized by this man."

Esther was scared. Marjorie put her arm around her mother's shoulder. "You can't worry. It's too silly to worry. He's a good teacher and an interesting, weird man. The whole class is mesmerized by him, the males, the females, the ones who haven't decided yet."

"Maybe you could rehearse next time where there isn't a place to sleep."

"Maybe."

Marjorie had meant it when she comforted her mother, but less than twelve hours later, she lay naked between the plain white sheets of Lucas Morgan's bed. Since both their stomachs had started embarrassing rumbling, he had gone out for Chinese food, giving Marjorie instructions not to move. She felt both excited and silly. Excited from being in her teacher's bed, silly because now that the lovemaking was over, she didn't feel like being alone and naked.

She had gone to Lucas' apartment to improvise. They had improvised scenes in twos and threes in class from the first day. Then during the fourth week of rehearsals Lucas had scheduled each of them to have a private session with him, dealing with the characters they played in *The Fifth of July*. Saucy had come back from her session elated. "For the first time," she said, "I really knew what acting was about."

It was Marjorie's turn the same day that Esther had warned her not to go to Lucas' apartment. On the way there, they had stopped at a luncheonette, got cartons of hot, black coffee and carried them up the four flights of steps. When they got there, a maid was just finishing up and Marjorie was surprised to see a housekeeper in the tiny, dark apartment. Lucas introduced her as "Mary, whom he had known all his life," paid her and gave her kisses on both cheeks. He made Marjorie tell him that the place was sparkling, which it was. (Months later, Marjorie would admit to Amanda that if the place hadn't looked so clean, and if she hadn't been sure the sheets were fresh, she might not have gotten into bed.)

"Tell me everything you know about Shirley Tally," Lucas said after they had tasted their coffee.

"I've told you. I've been playing the part for a couple of weeks."

"Tell me again."

"She's about thirteen, very dramatic, has a feeling that she's going to be something wonderful in the arts. She's . . . she's a love child and as a result of that, she's swung back to morality. The thought of people doing all those dirty things gets her crazy. Yet she's curious. She'll look in the windows to catch someone naked. In some ways, she reminds me of Julie. They're not that far apart in age. Mainly it's the innocence. They haven't been touched yet and their virginity shines through."

"Can you be her?" Marjorie was puzzled by the question and Lucas didn't help her out until he finished his coffee and crushed his cup as if it were a beer can.

"Really be her or act like her? I can act like her."

"Just for tonight, be her. Put her in any situation you want." Marjorie thought for a moment and then sat on the couch, her knees apart.

"OK, but this better not take too long because if it does I'm going to have to call my mother," she said.

"You are a mother, you don't call mothers."

Marjorie was disappointed that Lucas hadn't realized she

was acting. "I was being Shirley. She would have to call her mother. I thought you wanted me to be her."

"Not so fast. You have to give a person a chance to take a leak," he said, unbuttoning his jeans.

"You're running away because I tricked you," Marjorie said, staying in character.

"I'm leaving because I have to pee and although the rug is pretty crummy I don't want to add to its corrosion."

"Can I watch? My mother hardly lets me watch anybody urinate and if I'm going to grow up and be somebody as terrifically famous as Bette Davis, I am going to have to experience everything," said Marjorie with her best thirteen-year-old smile.

"Anyone in my acting class can watch me pee and that includes their mothers and fathers. Shirley Tally cannot." Lucas headed down the hall and Marjorie wasn't quite sure whether this was part of her improvisation or not. She had thought from the first day of class that the best thing about Lucas Morgan's acting was that you couldn't tell he was doing it. She followed him down the tiny dark hall. He had left the door open so the view was no problem, but both Marjorie and Shirley decided not to look into the green-and-black bathroom, decorated in an era when men spent time tiling bathrooms.

"You're invited in," he said, taking the longest pee in the history of the world.

"I've decided that my education can do without observing the common things in life. If you were making a soufflé then perhaps I would watch. Certainly I can go on to become one of the most famous people in the arts without ever watching anybody eliminate anything." Marjorie was feeling Shirley inside her by now.

Back in the living room, drinking orange juice straight from the bottle, Lucas asked Marjorie if she was ready to begin. Marjorie, who had felt she had been Shirley Tally for quite a while, was confused.

"You're into character, but I'd like to get you into your

'situation. You tell me where Shirley is and together we'll develop a scenario the world won't forget.''

''You mean a setting? Like in a park or something?''

''Have you been to a park lately? I find, and stop me if I'm wrong, that people from the suburbs have all the grass they need in their front lawns. Parks are not part of their lives.''

''My bedroom happens to overlook Central Park if I sit on the windowsill and almost fall out,'' said Marjorie, in much the same way she would have said it in 1958 when trying to impress a boy, not with her father's earning power, but with her closeness to nature.

''I think the operative word is overlook.'' Lucas dropped the empty orange juice bottle into a wastebasket. Marjorie retreated to the edge of the living room to think through where she wanted Shirley Tally to be. Lucas sat in the center of the couch, his arms outstretched along the worn-out brocade. He played with tiny threads that had set themselves free even before he had inherited the couch. He liked the look of Marjorie thinking. Most of his students didn't work as hard as she did and, as her teacher, it was pleasant to see such a sincere effort. ''Improvisations work best in charged situations,'' he said.

''The diner,'' said Marjorie, knowing she had something. ''You remember the diner I told you about the first day of class? The diner that was robbed and the thieves made the people lie down on the floor and have sex. I want to put Shirley there.'' Marjorie was excited by her idea and it was less than twenty minutes from its inception that she and Lucas Morgan were in bed.

It was hard to tell if Marjorie Weissman seduced Lucas Morgan or Lucas took advantage of Shirley Tally. The improvisation started with Shirley ordering what she thought was exotic from the dinner menu. ''I'll have a raw grilled cheese,'' she said, ''and make sure there's plenty of onion. Where I come from, it's almost a sin not to have onion on everything.'' Lucas played the short-order cook. It was going well and Marjorie, either as Shirley or herself, leaned over the counter and kissed either the short-order cook or Lucas to prove that the imaginary onions could do nothing to harm the sweetness of her breath. It was here that Marjorie fell out of character, because no thirteen-year-old child would have delivered that kiss.

"You taste very good," said Lucas.

"I hope so," said Marjorie.

"Do you know what you're doing?"

"Do you mean has acting made me drunk? I know what I'm doing. I'm Marjorie Weissman and you are Lucas Morgan and together we are in a diner that is about to be robbed." This time he kissed her and soon after he took her by the hand to his bedroom.

"I can't believe they're making us do this," said Marjorie, indicating that there were robbers holding guns to their heads.

He kissed her by the side of the bed while they were both still dressed and Marjorie realized she was about to have unmarried sex. Married people started their lovemaking lying down.

Lucas pulled his shirt off. Marjorie had already seen his chest in the classroom, but she was surprised again that the Marlboro man had very little hair on his body.

Lucas was out of his jeans before Marjorie guessed that she was supposed to undress herself. She pulled her T-shirt over her head.

He was wearing boxer shorts. She thought of David. David wore jockey shorts, which were the only kind she liked in the sixties. On Lucas the boxers were fine, sexy, superior.

While she struggled out of her pants, he fished for a rubber in his dresser. He exhibited it to her and then turned away to put it on.

Another surprise. She was surprised to see this straight, large eraser coming toward her. She had forgotten erections happened by themselves.

Lucas made love with the same energy with which he acted. He pushed her to the bed and with his mouth pressed against hers, he swallowed her breath.

Her breasts gave her desire away. They were alert and waiting for his next move. She was embarrassed by their willingness. She hoped that he was not going to do anything strange. He was the director of their lovemaking. There he was at the foot of the bed, separating her legs. Her body strained toward him, hoping to be touched. He put a finger inside her and moved it to his own rhythm, not hers. Since they hadn't spoken since the living room, she didn't want to break any spells by telling him what to do.

There was no doubt that he was going to climb on top of her, but before entering her, he pulled her down toward the foot of the bed by her legs, explaining that he didn't want to bang his head against the wall behind them. It was obvious this was not the first time he'd entertained in this bed.

She helped him inside her and he asked, "Is that good?" she answered quickly that it was. Her goal was that he didn't stop.

Truthfully, it was not good. It was exciting. It squeezed the breath out of her. But it was not good.

She was not comfortable and the rubber was irritating. She adjusted her position twice. It still wasn't comfortable, but she didn't shift again. She never squeezed her body into the position it needed to be in to get satisfied. She wasn't going to try to climax because climaxing led to sounds and looks she didn't want him to see or hear.

When he came he screamed, "Oh, God!" and she thought, "God is my husband." She held on to him tightly, letting him know that he could stay where he was even though he was finished.

He asked her if she was all right and she said she was, wondering why no writer had ever really understood a woman's body. They always wrote scenes of total satisfaction with brand-new lovers. Didn't they know that you didn't want to say things like "a little to the left"? Didn't they realize there were adjustments to make and positions to find? Didn't they understand that the first time in a strange room, with a new man, just being there was good enough?

Or.

Was she the only woman in the world who was happy to have gotten through lovemaking without farting?

There was only one thing she knew for sure. It was the first time in eighteen years that she had sweated in bed.

"I love you," he said, as he rolled off of her. "I know I don't have to say that and I don't know how long it will last but for now I love you." He kissed her left breast and she was glad it was exposed.

"Do you tell everyone you love them?" asked Marjorie in a voice she didn't know was going to be shaky until she used it.

"Yes, but that's because I only go to bed with people I love. I'm not a promiscuous person. I'm celibate for months at a time. Do you believe me?"

"No."

"You should."

"I'm never going to love you," Marjorie said kindly. She took his hand to show she had no hostility. "I can only love one person at a time."

"They do that in the suburbs. Here in Manhattan you can love ten or twenty people at once." He bit her neck, which she pretended to like, but didn't.

"My husband cheated on me by loving someone else and I can't do that to him." Marjorie wondered why she was talking about David at a time and place like this.

Lucas kissed her again and she rolled over on her stomach, content and naked. She kissed him on his shoulder, smelling his sweat. "You have a lovely ass," he said, "not one pimple. Do you mind if I look more closely? It's rare that I see such a beautiful one." Marjorie was scared to be inspected, but it excited her. She hid her head in the pillow as Lucas caressed her bottom. The sex with someone new had been scary, but the before and after were great. The before was an anticipation that she hadn't known since Peter Gootkin had tried to get his hand inside her bra even though she had given him specific instructions to stay outside the cashmere. After sex with David was always calm and, although there was a feeling of warmth, there was no excitement just because the act happened. Lucas took small, quick bites from her behind and she realized that married sex had foreplay, but single sex had afterplay, too. She would have loved to take his fingers and get them to move about inside her, but she was too shy to ask him or even show him the way. She was embarrassed to let him know that she wasn't satisfied.

While she was still wanting to be touched, he was standing by the bed naked and lively. "We have to pay each other," he said.

"What?"

"You're married. You can't bring me home to mother. I'm fucked up. I can't bring you home to my mother because she had the audacity to go crazy and embarrass us all by proving we didn't come from strong stock. You have a child and I am a child so you would be stupid to accept any proposal. By the way, I can tell by the way you move you've had a lot of exercise classes, so I'm not going to let you go easily."

"What does that have to do with paying each other?"

"I want you in my bed and I'm willing to pay for it."

"Pay for it? You mean I should charge like a whore would?" Marjorie was more flattered than insulted by Lucas' proposition.

"No. Not like a whore. If you were to get an acting job, would you expect to get paid what a veteran actor would?" Marjorie shook her head no, fully understanding his point. "I mean I would expect to pay you what I think you were worth and you can pay me what you think I was worth." Marjorie looked at Lucas for signs of acting.

"Is this an improvisation or what?" She hugged the sheet.

"No. If we pay each other I won't feel guilty or responsible and you're more likely not to get sick when I hurt you."

"Why do I feel like we're in the middle of an acting scene?"

"No scene. No audience. Two people who risk the chance of getting too close." Lucas lay down on the bed and moved Marjorie on top of him. Although she felt a loss at having to give up the sheet, it felt good to be close again. She rested on his chest and he had to move her hair from his mouth before he could talk. "Don't leave me," he said.

"Don't pay me."

"Can you think of a better way not to fall in love?"

"No," she said, without thinking. "How much do you think I'm worth?" Seeing that Marjorie was beginning to like the idea, Lucas slid out from under her and ran for his checkbook.

"You do take checks?" he asked, removing the top of a fat Mont Blanc fountain pen with his teeth.

"Only if you do." Marjorie realized that her checkbook was in the living room and even though she was willing to be naked in bed, she was unwilling to stand up and walk without the protection of her clothing. She just wasn't prepared to be a wood nymph in a New York walk-up. "Would you bring me my bag?"

"What's the matter, lady, scared of the photographers?"

Lucas got the bag and they both thought before writing out the checks. He finished before she even began to write, and seeing that she was having difficulty, he reminded her that it was no big deal. She should just pay him what she thought he was worth. Marjorie bit her bottom lip as she wrote out the check. She deducted it from her balance and double-checked the figures. Next to memo, she wrote L. Morgan. At the last moment she folded the check in half and handed it to him without looking, as if she were handing a Christmas present to the mailman. When she looked at his check, she immediately asked for hers back.

"No. Fair is fair." He was holding on to his.

"I made a mistake." She reached for the check she had given him, but Lucas moved away, leaving Marjorie the choice of whether to fight for it naked or to collapse back onto the pillow defeated. "I just wanted to add a one," she said sadly.

"I don't know why you're so upset. The deal was we paid what we thought it was worth. I'm perfectly happy. You want some chinks, my treat?"

He didn't wait for an answer and was into his clothes before Marjorie admitted she was hungry. He slammed the front door, whistling. Marjorie couldn't figure out how the man could be so happy after writing out a check for two hundred dollars and receiving one for twenty-five.

The next night they didn't rehearse. They made love. He remembered why he liked women his own age. She kept quiet about her needs and enjoyed being naked where she shouldn't be. On the night after that, he told her he was afraid he was falling for her. Filled with his words, Marjorie felt it was too late to tell him he left her frustrated. She was angry at herself for not standing up for her rights in bed, but mostly she was amazed that she was in bed with a new man. Friday night David came into the city for dinner and when Esther finally closed the door, Marjorie took David to her room. She enjoyed the first orgasm of the week and learned she needed two men, one for excitement, one for orgasms. She didn't think at the time that David needed two women, one to sleep with and one to flirt with.

On Saturday night Lucas and Marjorie were Hepburn and Tracy. (She hoped the real Hepburn had been satisfied by the real Tracy.) At two in the morning, Lucas squeezed her too tightly as he put her in a cab. He told her that they were falling in love. She said Julie would be home in three weeks. The cab driver drove her away, she looked back for him and there he was standing in the street. They watched each other get smaller. Marjorie knew she was in trouble.

Thirty-one

"So, you want to tell me your news first or should I tell you mine?" said Amanda, after ordering the individual pizza at the Saloon. Marjorie had begged her to have lunch the morning after she first slept with Lucas, but children, husband and dogs (the cocker spaniel was throwing up) kept Amanda from coming into the city. Since Marjorie wanted to see the expression of her friend's face when she told her about her affair, she restrained herself from saying anything on the phone. Esther suggested that Marjorie go pick up some of those little prune Danish and make some eggs for Amanda, but Marjorie insisted that they had to eat out.

"Why?" Esther asked. "You have something to hide?"

"Just because somebody is meeting a friend in a restaurant doesn't mean there's something sneaky going on," said Marjorie, belting a white linen dress that she hadn't worn all summer because it looked too expensive for class.

"So, why are you telling me what I already know?" said Esther, who sometimes didn't expect to be answered.

Marjorie, who knew from curtain calls that going last was going best, let Amanda tell her news first. "I've started doing Jane Fonda's workout tape every day." Amanda stood up to show off her new body, which was exactly the same as her old body. The second she sat down, she buttered a breadstick and asked, "So, what's new with you? Have you been sweating in all your good clothes?"

Marjorie talked slowly. "Class is good, we saw Julie last week and I'm having an affair with my acting teacher." Unfortunately, Amanda had to swallow before she could scream.

"Your acting teacher? You're boffing with an asshole who thinks he's in show business while your husband is home waiting for you?" Marjorie had expected Amanda to be thrilled for her. Instead she was angry.

"I thought you'd be happy for me."

"Really? Maybe I'm more of a prude than you thought I was. I didn't know one was supposed to congratulate someone on having an affair. I voted for Reagan." Amanda went back to her breadstick.

"I thought you'd want to know all about it. I thought you'd be thrilled, not judgmental."

"I don't mean to judge. I'm just surprised. Maybe I'm not dancing around the table congratulating you because I saw David last night at Rexall and he looked like hell and all we could talk about was how we missed you. We had a little 'who misses Marjorie more' contest and I'm telling you, Marge, no one could tell who won. I can't believe you would do this to us." The waitress interrupted the conversation with their food. By the time she left, both women were slightly angry.

"It was dumb of me to think you'd be happy for me," said Marjorie, acting like a small child.

"I've always been straight with you so I'm going to have to agree. It was dumb of you. I'm a poor shlepper from the Bronx whose life dream it was to have a house with more than one bathroom. Have you ever once heard me to be happy about anyone's affair? Remember when Harriet Shaifer slept with the cantor's brother? Remember how it turned my stomach?"

"That was different. She was living with Hal."

"David thinks you just left for the summer."

"I can't believe your attitude, Amanda, people have affairs all the time."

"I'm sure they do. That doesn't mean I have to like it . . . Look, Margie, it doesn't change my love for you or anything. I'm still crazy about you. So, my best friend had an affair. I don't think you're doing the right thing but I'm not about to sew a scarlet letter to the front of your dress." For the first time since she had climbed into Lucas' bed, Marjorie felt guilty.

"I thought you'd want to know all about it. Do you know the first time we did it I kept thinking, I can't wait to tell Amanda."

"During?"

"During. I couldn't believe it. My body was there but my head was in your kitchen in Syosset. I couldn't wait for today. I thought you'd ask me a million questions."

"Look, maybe you got more sophisticated than I am." Amanda moved the ice around in her Tab and looked at Marjorie over her glass. "What did you expect me to ask, what size his shlong is?"

"It is weird. Have you ever seen an uncircumcised one?"

"Marjorie, I wasn't asking about his penis, I was just using it as an example."

"You're blushing. You're actually red in the cheeks." Marjorie dug into her pocketbook and came up with a Clinique compact to show Amanda the color of her face. "How can you be blushing? You have the dirtiest mouth in Nassau County."

"So, I talk dirty. That doesn't mean that I can sit happily in a restaurant and hear that my best friend is fucking some Gentile behind her husband's back."

Marjorie banged her spoon on the table and closed her eyes before speaking. "You're trying very hard to make me feel guilty, but I'm not going to take that shit."

"You've hardly ever said 'shit' in your life. Look how this city has changed you."

"It's me, Marjorie. The same Marjorie. All I did was have some unauthorized sex, which by the way I deserved because of what my husband did, and I have always said 'shit.' You just weren't listening."

They ate in relative peace, trying to talk about anything but the affair that Amanda disapproved of. Marjorie went from trying not to care what her best friend thought to hating herself for committing sins. By the time they had finished coffee, she was sorry Amanda had found the time to come to New York. She didn't need anyone to rain on the one little parade she had going.

"Why don't you pay the check and we'll walk up Columbus?" Amanda said finally. "I promised Warren I'd look for a clock in this Deco place. All of a sudden, out of nowhere, he's into Deco."

Marjorie signaled the waitress, got the check and had her money out before she realized what she was doing. "Why am I paying?" she asked. A month ago she would have fought Amanda for the check, but now she was thinking like a student.

Amanda stood up without reaching for her wallet, letting Marjorie know there was no room for compromise. "Because you have given me plenty of aggravation today. You should be happy I'm not asking you to pay for Warren's clock." Amanda was halfway out of the restaurant.

They walked up Columbus hardly talking. It was not the month they had spent apart that put the space between them, but the man. They both felt insulted, Marjorie by Amanda's disapproval, Amanda by Marjorie's betrayal of a way of their life. In the fifteen years of knowing and loving each other, this was the first time they had ever strained their friendship.

When they got to the antique store it was a relief to have something else to think about. Amanda took down every clock from the shelf and complained about their prices and Marjorie found some old movie magazines to look at. She thought of buying one that featured Tracy and Hepburn for Lucas, but decided against it because she didn't want to have to explain to Amanda or her mother why she wanted it. Amanda bought a clock, a lamp and an umbrella stand that she fell in love with and told the owner that one of her husband's trucks would pick it all up the next day. She wrote out a check for twelve hundred dollars and both she and the store felt they had cheated each other.

"Now what?" Amanda said once they were out in the street again.

"I have an hour before I have to meet Lucas," said Marjorie after checking her watch. "You want to come say hello to my mother?"

"Who's Lucas?" said Amanda, with no intention of moving. Marjorie, seeing that they were going to stand there awhile, shielded her eyes from the sun.

"Lucas is the man I'm having an affair with."

"Sorry. I didn't know he had a name," said Amanda.

"He has a name. He has a face. He has a profession."

"You have a husband."

"I know and this has nothing to do with that. Come on, Amanda, I could take criticism from my mother if she, God forbid, found out, but not from you. It feels like you're pulling away."

"I'm pulling away? You're the one who left me out there in Syosset with no one to play with. You're the one who is making a life here in New York. How am I supposed to feel when you're cheating on me and your husband?"

"I wish you would meet Lucas."

"I don't want to."

"You'd like him. He's strange. Like after we made love, he wanted to pay me. He'd adore you."

"Maybe I should go home early. Walk me to the garage." Amanda took off, making Marjorie work to keep up with her.

"I have an hour . . . For God sakes, Amanda. It's only a fling."

"I don't understand it. You look like the person who came to my son's bar mitzvah. What's this about being paid for sex?"

"It wasn't serious."

"He really did it?"

"Yes, but it wasn't serious."

"Well, you came to New York to make money," said Amanda.

By the time they got to the car, both women were happy to say goodbye. Marjorie had spent the last two blocks trying to explain that Lucas had nothing to do with her real life and Amanda had apologized more than once for being such a stupid prude. "I feel like I have to run home and make chicken soup," she said.

"To repent for my sins?"

"I need familiar around me. I have to feel and smell what I know. If you want to know the truth, Marjorie," she said, "New York scares the hell out of me. I was always better at being a big fish in a little pond. And what happened to you? You had to go swimming away to some crazy uncircumcised penis? Tell me, Marjorie, does this penis do wonderful things to you, things we don't even dream about on Long Island?"

"It's nice. It's exciting." Amanda looked smaller than usual on the streets of New York and Marjorie felt it was time for a hug so she took her in her arms. "I never climax," she said.

"So, you'll come home." Amanda turned and went into the dark garage, handing over her parking ticket to an attendant name Al.

At seven-thirty that night Marjorie was lying down beside Lucas. They had gone to bed improvising a love scene between a war nurse and a soldier. He limped into the bedroom. She put cold compresses on his brow. He mimed pain as he asked her to lie down beside him. She refused and tended to his dressing. He finally got her to sit on the bed by talking about his mama, the silver-haired lady back in Iowa who knew what to do with rhubarb. When the imaginary pain pills began to work he asked her to lie on top of him to keep him from floating to the ceiling. She got him to promise that if she did, he would go to sleep. He promised, but while she was there balancing on top of his legs, he fought his drowsiness and found his way under her skirt. She asked him to stop, but he reminded her that there was a war on and that he might not live until tomorrow. His silver-haired mama would miss him less if this good nurse would carry his baby to her. Seeing that his health was failing, she made the sacrifice and gave up her virginity while he gave up his.

When the war and lovemaking were over, Lucas asked, "Is there anything you want me to do differently?" He yawned and slipped into his jeans. It was a serious question, which she sensed he wasn't asking seriously.

"No. Absolutely not. You are a magnificent lover. You make love like . . ."

"Like a dying soldier."

"What's better than a dying man trying to feel alive with passion?" Marjorie drew the quilt toward her and kissed him.

"I'll be right back," he said when she let him go.

"Where are you going?" Marjorie was sorry she had asked. If she was going to be the perfect mistress, she felt she had no right to such questions.

"I just thought of something that applied to my 'We're Only Eighteen' theory and I want to write it down. It has to do with comedy. Did you ever notice how through the ages the things people laugh at are more and more sophisticated? There's proof there somewhere that we are emotionally getting older. The old Abbott and Costello movies are for children now. Do you see what I'm getting at? Punch and Judy shows were once considered very funny, even by adults. Four-year-olds still think so. They think it's hilarious all that hitting on the head. The world was once comedically four. I'll be right back.''

Lucas left for his typewriter and Marjorie reached for her clothes. She was very angry with herself. She had told him he was a magnificent lover, giving up the opportunity to tell him what she needed.

Thirty-two

Lucas was down in the office fighting the administration for permission to do *The Fifth of July* on the main stage even though it was supposed to be performed in the workshop. Rebecca Lewis, the administrative head of the school, reiterated that it was a workshop class and therefore had no right to be on the stage. Lucas, pounding his fists into walls, kept insisting that it would show off better on the stage and who the fuck cared what the policy was? He reminded her that they were talking about show business, and that they weren't finding the cure for cancer, so they should cut the crap.

Upstairs his eight students talked about him. At first the conversation centered around what a wonderful teacher he was and what a brilliant actor. "When he's up there on stage I can't take my eyes off of him," said Saucy.

"Yeah. Well, who can?" said Jake, lighting a cigarette although smoking was against the rules. "He's quite a hunk. For him I would consider going gay."

"You are gay."

"That's not true, I haven't decided yet. My shrink says I don't have to decide until I'm thirty."

"Choose women," said Millie. "With the women you don't have to wonder if they're pitchers or catchers. They're all catchers."

"You think he's as good in bed as he is on the stage?" asked Millie, not expecting anyone to know the answer.

"I personally have no idea. Although God knows I've tried," said Saucy, assuming the question had been directed at her. Marjorie, who was sitting on the platform, her chin resting on her knees, paid closer attention to her classmates. "I don't think he does it to students because I practically threw myself at him and a friend of mine, Dotti Mills, she's the one that does the whole Bloomingdale's makeup campaign, took his course last fall and practically begged him to sleep with her, but he wouldn't. I could tell he liked my tits because he kept looking at them, but that's as far as I got." Marjorie smiled and hoped satisfaction didn't show on her face. She looked at Saucy and saw what she had seen the first day of class, a gray-eyed, red-headed beauty whose abundance of hair always fell into place. One could describe her as flawless and not be wrong. Marjorie wondered in what way she had thrown herself at Lucas and how he refused without losing her admiration.

"It's amazing that he isn't a star," said Millie, dipping into her pocketbook and coming out with a large-sized bag of M&M's, the size that Marjorie always bought for Halloween and hoped that Julie wouldn't finish. "I mean he has everything going for him, looks and talent, and a friend at William Morris. Maybe he's one of those self-destructive types who deliberately does something wrong every time he gets close to succeeding. Hey, you're awfully quiet." Marjorie didn't realize that Millie was talking to her until she looked up and saw her holding out a handful of M&M's.

"Sorry. I didn't hear the question," said Marjorie.

"There was no question," said Millie, and assuming that her candy was being refused, she ate it herself. "I was just saying that Lucas might be self-destructive because he's not a star." Marjorie wanted to defend Lucas, but anything she said would set her apart from the rest of the class. She leaned back on her elbows and said, "Maybe he likes his life the way it is."

"Then he's an underachiever who enjoys being an under-achiever," said Mike, who rarely talked and thought what he said was brilliant when he did.

"All I know is he didn't go for me or my tits. I'm not saying everybody has to, but I don't get rejected much and Dottie practically makes a career out of turning down men. Maybe he's gay." Marjorie made the mistake of standing before talking. Had she stayed seated she would have been part of the conversation. Now that her head was higher than the others, whether she wanted to or not, she was about to make a statement.

"You guys are really something. Here we all agree we have a great teacher who is knocking his guts out downstairs trying to get us the main stage and we're up here knocking his sexuality. Why can't we just accept him for the brilliant man he is and leave the bedroom out of it?" Marjorie left the platform downstage center, and with no place else to go, she headed for the window and, knowing beforehand that the sill was coated with dust, leaned on it.

"Wow," said Saucy. "It sounds like you really have the hots for him, lady."

"Well, I don't," said Marjorie, reading the names that had been written into the dirt on the window.

"You don't?" Lucas Morgan's voice boomed from the doorway. None of them knew how long he had been there or how much he had heard. "I got you the main stage, the least you could do is have the hots for me." He opened his arms and Saucy and Jake, confident that they would be hugged, fell into them. Marjorie didn't expect to be jealous, but she was. For one brief moment, Lucas caught her eye and winked. As he was telling them that they would have to work twice as hard now that they had a classy place for their showcase, Marjorie, with her best manicured nail, scratched L.M. and M.W. into the dirty window. A moment later she thought she had better smear the whole thing away and a moment after that she decided to let it rest. She hadn't, after all, written that M.W. loved L.M.

They all marched down to the main stage and, like four-year-olds in a new playground, explored the place. Lucas sat in the back row. His arms surrounded the two vacant seats on either side of him and his feet draped over the seat in front of him. He watched while his protégés roamed on and off stage.

As usual Marjorie was less interested in lighting and the other backstage mysteries than she was in the glory of the stage itself. The theater was actually smaller than the one the North Shore Players used, but this was New York. Her feeling was punctuated by a subway traveling under her feet, rumbling its way from one end of the city to the next.

Before any of them could relax, Lucas asked them to take *The Fifth of July* from the top. They threw chairs together for their temporary set. With an energy that they had never had in their classroom, they said their lines with meaning and listened to one another for the first time. Upstairs Lucas had screamed that listening was as important as acting, but it wasn't until now that they were able to do it. Everything was almost up to performance level, the play taking on a life of its own, until Marjorie went up in her lines. The first time didn't hurt, nor did the second or the third. By the fourth, everyone started getting shaky. The concentration was gone and several of the actors looked toward Lucas instead of looking at one another. He finally stood up, waved the students to stop and signaled Marjorie into the hall.

"You still upset about your kid?" Lucas asked before she had a chance to say she was sorry.

"A little. Not as much. I got a letter from her yesterday and she seems to be doing fine. I worry, but I really can't blame it on her this time. I guess I'm just nervous."

"Would it help if I told you I love you?"

"You don't have to."

"But would it help? Sometimes that helps nervousness."

Marjorie ended up between a smile and a laugh.

"It helps. It helps. I don't exactly know what to do with the information, but it helps." He reached for her and she let him pull her toward him. He didn't have to lift her face for the kiss because by now she was expecting it. She wanted to leave her pale peach lipstick on his lips, but afraid of the consequences, she wiped it off with her hands.

"You think you can go back in there and do your job?"

"Yes . . . I wasn't nervous about us, you know. I mean I wasn't feeling insecure or anything."

"We're all insecure. You think I don't worry about the day that you go back to that wilderness?"

"Long Island is not a wilderness. We have major traffic accidents and everything."

"Do you have theaters that charge forty bucks a seat?"

"Not yet."

"Then it's a wilderness and I'm scared for you to go back there. You might get poison ivy or something. I must love you. I only worry about poison ivy when it directly involves the people I love. Now get in there and act your ass off. Cancel that. Don't act your ass off. Your ass is spectacular. There's a crack in it, but as soon as I get my hands on some cash. I'll have it fixed."

Marjorie entered the theater smiling, even her walk so joyful that her gauze skirt danced with her. And she remembered her lines.

That night she told him that she thought Millie knew. He said he was glad. He wanted the world to know and that Marjorie should come and live with him happily ever after. He made her go to the movies with him without any underwear on and when the feature started he found his way under her skirt, one hand on her, and one hand on the popcorn. When they went back to his apartment, she fell asleep in his arms, woke up at three and called Esther to let her know she was on her way home. Esther said one sentence, but it was so loaded that Marjorie ran it over in her mind to the tempo of the taxi meter. "David has been calling every ten minutes since nine o'clock and I don't have to tell you what that means." Esther was right. Marjorie knew what it meant. It meant that she was upsetting the people in her life.

"I fell asleep on the couch at Millie's." Esther stood in the hallway, her pink bathrobe belted under sagging breasts, her arms folded in front of her. She blocked the door with her body and it looked as if she wasn't going to let her daughter in, but Marjorie knew that her mother would never throw her out at three-thirty in the morning or any other time so she squeezed past her, mumbling something about a terrible headache and hoping to get to her room without having to tell any more lies about Millie's couch. "Your husband wants you to call. He said it didn't matter what time you came home. He's a very patient man, Marjorie." Her mother's taking David's side really got to her.

"That very patient man was spending night after night at the hospital with a beautiful young woman. I was up at three and four in the morning hurt by what he was doing."

"He was probably just helping her."

"Right. And I was just helping Millie Klein."

Marjorie called David, waking him, telling him everything was fine and promising to call in the morning. She fell asleep wondering if Lucas had been serious about asking her to live with him. She could go to movies without underwear every night of the week. She surprised herself by forgetting her husband, her daughter and the closet space that she needed in order to live. She knew it was a fantasy and fantasies were terrific for falling asleep.

On Friday night, David came for dinner. Esther made brisket for twelve and took her books to sleep early. Marjorie and David made love and they had an orgasm apiece. He didn't beg her to come home because the summer was ending and he decided he could hold out until Labor Day.

Thirty-three

The members of the class sat at the edge of the stage as Lucas talked to them before the performance. He assured them that his friend from William Morris would be there. "I don't want you to be nervous just because he can change your entire life." Lucas smiled but none of them was calm enough to smile back.

"How much makeup do you want us to wear?" Saucy asked, clinging to a huge bag full of model's supplies.

"No more than during the dress. The lighting will be exactly the same." Lucas picked up his clipboard and seeing that he had everybody's attention he read his last-minute notes, crossing out each one as he went along. "Mike, make sure that the lower half of your body is a constant dead weight. I think I saw your toes wiggle last run-through. If the audience catches that, they're not going to buy that you're paralyzed. Also, the line is 'Where have you been hiding all afternoon?' your second line in."

"Isn't that what I said?"

"No. You said, 'Where have you been?' 'Hiding' is important. It's a loaded word." Mike nodded, whispering the word "hiding" a few times, carving it into his mind.

"Jake, I don't want to see one ounce of gayness. Jed may be a homosexual, but there's nothing gay about him."

"I'm not gay."

"Nobody said you were. Millie, you're still getting teary

252

toward the end of Act Two. You know by now that if you cry the audience won't.''

"Sorry. When I was rehearsing with Marjorie the other day, she liked the tears.'' Marjorie was embarrassed by this minor betrayal.

"Yeah? Well, I'm the director.'' He turned to Marjorie, still checking his notes, and said, "I want you to remember the entire time you are up there that Shirley is very young. During the last run-through, every once in a while, I saw the woman in you.'' Marjorie took the criticism and promised herself she'd remember to be a child. She suspected he saw the woman because he knew her so well.

"I want you to know before you go out there tonight that you are the finest group of actors I have ever met,'' Lucas said very softly. "And I'm a hard man to impress. You guys have done nothing but impress me. I'm proud of you and I love you all.'' He followed this speech with the hugs and kisses that show business is famous for. Marjorie forced herself to join in, but hearing Lucas say that he loved them all made her doubt his love for her. Marjorie was always crazy before a performance and needed Amanda to tell her she was brilliant.

They dressed in two classrooms, temporarily set up as dressing rooms, one for the men, one for the women. Marjorie, Millie and Saucy squeezed past one another reaching for makeup and clothes, trying to hide their nervousness. After spilling an entire bottle of Clinique Clarifying Lotion and attempting to mop it up with Kleenex, Millie said, "So why am I a wreck? My parents are out there, but I haven't been nervous in front of my parents since I was nine and I told them to butt out of my life. Since then my father and I haven't spoken to each other and my mother and I have traded sex stories. She tells me every time my father gets frisky and I tell her how big the guys I fuck are. I'm certainly not worried about anyone else's friends or family.''

"Could you please keep quiet, Millie? I'm really trying to prepare for this performance tonight.'' Saucy's preparation was smoking pot. Marjorie had been around too many nervous doctors to be surprised.

They were all quiet for a very short, tense time and then Millie spilled a bottle of Tea Rose perfume. "Who does he think he's kidding with that William Morris agent shit?" she said, trying to cover her fear. "If he signs anyone it's going to be you." She pointed to Saucy. "There's only room for one ugly actress a decade and Bette Midler has it all sewed up for a while. You're the only one who has a chance. I'm too dumpy and Marjorie is too old. Only older men get to make it in show business after thirty-five."

Marjorie didn't know she had it in her but she found the strength to sock Millie in the back. Millie pushed Marjorie back and as Saucy begged them to stop, Millie took the lilies out of a vase and dumped the water on Marjorie, missing her head, but drenching everything else.

"How am I going to act with a wet bra?" Marjorie didn't care that she was screaming.

"Don't wear a bra, cunt. You're playing a thirteen-year-old who doesn't even know what tits are." Marjorie went for her hair dryer, holding it threateningly, as one would a gun. The most she could have done to her opponent was blast her with hot air, but she never got the chance since Lucas, acting as stage manager, knocked on the door, telling them if was five minutes to show time.

The women rushed to dress and Marjorie, feeling soggy, took off her bra and hoped that no one in the audience could tell that the right one was going faster than the left. At one minute to show time they headed down the hall and Millie whispered in Marjorie's ear that she was sorry and ashamed. "I've been hostile toward you ever since I realized you were sleeping with Mr. Morgan." Marjorie took a long pause before forgiving her. They were running down the hall to make curtain time and both her breasts were letting her know that they were there.

The play was magic. The audience laughed and cried in all the right places and the applause would have been thunderous had there been more of a crowd. Lucas led the bravos and brought the audience to its feet, including Esther and Nancy. After the final curtain everyone was invited on stage for champagne in paper cups. Nancy wanted to know more about Marjorie's handsome teacher and Esther asked why they couldn't find some place for Marjorie to sing and why she didn't wear a bra.

Lucas, with his arm around a man in a Duke of Windsor plaid, congratulated each of the students and told them how great they were. He was introduced as Burt Lansky and everyone knew that this was the man from William Morris. When they got to Marjorie, Lucas tried flirting with Esther. "Of course you're beautiful," he said. "Look at your children."

Esther, who was too smart to be charmed, said, "My children are more than beautiful. They have a commitment to home and family." It was the best way she knew to tell him to leave Marjorie alone.

"Of course she loves her family," said Lucas. "Marjorie could have invited anyone here tonight, but she brought her mother and sister."

"Her husband couldn't make it," said Esther, just in case Marjorie had led him to believe she was single. She hoped he heard her, since he was already off with Millie and her parents.

"You're very talented," Burt Lansky told Marjorie. "Lucas said you were and I agree with him. I'd really love it if you'd give me a call at the office because there's something I'd like to send you up for." He opened his wallet and gave Marjorie one of his cards. She looked at it, and seeing the official William Morris logo with the M and W entwined, she felt successful.

"She'll call you after she consults her lawyer," said Esther.

Marjorie purposely waited until Millie was out of the dressing room. She hadn't seen Burt Lansky give anyone else a card and she was not ready to be congratulated or hated for what had just happened. She dressed slowly, seeing her future as having it all. No wonder Millie had wet her down. Women who had husbands, children, lovers and talent were not easily accepted.

Marjorie wanted to go to Lucas' and play with his few chest hairs. When she left with her mother and sister, he told her again how wonderful she was and she told him she would see him in class tomorrow. She looked for him to give her some signal, but it never came. She hoped it was because he was too smart to hint at anything in front of Esther.

Marjorie thought she was going home, but, as a surprise, Esther and Nancy took her to Elaine's. She had gone there after the theater with David several times and, although it was fun to sometimes catch a glimpse of Woody Allen, she had always felt touristy having to wait for a table while others were ushered in. Tonight, however, it was as if the whole place knew that Burt Lansky had given her his card. The crowd at the bar parted for her. Elaine waved her in and the table they were given was vintage. Woody Allen wasn't there, but that was OK with Marjorie because she didn't need the competition. With the card in her purse, she knew that it was time that she stop looking, and start being looked at.

When the wind was poured, Esther raised her glass and, forcing Marjorie's and Nancy's up with hers, she made her toast. "To my daughter, the actress. May her star or her light or whatever they say in show business shine on Broadway." They touched one another's glasses and sipped the wine.

"I thank you and thanks for coming to the show."

"Did I ever miss you in a school play?" said Esther, making Marjorie feel slightly less professional. "You always used to have the lead. You did a beautiful job tonight even if you didn't have a lead."

"There were no leads," said Marjorie.

"I thought the man on the crutches was the lead," said Esther, buttering a roll.

"So, what's the difference?" Marjorie was being as temperamental as she had been at seventeen.

"Come on, Marge, you're overreacting. I'm sure you are way past counting lines. Mom was just trying to tell you you were good." Nancy reached for the bread and smiled.

"Thanks. It felt good. It felt great being up there."

"Whose crazy idea was it that you should play someone a quarter of your age?" Nancy could no longer suppress her hostility. She never played leads.

"Lucas did all the casting."

"Lucas is the teacher. They call him Lucas." Esther felt she had to explain.

"He has crazy casting methods. They should have warned the audience or something. At first I didn't know you were a teenager. I thought you were retarded or something." Marjorie had forgotten how Nancy could hurt her. When they were young Nancy was always there to tear down any of her sister's glories. When Marjorie got her first bra, Nancy said it looked to her like a cut-off undershirt. When she married David, Nancy said, "All the luck in the world, kid. I think you made the right choice. A good career isn't for all of us." When Marjorie had Julie, Nancy said, "She's beautiful. As long as you're tied down it might as well be with a beautiful baby." Marjorie had made Nancy crazy by being the star of the family. When they were kids she had tried to hurt Nancy back. Now that she was faced with a forty-nine-year-old woman, who had had little love in her life and no bank account, Marjorie tried not to fight back.

"I knew how young she was supposed to be. She told me weeks ago," said Esther.

"Whatever. All I'm saying is it was strange at first. You want to split the pork chops and get two sides of pasta? I make every restaurant I walk into Chinese."

Marjorie could be civil to her sister, but she couldn't

share pork chops with someone who had spent a lifetime attempting to bury her. They ended up ordering completely separate meals, which didn't stop Nancy from piercing her fork into Marjorie's food. They talked mainly about the past. Fortunately for the three of them they could laugh at times that weren't funny when they happened. It wasn't until dessert (Nancy ordered two cheesecakes and three forks without consulting anyone) that the play came up again.

"I could never be in the theater," said Esther. "I could never remember all of those lines."

"I had trouble with that myself. Lucas was pretty patient."

"It seems Lucas was a lot of things," said Nancy. By now she had both pieces of cheesecake in front of her and was alternating forkfuls.

"He's a good teacher."

"He's a good teacher. He's a patient man. He has a great sense of humor. You have also told us he is talented, brilliant. No, more than brilliant. You have compared him to Darwin. He has a theory that rivals *The Origin of the Species*." Nancy was telling Marjorie that she wasn't buying any of it.

"I brought that home from the library once but I never could read true things," said Esther.

"The big question is why my little sister hasn't fixed me up with this God yet."

"I'll ask him what his situation is, the next time I see him."

"The next time she sees him will probably be in his apartment at night," said Esther, knowing she was loading her information.

"What're you saying, Mom? Are you telling me our little Margie is having an affair?"

"That's not what she's saying," said Marjorie, getting into the cheesecake for the first time. "I rehearsed at his apartment. The whole class rehearsed at his apartment. I fell asleep on his couch once and didn't get home until three in the morning, but that's it.'' Esther pointed her finger at Marjorie, but she spoke to Nancy. ''That night she told me that she had fallen asleep on the Klein girl's couch. She fibbed to me about whose couch it was.'' Esther pulled the sugar toward her and pushed it away, remembering that she took her coffee plain.

''Open your eyes, Mom. She falls asleep on his couch and lies about it. She thinks he's a genius and nobody has ever heard of him. And . . . I can't stress this enough, she was afraid to introduce him to her sister, which usually means she wants the man for herself. So am I right? Is our little Margie having an affair?'' Both Esther and Nancy listened hard for the answer and Marjorie found them less frightening than she had expected. Her mother, with all her years of moaning, had never hated her for anything she ever did. Marjorie would have a hard time getting Esther to stop loving her.

Nancy had never liked her. She had been a big-boned eleven-year-old who didn't need the arrival of a small, sweet, pink package in her life. If Marjorie had been beautiful, but not smart, Nancy could have carved her own place. Unfortunately for the frizzy-haired older sister, Marjorie was smart and talented. Although Nancy always tried pulling the rug out from under her, she never jerked it away completely. Marjorie always had the feeling that Nancy would never let her hit the ground.

Marjorie let the waiter pour her more wine, but she spoke before drinking any of it. ''I don't want to shock you,'' said Marjorie, watching the waiter clear the water glasses, ''but Lucas and I are having a thing.'' Had she had less wine, she would have revealed her affair with at least a little poetry.

''A thing?'' Esther said, and turned to Nancy to ask, ''Like the thing Mrs. Balaban from three B once had? Her husband Lou never found out. One Chanukah the boyfriend and the husband both gave her fur, a stole from the friend and a full coat from Lou, mink, all female skins. This is what Marjorie is having, a thing?''

"Yes, Mom, but without the fur," said Marjorie, happy that she had told her nearest and dearest her deepest secret and lightning had not struck Elaine's.

"You're going to stop this thing or what?" Esther asked, more for information than confrontation.

"Why should she stop? She has a husband paying the bills. She has this hunk in the Village. From what I understand, the husband will take her back and the hunk will let her stay as long as she wants to. I know about ten thousand women right here in Manhattan who would be willing to punch you out, including me."

Marjorie expected to be made to feel guilty for having an affair, but not because she had her unfair share of men. "It's not as wonderful as you think it is," she said.

"Not as wonderful as I think it is? You know what, Margie? I don't care about the details. I'm just goddamn pissed that you have your choice between two pairs of biceps and I don't have any." Nancy looked to Esther for help and it came.

"So maybe you could, I don't know, stop this craziness, go home to David and get Nancy together with the teacher." Esther, although not at all happy with the situation, was pleased with her solution.

"He's not Jewish," Marjorie said, hoping to have Esther push less. She couldn't tell her mother that she and her sister were not interchangeable.

"She doesn't have to marry him," said Esther. "She just wants to go out and have a good time. He'd probably like her, since they're both teachers. Am I right, Nancy?"

"Mom, please, drop it. Just because this guy is into Marjorie, doesn't mean he's going to be interested in me. We're different, or haven't you noticed." Nancy zipped her handbag as if she were leaving, but she made no other movement to go.

"Don't put yourself down all the time," said Esther. "If you gave this guy half a chance maybe you could have some fun. The least that could happen is you go out to dinner a few times. Does he take you out nice?" Esther asked Marjorie.

"He knows some great places in the Village," Marjorie lied, not wanting her mother to know that going out to dinner was not their prime activity.

"Those small, dark places with no carpeting or anything or someplace nice where Nancy could get a good meal?"

Marjorie, who was thrilled that Esther wasn't disowning her, was willing to talk about restaurants all night. While she was describing Joanna's, a nice place that she had been to with David and not Lucas, Nancy asked for the check. Marjorie demanded to pay, but her mother and sister insisted it was their treat and Marjorie, noticing for the first time that Nancy's sweater was too well worn, felt sad. They parted at the curb with Esther pleading that Nancy take a taxi and Nancy heading for the subway. Marjorie and her mother got into a cab, the daughter climbing in first so that the mother would have an easier time getting in and out.

"You shouldn't spend too much time with this man," Esther said as they headed through the park. "Women confuse love and sex." It was the first time Esther had admitted her daughter was involved sexually with Lucas.

"I'm already attached, Mom." Marjorie's words sounded like a plea for help.

"Don't see him again."

"I have to see him again. I have class."

"To heck with class." Esther looked out one window and Marjorie the other.

"I'm going down there now. He . . . taught me so much. It was because of him that I'm getting an agent. I have to. I don't know why, Mom. It makes me feel good."

"Mr. Robinson from eight D, you remember him, when his wife was alive, poor thing, may she rest in peace, they broke through to eight C and we laughed at how they had an apartment with two kitchens. Anyway. I met him in the elevator and he asked me down for a drink. I'm sure he meant coffee because he knows I'm not the one you ask for a drink, but I said no. Not that I don't trust him and not that I don't trust me. I just remembered how in *Tess of the D'Urbervilles* she got into all that trouble and I didn't want any part of it. Do you know what I'm telling you?''

"It's too late, Mom. Don't wait up for me.''

"I wait up for everyone. You think I sleep? You have underwear, just in case?'' Marjorie shook her head no and had the feeling that Esther was disgusted with her daughter's disregard for cleanliness.

When the cab stopped at West Seventy-sixth Street, Marjorie leaned forward to tell the driver not to stop the meter, that she was going down to Eleventh Street. She then turned to Esther, who looked too weary for a fight. "I love you, Mom,'' she said.

"I know you do. The trouble is you love too many people.''

Esther walked slowly to the front door of her building and Marjorie wouldn't let the driver leave until her mother was safely in the doorman's hands. She was jostled all the way to the Village. The night was cool and although August hadn't yet run out of heat, there was a reminder that fall would be there as usual. Marjorie didn't look forward to autumn. She had set herself free for the summer and September would take care of her freedom. Her mother was right. Marjorie loved one person too many. Ideally, she would have Esther return to Florida and she, Lucas and a new, thin Julie would live on Seventy-sixth Street with regular visits from David. They would get the fireplace in the living room to work for the first time. (Jewish families were always afraid of their fireplaces and put flower arrangements in them instead of wood.) Her new agent would drop by for a drink. Burt and David would probably get along great. Thinking of Burt Lansky made Marjorie reach in her pocket to see if his card was still there. Feeling the raised print made her feel that all was well with her immediate world.

Lucas was awakened by the bell and came to the door naked and confused. He asked Marjorie what time it was as if they had had an appointment that he had slept through. Marjorie just told him that it was late and pushed him away from the door and toward the bedroom. "Are you supposed to be here?" Lucas asked, still not awake. Instead of making it to the bedroom he fell onto the couch, sitting properly as if he were in a suit and tie.

"I finally told my mother about us. She didn't go completely berserk so I get to stay over. We get to have breakfast in bed, or lunch if we sleep late."

"I always eat standing up," said Lucas, and Marjorie was hurt for the first time since the relationship began. She was not the first woman to surprise a lover in the middle of the night and certainly not the first to be hurt by it. She had imagined that they would be in each other's arms by now but he refused to give her the warmth she needed. Had he been hostile she could have fled. He just sat there, causing Marjorie to work harder to keep their attraction alive. She finally got him to say that he was happy she was there, but his tone kept her from believing it. She pulled him to his feet, and without begging for attention led him to bed. He fell asleep so easily that she was insulted. Sadly, Marjorie undressed in the dark. Nancy could have told her younger sister that love in New York was not so much about two people coming together as it was about one person giving love and then taking it away.

"I'm sorry I conked out on you," said Lucas, screaming from the shower the following morning.

"Hey, that's OK. I'm sorry I came down unannounced." Since there was no answer, Marjorie stopped making the bed, and yelled her apology from the bathroom door. This time she was sure Lucas heard her. He got out of the shower, whistling, and Marjorie felt good enough to finish making the bed.

"What're you going to do today?" Lucas said as he put on socks. David had always put his shorts on first and it was astonishing to see a man dress from the feet first. He looked like he was ready for a clean-cut porno film.

"First I think I should call Burt. Is it too soon? I mean will I look desperate?"

"What for?"

"What for? Didn't he tell you? He's signing me. I really didn't think he would but . . ." Lucas stopped dressing and looked at Marjorie, confused.

"He said he was signing you?"

"He gave me his card. I know it's crazy because I'm probably not a great commercial risk, but every once in a while someone my age . . . what's her name, Elvis' wife, Priscilla, I know she's making it on his name, but still she's thirty-seven . . . and Victoria Principal made it late."

"I had a long talk with him last night," said Lucas. "We went out for a drink and he said he was going to take on Saucy, but in a nonofficial capacity because the business was slow."

"And he never mentioned me? He gave me his card." Marjorie must have looked forlorn because Lucas drew her to him. It was the first sign of affection that she had received since arriving at his apartment. There with his muscle surrounding her, she cared much less about getting an agent and much more for her lover's touch.

"I'll ask him what it's about." Lucas let go of her before she did of him.

Burt Lansky had a client who was putting together an Off-Broadway revival of *Witness for the Prosecution,* and although the William Morris Agency couldn't handle her at this time, a lot of their own people were out of work, he would be happy to set up an audition for Marjorie. Would she be interested? She was definitely interested.

Since the production was just in the planning stages, she was to meet the producers in their offices on West Fifty-seventh Street. The reception area, headed by a perfectly put together Calvin Kleined receptionist, revealed that Sugarman and Nesbitt did more than try to produce plays. They were, according to their walls, importers of fine Italian furniture. There was, however, a neatly framed review touting a dinner theater production of *The Gingerbread Lady*. Sugarman and Nesbitt, as the producers, were praised for bringing great theater to Syracuse. Marjorie, and anyone else who was asked to wait in the reception area, could see that the importers had the theater bug.

Marjorie was buzzed into the inner office and there among the beautiful Italian leather and chrome furniture were a tall Nesbitt and a short Sugarman, both with friendly handshakes. "I'm Jack Nesbitt and this is Al Sugarman and we know who you are. Sit. Sit. Did Jennifer offer you some coffee? You want a real drink?"

"I'm fine, thanks," said Marjorie, slightly exposing her long legs as she sat. Nesbitt and Sugarman both appreciated the exposure. "I don't know how much Burt told you," said Nesbitt, leaning against a large Deco desk.

"He just told me that you were doing an Off-Broadway revival of *Witness for the Prosecution*."

"He said that? He said we were the producers? I told you he took us seriously, Jack."

"Who told who? I'm the one who told you that he was impressed with the review. If he had flown up to see it, he would have really been knocked out." It was obvious to Marjorie that the two men were very proud of their recent status as producers. She relaxed, knowing they were new at it.

"Did Burt mention what was happening with the rights?" asked Jack, leaning in for an answer.

"What're you asking her for?" said Al. "You think he's going to tell her before he tells us?" And then to Marjorie, "There were some problems because CBS, of all people, bought the television rights and are putting Sir Ralph Richardson in it, but we have the exclusive New York stage rights."

"We hope we have the exclusive New York stage rights," said Jack.

"It's ninety-nine percent sure we do."

"Ninety percent. I'm telling you, there's a ten-percent doubt."

"We have the papers."

"That's true. We have the papers. So, let us assume that everything is in order. Is that all right with you, Miss Weissman?"

"That's fine with me." Marjorie didn't know why she was being consulted, but as an actress up for a job, everything was fine with her.

"You would be right for more than one role, you know that?" Marjorie felt herself sitting taller than she had since she was a cocky kid.

"I saw the play years ago. My mom and I went to a Saturday matinee and to tell you the truth all I remember was a woman with a scar and a huge scream from the audience at the end."

"That's what everyone remembers. I told you, Jack, the audience goes berserk. Jack never saw the original on account of he was still back in Chicago. Tell him how crazy the audience got."

"They screamed," said Marjorie. "I remember clinging to Mother and I'll bet she grabbed me too."

"So, was I right, Jack? You might have been right about the Mastrioni chair, but I'm telling you I'm right about this one. The audience yells, they pee in their pants."

"I got hold of a copy of the play and read it last night," said Marjorie, trying to get the attention back to her and her reason for being there. "I must admit, I didn't know which part you wanted to read me for."

"Which one most interests you?" asked Al. Marjorie, knowing show-business horror stories and not believing the privileges that she was being given, turned to Jack before answering. Since he seemed to be waiting for her answer too, she spoke quickly, fearing that they would soon realize that she was only an actress from the North Shore Players and not worthy of being on their couch.

"If it was up to me, I'd take the lead." Marjorie raced on,

fearing that she would hear laughter. "But I don't have to tell you that there are several juicy parts in the play and I would be honored to read for any of them. And . . . I know this great actor, Lucas Morgan, if you need him. He's wonderful. Really wonderful."

"Good. I was hoping you would stick with us. I'd like you to meet our director, Mike Howard. Do you know who he is?" Marjorie didn't but she nodded, not wanting to reveal her unfamiliarity with the theatrical world. "Good, because I want you to meet him." She thought of mentioning Herm from the North Shore Players but quickly realized it would be better for both of them if she got in first.

"And we would like you and your husband to come to our next backer's audition. It's not really an audition because it's proven material. We call it a backer's audition because we're still raising money for the production."

Al walked her to the elevator and just before the doors closed pressed a prospectus of the show's budget into her hands. Marjorie felt it had gone extremely well and over hamburgers at the Bagel Nosh on West Fourth she related as many of the details as she could remember to Lucas. When she finished she looked up for congratulations.

"Those assholes," was his only remark.

"Assholes for liking me?"

"You are new at this. You didn't get it, did you? They had you up there to try and get you to invest in their show. Burt is going to be really pissed."

"I think they're going to offer me a part. You jealous or something?"

"I think they're full of shit. That part could cost you fifty grand and they'll give you one line. You willing to pay five thousand dollars a word?"

"Maybe . . . maybe they think I'm talented. They want me to meet the director." Marjorie angered.

"Those shits."

Marjorie was not quite ready to accept Lucas' point of view until she spoke to Burt. When she called him, he was so angry he said he wasn't going to represent them anymore. "Let them stick to their fucking wop furniture. I don't handle producers who hassle actresses into investing. I'm sorry you wasted your time with those jerks. I'd love to schmooze, but the Coast is panicked. They haven't learned yet that there is no such thing as a showbiz emergency."

Thank God Lucas was there to receive her tears. He took her back to his apartment, reminded her she was a good actress and led her into an improvisation. She was a patient and he was a gynecologist.

"What seems to be the problem?" Lucas asked, parting her legs and putting them in imaginary stirrups.

"No problem," said Marjorie, looking at Lucas through the thighs she had worked so hard to keep firm. "I was looking at my appointment book and I realized that I'm three months overdue for my yearly appointment."

"Well, let's take a look." Which was exactly what Lucas did. Marjorie laughed at Lucas' concept of what went on in a gynecologist's office.

"Aren't you going to give me an internal?"

"Yeah, sure. I'm . . . uh . . . I'm all out of . . . those rubber gloves. I hope you don't mind."

"How many patients ago did you run out?" said Marjorie, her knees coming together. Lucas separated them again.

"I just ran out five minutes ago. I've only seen seven patients since then. Let me know if my fingers are cold." Lucas began his "examination" and soon the "doctor" was on top of her. "I just want to see if everything is working properly. Standard procedure."

"Do you do this for everyone?" asked Marjorie. It was hard to talk under Lucas' weight, but she didn't want to give up the sketch they were creating.

"I'm very thorough with my favorite patients." Marjorie moved her body with his. She tightened her legs around him and received his pleasure without, once again, trying for any of her own. He relaxed on top of her and she scratched her name into his back. He received the message, gently moved back her hair and whispered "I love you" directly into her ear. She received his love with pain instead of joy. Her heart was hurting in anticipation of what this love would cost her.

"Now what?" said Marjorie, once Lucas was lying by her side. She knew it was an impossible question to answer.

"Now, I call Burt and give him hell for what happened to you."

"I meant now what happens to our lives?" Marjorie was not happy considering she was a woman in love. Her clothes were at her mother's. The daughter she worried about was out of reach. Her husband was among her lifelong possessions on Long Island and she had forgotten his birthday. Her best friend did not understand and the man she was giving her heart to had no intention of making room for her underwear in his drawers.

Thirty-four

Dear Emily,

I can't believe how fast the summer is going. This letter will be getting to you just a little while before I will. To tell you the truth, I can't wait to get home even though I know there's trouble ahead. Maybe you'll be there when I tell them. With you there things will be quieter.

At lights out, the girls in the bunk talk in the dark for hours about what sex must be like. I can't believe what they say. They think it's heaven on earth and violins and all that garbage that all those old movies talk about. It's really funny when they talk about orgasms. Sometimes I have to really work hard to stop myself from laughing. I mean don't get me wrong, orgasms are great and everything, but they're really not what virgins think they are. I mean it just happens when a guy does it to you and you sort of feel hot and throbby.

Now for my good news. I've lost seventeen and a half pounds. I've sort of hit a plateau now and I haven't lost in three days, which is enough for me to want to throw myself in the lake, but I'm trying to be patient. Kim, one of the twins I told you about, was on a plateau for five days and then she lost two pounds in one day so I guess there's hope for me. The bad part is, now that I'm thinner I think I'm looking pregnant. Maybe it's just my imagination so I'm counting on you to tell me the truth. I'll be home in a little over two weeks. I can't believe how fast school is starting and with my luck I'll have the baby over Christmas vacation and I won't get to miss a lot.

Anyway, I only have a few minutes left to write if I want to get some rest. I can't wait to get home, but I have to admit that I have grown to like some of the people here and I'll probably even miss them. (Not like I miss you, but some of them are pretty nice.) I keep wanting to tell Kim about the baby because I think she'll understand and maybe even Myrna, my counselor. So far I'm keeping my mouth shut, but maybe when the baby is born I'll invite them to visit. I hope it's a girl because I'll feel funny about changing a boy's diaper.

I've been thinking a lot about how many parents are going to react. I used to think that they would scream and be really angry. Now I think they'll mostly be embarrassed.

Love ya,
Julie

P.S. I wrote a short, really short letter to Finkle. I have no idea why and sometimes I wish I didn't mail it. I still think he raped me in a social situation.

J.W.

Thirty-five

"Are you secretly happy that I'm not going to be a star in the near future?" Marjorie asked while lying next to Lucas, naked and happy.

"Yes."

"You would be jealous, wouldn't you, if one of your summer students was the toast of the town?"

"No. I don't want to be the toast of any town. My work for the next ten years has got to be on my theory. I've been thinking about recapitulation. You've got to remember. I'm only referring to Western civilization, but listen to this. Ptolemy thought that the earth was the center of their universe. Therefore, and I'm not the first one to think of this, each man recapitulates the universe. This had been proven on the physical side in the Ontogeny Recapitulates Phylogeny theory that has to do with us starting as one cell and the universe starting as one cell and going through our fish stage and all mammals going through their fish stage. You follow?" Marjorie nodded that she did. She was thinking of her own recapitulation, her old bedroom, acting class, hoping for a career. He squeezed her thigh and let his hand rest on her knee. She wished he would move it just a little to her right, to that part of her body that needed his hand. "I'm going to have to get a better typewriter one of these days. God, I've been saying that for a very long time. This fall. Right after Labor Day. I'm going to sit down at that fucking typewriter right after Labor Day. Don't let me get up until I'm finished. Forget your career. Sacrifice yourself and be the woman behind the man. I'll dedicate the book to you. Is ten years too much to ask?''

"How come we keep forgetting I'm married?"

"Because we're totally selfish people.'' And he removed his hand from her leg. She turned to look at him and realized that he had the lashes she had always wanted. Hers were long and thick, but his were longer and thicker and her heart didn't understand that one doesn't ruin one's life over lashes.

"My daughter is coming home in about two weeks.'' Lucas didn't say anything, as if what Marjorie was telling him didn't affect his life. She couldn't help asking, "Is this a summer romance?''

He played with her hair before answering, making a curl where there hadn't been one before. "It's anything you want it to be.'' He saddened, remembering Suzanne, who wanted to bring a few of her things into his apartment after they had been seeing each other for a while. She wanted a towel of her own, her pillow on the bed, a picture of her family in a silver frame, a vase she had bought on sale at Bloomingdale's, throw pillows for the couch, a blender and other insignificant kitchen items, and a quilt she had had since childhood. He tried for a month to live with her things, but after a very short while, those were the only things he saw. They strangled him as he entered each tiny room and when he could no longer breathe he asked if they could continue to care for each other with forty city blocks between them. She was the first and last woman to have her pillow on his bed.

"What's your fantasy for us?"

"That the summer will never end. What's yours?''

"That you and Julie and I live on Seventy-sixth Street. And that David comes to visit.''

"One man isn't enough for you?'' he said, smiling, letting Marjorie know his question wasn't serious. It was serious for her and if she had to answer it truthfully she would have had to say, "A woman like me, or maybe even every woman in the world, needs two men, one to make love to and one to make love to her."

"It was just a fantasy."

"What's the reality?"

"The reality is we all go home. My mom goes back to Florida. Pop called the other night. He has a bad cold and he wants her. She may even go home early. Julie comes home and I go home." And then Marjorie remembered a promise. "I'd like you to meet my sister. You might like her."

"The one who came to the show?"

"Yes. She's very bright. She teaches at Columbia . . ." Marjorie saw Lucas wasn't buying and stopped her sales pitch.

"You'll hurt me. I told you not to fall in love with me."

"How do you know I did? You're the one who has been whispering in my ear."

"It doesn't matter. You attached yourself around me, through me, under me. How are you going to untangle that?" Lucas said, pleased at having given her an unsolvable problem.

"Run away?"

"I doubt it. You didn't run away from a husband who didn't satisfy you for twenty years." Marjorie momentarily felt she wanted to save David's reputation. She wanted to tell Lucas that her husband did satisfy her, but even though she was new at it, she knew not to talk about her husband's lovemaking with her lover.

They talked for over an hour about what was going to happen to them. It was clear that they weren't ready or willing to let go. He couldn't come to Seventy-sixth Street because he needed his things around him. She couldn't move to the Village because she had a daughter and because he could more easily let a woman into his heart than into his apartment. She couldn't cut David out of her life. It finally became too difficult to talk and they made love. It scared the hell out of him and left her more frustrated than usual.

Thirty-six

The next evening, knowing the summer would eventually have its closing night, Marjorie asked David if he could meet her at her mother's as soon as possible. He was expecting either a confrontation or an explanation, since he had guessed by now she was having an affair. All the way in, he rehearsed what he would say, mainly words that would ask them to forgive each other. He wished with all his strength that the summer was behind them and that she hadn't had enough time to be anything but infatuated with the man she had found in New York. He blamed himself for the gap in their marriage, not Marjorie or her lover. He just hoped that all they had found were each other's bodies and nothing more lasting than sex in the dark. He was pretty sure she'd hear his plea. Maybe she would even like his moustache.

When he got there it was clear that Marjorie didn't want to talk. She walked him softly past her mother's room and drew him, fully dressed, on top of her. When they were sufficiently naked, he made love to her in the same familiar way he had for the last eighteen years. She had her customary climax and felt she deserved it. It was lovely having a guilty husband in her bed.

When it was over, he asked her to come home, using the script that he had written in the car. She ran her hand through his hair and told him his moustache would someday be nice. She didn't tell him she would return, but she did smile and worry about his welfare. He decided not to push her, since Julie was coming back so soon.

He spent the night and they parted in the morning as if all he had come for was orange juice and sex. At the door, she shyly asked if he would be back on Thursday. He would. In the meantime, he planned to shave and slowly take back his patients from Solomon. She watched until the elevator door closed behind him and Esther watched her watching him.

"You know what I think? I think you don't know what you want. That's what I think." Esther was sure she was right.

"I do know what I want. I want them both."

"When you were sixteen, no, almost sixteen, and I took you to buy a dress for your Sweet Sixteen. Remember? Well, I do. There was a black velvet from Saks that looked lovely on you, only I wasn't too hot for black for such a young girl, but I said we'll see. We found a beautiful pink at Lord and Taylor. You remember? Good. So you remember when I asked you which one you wanted and you said both and tried to convince me that you needed both because they were so different?"

"And you bought it," said Marjorie, enjoying the recollection. Her mother had never been easy to convince about anything, but it was always energy well spent because she usually caved in, giving Marjorie a chance to be victorious.

"You're right. I bought them both and believe me, now I know it was a big mistake." Esther sat down to drink her tea. She was up before she started, having forgotten the milk.

"You're right, Mom. Because you bought me both dresses, I never learned that I could have just one of anything. Now I want two men." Esther missed her daughter's sarcasm.

"Don't you think I understand the differences between dresses and people? I was just pointing out that you always fought for more than you needed." Marjorie shrugged her shoulders as if she couldn't do anything about it, which she couldn't.

"I know what it's like to be your age. Nancy was twenty. You were nine. I wondered why the life I was leading was mine. It's a stage. You'll outgrow it. You remember in *Diary of a Mad Housewife*? She had a lover she had to give up? You can't have both!" Esther banged the table with her small fist and a spoon jumped.

"This time you're wrong, Mom. I can't have either one. I can't have David. I never had him. All through our marriage he's sent flowers and given romance to other women. I have him at night in the dark, but there are whole days when he's out there flirting. And I can't have Lucas. He can only love me until I love him back. I left a letter from Julie on his dresser one day and he put it on my pillow that night as a reminder to take it with me. I can't even feel comfortable taking a shower at his place. Lucas isn't working now, so I can have him during the day. And David at night. You get it, Mom? Together they make one hell of a guy."

Lucas wanted to know where Marjorie had been the night before and she told him Esther wasn't feeling well. It was hard for her to keep from laughing because it struck her very funny that she was cheating on her lover with her husband. It would be nice to find a psychiatrist who really understood what was happening. "You see, Doctor, I have this lover who frustrates me and a husband who is satisfying. I can't tell the lover he's frustrating because I let too much time go by without telling him. If I get rid of the lover, my husband will bore me again. If I get rid of the husband, the lover will run away. I need them both, but having them both takes all my energy. The lover is good before and after sex and the husband is good during. Most of all I want to be an actress, but I can't be anything if I use my energy just trying to climax. By the way, Doctor, in case I didn't tell you, the whole problem came about because I realized I was thirty-eight years old and doing all the work in bed. I'll be responsible for my own orgasm but should it be that much work? Can you help me quickly? My daughter is coming home from camp.''

Like all couples having affairs, they started out having fun and making love. When they learned they could hurt each other, they made less love and talked about their relationship. In the case of Marjorie and Lucas, they tried to figure out how not to hurt themselves by keeping each other in their lives.

Everyone who didn't have a working air conditioner was out. It was one of those summer nights in the Village where everyone was too hot to be kind and fires started. The streets were crowded with different colored people wandering for enjoyment and buying different forms of sugar. Black men played basketball across the street from the Waverly Theater and small white men, arms around their dates, wished they were them for the night. There must have been drugs around, sold, stolen, consumed, but Marjorie didn't see any. Three-card monte dealers set up the cardboard boxes at every corner, hoping to catch high-school boys from New Jersey. Stores were open, hoping for eleven o'clock sales. Old people found benches and young people found each other. It was a classic summer night. Amanda had once asked Marjorie why so many novels had taken place during the summer and Marjorie had thought that writers liked writing about beads of sweat. Now that she was living the drama of her life in August, she was sure novelists were fascinated by lovers in the heat because they stuck to each other. Her hand was attached to his because it was summer.

Marjorie and Lucas walked among the girls in their cotton dresses and boys in their T-shirts and jeans. Many wore strong colored bandanas, pretending that they caught the sweat of their brow. Looking for a way to keep her, Lucas proposed that Marjorie stay in the city and keep the life she had now, trading in her mother for her daughter. She explained that she couldn't stay on Seventy-sixth Street with Julie. ''I could sneak around behind my mother's back. It was great trying to fool the woman who raised me, but I'm not about to sneak around behind my daughter's back."

"Don't sneak. Tell her what's happening."

"That's the problem. What's happening? I can't tell her I'm leaving her father. That's not true. I can't tell her I'm having a serious relationship with another man. That's not true."

"It is true."

"It's not true. In serious relationships, nobody is scared as we are."

"So we have a semiserious relationship."

"Nope. In semiserious relationships the couple owns at least one piece of furniture together. They start with an ashtray that they steal in a restaurant and then work their way up to a chair."

"For a lady who has been locked up in a marriage her whole adult life, you're pretending to know a lot about men and women and what they do with their spare time." He squeezed their fingers together, causing her wedding band to dig into her hand. It was a great reminder that she shouldn't have been having this conversation in the first place. She adjusted her fingers so that the symbol of her marriage no longer hurt.

"You know nothing about Jewish girls. We got on honor roll, every one of us. We went to the best colleges and wrote the best term papers simply because we had the best minds. And we learned to read men. We had to, because we had to know which ones would mop the floor with us, which ones would get us to mop their floors, and which ones would get us a maid to mop. That doesn't mean we didn't make mistakes. We all cried our hearts out over the wrong men who we desperately wanted, and we did it over and over again, but it was all part of our education. How else would we know who to choose as the fathers of our children? We had to learn to spot the nuts, because if, God forbid, one of us married one, we ran the risk of having our mothers throw us second-class weddings. Gloria Packer married a poet and her mother made a wedding at the Hotel Manhattan.''

"And I'm one of the nuts?''

"Of course you are. Your fly is always open.'' He quickly looked down at his pants to find that Marjorie was wrong. The buttons on his Levi's were only half open. He didn't think it was worth it to close it entirely just to prove he was sane.

"And where does that leave us in terms of our relationship? I'm asking you because you know everything.'' They were still holding hands and he wasn't at all afraid of her answer. The lamp post behind her haloed her hair the way medieval artists painted angels and rock stars appeared on their album covers. He was prepared to keep her.

"We are infatuated, in love, crazy about each other, but only because I think of myself as beyond child-bearing age.'' He drew her to him, leaning her head on his shoulder, wondering if she brought her halo with her.

"You'll stay in New York?''

"I have a daughter.'' They sat in the dark of the park for a very long time. Everyone around them was screaming and moving. They were very quiet and still.

One would have thought that the battle for Marjorie would be waged between Lucas and David, but as it turned out, it was fought between Lucas Morgan and Amanda Fine. In this corner, weighing one-seventy-five, tall, beautiful, sexual, and selfish in the jeans with the open fly, Lucas the lover. In the far corner, as far as Syossett, short, hair too thin, wearing new fall clothes in the heat of August, Amanda the friend. They met, at Marjorie's request, one day at lunch in the Russian Tea Room and both immediately recognized each other as the enemy. He snarled over his eight-dollar bacon and eggs and she won round one by asking what gave him the right to teach acting. Round two was at the curb when Amanda, getting into the Rolls, politely said she hoped to see him again, and he called her a fucking liar. She almost made a recovery by admitting she never wanted to set eyes on him again, but clearly he had tied the score. Had they met as two strangers, at a dinner party, they probably would have laughed together, but they weren't just fighting for a title or prize money. Marjorie Weissman was at stake.

The battle lasted for days and it wasn't until round fifteen that they both brought out their big guns. Amanda got Warren to secure the community theater rights to *Evita,* a show Marjorie worshiped. If she came home, she got the lead. Lucas got Burt Lansky to get Marjorie an under-five role in a play that was due to open at the Public Theater in October. It was a tiny part, but she got to play a heavy. It paid one-twenty-five and would force her to stay in New York.

Marjorie's head hurt from the decision. First she was Evita, wearing a blonde wig, her arms outstretched, speaking to all Argentina. Then Evita on the diner floor, forced to make love to Warren at gunpoint. Then she was at the Public and in an article in *The New York Times* about actresses over thirty-five. Then she was back on the diner floor, forced to make love to Joseph Papp.

Esther said, "What're you, crazy? Go home." And she herself packed her own suitcase for the trip back to Florida. "You don't know it now, but David is the person you'll want for your old age. If anything ever goes wrong, God forbid, he'll get you the best medical care."

Burt Lansky said, "I have to know by Wednesday, noon, at the latest. It's not the best part in the world, but I have fifteen ladies who would love to get their hands on it. It's work." For a brief moment Marjorie was on the floor of the diner with Burt, but even at gunpoint nothing happened.

Lucas said, "There's no decision. Either you want to be an actress or you want to disappear."

Amanda said, "My friend Doris Schneider had a couple of lines in a Broadway play once and the whole cast treated her like shit."

David said, "Julie is coming home a week from Thursday."

Julie wrote, "I can't wait to see you. I miss everything. The first thing I'm going to do is listen to Talking Heads on my stereo full blast so don't say I didn't warn you."

Marjorie said to herself just before falling asleep, "I'll bring Julie to New York with her stereo. It's my shot. I have to take it."

"Name one person who had a pisher part and went on to stardom," said Amanda.

"There must be hundreds."

"Hundreds more that went on to nothing. Look at Meryl Streep. She swears her child and family are the most important things in her life."

"And if that doesn't fulfill her at any given moment, she can always fall back on her stardom."

Sixteen years before, Marjorie and David had sat in a small cheap restaurant, eating chicken and trying to pretend that they were out on a night on the town. Marjorie was pregnant and David had a good offer from North Shore University. Now, as she sat facing David, in the Ginger Man, although the food and drink were more expensive, the issue was strangely the same. His work was forty miles from Broadway. Commuting would be impossible because sane people didn't take public transportation at midnight and actresses who played the Public didn't take limousines.

She asked him if he could move his practice to New York. He couldn't, he said. The heart specialists who had been practicing in Manhattan for the last twenty years already had the city carved up. He had worked for sixteen years to become God on the North Shore of Long Island and he couldn't start somewhere new where the most he could be was a saint. He had just shaved his moustache and gotten back to his case load and his patients were so grateful to see him, he couldn't possibly desert them again. Marjorie reached for his hand and told him that she wouldn't ask him to choose between her and his patients. "How would it be," she asked, "if Julie and I lived here just while I'm doing the play? It would be good for Julie to get some street smarts. She's a very innocent kid, you know, David. The play might close in an hour, so what's the big deal?"

"And the man?"

"How do you know there's the man?"

"I don't. Is there?"

"Yes, but no one who will mean anything in the long stretch." Marjorie didn't need the wine to fortify her, but she drank in the hope the conversation would end.

"I don't want to be a schmuck. I'm not too thrilled with the idea of you balling a guy while I have visitation rights."

"We were talking about me having the chance to work in theater. Why are you getting so crazy? I was a pretty big schmuck at the beginning of the summer while you were spending nights in that girl's room."

"So, now it's your turn to dump on me."

"I have a job in the theater. Do you know how hard it is to get a real job in the theater? I know it's only twenty-four words but they're going to be said in front of strangers. For once in my life the whole audience is going to be full of people who didn't come to see me."

"What if you get another part?"

"I won't."

David looked down into his coffee cup even though there was nothing to look at. Marjorie wanted to swear to him that she wouldn't get another part, but now that she was negotiating for a husband, marriage, a lover and a career, she didn't want to have to swear or make any irrevocable promises.

"I can see you wanting to do the part. I understand. Christ, it's exciting to me to know that you were good enough to get the role and I sure as hell don't want to stand in your way. So, stay at your mother's. I'll come in. Just do me a favor. Stop with the guy. I don't want to be a complete schmuck."

"It's nothing."

"I don't care what it is in your head. I don't want you seeing him. That's my condition. I'm jealous. OK? I'm not going to be a supportive idiot." David drank the last drop of coffee that wasn't there. "What if you get another part and another part and you never come back?"

"Why can't we worry about that if it happens, and it's not going to? They don't make middle-aged women stars. Will you let me pay for dinner? I haven't gotten paid yet, but on a hundred and twenty-five bucks a week I can take my husband out to dinner."

David spent the night. She played the part of an actress who was about to emerge on Broadway and he was David as usual. She wanted him to play with her, but after eighteen years of marriage, going to bed with his wife was a serious thing.

First she told herself that she wasn't going to see Lucas anymore. Then she was going to see him to explain things and say goodbye. Then when she went to say goodbye, she ended up in his bed. She convinced herself that it would all be over when her mother left and Julie came. Her mornings were full of promises and her nights were full of deceit. When David asked why she didn't come home until rehearsals started, she lied and said there were meetings with the producers and costume fittings. When David came into the city, he smiled at her and she hurt inside. Her sex with Lucas had never been satisfying; now it was sad.

Lucas' phone rang at eleven-thirty one night. She knew before he picked it up that the call had to do with her and she was frightened.

"David wants you to call him," Esther said. "He says it's important, but he told me not to worry. I am worried. So, call him back and then call me back and let me know what's happening." Marjorie looked for Lucas, but he had retreated to the living room. She hoped he was giving her privacy. It felt like he had disappeared, taking his comfort with him.

"David wants me to call," she yelled shakily.

"Feel free to use the phone," said Lucas, as if they had met that night.

"Are you scared he found out about us?" She stood in the doorway, a sheet around her. He sat naked on the couch, stiffly, waiting to see the principal.

"Yeah. If he climbs all over you and you buy it, then it's going to hurt us." She thought Lucas might by crying and then she remembered he was an actor and she thought he might be faking tears.

Marjorie sat on the bed and carefully dialed David, not knowing how she would answer any of his questions. She punched each number, carefully, imagining that the phone was some sort of bomb that would explode when the final six was pressed. He picked up on the second ring and told her, in the simplest terms he could, that Julie was in a hospital in Connecticut and that he was on his way to her.

"What's wrong with her?" Marjorie screamed in anguish, a mother's pain.

"She collapsed. They took her in about half an hour ago."

"Can you find out more?"

"Not until I get there."

"I'm coming with you. Can you pick me up at my mother's?"

"Are you sure your boyfriend won't mind?"

"David, please. Please don't."

He said he would pick her up in forty-five minutes and Marjorie dressed and called Esther at the same time. "Julie doesn't feel well and you know what a Jewish mother David is so we're going up there. I'll be home in fifteen minutes. Nothing to panic about."

"Thank God. You know, Marjorie, David seemed a little angry when I wouldn't give him your number. You'll patch things up?"

"No problem, Mom. We're going up there together."

When she was dressed and ready to leave she hugged Lucas and said goodbye. She'd let him know what happened.

He told her not to worry, which they both knew would do no good. In the cab on the way uptown she blamed her affair for Julie's collapse. If she hadn't been with Lucas, maybe she would have brought her daughter home. She cried and wiped her tears on her T-shirt and overtipped the driver in an attempt to absolve herself.

The ride up to Connecticut County General was mainly silent. They were both too worried about Julie to worry about their own lives. She aaked David several times not to be mad at her, but wouldn't admit what she was asking forgiveness for. He refused to look at her. Marjorie ran all the "if onlys" of her life through her mind, beginning with "if only she had taken Julie home on visiting day like she had wanted to." She asked David what collapsing could mean and hated him when he said "any number of things," keeping his medical knowledge to himself.

"Why didn't you ask them what was wrong?" Marjorie begged when they reached Connecticut.

"I did. The camp director didn't know any of the medical details."

"What did she say?" said Marjorie, pulling off her longest nail.

"I told you."

"Tell me again." Marjorie had caused her finger to bleed. She brought it to her mouth and was comforted by the taste of her blood.

"She said Julie collapsed and they took her over to the hospital. I didn't ask her for a long, detailed medical interpretation, because I knew that I was heading straight up there."

"Stop yelling at me." David hadn't been yelling, but it felt to Marjorie as if he had and she put her hands over her ears. "She didn't say anything about why she collapsed or how or what condition she was in? You didn't ask or she didn't tell you? Jesus, David, you can hate me for the rest of our lives, but you can't not talk to me about our daughter."

"Marjorie, I'm telling you everything I know. We'll be there soon. I'll find out everything."

"No. We'll find out everything. I don't want this doctor-to-doctor bullshit where you go off and whisper in corners. I'm her mother."

"I know you're her mother."

"I wanted to take her home. Remember? I thought she looked as if something was wrong. Even though she was tan, she looked wrong. Why the hell didn't you let me take her home? You wouldn't be mad at me. She wouldn't be lying there." And then without a breath, "I'm sorry. I don't in any way blame you. I don't."

"Will you please stop? It might have been something she ate or sunstroke or a million minor things. By the time we get there, she might be back in camp."

"I'm not letting her go back. I don't care if it's for four days. She's coming home. You can't fight me on that. I'm bringing her back to . . ." Marjorie got very frightened when she couldn't finish her sentence. Never before had she not known where home was. "She needs to come home," she said, hoping David didn't notice that she couldn't fill in the blank. She looked out the window. The trees looked dead in the dark. "We've been so mean to each other."

David pulled off the road, Marjorie thought to confess something. He had sped his Porsche all the way up to Connecticut so Marjorie couldn't understand why he would choose this dark, scary moment to talk. She felt that he had driven off the side of the road at the edge of a cliff and that if she opened the door she would fall and roll to the bottom. David turned the car light on and read the scribbled directions he had. With the paper in his mouth and the car light still on, he screeched back onto the road, continuing to speed toward Julie.

When they reached the hospital, he pulled into a doctor's parking space, knowing that his M.D. plates would protect him. He parked the car and ran toward the hospital, moving faster than Marjorie could. At first she tried to keep up with

him, but he got farther and farther away from her so she
shouted for him to stop, which he did the third time she
asked. "It's our child," she said when she caught up with
him. "We've got to be together on this."

"You're an actress. You can pull things like togetherness
off."

"David . . ."

"I'll try. For her I'll try."

Marjorie and David entered the hospital together and together they stepped on pads that opened automatic doors.

Julie had not felt well the night before, but Heather didn't
feel well either so Julie wasn't concerned. She woke up to
find two tiny spots of blood on her white underpants. She
was still sleepy and thought nothing more than she had gotten her period. She sat on the toilet trying to picture where
she had her Tampax when she remembered that she was
pregnant. "The doctor must have been wrong," she
thought. She was relieved that now she would never have to
tell her mother.

By the time she went to breakfast, with a borrowed maxi-
pad in place, Julie had a feeling of calmness the she hadn't
known in months. She would have to write Emily and tell
her. Maybe when school started she would be thin enough to
get a real boyfriend. If she did, she wasn't going to sleep
with him. Maybe after they had been together for a few
years and she was in college she would. It wouldn't be hard
to pretend she was a virgin because no one in the school
even knew that she and Finkle ever went out. Funny, the expression "going out." All she and Finkle ever did was
"going in" to his room.

After dinner, bunk twelve played basketball. The score
was only four to two when Julie collapsed. She felt her legs
give way and there was nothing she could do about it. Her
teammates tried to reach her, and someone threw the basketball in the air, only Julie never heard it land. When she
opened her eyes again she was lying on a bed in the infir-

mary, hearing Helen making plans for her to go to the hospital. She didn't want to go, but she didn't want to sit up and pretend that she was fine either.

Helen gently walked her to the camp station wagon. Her friends stood around like worried mothers touching the sides of the car as it was driven away. They told her that she was just trying to get out of clean-up and she told them, with the little energy she had, that her team would have won the basketball game if she hadn't fallen asleep. They all tried to laugh, but they were too old to laugh when friends were being taken to hospitals.

Helen drove and tried to keep her eyes on the road and Julie at the same time. "How're you doing, kid?" she asked more than once, and Julie always said "OK."

"You'll be great, kid."

"Maybe."

"I don't think it was anybody's fault. I mean it wasn't anything anybody did to you or the fault of the camp or anything. It just happened. Right, kid?"

"Right."

"You're a good kid. You've got good camp spirit. I've noticed that. Camp spirit is written all over you and that beats being the best athlete on the block."

Julie wanted to tell her that maybe she had the wrong girl. After the incident on the train, she couldn't remember one time the whole summer that Helen had noticed her. She didn't say anything because it was easier to be quiet.

At the hospital, Julie told the young doctor not to worry, that she was probably this sick because she had gotten her period for the first time in over three months. She told him only because she wanted him to leave her alone. He didn't. He and others started feeling and looking and testing. She was too scared to tell them to stop. They put her in a white gown and moved her from room to room. They had conferences with each other in the corners and outside of doors. At first she sobbed and only heard part of what they said. Words like ultrasound and gestation whirled around her head and although they tried to explain everything, she didn't want to hear what they were saying. Helen came into the room, took her hand and told her that she had called her parents and they were on their way. Julie was happy they were coming. They would protect her from all the hospital machinery. Her mother would understand that she had just gotten her period.

"Why can't I just rest?" she asked a nurse.

"Dr. Mitchner ordered an ultrasound. Nothing to worry about. It won't hurt."

"Nothing to worry about," Julie repeated to herself. She was wheeled down the hall and lifted onto a table. She closed her eyes, not wanting to know anything.

"We're going to take pictures of your baby," Dr. Mitchner said, confusing his patient more.

"Is it here?" Julie asked, wondering how pictures of her nonexistent baby were going to be taken.

"Right here. You look at that screen and through the magic of modern medicine you'll see your baby."

"I got my period today," Julie told the doctor so he wouldn't be surprised that there was no baby.

"That was just spotting," Dr. Mitchner explained. "If we can keep you quiet, everything should be all right."

Then there it was, the white outline of a baby from outer space. Everyone in the room focused on the screen and what it was telling them. Again strange words were heard. They talked of the stage of gestation again and there was mention of a placenta previa. After a long time, she was taken up to a private room with Dr. Mitchner following. Once she was in bed, an IV was attached and for the first time she felt she was dying. She looked at the clear solution attached to her arm and she cried. Dr. Mitchner sat in the chair by her bed and took her hand. His bedside manner had always worked with his women patients, but Julie was a child and she took her hand back. "Is there anything you want to ask me?" he said.

"Do you think my parents will feel sorry for me?" Even

though he knew she was sixteen, for the first time, he realized how young she was. He had a daughter of fourteen.
Shyness had always kept him from talking to her.

"I think they'll be happy to know you're being well taken
care of."

"Am I going to die?"

"No. You're going to be fine. We're just giving you
something to help bring your blood pressure up and if
there's no further bleeding, you'll be out of here soon."

"Back to camp?"

"I'm sure your parents will be wanting to take you
home."

"I guess."

"You rest now. I'll talk to your dad when he gets here."
Dr. Mitchner got up to go, but before he left, Julie spoke
again.

"Am I pregnant?" she asked.

"You still have your baby. You knew you were pregnant,
didn't you?" Dr. Mitchner's eyebrows showed Julie his
concern. They went up, then down, and positioned themselves in a V across his forehead.

"That's what the doctor in New York said, but then when
I got my period today . . ."

Dr. Mitchner almost sat down again, but knowing he had
little more to say, he stayed on his feet. "You're not
menstruating. You were spotting. That tells me there may
be a problem with the pregnancy."

"I was playing basketball," Julie said, closing her eyes,
and before Dr. Mitchner got to the door, she asked one last
question. "Will you tell my parents? It's just that . . . I
don't know. They think I'm great or something. If you tell
them, maybe they'll feel sorry for me." He said he would
and Julie fell asleep. He wanted to tell her he would be there
for her. He wanted to tell his own daughter he would be
there for her, but he never did.

Upon finding out that David was a doctor, Dr. Mitchner
did exactly what Marjorie had feared he would. He related

to David as a colleague using highly technical terms she had trouble understanding. But in the end he couldn't avoid telling both parents that their daughter was pregnant. The fetus was in its eighteenth week of gestation and it was still early enough to abort. She had had some spotting that morning, but so far there was no hemorrhaging.

David and Marjorie absorbed the news. They knew they all would have to make a lot of decisions, but first it was a time for analyzing, a time for talking into the night about what had happened and what they should do about it. First, they had to see their daughter, to make sure she was alive. They rushed into her room to find the lights on and Julie sound asleep. The IV frightened Marjorie, in the same way it had frightened her child, but Julie's face looked fine. The loss of weight had started defining the features that they had known were there. Neither one of them saw the pregnancy.

"The desk has my home phone, if they need it," Bill Mitchner said, in a voice that should have awakened Julie, but didn't. Marjorie nodded and David shook his hand. Marjorie sat in the chair by the bed and David pulled the chair by the window to his daughter's other side.

"She looks fairly well," Marjorie whispered but David signaled her to be quiet. Marjorie knew that she had spoken much more softly than the doctor and hated that David forced her into silence. They sat there for forty long minutes facing each other and facing their daughter. Marjorie looked at Julie and David, but David only stared at his child. Not able to sit any longer, Marjorie motioned to David that she was going to call Esther. He acknowledged her leaving, but went right back to Julie, who was sleeping peacefully. "She's going to be OK, Mom. She's in the hospital, but we had a long talk with the doctor and everything seems to be fine." Esther wanted to be relieved, but she wasn't.

"She's in the hospital. What're you telling me nothing is wrong? They don't put you in the hospital for a nap."

"The truth, Mom? She collapsed. She was so interested in losing weight, she hasn't eaten in days."

"I'll tell you something, Marjorie. You're a good actress. You almost have me convinced that you're not lying. Unfortunately, I'm your mother and I can always tell when you are reading lines. Please, Margie. I've lived a long enough time to hear what's wrong. I want to know. Please."

"It's not that terrible, Mom. She's pregnant. Everything's under control." Marjorie leaned her head against the booth. She was in the middle, having to be calm in front of her mother and her daughter and having nothing but a phone booth to lean on.

"Pregnant? Did she go out with boys?"

"I guess so. I guess she did. She's only a baby, Mom. She looks like a baby lying there in that bed."

"She's not a baby but she's not old enough to have one either. Oh, God, Marjorie, didn't you tell her anything?"

"I told her everything. There was a whole sex education program at her high school. I don't know."

"It's not your fault. Kids today live different lives. These are very modern times. You'll help her get an abortion?"

"I haven't thought about it. I just want to talk to her. She's been asleep since I got here."

"You have to guide her. She doesn't know."

"She'll be OK."

"You know, Margie, it's really crazy. Here you are maybe going to be a grandma and we're so sad. Tell her I love her. I better hang up. I feel tired and that happens so rarely. I've got to take advantage of it. You tell her to have an abortion, dear. Goodnight."

"Goodnight, Mom."

Marjorie meant to go straight back to the room, but she found herself calling Lucas. In a very brief conversation, she told him Julie was going to be all right and he said he was happy. She tried to believe him because despite everything that was happening, she still wanted them to love each other. As she walked back to the room she was surprised that while her daughter was in such deep trouble she had even thought of that crazy man in New York. Maybe if David had looked at her . . .

They took turns stretching in the hall and, once while David was gone, Marjorie thought of herself as a grandmother in jeans and sneakers, holding a blanket, getting a chance to play with another doll. Once when David was there, she remembered that she loved him. She loved the curve of his face and the way he knew enough not to lose his hair even though all his friends had. She made the mistake of whispering, "We have to talk," but David refused to go out of the room with her. Marjorie drew her legs up into the chair and closed her eyes, praying silently. "Let her be happy, God. Happy and well and happy."

When she opened her eyes, Julie saw David first. "Hi, baby," he said, and Julie said hi to him before she turned toward Marjorie.

"The doctor told us. It's going to be fine," said Marjorie, kissing Julie's forehead.

"Did he say I could have a drink?"

"Sure. Wait. Here you go." David poured some water out of the waiting pitcher and while Marjorie lifted Julie's head, he held the glass for her to drink. When she had had enough, Marjorie slowly brought her head back to the pillow.

"Is the baby OK?" Julie asked.

"The doctor says it is," said David.

Julie closed her eyes and appeared to be asleep again, but a few seconds later, she said, "That's good."

"Go back to sleep. We'll be here with you so don't worry." Julie nodded, she opened her eyes, but didn't say anything. Marjorie and David were quiet too, concentrating on loving their daughter.

An hour went by before a nurse entered to take Julie's blood pressure and pulse and, in a cheerful nursey way, she asked how the patient was doing. They all three said fine and smiled false smiles as if it were important to them for the nurse to think that all was well. She changed the intravenous and once again Julie and Marjorie were afraid of the hanging bottle. When the nurse left, Julie looked at her father, then her mother and back to her father again. It was as if she was deciding whom to talk to first. She chose Marjorie.

"Can I listen to music?" she asked.

"Sure," said Marjorie. "Sure, why not?"

"I have my Walkman at camp. Maybe they could bring it over. And my tapes. I'm gonna need my tapes. My Neil Diamond, Ma. I really need Neil Diamond now." This was said weakly, since Julie's strength was still lost.

"You're not going to be here that long, a couple of days," said David.

"The truth?" Julie's eyes opened wide.

"Cross my heart."

"God. I thought I was going to be here for months. God." Julie closed her eyes again. It was hard for either one of her parents to tell whether she was going back to sleep. After a few moments, however, her eyes opened again. "I remember, the doctor told me I wasn't going to be here that long. He said the same thing you did." She turned to Marjorie. "Mom?"

"Yes, sweetheart."

"Can I have my Walkman anyway? I mean even though it's not going to be that long. I kinda don't like to be without it, in case I get bored or something."

"We'll get it," said David.

"Thank you." This time she fell asleep.

When she got tired of watching her daughter, Marjorie walked out into the hall. It was quiet and bare. She walked past the nurses' station where the ladies in crisp, white uniforms were pretending it was the middle of the day even though it was early morning. Marjorie smiled broadly, straining muscles, wanting to be liked even if only for the moment. She tried calling Amanda, knowing, because of the hour, that the phone was turned off. Opposite the elevators were two armless vinyl-covered chairs pushed together to make a small couch. Marjorie sat down on the orange one and then, feeling exhausted, lay down as best she could on the yellow one too. There was no comfortable position and, even if there was, her thoughts kept her awake. She would have bet anyone that Julie was a virgin and here she was pregnant. Pregnant like the unwed mothers of the fifties. There was one girl at Hunter High School a year older than Marjorie, with washed-out blonde hair and immigrant parents. A week after she disappeared there were rumors that she was pregnant and when she didn't come back, everyone accepted the rumors as truth. Some said she had tricked the grandson of Macy's into marrying her, others said her parents were making her live in Puerto Rico until she had the baby. No one talked of abortion. As she looked back now, she realized that abortions were arranged, mostly illegally. They were a generation of girls who cried during *Love With the Proper Stranger*. Marjorie and all her friends thought abortions were made up in Hollywood to make girls who went to the movies on Friday nights cry their eyes out.

During her consciousness-raising days, Marjorie was definitely proabortion. Every woman in her group had her children and since it was the era in which you were supposed to "Try for Two," and save the universe, they were all sure that if they conceived they would get rid of it. Marjorie had tried for the second baby but twice she had miscarried. She wondered if her daughter hadn't done it to have a sister. Dangerously, it was a baby which could rob Julie of her youth. When Marjorie was awake enough, she slowly moved back to Julie's room. Her steps were small and slow, like the grandmother she was about to become. When she passed the phone, she remembered she loved two men. She still needed them both, one to worry with and one to talk to.

David sat in the same chair she had left him in, reading a copy of *Time*. A copy of *Newsweek* was waiting at his feet. Julie was still asleep so Marjorie sat and rested her head on the edge of the bed. She fell asleep for the hour and a half that made up the rest of the night.

The early-morning voices of David and Dr. Mitchner,

whispering in the hall, awakened her. She went into the hall to join in any discussions they were having. David was talking about how he thought silver was a great buy for under eleven dollars an ounce but he stopped talking the second he saw Marjorie. There were unnecessary good mornings and Marjorie questioned the doctor with her eyes.

"The bleeding hasn't stopped. As a matter of fact, it's increased. She's not at the point of hemorrhaging, but the spotting is still significant. There's a good chance of spontaneous abortion." It was a time for tears and Marjorie cried. There was no baby, but there had been a possibility of one and supposedly they were being robbed.

"And Julie?" she asked.

"She should be fine, weak for a while. We're going to keep her here until we know one way or another." At that point he looked at David, asking him to explain further. This was the first time Marjorie knew that an important conversation had taken place behind her back.

"If the bleeding does stop, there's a further decision to be made." David was talking as a doctor and Marjorie resented it. "There's still time for an abortion and we have to think of her age and her future. She's a high-school kid."

"I know what she is," said Marjorie.

"Let me know if you need me. My office is only a block away. I'm available." Dr. Mitchner backed down the hallway.

"We have to talk," said David.

"I've been saying that for the last twelve hours."

David moved away from Julie's door so what they said could not be overheard. "I think we have to be together on this. Julie was obviously afraid to tell us what was going on . . ." David talked to the wall behind Marjorie.

"You don't know that for sure. Maybe she was confused. Sometimes kids don't know themselves. Sometimes . . ."

"She asked Mitchner to tell us she was pregnant. So it's a pretty accurate guess that she was scared."

"I told her she could tell me anything. I did."

"Obviously she didn't believe you. She didn't believe me either when I said she could come to me with problems."

"It's no use blaming ourselves," one of them said, but there was nobody to blame but themselves.

"There's nothing we can do about the past," David said, as if Marjorie didn't know that. "And I think we should have a united front about the future." Marjorie nodded, which encouraged David to continue. "There's still time for an abortion. It's no big deal. They could do it right here in the hospital by the end of the week. We could take her home, probably that same day. She's very young."

"Maybe that's what she wants too," said Marjorie.

"I hope to God that's what she wants. What the hell are our alternatives?"

"I'm not sure. There must be alternatives. Every situation has different possibilities."

"Do you have any idea who the guy was? Did she go out with someone when I wasn't around?"

"The only one she ever went any place with was that Michael Finkle and I think they're just friends. They went to a couple of movies. I saw them together. You saw them together. Did it look romantic to you?"

"I thought they hated each other. No, hated is too strong. They did spend time together. I thought they couldn't stand each other. She punched him in the back once. Hard. Not playing around. Just socked him." Marjorie had one terrifying thought. For one brief moment, she imagined Julie on the diner floor. She forced the image from her mind.

They were leaning against opposite walls and then, as if on cue, they switched walls and faced each other again. "Let's just hope she loses it," he said, needing the wall he was leaning on.

"Why do I have a hard time hoping that?" Marjorie said with a sigh.

"Don't get sentimental on me." He closed his eyes and twisted his face as if her sentimentality was his pain.

"Babies are nice."

David reddened before he spoke and Marjorie could see his anger rise. He pointed his finger, before beginning to speak. "If babies are so nice go have one. Don't expect your daughter to have one for you just because you don't want to be out of shape for nine months. The world may not know why we never had another kid, but I know, Marjorie. You hated being pregnant."

"I miscarried twice," she said, as loudly as she dared in hospital halls.

"For no apparent physical reasons. You gave up on a second child more quickly than most or all women would."

"Not because I wanted to wear a bikini every day of my life."

"I'm sorry," he hissed, even though the apology was out of sequence.

"I'm sorry too." Her voice was no kinder than his.

They watched each other and knew, although they were still angry, they had apologized for the summer. It was too soon to kiss and make up, but at least they heard each other. David breathed deeply and Marjorie almost smiled. If he didn't see the first look of love in her eyes, he saw the second.

"Did you ever laugh with her?" asked Marjorie.

"With who?"

"With your infatuation. Did the two of you laugh?" She asked this as if laughing was a more serious crime than having sex.

"No. She had no sense of humor. None."

"Thank God," said Marjorie.

A nurse wheeled a breakfast tray into Julie's room and David and Marjorie followed it in. For the first time since they arrived at the hospital, Julie was sitting up and totally alert. She was uninterested in the breakfast of boiled eggs and very curious about what her parents thought of her. In a family that contained two stars it had always been hard for Julie to get center stage. For years she had done it by being fat. Now she knew a better way, getting sick. They were hers for as long as she stayed in that bed even though she had done something as horrible as getting pregnant.

"How do you feel, baby?" Marjorie touched the sleeve of Julie's hospital gown.

"Pretty good, not so hot," was Julie's confused answer.

"You hungry?"

"Nope. I haven't been hungry in a long time. They told us at camp if we ate less we wouldn't be so hungry and they were actually right. What did Dr. Mitchner say?"

"He said . . ." David started. How many times he had had to tell patients news. They looked into his face for the information, sometimes before he even knew it. Julie was looking now, her eyes, the exact same color as his own, wanting answers. "He said there is increased bleeding and if it continues there's a good chance that you will abort."

Julie grew angry and frightened. Her blue eyes dampened and she clutched her heart. David had seen Marjorie do this same gesture many times, but Julie, up to this day, had been too young for this type of clutching. "I won't have an abortion. I can't. I really, really can't. I have a name for this baby and everything. I swear I'll take care of it. I know I don't clean up my room and I didn't clean out the fish tank, but I swear I'll take care of my baby. You won't have to do a thing." Both mother and father couldn't help thinking that she was pleading for a puppy. They had been through these words right before they bought her Max, the cocker spaniel that Marjorie ended up taking care of.

"I didn't say anything about having an abortion." David felt he had done a good job explaining.

"I'm never going to do it," Julie said. "I don't believe in abortion."

"We'll talk about it later," said David.

"I don't want to talk about it later. I don't want to talk about it ever. It's my baby and my body," Julie screamed. "I'm sorry, I'm really, really sorry about what happened and I promise I'll never do it again. I mean I won't even go out with anybody ever again if you don't want me to, I promise I'll never, ever have sex with anyone, but you have got to know that I want this baby. Do you think I'm going to have a miscarriage?''

"There's a chance . . ." David said, stopping when he saw how hurt Julie was by the information. Part of his life had been spent telling patients bad news. It was always hard. To tell his daughter that she might lose the baby that she was so desperately trying to hold on to was impossible. Sensing this, Julie turned to Marjorie.

"Mom?" Marjorie took her daughter's hand and found it to be the same size as her own.

"You're bleeding, spotting they call it, and that lets the doctors know that something is wrong. If the bleeding continues, there's a good chance that you will miscarry. That's exactly what the doctor told us."

"We've got to pray," said Julie with urgency. "I can't lose this baby. We've really got to pray. Hard." Marjorie remembered bleeding and praying. The babies she had lost also had names.

"You're not thinking carefully, honey. A baby is something major . . ."

"You think I don't know that? I know that. If this is going to embarrass you, I could go away. I've thought this out so don't think I haven't. What I'll do is ask Grandma if I can stay in her apartment and she'll probably say yes because nobody is there all winter. I have twenty-two hundred dollars in my bank account so I could get some sort of job and—''

"Julie . . ."

"No, let me finish. I could even go to school, only in New York, and you could visit, so it's not like I'm running away. We could see each other every weekend. And here's another exciting part, I mean besides having the baby. If I'm living in New York, I was thinking I could take singing lessons. They have the best teachers there and maybe I could be a backup singer for commercials or something. Who knows? Maybe someday I'll get someplace. I mean I don't expect to be a star but I think it would really be good for me and my baby if I had a career and singing is what I really can do.''

Marjorie brushed the hair from Julie's forehead with a graceful hand.

"You don't have to go to New York. If . . . if, and we should still discuss having the baby, if you do have the baby, Daddy and I will want to be right there for you.''

"Going to New York isn't my first choice. Coming home is my absolute first choice. I like my room. I like my school and I really want to be close to Emily. She knows all about this and she's going to help me and everything. I love her, Mom. I really do.''

"Are you sorry you never had a sister?'' Marjorie's voice was kind and motherly, making Julie feel safe.

"Yeah. Sure. It's not your fault or anything.'' Julie had no idea that her mother was playing psychiatrist and concluding that Julie was giving birth to her own sibling.

"You could take singing lessons. You could do anything you want to. You don't have to have this baby,'' said David, still campaigning for the abortion.

"I do,'' said Julie, starting to eat her breakfast. She reached for the jam and than rejected it.

"Remember how we talked about your going away to college? How can you if you have a baby?''

"So I'll go to Hofstra.''

"They may not let you stay in high school.''

"Emily said they do. She said there was a girl at Valley Stream Central who got pregnant. It was a big legal thing and she won because she had a right to an education. They didn't make her take gym, which is great with me. I hate gym.''

"If you don't have the baby, I'll see to it that you don't have to take gym,'' said David, believing that his proposition would help.

David and Julie argued for a while. She knocked down each one of his obstacles. When he said that pregnancy

would get in the way of going out with boys, she said,
"Who goes out with boys?" and quickly added, "And
please don't ask me to tell you who did this to me because I
am totally dedicated to not telling. I really don't want to
marry him or anything so what's the use in telling just to get
him in trouble." Julie leaned back into her pillow, tired
from the conversation and the fight to keep her baby. "I'll
die if you make me have an abortion," she said tiredly.

Hours later, with Julie's condition unchanged, David was
back on Long Island and Marjorie was on the phone with
Amanda.

"I'll be there as soon as I can," she said.

"She's not sick. If she were sick I'd let you be here."

"What're you going to do, Marge? She's a baby. You
can't let a baby have a baby."

"I don't know. I'm very tired. I'm not even sure the decision is mine."

"Of course it's yours. The kid couldn't pack her camp
trunk alone and you're thinking she can have a vote in
whether to keep this mistake."

"I think she can have more than a vote. It's her body."

"It's your body. As long as you pay for the haircuts, the
body is yours."

By the time Marjorie hung up, she was convinced Amanda was right. If she hadn't had any more change, she might
have gone to Julie with reasons to abort. The change went to
call Lucas.

She told him what was going on and he was as sympa-
thetic as a lover could be. "You can't ask an ex-Catholic
choir boy his views on abortion," he said.

"You know what I learned today?"

"What?"

"You're right. You are brilliant and your theory deserves
all the prizes it can get. We're only eighteen. All of us. Julie
started talking about taking singing lessons in New York
and she sounded just like I do. I have the same aspirations,
hopes, dreams, as my adolescent daughter. She wants to

make it and I want to make it and we're both willing to play the maid."

"You should be proud of her. You know how many people lack dreams?"

"How many?"

"Billions."

"But not you."

"And not you. So how can you expect your daughter not to have any?"

"The big question is . . . Can a grandmother start an acting career?"

They hung up uncertain when they would see each other.

When David returned, showered and changed and with fresh clothes for Marjorie, there were more talks in the hallway. Marjorie felt split loyalties. Her daughter wanted her to pray and her husband was hoping for a spontaneous abortion. She saw all sides, including her own. Julie's first choice was to go home and have her baby. She knew she had years ahead to fulfill dreams. Sixteen years ago Marjorie went to the suburbs to have her child thinking she had time. She didn't want Julie, with her perfect pitch, to disappear the way she had. Yet her daughter had asked her to pray.

Marjorie went to talk to Julie. When David followed her to the room she turned, before entering, asking him to leave them alone.

"Don't give her a romantic idea of motherhood," said David, not realizing that every woman who didn't have an infant at home had a romantic view of motherhood.

"I hope the baby looks like you," said Julie.

"We look alike."

"Yeah, one of the nurses thought you were my sister."

"That's because I cover the gray in my hair."

"You do? You never told me that."

"I guess we both have secrets," said Marjorie. She had stretched her leg across the bottom of Julie's bed and now noticed that her tan had faded from the summer in New York.

"How come you didn't tell me?"

"About being pregnant and all?"

"Yes. About being pregnant. I thought we were friends."

"You're my mother, not my friend. How many kids my age do you know who have real friends in their thirties?"

"That's still not an answer."

"I dunno. I didn't want to ruin your summer. I was scared you'd yell at me. I thought it would go away if I ignored it. I was going to tell you as soon as I came home from camp. Maybe I wanted it to be this way. Emily says there are no accidents, that what happens, we make happen. So, maybe I made it happen."

"You're too young, Julie. You know that. It's a fantasy to think you can go to school and take care of a baby. It seems like a good idea now, but you'll be sorry. There'll be things you'll want to do that you're not thinking of. Daddy was right, you did want to go away to college . . . You look so pretty now . . ."

"Were you happy when you were pregnant with me?"

"Of course I was happy and don't try and trick me into saying something I don't want to. I was thrilled. I was also married, older, and had finished college."

"Maybe you should have waited until you got your career started."

"Don't you think I tried to break into show business before you were born? I was out there every day hanging around agents' offices, going to open auditions, buying *Variety*. I was rejected everywhere. And that was on good days. On the bad days I couldn't even get in the door to get the rejection. I was ready to quit. Believe me, honey, my ego wasn't strong enough to take all those nos."

"So you had me because you were scared to keep trying."

"I had you because I wanted a baby. I always wanted a baby."

"Maybe high school is for me what show business is for

you. Every day I go there and every place I look there's some guy with some girl. Talk about rejection. Remember last year I decorated the gym for the spring dance and then didn't go to it?''

"I remember. I cried too.''

"I didn't know you did.''

"More secrets.''

"Yeah.''

"Having a bad time in high school is no reason to have a baby.''

"I wish I'd told you sooner.''

"Why?''

"Because months ago I didn't care about it. In June I was hoping it wasn't true and that it would just go away. I would have agreed to an abortion. You know what, Mommy? I felt her. And I felt her just before so I don't care what the doctor says. I know she's all right. Sometimes a woman knows her body more than the doctors do and you don't have to feel guilty about sending me to camp. I ate well. Really. Really. Healthier than usual. They didn't hurt me. Did I feel like a butterfly running across your stomach before I was born?''

"Yep. You did.''

"In June I would have given it up. I can't now. I can't, Mommy. I felt her. Maybe she'll sing like us.''

There were more discussions, in twos, threes, fours when Dr. Mitchner was around. Julie held on as long as she could. Then, with blood and pain, her unborn child left her. David, Amanda, Emily and Esther said it was best. Marjorie and Julie wet each other with their tears.

"I've never been this sad,'' said Julie between sobs, but she would be happy again long before Marjorie would.

Thirty-seven

By the time summer was deciding to quit, everyone's story was completed but Marjorie's.

Esther was back in Florida complaining to her husband about the lack of culture in Miami.

Amanda was sweltering in the new fall fashions and promising the theater more lighting.

Emily was redecorating her room in hi-tech and worrying that Julie was going to be anorexic.

Julie sometimes had waves of sadness land on her. At other times she was the sixteen-year-old she should have been. She hadn't yet learned to love her new body, probably because she missed her pregnancy more than her fat. She did two things that were surprisingly mature. She told Mike Finkle that she never wanted to go out with him again and she told the salesgirl at Sport Togs that she wasn't really married.

David planned to take his family on a weekend to Montauk, but being a white-water man, he never consummated his plans. He spotted a beautiful woman in the hospital and stopped himself from smiling. He gave himself a lot of credit for letting her go.

A week after Labor Day, when Julie was in school and David was at the hospital, Marjorie had the urge to pack. The symbolic suitcase she wanted to fill was at Lucas' and although she had none of her things at his apartment, she needed to move out of his life.

He served tea, one bag for both of them. She sat on the couch and he sat at her feet, which made the whole thing more difficult. She felt like patting his head as she spoke.

"I'm crazy about you," she told him, and he brightened.

"I thought you came here to tell me that you were staying in Syosset." He buried his head in her lap.

"I am," said Marjorie. Her cup rattled, reminding her that she was nervous.

"You want to tell me why?"

"It's home. Every clock I've ever owned is there. All my guilts. And my daughter. And my husband." She kissed the top of his head where his hair had thinned. He didn't seem to know about the missing hair or the kiss. "I love them both," she said with a small smile that she knew he couldn't see.

"And me?"

"I love you, too. My mother said I love too many people."

"Your mother was right." Now he sat up and looked to her for an explanation. She could only shrug her shoulders.

"You don't really want me. Not for anything like nesting."

"I do. Especially if you tell me I don't."

"My daughter comes first. If the two of you were drowning, I'd save her."

"I can swim."

"This isn't about swimming and you know it." He scratched the back of his head as if he didn't know anything.

"And your husband?" He leaned back for her answer. Since he had known her, he had beaten out the husband.

"I'd save him, too."

"So, I come in third."

"I told you, you don't want me." Marjorie knew she was saying goodbye and got scared. She embraced the back of

his neck as she talked, wanting to tell him that she wasn't
going yet.

"I do want you. What can you offer me?"

"I can ask you to always let me know where you are in
case I ever need you. It's totally selfish."

He grabbed the hand on his neck and held it tightly. Still
they didn't face each other. "What love isn't? he asked.

"I can promise I won't do anything with David that I did
with you."

"Good enough. Not really good enough. I'm sad. You
made me fall."

"I'm so sorry. I didn't know I could do things like that."

"You're the last innocent woman I'll ever get involved
with."

Because neither of them was ready to let go, they sat holding on to each other. He thought she might change her mind
and she thought she liked the strength of his back and that
there'd be time to make a turkey breast for dinner. He spoke
first. "Shit," he said, "we're doing this all wrong. Nobody
would believe we're breaking up. With this awful scene we
wouldn't sell one fucking ticket."

That's when they both cried and moaned. He stood up
and brought her to him. (Had he brought her to the bedroom,
she would have gone.) They cried on each other's shoulders, and kissed each other safely on the lips until their eyes
were red and their legs were tired. Then they sat down together and moaned some more. Finally, when their teeth
marks were in each other, Lucas had played out the scene
that he needed. Someday they would recount the good
times.

"Why are you going back?" He held her so tightly she
had trouble answering.

"David needs a wife. Julie needs a mother. And they're
no accident. I chose them once and I'm choosing them
again. I'm crazy about you."

"You're not happy."

"Yes I am," she said with a face full of tears.

"You're not."

"I am."

"Prove it." His lashes were wet and appealing.

She had a hard time thinking about what would prove to him that she was happy in Syosset. It was a long minute before she spoke.

"Promise you won't laugh," she said.

"I promise. I'll never laugh again." He looked sincere.

"I never wanted to do that Joe Papp thing. I'm not very good with twenty-four lines. I can't wait to do *Evita*."

He broke his promise. She hugged him and when it was time to leave, she went home with the pain of needing two men.